SAVING EVA

Table of Contents

Saving Eva..1

1 3

2 17

3 33

4 41

5 55

6 67

7 73

8 83

9 93

10 99

11 109

12 119

13 127

14 135

15 143

16 159

17 169

18 179

19 191

20 203

21 217

22 223

23 241

24 253

25 265

26 269

27 279

28 287

29 295

30 305

31 313

To the Amazing Pancake Rabbit who had no idea what to say.

Morning glories threatened to pull down the corn. Intent on remedying the situation, Eva and Lora tromped through the glistening humidity and breath-stealing heat of Alabama in July to retrieve their garden hoes. As Lora pulled open the warped, wooden door and Eva stepped inside, a frightened, shaky voice from the shadows whispered, "Please Miss Eva! Don't tell'em I'm here!"

Alarmed, both women rushed into the small enclosure. Eyes adjusting to the gloom, they saw a young Black man with wide, white-rimmed dark eyes shivering in the corner, hunkered down behind the dented wheelbarrow. Recognizing him at once, Eva knelt beside him in the dirt, took his trembling hand in hers, and asked, "Leon, what's happened? You can tell me."

"Yes ma'am. Yes I can, that's why I came here. To you," Leon gulped. Lora knew his face. He was about her age and often stopped in to say hello to her grandmother when he wasn't working. His mama, Myra, was Eva's closest friend. They listened as he continued, "I don't know how to explain it and you might be mad, but, see, I take your big ol' plate of biscuits every day. I'm not stealing!" He whuffed a deep breath and picked at a ragged fingernail. "Well, I suppose I am but not for myself! I take them to the Johnson's house and leave'em. I just had a way-down, gut feeling one day a few months back that I needed to do something for somebody. Almost like starving but not really. Never felt nothing like it before...Anyway, I followed that feeling straight to your biscuit plate and toted it all the way to their back door. I been following that feeling every day since."

Knowing Lora would need a moment to process his revelation, Eva glanced over Leon's head and said, "Lora, maybe Leon would like a drink of water? Can you get a glass from the kitchen?"

Lora immediately dashed across the yard, through the back door to the sink. Her mind spun in ninety-seven directions at once. *Leon is the person who takes Gram's biscuits every day? The forty some odd biscuits she makes every single morning because she had a deep, wrenching ache in her heart back in the spring that told her the Johnsons needed food? How could that be? How could he know? Did he have the 'knowing' too?* Snatching the glass from under the tap, Lora ran back to the shed as fast as she could, hoping for answers.

She swept back into the sweltering, earthy darkness, pressing the glass into his hands. Leon was explaining how he came to be huddled amongst the hoes and shovel's in Eva's shed. He'd taken this morning's biscuits from Eva's sideboard, across the shallow creek, and through the cemetery in the woods which backed up to the Johnson place. He had put the biscuits on the counter, just inside the back door like always, and was turning to leave, silent as dawn, when he'd run smack into Mr. Johnson coming in from the barn. Both men were surprised. Leon, because he knew there was no way he could explain why a Black man would have any business in a white man's house so early in the morning. Mr. Johnson, because he couldn't imagine any reason for a Black man to be on his property at all.

Leon had bolted across the Johnson's yard and back to the cemetery with Mr. Johnson lagging only far enough behind to allow him to grab his shotgun from behind the door and give chase, raging and snorting like a wounded bull the whole way. Leon had run to the first safe place he could think of. Eva's garden shed.

While he spoke, Lora's head hurt, just above her left eye, and her vision shifted. She saw the truth of his story. Leon had left out something important. She touched him gently on the shoulder. "Leon, did something else happen?"

He dropped the glass. Water swirled and eddied in the dry, dusty dirt before collecting itself into thirsty little balls of mud. His mouth dropped open and his eyes bulged wider in renewed panic. "Miss Lora," he whispered, "how do you know?"

Eva nodded for her to continue.

"Nevermind that. It's just, I, we...can't help unless you tell us everything."

Leon sucked in a shuddering breath and closed his eyes. "Well, you know Bumpus? The drunk man who wanders all over shouting at nobody? I...while I was running through the graveyard, I run slap into him! I bounced off him an' kept on running. But...he fell! I think I heard a nasty crunch but no way was I slowing down to check. Not with Mr. Johnson hot on my heels!"

Eva and Lora looked at each other while he held his head and cried. Eva patted her knees and, in tribute to every Southern grandmother who'd come before her, spoke to him like he was her own. "Well Leon. Hiding in my shed for sure isn't going to work. You come on in the house and we will get you sorted. Lora, I need you to go to the creek, down by the graveyard, and gather up some wild lettuce. I think Leon could use some tea."

If Leon had been paying closer attention, he'd have noticed the look on Eva's face and understood better. He'd have realized that Eva didn't care a leaf about wild lettuce; she wanted to know if Bumpus was still in the graveyard. If wild lettuce tea would help calm Leon's nerves, well, all the better. Eva stood, her knees complaining at the effort and reached a hand to Leon to help him to his feet. He clung to her firm grip as he stood, not trusting his wobbly legs to support him.

• • • •

WRAPPED SNUGLY IN THE sedating effects of steeped wild greens, Leon dozed uneasily on the sofa. The women retreated to the kitchen to discuss the next move. Lora had found more than a mess of lettuce; she'd also found Bumpus. Dead in the graveyard from a sharp blow to his head. A browning smear of blood on an ancient stone corner bore grim witness to the fatal wound.

Lora nervously twisted strands of her thick brown ponytail around a finger and chewed on the ends in an effort to calm herself. Her thoughts scattered like chicken feed. Her nerves frantically scrambled to gather the pieces as she whispered, "Gram! We have to tell the police. Leon killed Bumpus and knows it. We know it. We have to do the right thing!"

In the soft morning light from the kitchen window, Eva studied Lora over her water cup. Her shrewd blue eyes watching every flash of emotion as her granddaughter spoke.

Setting her cup on the counter and making an obvious effort to keep her voice low, Eva asked, "Is that what you think we should do? Turn him over to the law? Over an accident? Use your head girl!" She snorted and turned away, shaking her head.

Lora was stunned. Her grandmother was rarely short with her and even worse, they rarely disagreed about anything. Could she really be suggesting they shouldn't turn Leon over to the police? Sullen and indignant, she snapped back. "You ought to use yours!"

Eva spun around with a wrinkled finger jabbing into Lora's chest and replied in a harsh whisper, "Lora, listen to me. Bumpus was a nasty old buzzard who beat his wife and children bloody if they breathed wrong. So bad, and so often, that she killed herself and those babies! Burned their house down with all of 'em in it! And everybody knew it! Your granddaddy and me wanted to help but we could only do so much. The law knew it and said it wasn't their business what went on between a man and his wife. The law turned their back on her so she took the only way out she could find. When she did what she did, he lost what was left of his mind."

Eva shook with simmering fury and hissed through her teeth. "Don't you dare go feeling sorry for him. He did it to hisself and if anybody ever needed killing, it was Bumpus. You'll have to forgive me if I'm not interested in sacrificing Leon for that man." She flung her water glass into the sink with an echoing thud and stalked away.

"Gram! Wait!" Lora snatched at her grandmother's arm, catching hold of her worn sleeve. "Fine! So Bumpus was no good, but really? You want to play judge and jury here?"

"No Lora, I don't. Life has done taken care of that. Bumpus got what he deserved, even if it did take ages too long." Eva's nostrils flared. "What I want, what I have to do, is help Leon."

Eva's face lit on an idea as she continued, "Why don't you use your talent and see what Leon thinks will happen to him if we handed him to the authorities." Until now, Lora had only seen events with the advantage of hindsight. Now, they needed to know if Lora could see the truth unfold in the future. Eva wanted to know if her granddaughter had the strength to do the right thing; the difficult, hard thing.

Lora glanced into the living room at the young man fitfully napping on the sofa. His feet twitched beneath the crocheted granny-square afghan. Judging by the grimaces contorting his features, his dreams carved waves of grief and horror across his face. Sleep was no peaceful escape from the terrors of the morning. Lora, afraid of waking him, kicked off her garden boots and padded softly across the house. Taking one of his dark, calloused hands into hers, she closed her eyes, focusing only on him. As her mind calmed, her left eye again felt as if it would rupture in its socket and she was thrown into a maelstrom of hate and fear, blame and grief. Letting go, she looked back at her grandmother, tears winking from the corners of her eyes. "Oh Gram, they'd say it was murder! They would want to hang him!"

The soft lines on Eva's face hardened. "I know. What's important is now you do too. How's that for justice? Your trust in the law? It's not just, it's not right. We gotta figure out what to do next." With a jerk of her chin in Leon's direction, she said, "For his sake."

· · · ·

EVEN THOUGH IT WAS later than she'd normally drink it, Eva brewed a pot of coffee in the Montgomery Ward electric dripper she'd gotten as a Christmas gift last year. Once the pot was full, she and Lora sat at the kitchen table and tried to work out the next steps. Lora was unsure how to handle Bumpus's death and what should be done about it.

Eva's answer was matter-of-fact. "Nothing. Don't nothing need to be done about it. Drunks fall over and crack their heads all the time. This particular drunk just happened to fall in a graveyard and die. Saves the undertaker a trip! Nice of Bumpus to be considerate in his last moments, isn't it?"

Lora was shocked by Eva's macabre, nonchalant sarcasm. Her grandmother shrugged off the problem of Bumpus like he was an uncomfortable jacket on a too warm day.

"Gram. Are you seriously suggesting that we just leave him there? To bloat and rot, and God only knows what else, until someone else finds him?" Her nerves were still taut as bowstrings, one more crank and they would snap, sending her straight to the loony bin.

Eva's low chuckle nearly did the trick as she blew across the top of her coffee cup. "Of course not. I'm just thinking that right now, our biggest worry is laying on my couch. How about we focus on the living and leave the dead for later? Now, what do you reckon we can do to help young Leon over there?"

"Well, I really don't think he can stay with you."

"No. He can't. Of course, I'd be willing but I can't keep him cooped up here forever and somebody would see him eventually. Obviously, that'd court more questions than answers."

"Could he go somewhere? Does he have family anywhere that he could stay with? I guess we could send him to Detroit. Mom and Dad might take him in for a while...maybe." Even as she said it, she pursed her lips in contemplation, not relishing the idea of trying to explain to her parents why she was sending a random Black man to stay with them. They may live in Detroit, and they might pay lip service to the recent civil rights efforts, but they were still red-clay Alabama at heart. In truth, she had no idea how they would react.

Eva and Lora were so intent on their conversation they didn't hear Leon moving around until he spoke. Leaning against the door frame, in his dusty jeans and plaid work shirt, he cleared his throat, "Excuse me, ma'ams? But I can't be going anywhere. My mama needs me to help with the farm and my brothers ain't big enough to do all that needs doing by themselves."

Leon picked at a spot on the door frame where white paint was peeling away, revealing the bare wood underneath. He smiled at the lines and scribbles marking height measurements and ages of Eva's family as they grew. "My mama's got one of these," he murmured. He stopped picking and ran his hand gently over the markings.

Passing a coffee cup and inviting him to sit, Eva shook her head and said, "Leon, you getting all tangled up with these ignorant people around here won't do your mama no good either. Yeah, Bumpus is dead but you didn't kill him. He's been walking dead for years. We all know that won't nobody miss him but the man who sold him 'shine. Don't you worry about your mama. I'll talk to Myra and explain everything. She'll understand. And, I'm sure I can round up some help when it's needed." With that, she took a sip of her coffee and winked at them both over her cup.

The three of them spent the afternoon making plans. Leon suggested he go stay with his older brother in Chicago. Maurice had been pestering him to come visit anyway and, if Leon was interested in staying, Maurice thought he could get Leon a job with him in the rail yard. If he got the job, Leon could send money home to help with the bills, just like his brother did. Eva and Lora thought his idea was worlds better than anything they would have come up with and readily agreed.

. . . .

OTHER THAN HER OWN mother and grandmother, Eva had never known anyone with a talent like hers. She called it 'the knowing.' And yet, here they were. Two! One of them not even related! When they questioned her about what their own talents might mean, she explained it the best she could.

"Well, it ain't magic, but we just...know things. We know how to help people the way they really need helping. I get a feeling like my heart is being squeezed and it keeps on squeezing until I figure out who needs my help. Lora, your head hurts right behind your left eye and you 'see' the truth. Leon, it sounds like your stomach clenches, letting you know someone needs something done, right?"

Leon nodded, hovering a hand briefly over his abdomen, and Eva continued, "The old folks in my family used to call us bearers. Because we know the burdens of the community and do what we can to help bear them. I never dreamed there were others. None other than the ones I grew up with, anyway. And, I reckon I thought it was dying out because nowadays, the community ain't what it once was and people don't share like they used to." She slapped a palm on the table and grinned in delight. "Looks like I was wrong!"

Eva was glad to be wrong. She marveled at the strength Lora and Leon didn't know they possessed; the strength they would need to meet the demands which would be placed on them for the rest of their lives. Lora's gift hadn't shown itself until last summer. She was certain this shared burden encapsulated the tie which bound her so tightly to her only granddaughter. And, she wondered if helping the Johnsons was the first time Leon had felt this unusual type of hunger. Setting her musings aside, she turned her attention back to the young people at her table. Here they sat, in her kitchen, drinking coffee, and learning to carry the weight of the world together. Watching them with their heads bent towards each other, smiling, and occasionally laughing with the unwavering resilience and optimism of youth, she smiled slowly in response. Right now, she knew they felt overwhelmed and more than a little lost. She was thankful she was here to help them examine the gifts they'd been given.

Eva's burden was one of charity. She knew when her neighbors were truly in need and had no way to sort themselves out. It came to her as a heartache, a soul wearying sorrow, and the only balm was to provide for those who couldn't provide for themselves. She'd long ago learned to concentrate on her feeling while thinking about her neighbors in turn, knowing the answer to "Who needs what?" would come to her if she sat still and listened to her heart. That's how she knew the four Johnson children had no mama in the house and Mr. Johnson was too proud to let the community know his wife had run off. She knew Mr. Johnson struggled to keep all his irons turned and ends meeting. And that's why she made forty extra biscuits every day. Until Leon turned up in her shed, she'd never known how her biscuits made their way to the Johnson house. They simply disappeared from her kitchen sideboard every morning. Yesterday's empty plate was always waiting in their place afterwards.

But the burdens of these two? She suspected Lora's gift was truly heavy, the weight of truth could be difficult for even the strongest and wisest to carry. Based on what they had learned, Lora saw the truth at its most naked and vulnerable. Not truth of perception or interpretation, but that elusive idea of vulnerable truth with no bias or filter. While she knew even less about the weight Leon carried, she had an inkling it was a call to action. She worried over that a little. With Black people rightly protesting the way they were treated, young folks of all colors protesting the conflict in Vietnam, and that same gluttonous war chewing up young men faster than they could come of age, she knew his burden could place him in situations more dangerous than just bumping into a drunk in a graveyard.

• • • •

ONCE THE PLAN WAS IN place and potential obstacles identified, Eva walked the mile or so to the corner store to use the telephone. She didn't have a phone in her house yet; most people in the area didn't. Those who did generally had party lines which meant you couldn't trust private conversations to stay that way. So, she called down to Leon's church, Better Day MBE, and asked the pastor's wife, Mrs. Wiggins, to let Myra Strong know she had blackberries ready for picking and ask if Myra would mind coming to help bring them in. Eva trusted Mrs. Wiggins to get the message to Myra, who lived next door to the church. Eva beat Myra to the house by a scant fifteen minutes.

Carrying her empty blackberry bucket, Myra was huffing and sweating as she jerked open the back door without knocking. Blackberry picking had been a code-word between the two women for years to let the other know there was an emergency which needed handling. She was startled to see her son cradling a coffee mug at Eva's table and blanched when she realized he was part of the blackberry problem. Eva ushered her friend into a chair and poured her a cup of coffee with two spoons of sugar, just the way she knew Myra liked it.

Together, carefully leaving out any mention of secret biscuit deliveries, Eva, Lora, and Leon explained what happened in the graveyard that morning. Myra already knew her son helped a neighbor early every morning, so she didn't question why he was cutting through the cemetery. Hearing he'd knocked over Bumpus and now Bumpus was dead was an entirely different matter however. When they obliquely suggested Mr. Johnson may have seen Leon in the area, Myra exploded from her chair in a fit of panic and worry, her hands fluttering like dragonflies unsure of a safe landing spot.

Leon captured her hands in his with a gentle smile. "Mama. Everything is going to be fine! Calm down, please. Miss Eva and Miss Lora are helping me!"

Myra snatched her hands from his, freeing them to flutter about his face again, and shout-whispered, "Leon! Don't you be telling me to calm down! You might have killed a white man! Accidental or not, Lord have mercy! You don't understand the kind of trouble you could be in!"

Once they'd fanned her down, warding off what was shaping up to be a full-blown, wet hen conniption fit, they laid out the immediate plan. Leon would stay the night at Eva's. Tomorrow morning, she would drive him to Decatur where he would catch a Greyhound bus for Chicago and Maurice. They found comfort in the hope that Maurice could come through with that job. Leon would call Maurice's boarding house from the bus station to let his brother know where to pick him up.

While Myra went home to pack his bag, Leon sat at the table with his eyes closed. When he spoke, his voice quivered and his lip trembled, but his tone was resolute. "Miss Eva. Miss Lora. I never expected y'all to take me on like this. If I'd known carrying biscuits would turn out this way, I'd have ignored that feeling in my gut!"

With a "Ha!" Eva reached across the table and tightly gripped his hand. "Leon, I've been trying to ignore my guts for ages. Trust me. It can't be done. You'll go crazy! You did what you were supposed to do. My guts told me to make the biscuits. I knew I was making them for the Johnsons but never knew how they got there, until today. My gut told me to make them, not deliver them. Looks like me an' you've been silent partners for a while now!" She said this last bit with a smirk, 'silent partners' made them sound like fancy businessmen instead of farm neighbors eking out meager livings one season at a time. She carried on telling them both what it meant to be a bearer. Just like a seed knowing exactly the right time to send up a little green shoot; somehow their souls, their feelings, knew the exact need and wouldn't allow them to ignore it. Leon was none too pleased with this particular revelation and grumbled again that he'd still have tried.

"Miss Eva, I ain't never been away from home. Never wanted to be. I'm scared. I know you're risking yourself by helping me and I appreciate it. I can't tell you how much." Leon's voice cracked. Eva gathered him up in a fierce hug and kissed his head.

"Hush now. You didn't do anything wrong. You believe that; believe it with all your heart. You are a good man. Me and Lora aren't about to let this ruin your life because some people don't understand accidents. Not if we can help it. And we can. You're going to go to Chicago and be brave. We'll take care of everything here. Don't you worry."

He sank into Eva's hug with relief and seemed right at home. When Eva finally let him go, Lora chimed in with a grin and hug of her own, saying, "And unless you want me to start calling you Mr. Strong, please call me Lora. No more ma'am and Miss? It's just weird."

· · · ·

MYRA WOKE THEM UP BEFORE the sun rolled over in its bed. With her three younger boys in tow, all carrying blackberry buckets just in case, she hugged Leon and patted his chest, patted his face, swallowing oceans of air in every breath. With herculean effort, he controlled his tears, promising her everything would be okay. She kissed his forehead and stepped back, gripping Lora's hand in a shaking squeeze as they stood inside the back door watching Eva and Leon leave in her ancient, but reliable, International pick-up. When the taillights blinked out of sight, the five of them swished through dew-covered grass to the blackberry bushes and silently reached into the thorns.

No biscuits were made, or delivered, that day. Myra and the boys walked home not long after dawn, blackberry buckets full and hearts empty. Lora spent the morning pulling weeds and mulling over her thoughts. Eva returned just before noon. She joined Lora in the garden and, as casual as commenting on the weather, said, "He's on his way. We need to gather fresh willow bark from the creek. On our way home, we'll stop at the store, all distraught and helpless, to tell them we found Bumpus dead in the graveyard. The men will take it from there. If anyone mentions Mr. Johnson's visitor yesterday mornin', we don't know nothing."

Lora rested on her haunches, squinting into the morning sun limning her grandmother in a golden glow, and nodded. "Agreed. It's not perfect but it is right. And that's all we can do for now."

2

On Sunday, Eva and Lora made their way to morning services at Holley Hill Church of Christ. Naturally, between preaching and Sunday School, the entire congregation chattered and speculated about recent events in the graveyard. Most knew that Eva and Lora had found Bumpus's body in the cemetery; some were eager to pluck carrion details off their grisly discovery.

Agnes Crawford, in a suffocating cloud of Avon fragrances and layers of wilting pink lace, tittered, "Oh Eva! Bless your heart! How upsetting! Did he smell something awful? Had he started bloating up yet?"

Margaret Clem, adjusting her veil, looked down her long nose and sniffed, "I'm sure every critter and bug in that cemetery was as drunk as he was after they'd had a nibble of him. That man was probably just fermenting in this heat. Tell me, was he still holding on to his bottle?"

Helen Fudge, the preacher's wife, waved her cardboard fan to swirl the stuffy air, and hooked her fleshy arm through Eva's. She pulled Eva into a moist embrace and chimed in with, "Dale said it was just awful and sad. To see a good man lose his way and his life in such a sad place. Was he leaned up against the stones of his wife and children? How sad. Please Eva, tell us everything. You'll feel better if you let us help you deal with the shock."

Eva Burnette was a sturdy, silver-haired, plain-spoken country woman made of no-nonsense practicality and a sly sense of humor. She was salt-of-the-earth and fragile was the last word anyone would ever use to describe her. Still, cool as a cucumber, Eva masterfully played the 'fragile lady' part in response to her friends' squelching concerns. She was so convincing even Lora almost believed her. She watched her grandmother clasp their hands as the sympathetic vultures disguised hovered and crooned. Eva shook her head, dabbed her eyes, and explained it was just all too horrible to discuss. Their faces fell when they realized there would be no juicy bits offered up for contemplation and consumption.

Glancing away from the wheedling matriarchs to the congregation gathered in the hall, Lora smiled to herself a little. The teenagers fidgeted around the water fountain while the men huddled around Mr. Johnson just outside the double doors leading into the sanctuary. From their stiff postures and sharp gestures, it appeared their conversation was more intense than that of the ladies, so she drifted closer, pretending to look at last week's sermon notes, 'God's Grace,' which were tacked to the bulletin board.

"I'm telling you! I chased a nigger off my property last Monday! Followed him all the way to the woods before I lost'im! The day before Eva Burnette found Bumpus in the graveyard!" Mr. Johnson croaked, spitting Eva's name as he said it.

The men sucked in sharp breaths. Lora didn't know his name but an elderly man, gripping the brim of his hat with angry, arthritic knuckles, leaned closer to Mr. Johnson with an unsettling glint in his eye. "Hal, what was he doing at your place? Would you know him if you saw him again?"

"I don't know. I might. All those darkies look the same to me. 'Sides, it don't matter what he was doing! He was coming out of my house. I ain't never had a nigger in my house and I never will! If I coulda caught him, I'd have made sure he didn't make that mistake again."

Dale Fudge, the preacher, put a steadying hand on Hal Johnson's shoulder and said, "Easy, Hal. Do you think this boy had something to do with Bumpus's accident?"

Hal Johnson hissed, "I don't know, s'possible. My sister tol' me to call the law about the trespassin' though." Mr. Johnson took a deep breath and schooled his expression into one of superior citizenship. "So I did. Early said he'd ask around. Maybe he can dig up something." He gripped his worn bible so tightly it looked like his fingers would punch right through and meet in the middle.

Lora's heart leapt into her throat, where a heart has no business being, and felt her face turn red. Alarmed and worried, she drifted back to the women's group. She laid her hand on Eva's arm and said, "Gram, I'm not feeling very well all of a sudden. Would it be alright if I went back to the house to lie down?"

The flush of her skin lent truth to the lie as Eva gently touched the back of her hand to Lora's forehead. "Child you're warm! Of course! Come on, I'll take you home." Nodding excuses to her friends, she put her arm around Lora's shoulder and walked her out of the building, ushering her into the sweltering heat of the pick-up.

• • • •

ONLY WHEN THEY WERE safely away did Lora tell her grandmother what she'd learned with her eavesdropping. Eva's lips whittled themselves into a thin line as she thought for several long moments. "You didn't hear anything about Leon specifically?" she finally asked.

"No ma'am but Gram, this is a small community and Black or white, it won't be long before word gets around that he's been gone since about the same time! And what about the hateful way Mr. Johnson said your name?" Lora was starting to feel more than a little panicked. She plucked a lock of hair from her ponytail and twisted it through her fingers, brushing the ends across her lips.

Eva pulled Lora's hand away from her face. "Well, you're right about that. I don't suppose Hal Johnson bothered telling'em there were biscuits in his house that wasn't there before he went to the barn that morning? These men! Always assuming the worst and needing to be offended by something. Pfft! They wear me out. Don't you worry about Hal Johnson and his opinion of me or my name. You'd just be wasting your time."

Shaking her head, Eva reached up and snatched off the circle of white lace which served as her head covering for worship and flung it onto the truck seat. Pounding the heel of her hand on the wheel with every word, she muttered. "Good God Almighty! This is 1966 not 1896. When are folks gonna learn? At least we know Leon got off to Chicago with no problems and is safe for now. But we do need to get word to Myra. Sounds like we need to put it out that he left at least a week ago."

Lora felt a smile spread across her face and realized she'd never seen her grandmother like this before. At that moment, if Eva said she'd marched from Selma to Montgomery with Dr. King last year, Lora would have believed her. It was looking like Eva was a sneaky little activist! Lora loved her all the more for it and started to feel quite rebellious herself.

When she saw Lora grinning like a mule eating saw briers on the other side of the truck cab, Eva did a double take and grinned back. "What? What are you grinning about?"

Lora asked, "Are you following your knowing or just doing what's right? I've never seen you so worked up!"

Eva's grin slipped for a heartbeat but quickly repaired itself. "I don't think the two are all that different. See, everybody has a different idea of what's right. Problem is, most of those interpretations are clouded by what they want or what they're scared of; not what's actually right. I've always tried to study things and figure out what's right, not necessarily what I want."

She gripped the steering wheel and swerved to avoid a stray dog as it darted across the road. "Do you think I wanted to make four dozen biscuits every day for the past few months? No. The knowing told me I needed to help feed the Johnsons and so I had to. I had no choice. I reckon I could have told the church about it and the women would've started a collection or carried stacks of casserole dishes over to his place. But no, I just knew it was a matter of pride for Hal and to keep it to myself. Besides, how would I have explained it to them? I knew my biscuits would meet the need so I made them. Would I have helped anyway? Of course! So, there you have it. The knowing and the right are the same. You know what's funny though? I ain't made any extra biscuits since the day we found Leon in my shed. And haven't felt like I should."

Lora considered what her grandmother said and asked another question. "Gram, how could Mrs. Johnson just up and leave her kids? And why didn't you take the biscuits yourself? You knew she left. You knew he was struggling. You could have taken them and told him his secret was safe with you. Everybody around here knows you don't gossip. No matter how hard they might try." She giggled a little at the memory of the church ladies prodding Eva for details and coming away empty handed.

Turning the truck into the yard, expertly dodging the wash-out where the drive and the road met, Eva replied, "Mm hm. Arlene Johnson was Hal's second wife. She was slip of a girl, only about ten years older than Maggie, his oldest. His first wife passed away birthing their youngest. Hal needed a wife and Arlene needed, well, something. I don't know what she thought she'd get from being married to Hal." She parked behind the house and gathered her things before swinging the door open to a welcome gust of breeze. "Anyway, that first day, I intended to take them. I made the biscuits. Piled'em up on a plate and went to change outta my housedress. When I came back to the kitchen, they were gone and I just had a feeling my part was done. The next morning, I made a mess of biscuits again and went to change. Same thing. The biscuits were gone."

She cut a sharp look at Lora and said, "I had no idea Leon was runnin' them though. What I figured was one of the Johnson kids was coming to get'em, especially since the empty plate from the day before was always left behind."

• • • •

CONVERSATION CONTINUED over a quick lunch of fried-bologna biscuits with mustard while Eva explained the difference between being stupid and being ignorant. Being stupid can't be helped; some people are just not smart and that's no sin. Being ignorant can be remedied and was, in her opinion, inexcusable. She believed without doubt that growth wasn't solely reserved for children. Adults have a responsibility to continue growing, to curing themselves of ignorance. She often quoted scripture like I Thessalonians 5:21-22 which says, "Prove all things; hold fast to that which is good. Abstain from all appearance of evil," in order to support her philosophy.

To Lora, it sounded like Eva used the Bible to argue with her own church. When she asked about it, Eva lifted one shoulder and replied, "I go to that church because it is the church I was raised in. I love the people and we know each other. That don't mean I agree with them all the time or about everything. I push when I can but like the Lord said in Luke 4:24, 'No prophet is accepted in his own country.' I'm no prophet but I do think some of them are wrong in the way they think and act. All I can do is keep trying to teach them." She sighed, "Even though they won't listen."

Once the dishes were done, Eva suggested they run down to the creek and do a little fishing. She clearly thought sitting in the shade with the possibility of hooking a couple catfish for dinner was a better idea than doing any chores around the house. Lora agreed. After changing into well-loved overalls and faded men's work-shirts appropriate for getting muddy and fish-gutty, Lora mused aloud that Eva only ever wore breeches when she was fishing. The observation earned her a playful swat from Eva's sun hat but prompted no explanation. They slung bamboo poles from the shed over their shoulders and started walking.

When Lora wondered about bait, Eva slyly cut her eyes and said, "Well shoot! I knew I was forgetting something. I guess we'll have to stop in over to Myra's and see if her compost pile has any good worms in it."

Lora had no idea where exactly Leon's mama lived but wasn't at all surprised by Eva's completely justifiable explanation. She should have known Eva had an ulterior motive when she'd suggested this spontaneous fishing trip. After all, everything in the county still closed on Sundays and Eva had no way to call Myra's pastor.

Approaching the Strong's little house from the backyard, Lora couldn't help but notice the similarities and differences between it and Eva's home. Both houses had a window and back door with a little stoop where both women propped their floor mops to dry in the sunshine. The porch light jutting from the wall over the door was on. Lora wondered if Myra ever turned it off; Eva never did. Both houses had a hand pump for the well jutting up from the ground not too far from the back door. Lora wondered if Myra had indoor plumbing yet. She remembered when her dad and uncle paid to have plumbing run in their childhood home, carving a tiny bathroom out of one of the downstairs bedrooms and dropping a sink under the kitchen window. At ten, and as a child of the city, she didn't understand at the time why indoor plumbing was such a big deal. Now, she knew there were still folks who lived without it.

Flowers grew at the corners of both homes; Eva chose the brilliant oranges of daylilies, Myra preferred the towering majesty of hollyhocks in a rainbow of colors. While Eva's house was a crisp, happy white, Myra's was a faded gray. Not dirty, just a little sad, like the world was too heavy for its walls. But, there were bicycles propped up by the door and a slightly deflated football past its prime on the bottom step surrounded by a handful of tiny matchbox cars. Lora smiled. These were a sure testament to active children whose mama believed in the need to play as much as the need to work.

Lora knew there was history between Eva and Myra which brought them close and bound them together. She wasn't sure exactly what all the circumstances were but had figured out years ago that their relationship was unusual at the best of times. The two women shared a camaraderie and friendship which ignored social and racial barriers in private while still bowing to convention on the public surface. Behind closed doors, away from listening ears, Eva and Myra were close as sisters, despite the difference in their ages.

Eva ambled to the corner of the yard where a jumbled compost pile of leaves, potato peelings, eggshells, and other questionable kitchen detritus had been tossed. She scavenged a dented coffee can from the trash can beside Myra's shed and took hold of a shovel leaned up against a ramshackle outhouse building When the shovel sunk into the decaying heap, a swirling cloud of insects and rancid odors assaulted their noses and made their eyes water. Working fast, Lora and Eva soon had a healthy crop of earthworms who'd just been handed a death sentence. It wasn't lost on Lora that they hadn't seen Myra, or anyone, and she whispered, "Okay Gram. We got worms but we haven't seen anyone who could tell Myra we're looking for her."

Eva wiped her dirty hands on her breeches and shook her head. Not bothering to whisper, she said, "Don't worry. She'll know. Just because we ain't seen any body, don't mean we haven't been seen. I imagine Myra will come by the house later on. Now, let's go see if they're biting!" And with that, she turned and comically marched towards the creek, whistling the melody of "Onward! Christian Soldiers" and swinging the worm can. Lora hoped dizzy worms would catch fish as readily as steady ones and followed behind.

• • • •

LATER IN THE AFTERNOON, when the few fish they'd caught were cleaned, rolled in meal, and frying busily on the stove top, spitting grease and crispy grains of cornmeal, Lora thought she heard a knock on the back door. When she opened it, a fast-breathing Myra, still wearing her church clothes and hat, scooted into the kitchen and closed the door quickly behind her.

Eva turned from the stove and said, "See Lora. I told you we'd see her tonight. Hey Myra! Catfish is almost ready! You want some?" Folding her arms around Myra in a quick hug, Eva murmured soothing words to her distraught friend.

Myra impatiently waved her off. "No Eva...I'm good. 'Sides, I got chicken to fry when I get home anyways. I heard you was by my place after yo' church let out. I figured there had to be some other reason besides digging up my fishing worms since you could'a pulled them from your own heap. What have you heard? What's folks saying? Is it about my boy?"

Eva poured Myra a glass of iced, sweet tea and motioned for her to sit. Myra was breathing so hard Lora wondered if she'd run all the way from her house. She had no doubt Myra was strong but figured her job as a grocery clerk wasn't known for requiring cross-country treks. Myra was a short, but round, woman who probably didn't run very often. Her robin's egg blue, pillbox hat slipped a little off center, kept in precarious place with just a couple tenacious bobby pins. Myra's hands fidgeted with the hat, trying to adjust its hold, until she eventually just gave up and yanked it off her head altogther. Bobby pins skittered across the beige-speckled linoleum floor.

While Myra fanned herself and sucked down her tea, crunching ice cubes when she caught them, Eva explained that Mr. Johnson was telling people he'd chased a Black man off his property the day before Bumpus was discovered. Eva did not use the "N" word. She didn't need to say it for Myra to know Mr. Johnson had. Eva was quick to reassure her that no one had mentioned Leon specifically but thought it'd be a good idea to tell people he'd accepted his brother's offer to stay with him in Chicago and had left Mooresville at least a week before Bumpus died.

Myra, finally starting to calm down and catch her breath, agreed with nods which shook her whole body, right down to her broad hips. Sucking in a deep cooling breath over the ice in her mouth, she said she'd do just that. She also shared happy news, relayed by Mrs. Wiggins from a phone call received at her church, that Maurice had been able to get Leon on at the rail yard and the brothers were enjoying their time together so far.

Lora listened intently while Eva and Myra chatted. She loved the rare balance in their relationship. Even though desegregation had been legally codified in recent years, the Black and white communities in Mooresville continued to operate side-by-side but separately for the most part. Information and gossip broke the color lines while the people slid around each other on the streets pretending the other didn't exist. As a visiting Yankee, Lora straddled the fence between big city progress and small town recalcitrance. The entire nation was wrestling with civil unrest and to her, Southerners seemed to consider this movement as yet another indignity visited upon them by Northern Aggressors. It hurt her heart that so many good, honest people, refused to understand that just because things have always been a certain way doesn't mean that way is best.

Myra stayed just long enough to finish her tea and catch her breath before thanking Eva for the heads-up and heading home to make dinner for her own family.

· · · ·

MYRA HADN'T BEEN GONE more than ten minutes, just long enough to pull the catfish from the skillet to rest, when there was another knock, from the front door this time. Flashing Lora an irritated look of *What now?* and sparing a regretful glance for the cooling catfish, Eva bustled off to answer the summons. Lora was surprised to hear her call out, "Well hello Sheriff! What can I do for you?"

Eva opened the thick wooden front door wide to let the beanpole of a man into the house. The sheriff was unusually tall and thin with skin pulled tight over all his angles and silvery white hair cut close in a high-and-tight. Wiping her hands on her apron, Eva motioned for him to sit and offered him a glass of tea. Lora knew of the sheriff, Mr. Early Griffin, only through reputation and her grandmother's opinion of him. According to Eva, Sheriff Griffin was a staunch opponent of both equality and justice, especially if the benefactors happened to be anything other than white men. He was as out of place in her grandmother's kitchen as lipstick on a pig. Lora disliked him instantly.

As Eva made introductions, he nodded and took a sip of his tea, commenting graciously about how tasty and refreshing it was. He hadn't bothered to sit. Sheriff Griffin believed in good manners only as far as they went to win over undecided voters. With a smack of his thin lips and a deep sigh of satisfaction, he set his glass next to the stove, perspiration dribbling down the sides and pooling on the warm surface. He plastered sympathy across his taut face. "Mrs. Burnette, I understand you and your granddaughter were the ones who found Bumpus last week? In the cemetery?"

"Yes. That's right. We were gathering some greens and justa 'bout died when we stumbled across him. Just laying there! It was ghastly!"

"Gathering greens, huh? What kind of greens?"

"Well, not greens exactly but all the same," she waved her hand in dismissal, her voice thin and crinkly. "We went down to the creek bank to get some willow bark. I get these headaches, see, and nothing works better for them than willow bark tea. I don't care how many aspirins I take, willow bark is the thing. Lands! I certainly needed it when we got back to the house after finding poor old Bumpus in that awful state. Bless him."

Lora was puzzled by Eva's sudden frail, babbling old lady change of demeanor. Her grandmother's feistiness had melted away the moment the sheriff crossed the threshold.

Eva continued, "What's this all about Sheriff? Surely you didn't come all the way from town, at this hour of the evening, just to ask me about my headaches? I appreciate your concern but I reckon there's something else on your mind?" She made a convincing pitiful show of lowering herself into a chair, holding her back with one hand, stooping over just a little.

Sheriff Griffin puffed out his narrow chest in an obvious, and unnecessary, attempt to intimidate. His beady black eyes and smooth, nut-brown tanned skin managed that feat all on their own. Lora thought he resembled nothing more than a walking, talking mummy from a cheesy horror film at the drive-in. He said, "Well, we've gotten word that there was a Black boy running in the direction of the cemetery the same day Bumpus was killed."

"KILLED? Oh lands! We figured Bumpus was falling down drunk as usual, and well, that he'd just fell over and konked himself! " Eva drew in a sharp breath and clutched her chest in shock. "Sheriff! You don't think it was an accident? The blood on the stone! That awful gash on his temple! You can't be saying something different!"

Lora rushed to Eva's side and fanned her with a dish towel. For the first time, she addressed the sheriff directly. "Sheriff Griffin. Why would anyone think a Black man running had anything to do with Bumpus' death? I'm not sure I understand the connection."

Griffin leaned over to look her in the eye, resting his hands on his upper thighs. In a slimy, infuriating tone, he said, "I understand you ain't from here. Now missy, I'm the law and as such, I have to look for connections when anything suspicious happens in my jurisdiction." He spoke slowly, enunciating each word, the way one does when speaking to a child. "Hal Johnson says a Black man ran from his place that morning, towards the cemetery, and the next day you and your grandmother just happened to find Bumpus dead in that same cemetery. Who knows that boy didn't just decide to knock Bumpus upside the head a couple times and rob him? Your grandmother is awfully chummy with the negroes around here."

He straightened and spread his hands like his point was obvious. "And so like I said, I have to look for all the connections little lady. You never know what I might find."

In a sudden, startling shift from patronizing placation to near accusation, he stabbed his finger at her nose and asked, "Now, did you or your grandmother see anybody running through here the day before you found Bumpus? Did you notice anything unusual about the cemetery?"

Lora glanced at Eva and both women shook their heads. Eva, pulling the sheriff's attention back in her direction, said, "In the morning, you say? We don't usually get out of the house until probably nine o'clock or so. Breakfast and clearing away, you know. And then we spent all day pulling weeds and hoeing the garden that day. I don't reckon we looked up from the ground other than to come in for lunch. Lora?"

Taking Eva's lead, Lora folded her arms across her chest and added, "Right. After breakfast, we washed some canning jars, getting ready for vegetables to start coming in. Afterwards, well, with the big brims on our hats, it's hard to see much going on around us."

She waved her hand towards the hooks on the wall near the back door where their gardening hats hung. Both made of cool yellow straw with brims wide enough to shade the eyes and the backs of their necks at the same time, it was easy to believe any peripheral vision would have been limited. "And, as far as the cemetery goes, I didn't see anything unusual. I mean, other than Bumpus, of course." Lora shrugged, "At first, I thought he was just sleeping it off in the quietest place he could find. I'll admit, it was quite a shock to find a dead man above ground in a graveyard and we just ran for help as soon as we saw him."

Lora lifted her chin, silently challenging the sheriff to find fault with her logic or reasoning. Sheriff Griffin pinned her in place with a piercing stare for a couple heartbeats and held his hat by the brim as he started towards the door. In yet another sudden change of attitude, this time benevolent, he prevaricated, "I know it was awful for you ladies. And I'm sorry to have brought such disturbing ideas through your door. I hope you feel safer knowing me and my men are looking deeper into this. Rest assured, we'll be patrolling down here more often until we can be sure we've caught the responsible party. After all, we can't have anybody running around here beating war heroes to death." He stepped onto the front porch, put his hat back on and left without looking back.

• • • •

WHEN THE DOOR CLOSED behind him, and the screen door bouncing and banging in its frame, Lora blurted, "War heroes? What does that mean? Gram, do you feel safer with that man on the prowl?" As she spoke, the space behind her left eye burst into a kaleidoscope of color and pain. Her vision blurred and she froze in the spot where she stood. Forgetting her concerns about Bumpus being a war hero, she pushed a knuckle against her eye and gasped. "Gram. Sheriff Griffin has your plate. He thinks you had something to do with Bumpus' death!"

Eva grunted. "Well, that's a fly in the buttermilk. I hadn't even thought about that derned plate." For the first time that evening, she looked a little worried. Her brows creased and she shook her hands like she was flinging away a squashed bug. "Ooh! I don't like the idea of being in that man's crosshairs. He's a snake and liable to strike at anything that moves."

Lora agreed with her grandmother's assessment of Sheriff Griffin. Everything about the sheriff made her skin crawl, from the way his unlined face slid across his skull to his too-slick, better-than-you manner of speaking. After their brief interaction, Lora wanted to take a scalding hot bath. She hated it when a man talked down to her and Sheriff Griffin had crossed that line as soon as he'd hunkered down to eye level.

She asked, "How does he know it's your plate? Couldn't it easily be someone else's?"

Eva crossed to the cupboard, her steps and hands both a little unsteady, and took out a plate. Turning it over, she showed Lora a very small "EB" neatly penned underneath the maker's mark. "This is my marker. Most church ladies have one, or something similar, so we know whose dishes are whose. Church picnics, weddings, funerals...it's easy for dishes to wander off and never find their way home. The bigger question is where did he find it?"

Lora wrinkled her forehead and covered her face with her hands. Muffled behind them, puffs of breath fluttering her bangs as the air escaped between her fingers when she spoke, she said, "Gram. There are so many questions. Where did he find the plate? What's wrong with being 'chummy' with Black people? Why would he think a plate connects you in any way with Mr. Johnson or Mr. Bumpus? And what on earth did he mean by 'beating war heroes to death'?" Remembering the way Eva had all but cowered when the Sheriff walked in, she dropped her hands to her hips, pulling a face like she smelled something rotten and added, "And what was with the pitiful old lady act you put on while he was here?"

Eva chuckled and once again, Lora was buffeted by the winds of humor in situations which were most definitely not funny. She rolled her eyes at her grandmother and sucked in a deep, calming breath, waiting for Eva to speak. Hoping she would say something comforting, reassuring.

Instead, Eva gestured towards the television set and said, "How about we watch a little TV while I think on things a bit? *Voyage to the Bottom of the Sea* is on. I do like that show." Turning the knob and adjusting the antenna, Eva settled into her rocking chair, adjusting a brightly colored cushion behind her back and put her feet up on the worn leather stool in front of the chair. Lora knew there was no point in pushing for answers once Eva mentioned television. Watching television was Eva's one guilty pleasure. She especially loved taking mid-day breaks to watch her 'stories', also known as *Guiding Light* and *As the World Turns*. She was proud of her television and the big Magnavox console with built-in radio which sat proudly along the wall of the living room. It was a gift from her not-so-secret favorite, third oldest son, Anthony, just after he'd joined the civil service and moved to California. Eva was sure his life was filled with movie stars and limousines even though he lived in Sacramento and nowhere near Hollywood.

3

Lora suffocated through their voyage to the depths and as the credits rolled, tried again. In a voice that sounded like there was no more oxygen to be had, she asked, "Gram. What about Sheriff Griffin? Your plate? Bumpus?"

Eva ran her hands along the arm rests and pushed herself out of her seat. She switched off the television and with a heavy sigh, sat back down. "Okay Lora. Sheriff Griffin is going to try to make out like I am the connection between the Black man at Hal's and Bumpus's death. He and I have butted heads more than once over the years, even before he was elected, mostly over petty things. He'd like nothing better than to bring me down a couple notches. I pretended to be a meek old woman so as not to stir up any more trouble with him. I don't believe he'd outright accuse me of any wrongdoing but sometimes just hinting is enough. Wherever he found my plate has to be somewhere between here and the Johnson's. Leon mentioned he'd dropped it, remember? So I reckon that's why he stopped in. Just to see if he could fluster me. As far as Bumpus goes, well, that's a story."

"So tell me," Lora urged softly. She pulled her bare feet up underneath her and leaned an elbow on the armrest, propping her chin in her hand. Waiting.

Eva nodded and closed her eyes, leaning her head back against the rocker. She breathed deep, her voice thick with memory as she spoke. "'PRIVATE ETHELRED BUMPUS RETURNS FROM THE WESTERN FRONT' That was the headline in the Alabama Courier out of Athens when Bumpus was shipped home. I guess this was in 1918? And before you ask, yes, that was his real first name. His mama must have hated him from the get-go to stick a name like that on him when he slithered out of her womb."

She pushed into her feet, setting the rocker into motion. "Anyway, he came back with a slight limp, a cur-dog smile and more than a couple screws loose. He was discharged because of an injury to his right foot. Everybody assumed he'd been wounded going over the top of the trenches but in truth, he'd shot himself. On purpose. See, Bumpus was a coward before he joined up. He was always shootin' off at the mouth and then runnin' when anybody called him out. He was loud, coarse, whiny, and lazy. Acted like the world owed him something just for the privilege of breathing the same air."

Eva was getting agitated just talking about Bumpus, rocking the chair faster and faster, rubbing her hands on her legs and twisting her skirt in her fists. Lora was enthralled with this story she'd never heard before. She didn't like seeing her grandmother upset, but there was obviously something else about Bumpus which rubbed her the wrong way, something more than being a drunken nuisance to the community.

Eva wheezed a sarcastic laugh. "Problem was that before the war, none of us girls thought he was anything more than a pest and wouldn't have anything to do with him. He was handsome enough but Lord, when that boy started talking! Stupid just poured out in clumps like sour milk! When the Great War started in Europe, all the girls swooned over men in uniform. So, in nineteen hundred and seventeen, when he was seventeen, Bumpus decided he'd get himself into one of those uniforms. All he saw was the shine of the medals and the sharp cut of the jackets. He thought he'd go over there, show those Germans what for and come home to ladies fawning all over him."

She continued, "And, I guess that was the case for a little while. He managed to catch a sweet little girl from up at Belle Mina, Dot was her name, and it wasn't long before they got married and started having babies. Shortly after the first one came along, he started drinking too much and one night, in a blind drunk confession, he let it slip to Dot that he'd been so scared, so wrong, so out of place, he'd shot himself to punch his ticket home. Dot was sweet but by this time had seen him for what he was. A coward who cared about no one but himself. She told her mama, who told her sister, and eventually most everybody knew he hadn't been wounded in action. Bumpus didn't know his secret was out but he did notice he wasn't being treated like the hero he'd made himself out to be. He drank more and more, stopped trying to do any work, started beating his frustration into Dot and the children...and—,"

She waved a hand in Lora's direction. "Well, you know the rest. I don't need to repeat it. Folks said he had war neurosis and I don't doubt it. But, it's still no excuse for what he did to his family. He should have shot himself in the head and saved everyone a world of grief." With that damning statement, Eva abruptly got to her feet. She said she was going to bed and wished Lora a good night. Her bedroom door clicked shut behind her.

· · · ·

LORA SAT ALONE IN THE living room for a few minutes more, listening to the peaceful summer symphony of crickets, frogs, and cicadas drifting in through the open windows and trying to make sense of what she'd just heard. She moved softly around the little house, turning off lights and clearing away the catfish they hadn't had a chance to eat. She mulled things over and nagged at the unanswered questions rattling around in her head. Bumpus's story was sad from the beginning and tragic at the end, but she still didn't understand why Eva was so harsh and unforgiving. Sure, Bumpus was no-good but what did it really matter to Eva? Why did just the telling of something that happened so many years ago still upset her so much? Normally direct, Eva had side-stepped most of her questions and this tied her guts in knots, leaving her more unsettled than before. Deciding there was nothing more for it until the morning, Lora went upstairs to her room under the eaves and hoped it would rain during the night. The breeze wafting through her window smelled like it might but she couldn't be sure the heavens weren't teasing her.

When she opened her eyes in the morning, Lora laid in bed for a while, staring at the ceiling and listening to the low rumble of thunder in the distance. Tiny pinpricks of rust showed through the white plaster bearing witness to the decades long, slow seep of water from the tin roof above; it could be years before any real damage was done. She listened for the familiar sounds of her grandmother moving around and sniffed for the comforting smells of breakfast being made. The house was silent and still. Grabbing her dressing gown, she went downstairs to find out why.

It was too dark for this time of morning. When Lora looked outside, petulant black clouds loomed overhead and she knew the day's weather would keep them inside. Eva was not in the kitchen like she usually was; patting out biscuits, brewing coffee, frying eggs. Alarmed, Lora turned to Eva's room, her heartbeat thudding in her ears loud enough to drown out the approaching storm, and softly knocked. "Gram? Are you in there?" Worried, she pushed the door open a little ways.

Eva was still in bed, her back to the door. Gloomy dawn filtered in through the gauzy window sheers, an unseasonably cool breeze drifted along the sills of slightly cracked windows into the room. Outside, with a booming jostle, the clouds burst and unleashed a torrential burst of rain on the little house. Lora lifted the faded, soft quilt and curled up next to her grandmother, the way she'd done when she was little. She laid a hand on Eva's shoulder. "Hey...Are you okay?"

"No Lora, not really. I had a bad night and think I might just stay here today, if you don't mind."

"Are you sick? Should I go call the doctor? You never spend the day in bed!"

"No, I'm not sick. Not sick in a way a doctor could help anyways."

Lora pulled the thin quilt up over their arms and scrunched in closer. "You want to talk about it? I'm pretty good at listening you know."

Eva rolled onto her back and stretched, old joints cracking and popping as she worked the sleep out. She rubbed crust from her eyes and squinted in Lora's direction. "I guess I should. But before I do, why don't you go make us some coffee and grab a couple of yesterday's biscuits? We'll have breakfast in bed while I talk." Eva gave Lora a reassuring half-smile as she left the room.

Lord help me, Eva thought as she made her way to the bathroom while Lora went to the kitchen. *Why do simple things have to get so complicated?*

By the time Lora returned, the wind had picked up, blowing rain into the room and tossing the sheers across the bed. Eva was propped up on her pillow with the quilt spread across her lap. Lora stifled a giggle when she came in, balancing a platter with coffee, biscuits, and some honey to boot. Eva may have situated herself like the Queen of Sheba on her throne, but her tightly permed, silver hair was sticking out to give Medusa a run for her money. Lora passed the platter to Eva and closed the window. Thunder roared in protest. Curling up cross-legged on top of the blanket, facing her grandmother, Lora smiled as she pulled the dipper from the honey pot and drizzled a generous dollop of golden deliciousness on a biscuit before handing it to Eva. She'd intentionally brought up all of yesterday's biscuits so she wouldn't have to go back for seconds and left the coffee pot on a hot pad just outside the bedroom door for the same reason. If Eva was going to talk, she didn't want to ruin the tale telling with constant trips to the kitchen.

Eva took a sip of her coffee and immediately sucked in air to cool her tongue. After a bite of honeyed biscuit, she spoke. "Last night hurt my heart. Bumpus's wife, Dot, was my first cousin and best friend. Her mama was my mama's sister and we were thick as thieves when we were girls. She was a sweet thing with so much life in her! She laughed loud and loved hard. I've never met anyone with more backbone to them than Dot. I hated seeing her married to Bumpus but hated even more watching her wither away under his thumb.

"The day she died, the day she burned up, that was the one and only time my knowing set me an impossible task. I woke up that morning feeling like my heart was being yanked from my chest. I couldn't catch my breath! I studied and prayed over it, trying to figure out what I was supposed to do. I knew I was supposed to help Dot but couldn't figure out what exactly needed doing. I walked over to their place and she wouldn't let me in. She said the little one had kept her up all night, they had four kids by this time, one right after the other, seems she was always pregnant." Eva choked in a ragged gulping breath.

"Anyways, the baby was miserable; coughing and crying with the croup. She said they were going to try to sleep for a bit. Bumpus was nowhere to be found. I begged her to let me in, to let me help her with the baby, to take the others for a while, anything, but she wouldn't have it. She got mean and told me to mind my own damn business and leave. I got mad and left; my heart aching the whole walk back. It was everything I could do to put one foot in front of the other. I knew I had a job to do but couldn't figure out what it was or how to do it. I came home and told Dub about my feeling and how she'd treated me. He said I'd done all I could and it'd be best to forget about it. He figured everything would be fine; but it wasn't. I know now I was supposed to save her. I reckon I should have busted out a window or barreled into the door and forced her to come away with me, but I didn't. I was a coward."

Eva drew a serrated breath and twisted the quilt in her hands. "I was a coward." She paused for several moments, giving her words time to catch up with her racing emotions.

"When I looked across the fields after talking to him, Black smoke billowed up from her direction. Towering over the countryside like Beelzebub himself had stepped up out of Hell. I could smell it. Worse, while I watched the smoke, the ache in my heart went away only to be replaced with suffocating grief. A void. I just felt empty inside. I knew I'd failed my gift and, worse, failed my best friend in the process. That sweet woman, that incredible laughter, was gone. Gone forever. All because of Bumpus."

Eva's voice steadied and her steely eyes flashed with remembered, everlasting anger. "He didn't come back around until two days later. When he finally showed up, he was caterwauling and carrying on. Acting a fool. Of course some folks, including Early Griffin, said Dot was crazy and felt sorry for him, which is what he wanted. But most of us knew he was the real reason for her doing what she did. Early had been a deputy for only a short time when Dot set that fire, and he'd been one of those who said the law couldn't intervene in marital concerns. I blame him too."

She rubbed her weathered hands across her face. With a weary, penitent sigh, Eva looked at Lora, her eyes now dull and flat. In the short time she'd been talking, her wrinkles had deepened and her shoulders sloped with more than age. She looked as though all her strength had been sucked out like a tornado which pulls every last hay straw from a barn but leaves the barn standing, each board battered but whole.

Lora whistled low through her teeth and said, "Oh Jeez. How awful. For all of you." Her coffee had gone cold, and she didn't care. Her appetite was gone and her breakfast was threatening to make a return trip. Seeing Eva's devastation, Lora gathered the dishes and brushed crumbs from the bed saying, "Why don't you go back to

sleep and I'll go read or watch television for a bit?" Lora hoped
the mention of watching television would perk her grandmother up
a little. She was disappointed when Eva agreed and slumped back
down under the covers, turning her face away from the door.

Eva spent the rest of the day in bed, shrouded in memories of
a tragedy long dead. Lora peeked in every few hours to see if she
needed anything but was always met with little more than a barely
perceptible shake of the head or shrug of the shoulder. She felt
strange moving around the house by herself. All day long, furious
thunderstorms raged and pounded outside, insistently picking away
at the roof tin, threatening to drop the large oak tree in the front
yard onto the house and smash them to bits. She never turned on the
television, choosing instead to watch the storm's tantrum play out
through the kitchen window. Eva may have been mourning her dead,
but Lora was anxiously working to understand how she could have
missed the heaviness of this place.

She felt like she was trying to hold smoke in her hand,
desperately grasping at the unraveling threads of idyll peace of her
childhood memories. Had she been sheltered or willfully ignorant?
How did she not know these shadows? By the time evening rolled
around, and Eva hadn't done more than pop out to go to the
bathroom all day long, Lora had made exactly one decision. If Eva
agreed, she would not be returning to Detroit and her parents' house
the first of August. She wanted to stay with her grandmother and
help her weather whatever storms were brewing over the horizon.

4

E va was up with the cock crow the next morning, bright eyed and bushy tailed, ready to tackle the day. Sunlight strutted through the window over the sink, tempting her with promises of a gorgeous morning in the wake of yesterday's storms. She loved her little kitchen and cherished her early morning routines – each step the same as so many before. In those quiet moments, Dub's presence could still be felt in every strain and creak of the floorboards. There were days, when the humidity was low and the breeze was cool, out of nowhere, Eva would catch herself talking to herself, talking to him, and have to remind herself he was gone.

She chuckled under her breath as she patted out sausage patties, remembering the outdoor kitchen she used in the early days of their marriage. That first kitchen was just a small pole-barn behind the three room house on the overlarge farm they'd bought from his parents when they got married in 1918. Dub eventually cut a doorway in the back wall and enclosed the lean-to shed just behind the house. He wanted Eva to have a 'modern' inside kitchen.

The floor tilted slightly. Not enough to notice when you walked but enough that pencils and apples rolled off the table and under the stove if not laid down just-so. The cabinets were a hodge-podge of bespoke shelving and roadside finds with a kaleidoscope of counter surfaces from butcher block to faded, worn green Formica. Although the kitchen now boasted an electric range, indoor plumbing, and a small second-hand refrigerator, Dub's one extravagance for Eva's kitchen at the time was a large, Black, wood burning stove and oven which still held court from one end of the room. That big iron oven was still her go-to when she made biscuits. Everything else could be trusted to the newer electric appliances but her biscuits, well, that was a different matter altogether. She said a silent prayer each time she stoked the fire and closed the door on a fresh batch, thanking God for gifting her with Dub.

Family lore said he'd surprised her with it when she'd come home from a visit to her sister's house in Tennessee to help care for a sick child. They said Eva walked in the front door and thought the house was on fire from all the smoke. Dub wanted to have it lit, warm, and ready to cook when she got there but hadn't quite set the dampers correctly. All the smoke was pouring into the house instead of drawn up the stove pipe. She'd wound up cooking their supper on the old stove in the outdoor kitchen like always that night. In time, Eva mastered the new oven and was churning out big, fluffy biscuits like a pro.

Smiling at the memories and waving them away 'til later, Eva realized it had been ages since she'd frittered a day away in bed. So long, she couldn't remember the last time. Still, there wasn't much she could have done other than house cleaning anyway. The roiling storms of the previous day made sure everyone stayed indoors.

Padding barefoot down the stairs, Lora was relieved to see Eva bustling about the kitchen from sink to table to stove and oven like she hadn't missed a beat. She loved watching her grandmother juning around in her lavender flowered house dress and slippers, humming some nameless tune under her breath while she cleaned and biscuits puffed in the oven. In the background, the tinny voices of the "Sick Call" broadcasters crackled from a little transistor radio on the windowsill. Every so often, the broadcaster would mention someone Eva knew. She'd tsk-tsk and bless their hearts, all without missing a beat in the breakfast making. Lora peeped around the door frame just in time to see Eva reach into the cupboard for something or other.

Opening the cabinet door, Eva was nose-to-nose with a little gray mouse nibbling on a crumb, unbothered, on the shelf right at eye level. Without hesitation, she whispered, "Well fella that ain't it."

And quick as a snake, she snatched him up and popped his head off with her thumb. Not realizing Lora was watching from the doorway, she shrugged and said, "Got that dude!" before casually chucking the mouse and his head out the back door. Washing her hands, she muttered under her breath, "Unh-unh. I don't mind mice but I can't have them taking up residence in my kitchen. They need to know their place. Yes sir...vermin belong in the yard." Without another word, she went back to fixing breakfast like nothing had happened.

Lora jerked back out of sight and clapped her hands over her mouth, blinking her eyes back into her skull. Clearing her throat to let Eva know she was there, she opted to ignore the small murder she'd just witnessed and chirped, "Good morning Gram! You're looking better today! What's on our agenda this morning?" Picking up a hot biscuit and sausage patty, Lora crossed to the table, stopping on her way to get mustard and milk out of the fridge. Eva made a thoughtful noise in her throat like a cross between a grunt and a hum. Gesturing towards the back door with her dish cloth, Eva replied, "Well, I reckoned we'd go out, survey the storm damage, and clean up a bit before it gets too hot. You know where your mud shoes are?" Lora nodded while she chewed.

· · · ·

SMOOSHING THEIR WAY around the saturated yard, small puddles oozing up and sucking at their feet, they quickly worked up a sweat in the thick, still morning haze while picking up branches and trash which had blown down and through. Lora figured now was as good a time as any and said, "Gram? I was thinking. If you don't mind, I'd like to stay, move in here with you. There's no real reason for me to go back to Detroit in a few weeks. I mean, I was planning to go to the community college back home but that isn't a big deal since I can always go to Calhoun here. I thought I could help you out and still go to school. What do you think?"

Eva bit the inside of her cheeks for a minute before speaking. "Well Lora, I'd love that! But only if you're sure. You ain't just saying this because I had a bad day yesterday, are you?"

"No. No ma'am. Not at all. You know I love it here. I look forward to my summer vacations with you all year long. Especially when I'm freezing to death in Detroit every December! I've been thinking about this for a while now." Lora felt her cheeks flush just a bit at this small lie but was pretty sure Eva wouldn't notice. They were both red-faced from their exertions cleaning up the yard.

"Have you talked to your Mama and Daddy about it? Will they mind? You didn't run off to the store and call them while I was in bed yesterday?"

Lora shook her head and drug the back of a sweating gloved hand across her eyes to dislodge a wisp of hair from her eyelashes. "No, I haven't mentioned anything to them yet. I wanted to make sure it was okay with you first. Besides, no one in their right mind would have gone anywhere in those storms if they didn't have to." She picked up a branch and heaved it onto the pile in the wheelbarrow. "I don't think Mom and Dad will mind. They might even be glad to have the house all to themselves."

Lora was an only child and didn't mind that she had no siblings to play or squabble with. There were always plenty of kids in her neighborhood to fill the shoes of an older, or younger, sister or brother when necessary. These friends flitted in and out of her house with the same regularity as she skipped through theirs. Her entire street felt like one big family. Almost all the dads worked at the Ford factory and carpooled to work. Most of them were veterans and spent their drives either working out their personal demons or pointedly ignoring them. The moms planned neighborhood cook-outs and Easter egg hunts, Christmas caroling, and trick-or-treating. Coloring the children's days in primary colors and wrapping their nights in starlight dreams.

Although her parents, Charlie and Maeve, were as different as daylight and dark, she knew they loved her and she'd never felt limited by anything more than tradition and social expectations. Whether she was interested in archeology or ballet, poetry or oil changes, both always encouraged her to explore her ever-changing interests.

Her mother, Maeve, was the pragmatic disciplinarian and could be irascible. She pushed Lora to be the best, finish first, to always put her best foot forward. Maeve was shrewd but fierce and protected Lora with a sometimes frightening diligence. Charlie was indulgent and doting. He pushed her too, but in a different way. When she asked questions, he helped her find answers for herself. He was always willing to escape into her imagination and didn't mind playing the damsel in distress to Lora's conquering knight. As she matured, Lora thought her parents balanced each other. Maeve kept her grounded while Charlie gave her wings.

Wheeling the debris to the burn pile behind the house, they chatted and made plans for settling Lora in permanently and getting her enrolled at the community college. As they talked, Eva got excited about having a young person in her house again. She didn't mind living alone and enjoyed her routines but having another person to talk to was just so nice. She had dreaded Lora getting on the bus to leave again in a couple weeks. And, if she was honest with herself, she was glad to know Lora would be around to lean on while she sorted out whatever Early Griffin was getting up to.

• • • •

THE TWO WOMEN CHATTERED and worked in an effortless dance choreographed by familiarity and trust. They talked about painting Lora's room and what classes she'd take in the fall and looked forward to spending the holidays together. Despite the challenges of the last couple weeks, their confidence in each other had not been shaken.

After a lunch break to catch up on Eva's favorite soap opera dramas, with pockets full of nickels and dimes, they walked to the store to call Lora's parents. Not more than a mile or so away, along a shady stretch of road overhung by towering proud oaks and haughty maple trees, Monroe's Store was a community hub for gasoline, farm supplies, hot sandwiches, cold sodas, and most importantly, gossip. Steeped in the smells of dust, motor oil, farm sweat, and decades of tobacco smoke, Monroe's provided a welcome respite from the labors of the day. There was always a steady stream of hands pulling on the door and a constant song of "Hiddy-do?'s" and "Fine, just fine. How's yer mama?" ringing out. Occasional beats of "Lord, I ain't seen you in a month of Sundays!" or "Lands you got tall! How old are you now?" would interrupt the rhythms as long-lost friends returned to the chorus. Lora loved Monroe's Store.

Today, even though the lot was busy with farm trucks, when Eva crossed the threshold, hollow footsteps thumping on the worn floorboards, she was greeted only by Monroe's croaking boom, "Eva! Lora! Come on in!" and the soft twang of Loretta Lynn on the radio he kept in perpetual play behind the counter. Everyone else in the store was silent.

Monroe, a bullfrog of a man, squatted on his stool behind the cash register. Jolly and friendly, quick to laugh, and generous with his customers, Monroe was a fixture in Mooresville. However much Lora loved his store, she thought Monroe himself was a little scary. Maybe it was because even though he never seemed to move off his perch, he always knew when a child was trying to pocket a piece of candy. Maybe it was because she once heard him bellow her name when she tried to snag a piece of penny gum and peed herself in fright. Eva had been disappointed, which was worse than her being angry while Monroe was amused, his numerous chins and belly joggling with suppressed laughter. Lora had been mortified. Monroe hadn't been mean or judgmental and didn't treat her any differently the next time she was in the store. All the same, she was always slightly embarrassed each time she saw him and couldn't shake the feeling that the large, round man with the greasy comb-over and knobbly round head was watching her. Still, even though no one else greeted them when they walked in, Monroe hadn't changed.

Eva paused at the counter and he leaned his warty head in close, dipping beneath the overhead cigarette rack, to scratch out a whisper, "Eva, folks been talking about you and Bumpus. Something's going on and you need to be careful." Pushing himself upright with his meaty hands and reverting to his loud, toady self, he asked, "What can I do ya for today? Co-Cola? Maybe Lora needs a piece of gum?" This last bit was accompanied by a smirk and a wink as he patted the tub of Double Bubble next to the register. Lora grimaced. Eva chuckled and replied, "Not today Monroe. We just need to use the phone. Lora's going to stay with me for a while and we need to let her mama and daddy know." She moved to the end of the counter, past the jars of pickled eggs and pigs' feet, and emptied her pocket change onto the counter space next to the pay phone.

Lora leaned against the counter and watched the store patrons while Eva dialed long distance to Detroit. She noticed that sure enough, everyone greeted each other warmly, smiling and nodding, shaking hands and hugging, but when they saw Eva in the corner, their eyes squinted and lips thinned. Monroe was right. Folks had been talking.

When Lora's mother answered, Eva spoke her pleasantries and turned the handset over to Lora. Eva relaxed on the little bench Monroe provided for people to use while waiting their turn to use the phone, underneath a flickering, neon Dixie Gasoline sign. Lora had to do a little convincing but in the end she won out and got what she wanted. Her mom even agreed to load up the car and bring her things down themselves. Her mother was sure Lora's father, Charlie, Eva's second oldest child, would be glad knowing Lora would be there to help look after Eva and the place. After all, Eva wasn't getting any younger, even if she refused to admit it.

Saying her good-byes, Lora turned to offer the phone back to Eva and saw her grandmother holding her chest, her eyes shut tight. Eva swayed back and forth, murmuring, over and over, "Ask and it shall be given. Seek and ye shall find. Knock and it shall be opened."

Alarmed, Lora quickly hung up with her mother. "Gram! What is it? Are you okay?" She knelt beside Eva's knees, clutching her free hand, afraid Eva was having a heart attack.

After a moment, Eva opened her eyes and squeezed Lora's hand. In a low voice, she said, "I'm fine. I was having a spell. I sure hate when this happens in public." She motioned for Lora to help her to her feet before prying eyes in the store could get curious.

Eva glanced around to make sure no one was listening, "Tell me, did you bring a spare pair of shoes with you that you can do without? If not, we're going to need to run to town tomorrow morning."

Lora was confused. "What? Shoes? Why?"

Dodging the questions, Eva pushed herself to her feet and pulled two Cokes from the cooler, picked up a pack of peanuts, and told Monroe they'd changed their minds about the cold drinks after all. Monroe nodded and added the purchase to Eva's account.

· · · ·

WITH PEANUTS FIZZING and floating in the necks of the Coke bottles, Eva and Lora stepped off the store porch, into the harsh, brilliant sunlight, and turned towards home. Lora, between sipping and chewing the savory treat, asked, "Gram. What is all this about shoes? I'm so confused!"

Eva laughed and grinned, patting Lora's arm with a cool hand, wet from the perspiration dripping down her Coke bottle. "Yeah, I guess you are. While you were talking to your mama...I assume she agreed to let you stay?"

At Lora's nodded yes, she carried on, "Good. That's good. Anyway, while you were talking, my chest started hurting as it does and I had to concentrate. Lord, I wish this one didn't settle on Hal Johnson's doorstep too but, I guess there's nothing for it. His oldest, Margaret, you know her? Goes by Maggie? Fifteen or so?"

Catching Lora nodding again with a mouthful of peanuts and coke, she continued, "Well, she needs shoes something fierce. And, I reckon I have to get some for her. I just thought if you have a pair you can spare, those would do." Eva took a swig from her own bottle and kept on walking, little puffs of road dust following in her wake.

They'd reached the shady part of their walk by this time. Sunlight filtered and flirted its way through the trembling leaves in the canopy above. Butterfly shadows played across Eva's face as she raised her eyes to the canopy overhead. She may not want to help Hal Johnson but she would never turn her back on a child, even one of his. Eva was content, enjoying the slight breeze and the smell of honeysuckles it carried.

Lora, speaking through a thick, slurpy mouthful, said, "Gram. Sure...I have a pair of loafers I haven't worn much. But, how do we know they'll fit? I mean, I think I know which one she is. How do we get them to her? And what if she doesn't like them?"

Eva scoffed a little, which made her choke on her peanuts. When she'd cleared her throat, "Shoot! The knowing don't leave me completely in the dark! I just know your shoes will fit. Ain't you ever heard that beggars can't be choosers? Well, Maggie needs shoes that Hal can't provide for some reason, so she'll be happy to have them. Let's study on it. We'll figure it out." They kept walking, tossing ideas back and forth, keeping some, chucking others. Enjoying the last of their afternoon snack and feeling like conspirators in a game of Secret Santa at Christmastime.

Turning the corner to Eva's little white house, they stopped dead in their tracks. Sheriff Early Griffin stood on the front porch, cupping his hands to the glass of the living room window as he looked inside. Eva narrowed her eyes and set her jaw, gritting her teeth. She shooed Lora into the bushes along the property line, "Let's watch him. See what he does."

Few in the area bothered locking their doors. Eva often bragged that she didn't even know where her house key was. Besides, very few people had much of anything worth stealing, and those who did, trusted their neighbors not to. After a few seconds of window peeping, Sheriff Griffin tried the door. He pulled open the screen, turned the knob to the front door, and let himself in.

"Hunh! That little sneak! Come on, Lora." Eva scrambled out of the brambles, brushing leaves out of her hair and sticker burrs from her skirts, and crossed the yard at an almost run. Eva wanted to startle the slippery man and let him know he had no business helping himself to her house. Sheriff or not, some things just aren't done. Lora scuttled along behind her, swigging the last of her Coke and trying to keep up.

· · · ·

BURSTING THROUGH HER own front door, Eva called out sharply, "Sheriff! What can I help you with today?" Because she could see all the way into the kitchen from the door, Eva was gratified when the spindly man jumped, embarrassed to be caught off guard, or red-handed, as the case may be. It wasn't lost on Lora that the kitchen cabinet doors were hanging open and the Sheriff was holding one of Eva's plates in his hand. A hot flush crept up his neck and bloomed across his waxy cheeks. His face was so red, if his hair caught fire, Lora wouldn't have been surprised. He looked like a beanpole with eyeballs on a regular day but now, he looked like an over-sized matchstick; one good fingernail flick and he'd catch fire. Words failed him and the delay cost him his chance to reply.

"Here you are! Standing in my kitchen, rifling through my cupboards. I assume you can explain yourself?" Eva sounded like a mother scolding a wayward child but her face wore a challenge few could have pulled off. Obviously, she was no longer concerned with placating the Sheriff to stay out of his cross-hairs.

He took the bait and said, "Well, as a matter of fact, I came to see what your plates look like. And now that I know, I'll be leaving." Sheriff Griffin dropped the plate on the counter and started towards the door.

Eva snorted and waved a finger in his face. "Not so fast, Early. Why're you interested in my plates? You helped yourself to my house, while I wasn't home. You owe me more of an explanation than that."

Griffin inflated his thin, bird chest and glowered, "No. I don't. I'm the sheriff and can do what I please when investigating a crime."

"Crime? What crime do you think you're investigating?" Determined to goad the sheriff into revealing the cards he was holding, Eva thrust out her chin and poured every bit of her disdain for his investigative skills into the last word.

Sheriff Griffin rounded on her and glowered, stalking back into the kitchen like a rangy tomcat toying with a mouse. "One of your plates was found broken near the body of Bumpus in the graveyard. Now I'm thinking you didn't just find his body; I'm thinking you had something to do with his dying. And that, Missus Burnette, is the crime I'm investigating." He straightened and puffed his chest, pride in his deductive reasoning oozing from every pore as profusely as the sweat staining his armpits.

"Of course it is. Bumpus been harassing this town for ages and you think I just all of a sudden walloped him upside the head? That's the dumbest thing I've ever heard."

Sheriff Griffin's jaw clenched. He picked up the plate he'd dropped earlier and gripped it so hard Lora thought it would break. "I'll be taking this with me as evidence. Good day."

Faster than Lora imagined her grandmother could move, Eva snatched the plate from the Sheriff's hand and declared, "Oh I don't think you will!" She passed the plate to Lora and stepped to the Sheriff, pushing her shoulders and head back to look him in the eye. Through gritted teeth, she said, "See, you might not, but I remember my schooling. Mrs. Thatcher's class? We studied the Constitution and the Bill of Rights. You remember her and how she insisted we memorize what every amendment meant? I might be old but it's going to take a lot longer for me to forget those lessons!"

She took another step towards him, close enough to pluck the badge from his chest if she wanted. "And I'm right positive that the Fourth Amendment prohibits "unlawful search and seizure" which means your very presence in my house is illegal. Unless you found a judge willing to give you a warrant based on a piece of broken pottery? No? Then I suggest you get out and stop wasting my time." She pointed her finger at the door and jerked her head at him.

Crimson with anger, Sheriff Griffin waved his arms like an angry spider before collecting himself and lurching through the house. He made a show of slamming his cruiser door and threw a gravel-slinging temper tantrum as he spun out of the drive, hurling debris from under his tires at the house just so he could have the final word.

Lora didn't realize she was holding her breath until she exhaled like she'd been punched in the gut, bursting into laughter. "Gram! That was incredible! I thought his head would pop off when you started throwing the Constitution at him! Ha!" She doubled over, holding the plate against her belly and wheezing.

Eva laughed low and deep and sat heavily at the table. Her face was pale and her hands trembled. She knew she'd just torn the entire top off a can of worms and was certain he'd be back with warrant in hand. She sighed, looked up to the ceiling and whispered, "Lord, give me strength."

5

The next morning, Sheriff Griffin rolled up in his cruiser, waving a blue envelope out the window, grinning from ear to ear like a fat kid who'd eaten the last piece of pie. After he'd left the day before, Eva explained to Lora that while telling him off may have felt good, it would wind up causing more problems than it was worth. Watching from the front porch as he unfolded himself from behind the steering wheel, strutting like a barnyard rooster, Lora saw Eva was right. The man was practically vibrating, giddy with the idea he might catch Eva doing something illegal. He bounded up the steps and through the front door without so much as a sideways glance at Lora, calling out, "Eva Burnette! I have a warrant for your plates and your fingerprints! You're gonna have to come with me!" Lora could have sworn he was laughing as he hollered.

Rather than acknowledge him, Eva kept washing the breakfast dishes at the kitchen sink when he rushed in. Refusing to be cowed, she finished the pot she was scrubbing, laid it on the drying towel next to the sink and turned around, wiping her hands on her apron. "Well, Early, I figured I'd see you again. Glad you decided to do it legal-like this time."

Taking off her apron and hanging it on a hook by the back door, she continued, "Go on. Grab a plate. You know where they are. I'll just get my pocketbook so we can get this over with."

Having taken the wind out of his sails with her unimpressed response, she walked out the front door, saying over her shoulder, "I'll wait on you at the car. Don't take forever. It's hot out and I got other things to do today besides melt."

Sheriff Griffin trailed after her like a scolded puppy dog, wondering how he had managed to lose a fight he was sure he'd win. The plate in his hand dangled like a cheap participation trophy after failing to capture the grand prize.

Passing Lora on the porch, Eva said, "I doubt he'll want to bring me home so if you would, finish the dishes, then come on into Athens to get me. You know where the sheriff's office is?"

Lora nodded and took petty comfort in squinting her eyes at Sheriff Griffin as he crossed the yard behind her grandmother. When she saw he was putting Eva in the criminal backseat, she jumped and shouted, "Wait! Are you arresting her?"

Eva quickly jerked her head "no" to silence Lora's protest and climbed into the car. As Eva arranged herself in the squad car with her head high and purse in her lap, Lora heard her grandmother say, "I sure do appreciate you chauffeuring me into town, Early. Nice of you to save me the gas."

Lora smirked and shook her head at Eva's impertinence. She lifted a hand in a slight wave as he spun out of the drive for the second time in as many days.

Back in the kitchen, Lora dug around in the dishwater for the silverware lurking in the sink bottom and wondered if she should stop at Monroe's on the way and call her parents. She felt like someone needed to know what was going on. In the end, she decided against making any phone calls and in favor of just doing what she'd been told. Leaving the dishes to dry on the sideboard, she grabbed the truck keys and headed into town.

The ride from Mooresville to Athens took about twenty minutes and Eva was determined Early Griffin would not think she was worried about him, his investigation, or what exactly he thought he could prove with a dinner plate. Early was a vindictive, sad little man still playing cops and robbers, even if the stakes were higher than they'd been when he was a little boy. He'd only been with the sheriff's department for a few years when Dot burned her house down and Bumpus had gone off the rails. Eva vividly remembered a stand-off between herself and then-Deputy Griffin on the steps of Monroe's Store when she'd confronted him about the department's refusal to intervene in the violent goings-on at Dot's house. The bitter taste of gall rose to her mouth just thinking about his smarmy dismissal of her as a 'hysterical woman.' Griffin believed the tragic, tortured hero version of Bumpus and refused to see the drunk, wife-beating, rotten side of him. No, he knew the state of things in the Bumpus household and had turned a blind eye.

From the backseat of the patrol car, Eva watched the fields along the roadsides pass by in a blur of emerald greens and snow-white cotton blossoms and lush pasture lands clipped short by fat Holstein cows. Neither the cotton nor the cows noticed the patrol car speeding by under an insistent blue, cloudless sky. The cows may be indifferent but Eva knew the gossip mill would be working double-time and well into the night as she rode along, pointedly ignoring the sheriff and his childish, swerving attempts to discomfort her. Everyone knew if she was making a complaint, she'd be riding up front. Backseats were reserved for bad guys. *Well, there's nothing for it,* she narrowed her eyes, thinking, *Besides, what will my fingerprints on my own plate prove anyway? That the plate is mine?*

Sheriff Griffin pulled up in front of the station, the side facing the courthouse square, instead of going around back, and made a slow public show of pulling her out of the back seat. He gripped her arm above the elbow and came close to dragging her inside the boxy brown building. He was treating her very much like a criminal under arrest instead of someone just having her fingerprints collected.

By the time they got to the doors, Eva had enough. She jerked her arm away from the sheriff and hissed, "That is enough of that. I haven't done anything wrong, and you know it. Let's get this over with so I can get at least a little work done in the garden before church tonight." Instead of reaching for the door herself, she looked at the handle and then at him and back again, daring him not to open the door for her.

Finding himself red-faced again, this time in front of spectators, Sheriff Griffin snatched at the door and made a futile attempt to push Eva inside. She dodged his grasp and walked into the lobby by herself. Griffin removed his hat and with it in hand, pulled on a sarcastic face and flourished it in Three Musketeer style, indicating the direction they would be heading. Eva rolled her eyes and started walking.

When they reached the fingerprinting room, the door swung open and Hal Johnson barreled out, nearly knocking them both over. He skittered back a few steps, as surprised to see them as they were by him kicking the door open with his dusty boot. He had a handkerchief in one hand, attempting to scrub ink stains from the other, his dusty wide-brimmed farm hat tucked up under one arm. For a brief instant, he narrowed his eyes at Eva, before glancing at the sheriff and nodding, "Early." Sheriff Griffin nodded back, "Hal," and held the door open for Eva. Hal Johnson was soon out of sight.

Once inside, it occurred to Eva that she hadn't read the warrant Sheriff Griffin had gleefully waved around. Spinning on him, she said, "Before we do this, I'd like to read that warrant, if you please."

Immediately defensive, Griffin ballooned and huffed, "I told you what it says. That ought to be good enough for you."

"Well it's not. I need to read it for myself, Early. I could always start hollering about it if you want?"

"Eva, I left it in the car," he mumbled in exasperation.

"That's fine. I can wait." Eva crinkled her nose at him. "Run go get it." Finding a folding chair along the wall, she sat. She placed her purse on the floor next to her feet, folded her hands in her lap, and raised her eyebrows, giving him the same look mamas give children who are procrastinating at doing what they're told.

Sheriff Griffin muttered, "Fine. Wait there."

The fingerprint technician behind the print desk slunk silently down in his seat and didn't say a word.

When Griffin returned, he shoved the papers under Eva's nose and dropped them into her lap. Eva took her time reading every word.

"Huh! Sheriff, I'm not seeing a single word in here about you being allowed to collect my fingerprints. One of my plates, yes. But my fingerprints? Nope. Nary a word. Are you sure you have the right copy?" She a show of slowly flipping the pages. "No, looks like the judge's signature on this one. Clear as day. Maybe you're missing a page?"

Going through the pages one more time, "No, that's not it. Page numbers are all in order too. Hm. Ain't that interesting?" When she finished speaking, sounding for all listeners like a law school professor, she folded the warrant and put it in her purse. Clicking her purse closed, she heaved herself to her feet, metal chair feet screeching on the tile floor, and said, "Looks like I've wasted a trip to town. Don't worry yourself about taking me back home. Lora should be pulling up any minute." She winked at the fingerprint technician trying his best to be invisible, patted Sheriff Griffin on the shoulder and walked out of the printing room, back down the hallway, and out the front doors.

Chuckling under her breath and shaking her head, she looked around just as Lora was rounding the corner from Market to Jefferson Street. Lora pulled the truck into a space and jumped out, running to her grandmother. "Hey! What happened? I didn't expect to see you just standing out here on the sidewalk! Wouldn't they let you wait inside?"

• • • •

EVA HOOKED HER ARM through Lora's, threw her head back and laughed. "You won't believe this but Lord, I am feeling some kind of dumb right about now. It dawned on me once we got inside that I hadn't read that warrant Early was proud of. So, I asked him to let me see it and guess what it said? That he could take one of my plates. That's it! I fell for him strutting around my house like banty rooster and almost let myself be fingerprinted. Pfft! Anyway, I read it and once he knew I'd called his bluff, I walked myself out! Now, let's go to the drugstore for some ice cream." Steering Lora in an about face, she guided them towards the Limestone Drug Store on the corner of Market and Marion.

As they walked, Eva told Lora about seeing Hal Johnson at the station and how his squinted eyes were the only acknowledgment he'd seen fit to give her. "It looked to me like he'd just had his fingerprints done. Now, I wonder if he volunteered to do that or if he was suckered into it by Sheriff Griffin?"

Barely making it to the drugstore before the soda fountain closed at noon, Eva and Lora ordered cones to enjoy while they window shopped on their walk back to the truck. Peering in the windows at Sharp & Killen Shoes, and chasing drips of vanilla ice cream as it raced down the sides of her cone, Lora remembered Eva's shoe problem and Maggie Johnson.

"Hey. So, did we ever decide what to do about Maggie's shoes?" Because most churches in the area held Wednesday night prayer meetings, all the stores on the square closed at noon on Wednesdays if they opened at all. Shopping for new shoes for Maggie Johnson wasn't an option.

Eva leaned against a lamp post and shrugged her shoulders. "I figured we'd just take'em with us tonight and you could give them to her afterwards while everyone's talking. Nobody will think much of two girls just chatting, even if the girls in question are you and Maggie Johnson." Finishing her cone with a satisfied smirk and crunch, Eva held her hands out for the keys and said, "Come on. We still got time to get some chores done before church."

• • • •

THAT EVENING AFTER bible study, Lora spotted Maggie Johnson and her friends standing not far from the church doors, just a step outside the glow of the porch light. The light flickered against the barrage of fluttering moths and night bugs. The girls giggled and swished their skirts as they talked, careful not to look too long or with too much interest at the group of boys lounging next to a new Ford pick-up parked in the grass. The boys, having taken the time to slick their hair and don clean jeans and shirts with their dusty boots, were working just as hard not to be obvious while they studied the girls. Everyone enjoyed the cool breeze sweeping over and through the rustling corn fields across the road from Holley Hill.

Trying to slip into the rhythm of the younger girls' conversation, Lora stood at the periphery and felt the unexpected tug of maturity as she reckoned the difference in their ages. Only four or five years older than most of them, the events of the last couple weeks had clued her in to the world weariness parents often talked about when they thought their children weren't listening.

Within seconds though, the chattering stream trickled away to barely a drip. All eyes were looking at her. Lora cleared her throat and squeaked out a weak, "Hey." Tapping Maggie on the shoulder, she said, "Do you have a sec?" Assuming curiosity would get the best of the teenager, she walked towards Eva's International. Maggie took a few quick steps and caught up with her.

"What do you want? My daddy's going to be sideways if he sees me talking to you!" she whispered.

Lora hugged her Bible to her chest and whispered back, "I've got something for you and couldn't figure out another way to get your attention!"

Picking up the pace, both of them shot looks over their shoulders to make sure their departure from the crowd wasn't noticed. Once at the truck, Lora reached through the open window, dropped her things on the bench seat, and pulled out the pair of loafers. "My mom sent me these, but they're too small for me. I thought you looked to be about the right size and I'd rather give them to you. If you want'em. If you don't, I'm sure I can find someone else."

Maggie's mouth gaped for a second before snatching the shoes from Lora's hands. Her face was hard to read in the twilight shadows outside the golden glow of the church lights. When she spoke, the tone and timbre of her words shifted from longing to anger to shame in quick succession. "Oh! Why do you think I need your hand-me-down shoes? Do you think I'm poor?"

Lora was bewildered. "What? No! It's just...well, I can't use them and since I've decided to move here and live with Gram, I can't exchange them. So, I thought I'd give them to someone who might want them. Since you don't..." Lora reached to take the shoes back. Maggie twisted just out of reach. "No. I like'em alright. I think I'll keep them after all." Turning on her heel, she scooted back towards her friends, the loafers hugged tightly to her chest.

Lora shook her head and leaned against the tailgate. She looked up at the sky, noticing the last indigo tendrils of sunset stretching over the horizon, unsuccessful as always in fending off the darkness, and wished she was able to turn back time. Catching the slightest blur of movement from the corner of her eye, she was startled when Hal Johnson emerged from the shadows and grabbed hold of her wrist, pulling her in close.

"What business you got with Maggie?" he grunted. His stale, cigarette breath made her eyes water.

Thankful he couldn't see the flush creeping up on her neck, Lora gasped and stammered at the sudden burst of pain behind her left eye as his truth became clear in her mind.

"Oh, nothing really. Just girl talk, you know."

"Unh! I can't think of any 'girl talk' she'd be needing to share with you. You and Eva need to keep away from me and mine." He flung her wrist away and jerked the pack of Lucky Strikes from his shirt pocket. He lit a cigarette, flames from his match flaring, casting his features in craggy relief. As soon as he'd let go, the throbbing behind her left eye had receded, leaving behind only the knowledge she'd gained when Hal grabbed her.

"Hal Johnson! I sure hope you got a good reason for laying hands on my granddaughter. Otherwise, you might be meeting Jesus sooner than you'd expected!"

Scuttling back into the shadows, Hal Johnson jabbed the glowing end of his cigarette in Lora's direction and stalked away without another word.

Neither Hal nor Lora had noticed Eva headed in their direction; neither knew how much she had seen or heard. As Lora rubbed her wrist and scrunched her eyes shut against the fading headache, Eva thought it best to dissipate the tension until she and Lora could be alone. Coming up with nothing else in the moment, she softly whistled a mildly off-key rendition of "I Saw Her Again" by The Mamas and The Papas. Lora shook herself, hoping Eva wouldn't notice the flush of her skin. Instead, she managed a weak smile and laughed, "How on earth do you know a song by The Mamas and the Papas?"

Leaning against the tailgate next to Lora, looking up into the night sky, now full dark and pregnant with a waxing moon, Eva feigned a shocked, hurt look before chirping back, "I know a lot of things! Never underestimate me."

Nudging Lora with her shoulder, Eva said, "Come on. Let's go. On our way, you can tell me how it went with Maggie. And, what Hal had to say."

AS SOON AS THE INTERNATIONAL rumbled out of the church lot, Lora launched into her tale and the revelation she'd received when Mr. Johnson had grabbed her wrist.

Eva harrumphed. "Well, now. Isn't that interesting? I guess it explains some things. Hunh! Arlene Johnson running off with a Black man! Sure didn't see that coming!"

She steered the truck into her drive and pulled around back, parking in the hazy puddle of light from the stoop. "As for Maggie, I imagine she was a little embarrassed and thought you were poking into her business. Seems she's like her daddy that way. Still, she took the shoes so that's handled.

Dropping their purses and Bibles onto the kitchen table, Eva added with a shrug, "Hal Johnson is an idgit. I just hope he don't need something else."

Declaring a snack of cornbread and buttermilk before bed was necessary, Eva poured two tall glasses and sat down with a low groan and sigh. She crumbled cornbread into the glass and swirled the mixture around with her spoon. She pulled her checkbook out of the bottom of her purse. Giving her grandmother a questioning look, Lora eyeballed the checkbook and sat, waiting for Eva to explain herself.

"Just in case, I'm going to sign a couple checks for you to use if you need to. If you're going to be staying here, you might need to take care of paying the bills once in a while. We'll add you to my account next time we're in town. You could go ahead a pay your fees for school, too. I can cover those until we get all that worked out with your parents. Here's my register so you can keep up with how much you spend; don't forget to write everything down. It won't do to go writing bad checks all over town."

Thinking all of this made sense, Lora nodded as Eva penned her name across the bottoms of several checks.

"I embarrassed the sheriff today. He's not the type of man who takes that kind of thing laying down, much less from a woman. He'll be pretty ornery for the next little bit and I wouldn't be surprised if

I have to make several trips into Athens to sort him out. I just figure it's smart to be prepared," Eva mused.

She scooped a dripping spoonful of cornbread mash and slurped it into her mouth. Letting go with a sudden "Ha!" when a bit of buttermilk got away from her and dribbled down her chin, she darted to the kitchen sink for a dishtowel. "Oo-wee! I love this stuff but land's sake, I always seem to make a mess of myself! I knew I should have put on an apron."

Lora wasn't crazy about this particular treat and hadn't done much more than spin her glass between her hands. Preferring to eat them separately, she hadn't bothered with any cornbread in the buttermilk. Looking into swirling milk, she asked, "What kind of ornery do you think he's going to be?"

Dishtowel in hand, Eva sat again and with another dribbling bite, said, "Oh I'm sure he'll get a warrant for my fingerprints. And then he'll probably need me to come up and write a statement about the day we found Bumpus. He might even want us to make a trip out to the cemetery to retrace our steps. And you can bet he'll do all of these things separately instead of getting everything done in one day."

She grunted. "Wasting time, running the roads, strutting around like a peacock, acting all important." She tipped the glass to catch the last bits. Lora hadn't touched hers and felt a little guilty for the waste.

6

S ure enough, when Sheriff Griffin wheeled into the yard several days later, Lora spotted him through the front window and swore her grandmother could make a fortune as a carnival fortune teller. *Yep, strutting around like a peacock,* she thought. *Least he could have done is waited late enough for us to have finished breakfast! Maybe that's why they call him Early.* She snorted and decided maybe she'd inherited Eva's sense of humor after all.

Eva didn't see him pull up and was confused when Lora left her uneaten sausage biscuit on the table and went to the front door. She was more confused when Lora opened it for Sheriff Griffin and a deputy. She wiped her hands on her dressing gown and made a weak attempt to shape the sleep out of her hair, eventually deciding there was nothing for that particular rat's nest and giving up. Looking tired and without any smile whatsoever, she said, "Sheriff. Deputy. What can we do for you?"

"Eva Burnette. You are under arrest for manslaughter in the death of Ethelred Bumpus. We'll be taking you in. Now." Sheriff Griffin bounced on his toes like a kid on Christmas morning. He gestured to the deputy to take custody of the "suspect." Deputy John Ross shuffled forward, fumbling his handcuffs, looking every bit like he'd rather wrestle a dozen rattlesnakes than arrest an old lady.

Lora's half-chewed bite of biscuit fell out of her mouth as her jaw dropped, momentarily speechless. Eva suffered no lapse in loquaciousness and exclaimed, "You have got to be kidding me Early Griffin! I knew you were mean but to stoop to something like this?" She backed away from poor Deputy Ross until her backside was against the kitchen counter, her blue eyes flashing like heat lightning on a sweltering afternoon.

Lora pulled herself together just before the deputy reached out for Eva. "Hold on! Can't you at least let her get dressed? You can't take her in her house coat and slippers!"

Deputy Ross, a young man who sported a deep pair of dimples when he grinned, grimaced. With Lora's outburst, he drew up short and looked at Sheriff Griffin. From the set of his jaw and bright pink ears, it seemed he was of the mindset that Bumpus dying was no great loss and the Sheriff should leave well enough alone.

Sheriff Griffin considered Lora's request for a moment and decided he'd look bad if he didn't let her get dressed and fix her hair, so he sighed and acquiesced. "Fine. Deputy Ross, escort Mrs. Burnette to her room and allow her to change. Make sure there are no weapons or means of egress other than the door before you leave her alone."

Eva grunted and threw up her hands. "Lord have mercy, Early. What kind of crazy woman do you think I am?" She drew herself up tall, strode past Deputy Ross, and slammed the bedroom door. Lora and the deputy looked at each other and exchanged smirks. Sheriff Griffin, on the other hand, blew out a breath like a popped balloon and muttered, "I hate a proud woman."

· · · ·

EVA TOOK HER SWEET time getting ready to go. After slamming the door, she'd taken several long minutes to pull herself together. Upset didn't come close to describing how flabbergasted and mad she was. It took every ounce of self-control she could muster not to scream and throw things around just to get it all out. In the end, deciding not to give Early Griffin the satisfaction of knowing he'd riled her up, she took a few deep breaths and settled for tearing a couple pages from the notepad she kept by her bed into tiny little pieces. Satisfied with her homespun confetti, she pulled one of her best Sunday dresses from her wardrobe and changed. She brushed out her hair, shaping it into some form of acceptability and pinned in a half-hat with a tiny lavender feather on one side which complimented her dress. Figuring she'd left the sheriff stewing long enough, she opened the door and walked regally into one of the most uncomfortable silences she'd ever experienced.

• • • •

WHILE EVA CHANGED, the sheriff, Deputy Ross, and Lora stood in an awkward triangle, each alternating between glaring at and making pointed efforts to ignore the other. None of them spoke for the longest time, instead choosing to examine their fingernails or stare at the ceiling. Occasionally, one or the other would swat at a fly who decided it was too quiet in the house and felt it should make its presence known. Lora caught Deputy Ross studying her from the corner of his eye and then quickly looking away when their eyes met. She couldn't figure out why, although she was sure she'd have been more confident if she'd been dressed for the day instead of being caught out in just her short-pants pajamas and bare feet when the officers had barged in. It couldn't be helped now. Still, if he was going to peep at her, she thought it only fair to return the favor. The way he fidgeted with his hat and the splotches of discomfort blooming on his cheeks, she could tell he didn't want to be standing in Eva's kitchen. His close cropped, sandy blond hair was damp and dark with sweat in desperate need of a comb. Deputy Ross's face was tanned. Instead of making him seem washed out and leathery, as the sun tends to do with most fair-haired people, his sun-kissed cheeks made his sea-water green eyes more interesting. In different circumstances, Lora thought a closer look might be interesting.

Visibly irritated, Sheriff Griffin shifted his balance from one foot to the other and checked his watch every other second. Declaring she'd had enough time to "gussy up," he turned to hammer on Eva's door just as she walked back into the kitchen. Griffin's face fell, reminding Lora of Saturday morning cartoon villains whose plans go awry and mutter, "Foiled again!" Picturing him as Yosemite Sam's taller, skinnier brother, she had to stare at the floor to keep from laughing. She was certain the arrogant sheriff would not be amused by any comparison to a bumbling Warner Brothers character.

Griffin again ordered Deputy Ross to cuff Eva before escorting her to the patrol car. The young man blanched and shot Lora the most honest and apologetic look she'd ever seen. She figured he'd rather be carted off to jail himself than have to click handcuffs onto her grandmother's wrists. Still, he did what he was told and had the decency to whisper "I am so sorry" into Eva's ear as he gently took her arm.

Before being led away, Eva dug in her heels and asked, "Early, do you think it'd be too difficult for you to tell me on what grounds you're arresting me? You've told me what for, just not why."

Sheriff Griffin took a firm grasp on her other elbow, pushed her towards the front door and growled, "I don't have to tell you nothing."

The trio made their way in an off-kilter, clumsy waltz to the porch, trying to work 3/4 time into a 4/4 rhythm. Eva turned her head and told Lora, following behind, "You come on into town as soon as you've had a chance to eat and change clothes. Don't bother coming to the jail, go straight to Attorney Landon Cook's office and speak directly to him. I'm sure Early will take good care of me."

The bitter sarcasm in that last sentence could have been heard by a deaf man. Sheriff Griffin didn't say a word, he just tightened his grip and walked faster, bundling Eva into the car without bothering to protect her head from bumping on the door frame.

Deputy Ross sat stiff as a statue in the passenger seat while the sheriff drove back to town. The silence was overpowering and he gripped the door handle so tightly his knuckles were changing from white to pink with every beat of his pulse.

From the back seat, Eva stared into Sheriff Griffin's eyes in the rear-view mirror and tried again, "You know, Early, I still can't figure out why on earth you think I had anything to do with Bumpus being dead. You still nursing that ridiculous notion that I clobbered him with my own plate in the graveyard?" She knew she waded into some muddy waters by continuing to push him but truly, she never reckoned on being arrested for killing Bumpus. Instead, she'd expected Griffin to snuffle around underfoot for clues that didn't exist and eventually give up.

Sheriff Griffin met her gaze in the mirror and said, "Fine. Not only were your prints on the broken plate we found in the cemetery but some of Bumpus's blood was too. The way I figure it, you were toting a plate of something from Hal Johnson's place and came across Bumpus on your way back. He said something you didn't like and you cracked him on the head with the plate. He fell, hit his head again, this time on the marker, and you just left him there to die. Everybody knows you and Bumpus had sore feelings towards each other that go way back so it's not too hard to put it all together. Even for you." He twisted in his seat to give her a smug, gloating look before looking back at the road.

"Asinine," was the quiet response from the back seat of the patrol car.

7

L ora flew into action as soon as Sheriff Griffin pulled out of the yard and turned towards town. She finished her biscuit in two bites and chugged a few swallows of milk straight from the jug. Wiping the milky mustache from her lips with the back of her hand, she quickly washed her face in the kitchen sink and flew upstairs to change out of her pajamas. Her first impulse was to throw on whatever came to hand but when she remembered where she was going, she thought she might need to dress carefully. *After all, it's not everyday your grandmother is arrested and you have to go talk to an attorney*, she thought. Settling on a pink and yellow plaid shift dress, not too short, and a pair of white Keds, she brushed her brown hair and slid on a pink head band before sweeping some eyeliner and mascara across her eyes. Remembering to grab Eva's checkbook on her way out the door, she hopped into the truck and rumbled her way to Monroe's store.

She figured now was definitely the time to call for reinforcements and hit the wooden porch at Monroe's like a pastel whirlwind. Jerking the door with enough force to pull her own arm out of socket, forget the hinges out of the frame, she rushed past Monroe's too-cheery "Well! Good morning Lora! Where's the fire?" with a wave of her hand and made a stomping beeline for the telephone. Seeing Maggie Johnson jabbering away on the line set her teeth on edge and made her consider committing manslaughter herself. After all, none of this would be happening if it hadn't been for the Johnson family in the first place. Instead of jerking the handset out of Maggie's hand and whopping her with it, Lora settled for pacing back and forth and making exasperated noises every time the girl took a breath.

After an eternity which lasted all of three minutes, Maggie hung up and turned on Lora, over-plucked eyebrows raised nearly to her hairline and arms crossed over her chest. She was wearing the loafers Lora gave her the night before. The sight of those loafers took some of the wind out of Lora's sails and she muttered, "Sorry, but I really need to call my parents."

Maggie sneered, "Obviously," before heading for the door.

Lora fed her change into the slot and prayed her mother would be home to answer the call.

"Hey Mom."

"Yes, no. I'm fine, but things are definitely not."

"Well, Gram's been arrested. Manslaughter. When are you and Daddy driving down?"

"No...This morning. Yes, handcuffs and everything."

"Tomorrow? Groovy."

"Ugh...it's complicated. I don't think I should tell you over the phone."

"Yes! Mom, I don't have time to talk! Gram asked me to go see her lawyer and I just stopped to call you on my way into town. I have everything handled for now but...yeah, it'd be nice to have you and Daddy here to help sort things out."

"I know. I love you too. Bye."

She hung the receiver back in its cradle and rested her forehead against it for a second. Sucking in a calming breath, she turned and found herself eyeball to eyeball with Monroe. He'd waddled out from behind the counter and stood with his meaty hands dangling by his side. His warty face was a kaleidoscope of shock and worry.

"Did I hear that right? Eva's been arrested?" Monroe's voice was hollow, cracking with concern. "I wondered why you were all done up on a Thursday morning and off by yourself. Makes sense now. What can I do?"

Lora slumped and said, "Monroe, I wish I knew, but I don't."

The way he stood, out of place and untethered without the counter to hold him up, she was a little afraid he'd try to hug her.

She didn't want to hurt his feelings anymore than his eavesdropping already had but he was the last sweaty person on earth she wanted to hug. In an effort to avoid that possibility, she slid open the cooler door and pulled out a Coke, popping the top off with the opener on the side of the cooler.

"Wait. Actually, you can help. I need to see Landon Cook but don't know where his office is. I should've looked it up in the phone book before I left the house but…"

With unexpected alacrity from a man his size, Monroe scooted around behind his counter and whipped out the Limestone County Yellow Pages. Flipping to the A's, he found the Attorney section and slid his finger down to the listing for Cook, Landon. "Yes ma'am. Here tis…107 West Washington. That's just off the Square, about half-way down the block towards the railroad tracks. You know where I'm talking about?"

Lora nodded, raised her bottle in thanks, and flung the door open again. She did not see Myra Strong making her way to the front of the store as she left, eyeballing Monroe in a way which let him know she'd heard everything he did. The two shared a worried look as Myra laid her purchases on the counter. He wiped his brow with the tattered bandanna he kept in his back pocket, shook his head, and waved her on. "Don't worry about it. We got bigger problems today."

Myra gathered her items into her shopping bag and slid him a couple dollars anyway. "Mm hm. We sure do."

• • • •

LORA HAD NEVER MINDED that the International didn't have a working radio. She always enjoyed chatting about everything and nothing with Eva, or simply basking in the symphony of sounds and smells billowing around the cab through the rolled-down windows. Today, however, she'd have given just about anything for mindless chatter from faceless commentators, even the sad drone of "Sick Call" would have been welcome. Anything other than sweltering silence. She didn't know which would be worse - showing up at an attorney's office drenched in sweat or looking like she'd just crawled out the tail end of a tornado. She opted to sweat and kept the windows up.

Relieved to find a parking spot directly in front of "Cook, Cook, and Puckett - Attorneys At Law," Lora took a moment to collect herself in the shade of a spindly crepe myrtle on the sidewalk before walking into the offices. As she opened the heavy oak door, she was welcomed by a sharp blast of chilled air. *Thank goodness they have air conditioning!* she thought. Smoothing her hair to camouflage any rogue sweat beads plastering her bangs to her forehead, Lora crossed the thick-pile rug in the lobby and approached the secretary's desk.

The secretary, whose name plate read, "Lovenia Thigpen," did not look up from her typing. "Can I help you?" she scratched out from behind her too-bright, too-orange lipsticked lips.

"Yes ma'am. I need to speak with Landon Cook. It is an emergency. Thank you."

Adjusting a tab setting on the typewriter, Lovenia grunted past the pencil she held between her teeth and said, "He's busy. Do you have an appointment?"

"No. No appointment. I just need to see him. Please."

"Without an appointment, I'm afraid you won't be able to see Mr. Cook today."

Frustrated, and sweating again despite the arctic blast making her already moist clothes stick to her back, Lora leaned over the desk in an attempt to force Lovenia to finally look at her. As she leaned in, she noticed a small, silver photo frame with Sheriff Griffin's tight, smiling face staring back at her. Steeling her backbone, she tented her fingers on the desktop and gritted her teeth. "Is he here? Can you just go tell him I need to see him? Lora Burnette. Eva Burnette's granddaughter."

The leaning worked. Lovenia drug her eyes away from the typewriter and narrowed them at her, pulling the pencil from between her lips. Lora's lip twitched as Lovenia reached out a badly manicured hand to flip the photo of Sheriff Griffin onto its face. She breathed in a whiff of mentholatum and onions as Lovenia stood and tilted in towards Lora's face, her tortoise-shell, horn-rimmed glasses slipping down her nose. Placing her own hands on the desk, and blowing a cherry red stray hair out of her eyes, Ms. Thigpen breathed, "He. Is. Not. Here. You. Need. An. Appointment." Dismissing Lora, she sat and resumed typing.

Unwilling to be bullied, Lora looked around the office lobby and perched on the edge of a large wingback with slightly cracked, brown leather upholstery, crossing her ankles. She raised an eyebrow at the desk and said firmly, "I'll wait."

"Fine by me as long as you don't plan to talk the whole time."

Lora looked at her watch, a delicate silver ladies watch her parents had given her in May for graduation. *Eight-thirty in the morning. I suppose I am early. Maybe lawyers keep bankers' hours.*

Lora's instincts were right. About an hour later, a youngish looking man flung open the door, a surge of humid wind sending his tie flapping to the side as he shifted his briefcase from one hand to the other. "Good morning, Lo!" he called, not noticing Lora watching him from the side of the dark paneled waiting room.

Lovenia Thigpen did not immediately respond but rather fixed him with an annoyed look and made a point of sliding her eyes in Lora's direction. "Mr. Cook. You're late today. I'm sure you are late for court."

Landon Cook caught the not-so-subtle signal and turned towards Lora. "Oh hello. I'm sorry. Do we have an appointment? I do have court in a bit but if I'm late for an appointment, well, I can spare a few minutes."

Lora opened her mouth to respond but was interrupted by Ms. Thigpen. "She does not have an appointment. I told her she could make one and come back but she insisted on waiting."

Standing and reaching a hand to Mr. Cook, trying to seem assured and confident, Lora said, "Mr. Cook. I am Lora Burnette, Eva Burnette's granddaughter. She sent me here to speak with you. If you have a moment?"

Landon Cook's expression changed from genial amusement to serious in the blink of an eye, shallow frown lines creasing around his lips. He grasped her hand in a firm shake. "Of course. Please, let's speak in my office." He opened another heavy door and stepped aside to allow Lora to enter first. He risked a wide-eyed glance at Lovenia before he closed the door behind them.

• • • •

MR. COOK DROPPED HIS briefcase on the floor with a thump next to an over-flowing wastepaper basket. Settling into his chair, behind a desk piled high with papers and folders, pens, and at least two half-eaten sandwiches, he smiled, gesturing for her to take a seat in a leather wingback across the desk from him. "Okay, Lora Burnette. Why don't you tell me what happened? I'm sure you realize I've already heard one version of what happened this morning. That's why I was late getting here."

Lora studied him. He was average build, a bit disheveled, with mousy brown hair and chocolate brown eyes. He wasn't as young as she'd originally thought. Judging by the crow's feet just starting to march from his eyes to his temples, she guessed he was a little younger than her dad. She wondered how much to tell him and decided she'd stick to the facts. Eva could fill in other necessary details.

She twisted her hands around the handle of the purse in her lap. "Well, Sheriff Griffin arrested my grandmother this morning for murdering Bumpus a couple weeks ago. He called it manslaughter, but she didn't do it. She needs an attorney. And, she told me to come get you."

"Do you have any idea why Sheriff Griffin would think Eva did this?"

Lora shook her head. "She asked him before they left the house but he wouldn't tell her."

"Hunh! Did he say anything else?"

"No. Just that he had a warrant for her arrest. You really should talk to her."

Landon Cook leaned his elbows on his desk and steepled his fingers into a point just under his nose. He narrowed his eyes at Lora and asked, "Do you know anything about the Supreme Court?"

The flummoxed expression on Lora's face made him laugh.

"The Supreme Court? What does the Supreme Court have to do with this?" She left off twisting her purse strap and gestured wildly with her hands, her words climbing in pitch and volume.

"Well, back in June, the Supreme Court ruled that anyone who is arrested has to be apprised of their right not to answer any question which might incriminate them. That bit is in the Fifth Amendment. And, and this is important, the accused has the right to have an attorney present. That's guaranteed by the Sixth Amendment. Now, those rights are already Constitutionally guaranteed but the case in June, just last month, made it a requirement that law enforcement has to *tell* the person they're arresting they have those rights. Now, do you remember hearing either Sheriff Griffin or the deputy tell Eva anything along these lines?"

Lora blew out a big breath, flubbering her lips with the exhalation.

"No. I do not remember hearing anything like that."

"Hm. It's possible she was told on the way to town or once they arrived. I'll be sure to ask."

"Mister Cook. You've been swell but, can you go just over to the jail right now? Please?"

Landon held her gaze for an uncomfortable moment. Finally, he quirked up a corner of his mouth, checking his wristwatch, and said, "I really do have court shortly." Seeing her pulling together a protest, he smiled gently and put up a hand. "But. As soon as that's finished, I'll go straight to the jail and get her version of events. One piece of business though, you need to officially retain me as her attorney. My usual retainer is $100 but for Eva, I'll drop that to $25. You can leave a check with Lovenia on your way out."

He got up to escort her to the door, placing one hand on her shoulder the same way her father did when they went places together. She suddenly missed her parents. A lot.

"Um. Okay, great. You'll go see her but, can you tell me, what's going to happen next?"

He smiled again, exposing his slightly crooked teeth. "Sure. I imagine she will be arraigned tomorrow morning. At the arraignment, the prosecution will lay out the basic facts about the charges and Eva's alleged involvement. The prosecution will say she needs to stay in jail until trial. I will say she's not a flight risk or danger to the community and ask for bail so she can be released pending trial. Then, the judge will decide whether she stays or gets to go home."

Lora's hands flew to her mouth, her eyes wide. From behind her hands, she whuffed. "She has to spend the night? In jail?"

Landon squeezed her shoulder. "Unfortunately, yes. But we can hope she will come home tomorrow after arraignment. No promises though."

Lora's hands dropped to her sides, eyes wild with panic. "Surely the judge won't make her stay!"

"I hope not. Now, I have to head over to the courthouse. I'll see if I can find out anything else. I can come to the house tonight and let you know when arraignment is, unless you want me to call out to Monroe's?"

Clutching the shoulder strap of her purse, she grimaced. "No. Monroe's is fine. I hate for you to make a trip just for something everyone's going to know about before it happens anyway. He'll find a way to get the message to me. Thank you."

Mr. Cook opened the door, allowing her to walk out first. Lora, a bit too loudly, said, "Thank you so much for making time to discuss this important matter, Mr. Cook. I appreciate it." Landon chuckled under his breath and avoided Lovenia's eyes as he closed his office door. Lora wrote a check for the retainer and managed to keep a smug look off her face when she handed it over to the fuming secretary.

8

After processing, Eva settled into an antiseptic-smelling, cold, olive drab room for questioning. Her mug shot had been taken and fingerprints officially collected. Her purse searched and its contents noted before being logged into property holding. The sheriff crowed about concealed weapons when he found a small pocketknife lurking among wadded candy wrappers and rolls of breath mints at the bottom of the bag. Eva plucked at her dress and figured she ought to count her blessings that he'd stopped short of frisking her. Looking around the room, she felt fairly certain Sheriff Griffin would do everything in his power to get her to admit to something she didn't do. Eva huffed to herself. He could want in one hand and poop in the other. See which one filled up first. She most certainly did not kill Bumpus and there wasn't a chance she'd say she did.

Eva waited for what felt like hours, humming to herself, tapping her fingers on the small, metal table in front of her. The handcuffs on her wrists jangled an awful racket that bounced off the walls of the little room. *If that man don't hurry this along, I'm going to die of old age - or a busted bladder*, she thought. The idea of making water on the Sheriff's floor made her laugh. She was chuckling softly when the sheriff came into the room. He was none too pleased to see his prisoner comfortable enough to find something humorous in the situation.

"What's so funny, Eva?"

"Oh nothing Early—"

"In this station, you will call me Sheriff. It's my title and you'd be smart to use it," he interrupted.

"Alright then, nothing is particularly funny, Sheriff." She said, lacing the honorific with dismissal.

"But you were laughing. Surely you'd like to share the joke?" With a rictus grin, he pulled out the chair on the other side of the table between them and sat, leaning his elbows on the tabletop and staring into her eyes.

Unimpressed, she fixed her features into a bland, neutral expression and replied, "No. I don't think I would. What I would like though, is a trip to the restroom, and to see my lawyer."

"Your lawyer? You talking about that whelp of Robert Cook?" He scoffed.

"You may not have bothered to tell me I have the right to one but it don't matter, because I already know it. Landon Cook is my lawyer and I imagine he's already on his way. Or will be shortly. While we wait for him, Sheriff, how about you work on that restroom request before I let go right here in your dingy little room? I am an old woman, after all." Eva's eyebrows arched as high as her wrinkled forehead would allow and she pointed at the door, handcuffs clanking against the metal table.

Sheriff Griffin's tightly drawn face pulled back even further as he managed to speak without moving his lips. "Fine. We'll make a trip to the bathroom and afterwards, you and I can chat while we wait on Mr. Cook." The chair screeched across the floor as he stood, reaching across the table to unlock the handcuffs chafing her wrists. He pulled her to her feet, without bothering to be gentle about it.

"Oh, I don't expect you and I have much to say to each other, Sheriff," she replied calmly as he led her out the door.

· · · ·

BACK IN THE TINY, COLD room, Sheriff Griffin peppered Eva with questions. Why did you kill Bumpus? What was your plate doing in the cemetery? Why were you really in the graveyard? Did he threaten you? If he did, why didn't you report it instead of killing him? Eva answered each question with slow blinks and silence.

Eventually, he gave up and resorted to staring at her with his beady black eyes, occasionally pounding his open palm on the metal table. While the sudden table slaps made her jump, they didn't produce the results he wanted. She stared back, blue steel squaring off against gritty coal, and held her tongue, biting at the end of it with her front teeth. She knew she could wait him out. And she did, although she was sorely relieved when a knock came through the door and Deputy Ross stuck his head in. He risked a quick, dimple-flashing smile in Eva's direction before speaking. "Sheriff? Attorney Cook is here to see Eva."

Snorting long and hard through his nose, Sheriff Griffin clenched his jaw. "Fine. I guess we'll let him in."

Landon Cook hadn't waited for Deputy Ross to retrieve him from the outer offices, instead following closely behind. He didn't miss the sheriff's comment and countered, "Well of course you'll let me in to see my client!"

He pushed the door open and strode into the room, laying his briefcase on the small table with a satisfying thud. He nodded at Eva and then looked pointedly at the still-seated Sheriff Griffin. "Now, Sheriff, I'm sure you advised Mrs. Burnette of her right to an attorney when you tried to question her? Hm?" He threw a questioning glance in Eva's direction and was not surprised when she shook her head, confirming the Sheriff had done no such thing.

"No? Come on Sheriff Griffin! I know it's a new requirement but really...I'll make note of it. Now, if you'll be so kind as to allow us some privacy, I'm sure we'd both be much obliged."

He stuck his right hand out as if to shake the Sheriff's hand but when the sheriff clasped his, Landon Cook pulled the other man to his feet and turned him towards the door. Releasing his grasp, he put his left arm on the Sheriff's back and pressed firmly, indicating that it was time for the sheriff to leave. Sheriff Griffin whirled to glare down at the shorter, but more solidly built, younger man. "Watch how you touch me, son. You wouldn't want to be locked up in here for assaulting a lawman, would you?

Landon held his own hands up in a sign of surrender and smiled. "No. I sure wouldn't. Just like I'm sure you wouldn't want me to tell the judge you tried denying Eva the right to counsel. Now, please, leave."

Sheriff Griffin straightened to his full, impressive height and hitched up his pants. He spun on his heel and left the room, slamming the door behind him.

Landon Cook waited a beat or two before opening the door to be sure no one was lurking in the hallway outside, trying to listen to their conversations. He came face to face with Deputy Ross who had the decency to blush before walking away.

"Well, that was fun," he quipped, grinning as he gathered Eva up in an awkward handcuffed hug. "Now, what on earth is this all about Eva? Your granddaughter, Charlie's kid, right? She told me what the charges were and I'm damned if I have any idea why he'd think you could kill a person!"

Eva returned Landon's hug as best she could, squeezing her chin into his shoulder. "I can't tell you how glad I am to see you, Landon."

Letting go, Landon pulled his chair around to the end of the table so he could sit nearer to Eva and hold her hands while they talked. He wasn't her son, but he'd felt like one of her own for almost as long as he could remember. He studied her face, making sure she was alright before he got back to business and asked again, "Eva, what is going on here?"

She shrugged. "Bumpus died in the graveyard not too long ago. Lora and I found him while we were at the creek. We told the men up at Monroe's and they called the sheriff's department out. Apparently, one of my plates, a broken one, was found near his body in the cemetery and now, Early Griffin thinks I killed him. That's about all there is to it from what I can gather."

"Wait. So you're telling me that as far as you know, this entire case is based on a broken dinner plate?"

"Yep. That and some Bumpus blood on one of the pieces. You'll get access to anything else he might have though, right?"

Landon drew back and paused, cocking his head at a quizzical angle. "Yes, I should. But anything else? Can you think of what else he might have? I need to know everything Eva. I can't defend you properly if I'm broadsided by information."

"I don't really have any idea what he could have. I mean, he tried to trick me into giving up my fingerprints when he served the warrant to seize one of my plates. I almost fell for it until I remembered you telling us, when you were in law school, that a person has the right to read any warrant or writ for seizure before complying. I let that man bring me all the way to this building before I realized I hadn't actually read it. Once I did, I refused to let him have my fingerprints." She smirked, smug in her success, and leaned back in her seat.

"And that's all, nothing else?"

"One thing was odd yesterday. Hal Johnson was here and just about knocked me down when he was leaving. I don't know why he'd be here, it's not my business. But, he was wiping his hands when he left and they looked like they might have ink on them."

"What does Hal Johnson have to do with this?"

Eva shrugged. "Everything and nothing I suppose. See, I been secretly making biscuits for the Johnson kids every day for about the last 6 months or so. Hal don't know I know, but his wife left him, and I figured he could use a little help." She blinked at him sweetly before continuing, "I assumed one of his young'uns was taking them from my house every morning because the plate from the day before was always returned. Maybe that's how my plate wound up in the cemetery."

Landon studied her face for a minute and asked, "So, Sheriff Griffin didn't come asking you about a Black man running from Hal's place the day Bumpus died?"

"Well, yeah, he did. How'd you know about that?"

"Eva, Lovenia Thigpen is my secretary. You know she's Hal Johnson's sister. And, well, she's been stepping out with Sheriff Griffin. The idea of them as sweethearts makes my skin crawl but that's neither here nor there." He waved a hand like he was fanning away a sour smell.

"There's not much that happens in his house or in this department that she don't know. And yes, I already knew Hal's wife left him. Anyway, apparently, Hal called the sheriff about the incident and had him check into things. A running Black man in the area on the same day Bumpus died? I figure that ought to be the focus of his investigation instead of trying to catch you up over a dinner plate. Do you know anything about that? Or why Griffin has dropped the running Black man bit to go after you instead?"

"Nope. Sure don't."

Landon squinted at her. Her answer was conveniently short and made him think he was missing something. "You gonna stick with that story?"

Eva squared her shoulders, gathering her will and forcing it to the edges of the room, before saying, "I just told you I don't know nothing about a Black man running on the day Bumpus died. The first I'd heard about it was when Hal was carrying on about it at church the following Sunday. Sunday evening, Griffin came out to my place and asked me about it. That was the first I'd heard any yammering about it being murder. He didn't think it was necessary to tell me why he thought it." She lifted one shoulder to emphasize the fact her confusion mirrored his own.

Landon Cook was a quick thinker and made connections faster than most folks.

"Alrighty then, it would seem that Sheriff Griffin thinks, or thought, the running man and Bumpus and your plate are all connected. Any idea why?"

Eva's searching pause drew him up a little. He squeezed her hands in his. "Eva. Your granddaughter, Lora, paid my retainer fee. Anything you tell me, anything at all, will remain between us. You understand that, right?"

She nodded and said, "Yes. I understand but, I don't have anything else to add. Nothing that would make it any plainer or prove any better that I didn't kill Bumpus."

"Okay. Let's talk it through and see what we got." He opened his briefcase and retrieved a pad of paper. Pulling a pen from the breast pocket of his suit coat, he motioned for her to continue.

• • • •

"I DON'T KNOW WHAT MORE to say, Landon. I didn't kill Bumpus, and I don't know anything about a Black man running anywhere on the day Bumpus died." Eva took a deep breath, "Lora and I found him when we went to the creek that runs along the cemetery bounds. We stopped off at Monroe's and he called the authorities to let them know. Honestly, I figured Bumpus was blind drunk and conked himself on a tombstone. That's what I thought then. That's what I think now."

Sucking his breath between his teeth, Landon tapped his pen on the notepad and thought for a second. "Did you see your plate in the cemetery? I mean, did you notice it anywhere near Bumpus's body?" Growing up in Mooresville, he knew about plate markers and didn't bother asking how Sheriff Griffin figured out the plate belonged to her.

"No. Not that I recall, but, I didn't go poking around him too much either." She looked away from him and snurled her nose.

Clearly Bumpus was already pretty ripe by the time she and Lora had come across him.

Landon grimaced in agreement and dropped the pen. Leaving off his note taking, he leaned back in his seat, linking his hands behind his head, thinking aloud, "Okay, so we have Hal Johnson chasing a Black man off his property the day Bumpus died. Griffin, at least for a minute, thought the two events were related but has since dropped that angle because he isn't scouring the bushes for more suspects. We know your plate would have been at Hal's house, and we know that Hal was here at the station the same time Sheriff Griffin was trying to get your fingerprints. Is that the bare bones of it?"

Eva proffered a nonplussed nod. "That sounds about right. Besides, there's no reason to suspect Hal's running man had anything to do with Bumpus's dying."

Landon ran his fingers through his thinning hair, pulling it at the temples the way he'd done since he was a little boy deep in thought. The look on his face made it perfectly clear he didn't believe Eva was telling him everything she knew. Stifling silence crept into the room.

When he spoke again, he pleaded, "Eva, this case, on the merits I can see right now, is flimsy at best. But, if your plates are the angle that brought Sheriff Griffin to your door, I gotta have something to steer him in another direction. I have to have something or somebody else to present to the jury at your trial. If you're holding back...I need you to trust me. "

Shifting to sit as straight as possible, the chair beneath her creaked, anticipating the heaviness of what she was about to say. She looked him dead in the eye and said, "I do not want a jury trial, Landon."

Landon drummed his fingertips on his notepad and exhaled through his nose. "Eva, you know how this works. Twelve of your peers to hear the evidence and decide whether you are guilty or not. "

"My peers, huh? Since when did Alabama start letting women onto juries? We both know any jury won't be nothing but a bunch of gossiping men needing to feel superior. No. You ask for a bench trial. That's what I want. " She tried to fold her arms across her chest but had to settle for clasping her hands into a double fist in her lap. Handcuffs made it difficult for old women to gesture in defiance.

"A bench trial," Landon echoed. "Well, sure if you want to place your fate in the hands of one man instead of twelve but I still advise against it."

"One man, twelve men. It's all the same to me. At least a judge knows the law. I'm not taking your advice. I trust you with my life, Landon. Either you do your job or I go to prison. I'm fine with the possibility. I've lived long enough and my affairs are in order."

Frustrated, Landon ran his fingers through his hair one more and stood. "Alrighty then. I guess that's what we'll do. I just hope we both don't end up regretting it." He patted his hair down and sighed."Lora asked me to call down to Monroe's and let her know how our conversation went."

He picked up his briefcase and paused at the door before leaving the room. "I just don't know what I'm going to say to the kid." The door clicked softly behind him.

Eva raised her hands to her face and sucked in a wavering breath. She prayed in a faint whisper.

"Father God, I got your message. Having Early leave me waiting in this cold room while you squeezed the blood out of my heart was unnecessary but I got it. I will not exchange what's left of my life for the entirety of Leon's. This is how I'm supposed to help him. I understand. Your will, not mine. Amen."

She raised her eyes to the ceiling, hoping the God she believed in would change his mind. Divine recognition might sound like a blessing but oh Lord, the price is often steep.

9

Lora sat in the truck with the door open to the breeze when she left Landon Cook's office. She didn't have a clue what to do next. Waiting promised to be torture but she had no idea how to avoid it. She watched Mr. Cook leave his office, briefcase in hand, suit coat flapping in the stirring breeze, his mousy hair lifting slightly from his head. She decided that if she had to wait for news, she could manage just as easily from the courthouse square as she could back at the house. Besides, staying in town meant she didn't have to rely on the Monroe-relay to deliver any messages.

The Limestone County courthouse was a shining example of Classical Revival architecture wrought in a combination of limestone, granite, and marble. Taking up an entire city block, around which the Courthouse Square merchants plied their wares and trades, this courthouse had stood sentry over the city of Athens since 1919. Grand limestone staircases lead to double-door openings on all four sides, inviting visitors to participate first-hand in the machinations of government and justice. Broad Grecian columns reached for the sky from generous marble-floored porches at the tops of the stairs, only to be restrained by the weight of the clock tower and copper dome crowning the four story building. Towering oaks and maples on each corner of the lawn provided shade to any who needed respite from the blistering heat of summer in Alabama. Water fountains, hidden beneath the stairways in small tunnels which also provided entry into the imposing building, offered relief to thirsty white throats.

Hitching her purse strap over her shoulder, Lora followed Mr. Cook until he disappeared behind the double doors at the top of the steps on the east side of the courthouse. She thought she'd have enough time to do a little window shopping and maybe grab a snack at the drugstore soda fountain before making her way around to the

Jefferson Street side where the Sheriff's Office was. She wanted to know the precise moment he went to see Eva. She needed to be sure everything was happening in the way it should. Peeping in the Ben Jaffe's Department Store windows, she pondered the back-to-school supplies featured in the displays. Crisp white-and-black saddle oxfords rested next to brightly colored pencil pouches fanned out like peacock feathers. Protractors, rulers, and compasses strung on invisible fishing wire hung from the ceiling. Crates turned on end to serve as shelves supported piles of the newest offerings in crayons, school glues, and erasers. She remembered she hadn't yet enrolled in her own classes for the fall quarter and wondered if she ever would.

Continuing north on Marion Street, towards the drugstore on the corner, Lora felt like she was trying to swim through a vat of molasses. Time crept by while the people around her moved at the normal pace. She stopped in at the drugstore, considered ice cream, but opted for a cola and a bag of Golden Flake potato chips instead. Crunching and slurping her way towards Jefferson Street, where the Sheriff's office was, she took a few moments to examine the psychedelic prints and colors on offer at Wilson's Fabric. Electric pinks, purples, greens, and yellows swirled in dizzying patterns of ogees, geometrics, and florals as she strolled past. At the corner of Marion and Jefferson, she wished she had time to browse around in U.G. White's Hardware store. She loved the dusty, oily smell of farm tools and auto parts that drifted from the recesses and wafted up from the creaking hardwoods as she browsed the selections of dinnerware and flower seeds near the front of the store.

Still, there was no time for getting lost in White's. She turned the corner onto Jefferson just as Landon Cook crossed the street from the courthouse to the Sheriff's Office. Glad not to have missed him, she glanced at her watch and chose to have a seat on the bench just outside the department doors. Lora was determined to catch him when he left.

• • • •

AFTER THIRTY-OR-SO syrupy slow minutes, Landon stormed out the front doors of the Sheriff's Office looking like he wanted to punch someone, scream, cry, or all three at once. Lora startled and second-guessed her decision to wait on the attorney to make an appearance. Screwing her courage to the sticking place, she cleared her throat and stood.

"Mr. Cook? Excuse me. Hi. Were you able to speak with her?"

He whirled on his heel, shoulders relaxing as he realized who was asking the question. Schooling his expression into one of resolve, he said, "Yeah. We talked. Not that it did much good."

Acknowledging Lora's confusion, he continued, "She gave me the bare bones of a story and then clammed up!" He flailed his arms around while he spoke, his attempt at gathering himself crumbling with frustration. He drew the attention of passers-by and Lora gestured for him to sit down on the bench she'd vacated. He shook his head.

"No, I don't have time to sit. I need to get back to the courthouse to file some paperwork. Tell you what, I'll go ahead and come out to Eva's place tonight. Maybe we can figure out a way to make her come to her senses." With that, he patted her on the shoulder and turned to cross the street, thin hair sticking out in all directions. His agitation made him step a little too quickly in front of a car which slammed on it's brakes to avoid hitting him. The driver yelled and shook their fist out the window, but Landon Cook didn't check up. He kept, lost in thought.

• • • •

LORA MADE HER WAY ALONG the south side of the square to the truck and, with nothing else to do, drove home. Back at Eva's, she set to clearing away the breakfast mess which had been left unattended in the aftermath of Sheriff Griffin's sudden appearance that morning. The house was pensive without Eva's presence helping it breathe. Lora thought she might suffocate with worry and questions piling up in her head, pressing down and rooting her in place, making every movement twice as difficult as it should have been.

Once the kitchen was clean, Lora decided she needed the therapy of pulling weeds and, as busy as Sheriff Griffin had kept them in recent days, the garden had been neglected. She changed clothes, slapped a wide-brim hat on her head and, with several paper grocery bags in hand, went to survey the damage of inattention. She didn't bother with shoes. She liked the feel of cool dirt between her toes. Gardens are tricky things that many people make look effortless. Sure, initially it doesn't take much more than tilling under some dirt and shoving seeds into the ground. But getting those little nuggets of dormant life to grow and thrive? Pure magic as far as Lora was concerned.

The corn towered with spindly toes pushing delicately out of the ground; its silky tops just starting to burnish in the sun. Peas clambered up their strings but were shy about their accomplishment, hiding pregnant pods beneath broad leaves. Tomatoes sprawled in their cages and leaned against each other, heavy with fruits promising juicy delight to humans and worms alike. Okra stalks stood proudly, creamy blossoms with blood red centers swaying in the light breeze, belying the itchy arms she'd get when she cut the pods. Pepper plants and cucumbers argued along one edge of the plot while pinto bean bushes pushed back against invading tendrils from squash vines. Lora never understood why Eva kept such a large garden for just herself but there was nothing for it now. She needed to concentrate on keeping everything alive and happy until Eva came home.

Tackling the corn rows first and forgoing a hoe, she knelt to hands and knees and grabbed hold of a weed. She jerked the plant from the ground and pretended it was Hal Johnson she was throwing into the paper sack. This thought was entertaining and every weed she pulled and discarded became another irritation shoved into the sack. Hal Johnson, Maggie Johnson, Sheriff Griffin, Deputy Ross - no matter that she liked his face, Bumpus, even Leon Strong. They all found their way into a bag and when it was full, they were all dropped on the burn pile without ceremony.

She repeated the process until there were no more paper bags left in the kitchen. Lora pulled the wheelbarrow from the shed and kept on pulling. The sun grudgingly retreated behind the trees across the road before she stopped for the night. Her intention to spuddle around for distraction had generated worthwhile results. Surveying her progress, she saw she'd managed to clear all the weeds except the ones creeping in among the squash and cucumbers. *I'll get those tomorrow,* she decided, and went to wash up.

Realizing she hadn't eaten anything other than a bite of sausage biscuit all day, she was suddenly famished and wondered what she'd be able to scrounge up for dinner. Eva was an excellent cook and made meal preparation seem as effortless as gardening. No such thing as a TV dinner in Eva's house. When Lora checked the refrigerator and cabinets, all she found were ingredients. She sighed, dismayed at her inability to combine them into anything edible. After the day's exertions and worries, Lora doubted she could manage much more than a bowl of oatmeal or a bologna sandwich in her grandmother's kitchen.

10

While she contemplated whether to bother with the oatmeal, the back door swung open. Lora shouted and nearly jumped out of her skin. Easing her way up Eva's back stoop was Myra Strong. Myra's cheeks plumped as she smiled and she chuckled warmly. "You done a fine job on those weeds, Lora. I imagine some of 'em will think twice about popping up in that garden again."

Myra let the door close behind her and held her hand out to Lora. "Come on, let's get you something to eat before you fall out."

One hand still on her chest, trying to keep her heart from bouncing right out, she leaned over, bracing herself on her knees to catch her breath. "Miss Myra! You nearly scared me to death! What are you doing here?"

Myra's face flushed a little. "I was at Monroe's and heard your phone call with your mama. I figured you'd be needing somebody to talk to this evening. Couldn't stand the idea of you over here all by yo'self."

Myra moved around Eva's kitchen with practiced ease, somehow knowing exactly where everything was. Cabinets and drawers were opened and closed in a ballet of culinary grace as she hummed her own background music. Lora excused herself to change clothes, glad to have company in the house.

When she returned to the kitchen, enjoying the cool linoleum on her bare feet, she asked, "Miss Myra, why does my grandmother mean so much to you? How'd you two become so close? I mean, you have to be around the same age as my parents..."

Myra nodded and slid a scalding hot, cast iron pan of cornbread batter into the oven and said, "Well, that could be a long story but the Reader's Digest version is your grandmama and grandaddy have always been real good to me and my family. Not good on the surface but deep down, genuine good."

"How so? If you don't mind me asking."

Stirring the pintos simmering on the stove, Myra hummed a little more before answering. "My husband, Edward, grew up picking cotton as a hired hand on farms around here. Edward's family rented farmland from your grandaddy and his family for as long as anyone could remember. There was enough of those boys to pick their own cotton and earn a wage pickin' for other folks too.

"When me and Edward married, he wanted to buy his own place. A farm of his own, where we could raise a family. So, he started looking for places to buy. Problem was, no body wanted to sell to a Black man. And if they did, the land was no good for farming. It was either all used up or nothing but swamp. Your grandaddy carved out a piece of his own farm and offered to sell it to him."

"Well! That was nice of him!"

Myra peeked into the oven and hummed. "Mm hm. It was, but when Edward went to the bank to ask for a loan. They refused him. Ooohh...he was so down in the dumps! My heart broke for him, watching his dreams blow away like chaff in the wind.

"When he came over here to tell Dub he wouldn't be buying that farmland after all, your grandaddy told him not to worry about a bank. He'd sell it to us for a fair price, set a monthly payment, and not charge us any interest. Well, at $150 an acre for a hundred acres, that was still a pretty steep price tag for us. We could only afford about $25 a month back then and we were sure even your grandaddy would laugh in our faces. We'd be paying for that land for fifty years!"

She pulled a couple glasses from the cupboard and poured tea while they waited for the cornbread to finish. Myra lowered herself into a kitchen chair. "Ol' Dub didn't even blink! He just stuck out his hand and said, 'Deal!' As far as white folks around here knew, Dub was renting us the farm. Putting that word out kept us all safe. I've had a soft spot for your grandaddy ever since."

Lora thought for a minute and said, "What do you mean it kept you all safe?"

Myra crunched an ice cube and shrugged. "Well, lots of folks back then didn't think Black folks ought to own property and could make life difficult for anyone who disagreed. So, telling people we were renting instead of buying kept our names out the gossips' mouths and the busy bodies off both our places."

Lora swirled the tea in her glass, watching beads of condensation run down the sides. "Okay, I can understand that, but that was still just a business deal between your husband and Grandaddy. You and Gram are closer than that. How come?"

Myra held her hand to her heart, raised her head to the ceiling, and closed her eyes. She seemed to be praying. Lora noticed the lashes resting on Myra's cheeks were getting moist as she struggled to hold back tears.

"Five years after selling us that land, Dub died. The war was on and everybody with a son serving had learned to dread the sight of those big black sedans coming up the road. Your grandparents had two children overseas. Your uncle Walter, and your daddy. One morning, I saw one of those hateful cockroaches stirring up a cloud of dust headed this way and figured I'd follow it, just to make sure it wasn't coming here. Only...it was. That big car pulled up right in front and two men stepped out. One in an Army uniform, and another preacher looking type. Up on the porch, hats in their hands, they knocked on the door. Dub opened it and slammed it straight in their faces. Those men let themselves in, leaving the door wide open. All of a sudden, I heard Eva start hollering and carrying on like nothing I'd ever heard. "

Lora was holding her breath. She'd never heard this story before.

Myra heaved herself out of her chair, stirred the beans, and checked the cornbread. "Just a few more minutes. Anyway, when Eva started screaming, I started running. When I hit the door, Lord, I'll never forget it. Those men standing there useless. Dub on the floor. Eva holding his head. She'd stopped hollering by that time and was just whispering to him, "Oh Dub, it's okay, it's okay, it's okay," over and over, tears streaming down her face like a waterfall, rocking back and forth while she patted his cheeks. No doubt in my mind he was gone. Lora, your grandmama had just lost her son and her husband in the same day! How does a body recover from a blow like that?"

Myra wiped her eyes and sniffed. Lora pulled a handkerchief from her purse by the door and gave it to her. Myra nodded her thanks and continued, "I went on in and sat next to Eva. She just kept rocking and whispering. I looked up at the men and told them that unless they were going to help, they needed to say what they came to say and leave. She didn't hear them say the words but they said'em, and left. Said they'd come back the next day to make arrangements for Walter."

Lora whisked a couple forks from the drawer and a half-full jar of piccalilli from the fridge while Myra pulled the pan of cornbread from the oven and flipped it out. Spooning large portions of pintos onto their plates, Myra cut wedges of steaming cornbread and brought them to the table. As they sat down to eat, Myra kept talking."I sat with Eva for a good long while. When she didn't seem like she was moving, I made her look at me. Told her I was gonna run down to Monroe's and call the funeral home."

Crumbling her wedge of cornbread over the plate of beans, Myra said, "I could still run back then and that day, I ran like the hounds of hell were chasing me. Monroe didn't have a payphone back then, just the one to the store. I told him what had happened and he said he'd make the call himself. I ran on back fast as I could. She was right where I'd left her. Dub's head still in her lap. She'd stopped whispering at him by then but, I don't know, the silence was worse."

"What happened next? Weren't Uncle Anthony and Aunt Mable still living here then?" Lora interrupted, mashing her beans and cornbread together and spooning a generous helping of piccalilli on top.

"Naw. Anthony had just left to work in the civil service, he was in Texas at the time. Mable had gotten married the year before and her husband moved them off to Nashville. Anthony came as soon as he heard but he couldn't stay. Mable, well, she came back for the funerals but that's about it. That girl thinks her farts don't stink and decided she couldn't be bothered to help her mama." Myra grunted and waved a hand in dismissal. "Mm. She sends Christmas and birthday cards but that's about it. She don't even bother calling no more. No, Eva was alone here, 'cept for me.

"So, I took care of her. I helped with the funerals. I made sure she ate everyday, made sure she bathed. I kept her house clean and made her go outside. She was like a child, having to be told what to do and how to do it. I brought my oldest son, Maurice, with me. Eva enjoyed having him around, so I kept bringing him. That boy drew her out of her pit and gave her a small reason to keep on going. Edward took on most of my chores around our house so I could take care of Eva."

Lora noticed Myra hadn't taken a single bite from her plate and decided against asking another question. Myra kept talking anyway. "She says I brought her back to life. I just felt like I was being a good friend. I sure didn't realize she'd be doing the same thing for me when Edward passed."

Her voice dropping to a ragged whisper, Myra said, "Edward was killed in a cotton combine accident five years ago. Wasn't nothing that could be done to help him. I had to carry on, raising our boys, without him. Your grandmama stepped in and made sure I kept breathing. She deeded that land to me free and clear so I didn't have to worry about losing our home too."

Myra's eyes sparkled. "I keep on paying the rent though. Eva argued and refused to take it at first but I wore her down. I think it's only right. Besides, she'd done sold off most of their farm after Dub died. Nothing wrong with having a little money coming in regular."

With a deep sigh, she pushed her plate away and said, "I hate to waste it but I don't feel much like eating now. I just can't."

• • • •

ABOUT THAT TIME, BOTH women jumped up as the front door suddenly opened. Back-lit by the deep setting sun behind him, neither could see the man's features and yelped in chorus. Lora snatched up the nearest thing to hand, the jar of piccalilli, and hurled it across the house at his head. Fortunately for him, his vision was clearer than hers and he managed to dodge the flying missile, letting it smash into the wall behind him. Vinegar and pickled vegetables dripped down the plaster in chunks and glops.

"Hey! It's just me! Landon Cook!" the shadow shouted, holding his hands out, indicating he came in peace.

Lora whuffed in relief before laughing and saying, "Good grief Mr. Cook! I'm glad I threw the piccalilli instead of grabbing Gram's rifle!"

He smiled and returned her laugh, nodding in agreement at his good fortune. "She still keep it behind the washer next to the back door?"

Waving him into the kitchen, she grabbed a dishcloth and went to clean up the splattered jar while Myra topped off their tea glasses and poured one for Mr. Cook. Lora called from the living room and asked if he'd spoken with Eva again since she'd seen him earlier.

He cut his eyes at Myra and raised his eyebrows.

Lora huffed in frustration and put one hand on her hip, the other dangling the pungent dishtowel and its contents away from her like a hobo pack at the end of a bindlestick. "Miss Myra is my grandmother's dearest friend. You can say whatever you came to say with her sitting right here."

Landon inclined his head in acknowledgment. "I can't divulge details covered by attorney-client privilege but no. I didn't see her again. I figured it'd be a waste of time. I know Eva pretty well and once she's made up her mind about something, she's not in much danger of changing it any time soon." He took the offered glass and plopped down into one of the kitchen chairs, sprawling out like he was at home.

Lora noticed his relaxed posture and said, "You know Gram pretty well, huh? How's that?"

Myra moved the dinner dishes from the table to the counter next to the sink while Lora disposed of her self-defense mess. The heavy woman sat back down at the table, busily crunching ice cubes and listening closely. Lora took a seat next to Myra and propped her elbows on the table, holding her tea glass in both hands.

Landon took a deep draw from his glass and nodded. "Yes ma'am. I spent more time in this house than my own when I was growing up. Your uncle, Anthony, and I were best friends from the day we met on the steps of our first grade class."

"Is that so?" She looked at Myra for confirmation. Myra nodded once and kept on crunching.

"Yep. He was trying to get another kid to eat a worm and I stopped him. We scrapped about it. Got in trouble with the teacher and both our mamas. Naturally, we had to be best friends after that. Of course, he'll tell you it was the other way around but don't listen to him. I'm a lawyer and lawyers never lie." He wiggled his eyebrows at her to let her know he was teasing.

"It's been a long day so I won't stay. I just wanted to come out and see how you were. Looks like you're in good hands."

Lora was relieved he wasn't planning to camp out in the kitchen all night but that didn't stop her from asking one more question. She folded her hands on the table. "So, what'd she say?"

Landon set his glass down and leaned forward, elbows on knees, to look her in the eye. He was suddenly very serious. "Well, she said she didn't kill Bumpus," then he looked pointedly at Myra. "I heard through the grapevine that Hal Johnson chased a Black man off his place the day Bumpus died. When I asked her about the events of the day, she said Griffin had asked her about that too but claimed not to know anything. What about you? Do you know anything about that?"

Myra crunched a couple times and smiled sweetly back at Mr. Cook before saying, "No sir. Can't say I do."

As soon as he mentioned a Black man, Lora's neck flushed and a sheen of cold sweat broke out along her hairline. She shook her head. "Me either." Thankful her voice was steady, she asked if he'd like a refill and started to rise.

Landon reached out and grabbed her arm to stop her. He leveled a stern eye at her and said, "Look, I'll be clear here. The sheriff has Eva's fingerprints on both the broken plate in the graveyard and the plate he got from here. The plates themselves are a flimsy case for Griffin to try to stand on. But, if I can give him another suspect, I can blow a reasonable doubt hole in his case wide enough to drive a locomotive through. What do you know about this Black man?"

Not daring to look at Myra, Lora shook her head again. "Nothing," she said and changed the subject. "Will arraignment be tomorrow? What happens at arraignment? Will I be able to see her?"

He sighed, running his fingers through his limp hair, the moisture from his tea glass making it stick up like he'd been electrocuted. "Yes, it's tomorrow morning in Courtroom 1 at nine o'clock. I have also filed the paperwork for a preliminary hearing to take place as soon as possible, hopefully Monday."

Interrupting him with a sudden, frantic wave of her hand, Lora blurted, "Monday? You mean Gram might have to spend the weekend in jail? She can't—"

Landon responded to her flailing with calming gesture of his own and said, "I'll ask for bail at the arraignment. I'd be real surprised if the Judge denies the request given Eva's nonexistent criminal record, reputation in the county, and lack of flight risk."

Lora interjected again, "Bail? What does that mean?"

He smiled, understanding she wasn't fluent in the language of criminals, and said, "It means, if the Judge grants bail, she will be expected to put up something as surety that she's trustworthy and will comply with all of the court proceedings from here on out, including showing up for trial and staying out of any more trouble in the meantime. If he grants bail, she'll be released to come home as the rest of the trial progresses."

Mr. Cook took a gulping swig of his tea and continued, "The arraignment will consist of the charges being read and Eva's plea being entered. If the judge grants the request for preliminary hearing, we'll get a first look at any additional evidence or cause Sheriff Griffin may have used to support the charges."

"Okay, can I be there? Can I see her?"

"Oh, sorry. Yes. It's an open court procedure so you can be there. You won't be able to talk to her though. Still, I'm sure she'd like it, knowing you were there to support her."

Lora nodded and in a soft voice said, "Of course I'll be there."

Landon reached across the table and took one of her hands. His hands were warm and surprisingly calloused for an attorney. "I'm going to do everything in my power to make sure she comes home tomorrow. She's important to me too." Thanking her for the tea, he stood and took his leave.

11

After Landon left, Lora stood still as a statue. The house was quiet, except for the hum of the refrigerator and Myra's ice crunching. Slurping the last drops of tea from her glass, Myra said, "Hmpf! A Black man running." Her mouth twisted. "I guess now I know exactly where Leon took off to every morning. He was helping Eva. And she couldn't even tell me? I had to find out like this!" Her words were heavy with betrayal.

Lora was relieved Eva hadn't mentioned Leon to Mr. Cook. And she understood Myra's concern. This was just the sort of thing they'd all hoped to avoid. She also understood Myra's hurt feelings over not knowing the reason Leon was at Mr. Johnson's in the first place. Still, there was nothing she could do now except hope the judge allowed Eva to come home after arraignment. She pasted on a positive face. "Miss Myra. We both know Gram will never do anything to endanger Leon. You heard Mr. Cook. The sheriff's case is flimsy. Just the possibility of someone else in the graveyard makes the case weaker. He could mention the theory without mentioning Leon at all."

Myra shoved herself away from the table and pulled the tea pitcher from the refrigerator. Her hands were shaking as she waved the half-full, glass pitcher in time with her words, sloshing amber droplets with every swing. "That's all well and good for you to think. But that possibility points directly at my son! Even if no one 'sides us knows it was him! If folks around these parts think a Black man had anything to do with Bumpus's death, well, ain't no Black man safe!"

Myra's chest heaved with the force of her words. She slammed the tea pitcher on the table and glared at Lora, daring her to disagree. Myra exited out the back door, stomping down the steps and across the yard, muttering in frustration.

Lora couldn't pretend Myra was wrong. She flopped into the chair Landon had vacated and felt the emptiness deepen and widen with every tick of the clock.

Alone again, she listened to the deafening rise and fall of the whining cicadas in the trees outside. Lora envied their conversations and wished she had someone to talk to. She wished her grandmother was home. Under Eva's protective wing, Lora always felt she was as much a part of Mooresville as anyone else. In this moment, she thought maybe she really didn't belong.

With numb hands, she covered the pot of beans and put it in the refrigerator; the cornbread went back in the oven. She scraped the dinner plates into the scrap bucket and tiptoed through the moonlight and dew-tipped grass to dump the dregs on the compost heap.

Lora wandered into the living room and clicked on the television set, just for noise, before curling up in Eva's rocker. She wrapped the same granny-square afghan which had sheltered Leon just days ago around her legs and tried to find humor in *The Lucy-Desi Comedy Hour*. But, with no other lights on in the house, their flickering, black-and-white antics couldn't shoo away the crawling gloom of helplessness settling into the creases and corners of the little house.

Sure the Sandman would steer clear and sleep would elude her, she blearily watched the images moving across the screen. She drew the afghan up around her neck and wished things were different.

• • • •

MORNING DELIVERED A crick in her neck from sleeping in the rocker and a hammering, anxious fear she'd overslept. Running to check the clock on the wall in the kitchen, she realized she'd woken up with barely enough time for a quick bath before she'd need to head to town. Regretting not bathing the night before, as well as not sleeping in an actual bed, she zoomed around the house in a frenzy.

During the coldest, fastest wash-up she could manage, she wondered what someone wears to court for an arraignment. Finally settling on a black knee-length skirt with a powder blue sweater set and black flats, she grabbed her purse off the couch where she'd dropped it the day before and bolted out the door.

Her drive was complicated by tractors and hay-balers hogging the roadways. Still, finally swinging into a parking spot, she checked the clock tower and breathed a small sigh of relief, 8:50, just in time, barely. She flew up the courthouse stairs and lost no time locating Courtroom 1. Slipping into a seat as close to the dividing rail as possible, she took a deep breath and examined the cavernous space. The courtroom was paneled in dark wood with the judge's bench on the far wall, slightly elevated on a platform. This was the only room in the courthouse with a gallery level above the main seating area. Lora assumed there were stairs somewhere in the hallway which allowed people to gain access. Low-pitched conversations buzzed and drawled as spectators and petitioners filed in, choosing their places with care. The court reporter appeared from a previously hidden doorway next to the judge's stand and set up the odd-looking little stenography machine, clicking a few keys to confirm everything was working as it should.

The seats around her filled in. When she looked for familiar faces, she found more than she'd expected, but none she wanted to see. The Church Ladies, Eva's friends, were in attendance: Agnes Crawford, Margaret Clem and Helen Fudge. Each dressed in their Sunday best, still reminding Lora very much of vultures. Her grandmother may love them but Lora hated them for being there. She couldn't shake the feeling they were scavenging for gossip to add grist to the mill. Hal Johnson fidgeted in the row behind them. He hadn't bothered to dress up. Instead, he looked as if he'd come straight from the barn with bits of hay chaff still sticking to his shirtsleeves. The sneer on his face told her all she needed to know about why he'd come.

Just before the clock struck 9:00, Sheriff Griffin and Deputy Ross came in and took their seats behind the railing, behind the prosecution desk. Landon Cook followed them, spotting Lora in the crowd. He managed to toss a small wave and reassuring smile in her direction before taking his own seat at the defense table. The prosecuting attorney, a man Lora didn't recognize, sauntered down the center aisle at exactly 9:00. He was an ample, big-bellied man with a greasy comb-over who carried himself like a watermelon with legs stuffed into a $40 polyester suit two sizes too small. Still, he swaggered with confidence and pursed his lips with the seriousness of the business at hand.

As soon as the prosecutor's briefcase hit the table, the court bailiff called the assembly to order and announced, "All rise! The Honorable Judge Robert Underwood presiding!"

Everyone stood when Judge Underwood emerged from the hidden door and ascended to his seat. He muttered, "Be seated," while he arranged his robes around him and sat. He cleaned his glasses with a corner of his robe as he scanned the assembly. He slipped the temple tips over his ears and was perplexed to see there was no defendant accompanying Mr. Cook. He asked, "Counselor, where is your client?"

"Your Honor, that is a very good question. One which should probably be posed to Sheriff Griffin since my client is currently in his custody." Landon's head swiveled, deflecting the judge's gaze.

Judge Underwood peered down at the Sheriff and raised his eyebrows over his glasses and said, "I agree. Sheriff Griffin, your office is responsible for ensuring all inmates are present for court proceedings, is it not?"

Sheriff Griffin stood, hat in hand, obviously embarrassed. "Yes, Your Honor."

"Well. Why do we not see Mrs. Burnette here this morning?"

"Your Honor, I instructed one of my deputies to bring her before I headed over. With your permission, I will retrieve her myself."

The judge nodded his assent and shooed Griffin towards the door. Sheriff Griffin made it to the exit in three long strides, his face and corded neck on the verge of apoplexy.

Landon Cook cleared his throat. "Your Honor. While we wait, perhaps we could get your ruling on my request for a preliminary hearing on this matter?"

Underwood removed his glasses and made a show of considering the request while he cleaned them again. Without looking at Mr. Cook, he scratched at a persistent spot on a lens and asked, "Have the papers for this request been filed with my clerk?"

"Yes. Your Honor, I filed them with the court yesterday afternoon."

"Well in that case, as long as everything is in order, and the prosecution has no objections, I don't see why we can't go ahead and get that on the schedule." Judge Underwood perched his glasses back on his nose and considered the prosecuting attorney. "Mr. Beatty, do you have any objections to a preliminary hearing for this case?"

In a surprisingly squeaky voice from such a rotund man, Mr. Beatty stood and replied, "No, Your Honor. No objection."

The judge reached a hand to his clerk, who was already handing the docket schedule to him, and perused the calendar. "Are there any objections from either party to a preliminary hearing on Monday at 8:00 am?"

When both attorneys voiced their agreement, Judge Underwood penciled the hearing onto the official record. "Good. Good. We will proceed with arraignment as soon as Mrs. Burnette arrives." He banged his gavel on his desk, announced a 10-minute recess, and withdrew to his chambers.

• • • •

LORA STAYED ROOTED to her seat during the recess. She refused to miss the opportunity to be the first, possibly only, smiling face Eva saw when she arrived at the hearing. She pretended to appreciate the Church Ladies being there in support of Eva when they petted her shoulders and tittered hollow concerns in her ears. She pointedly ignored Mr. Johnson when he skulked out of the room and returned, wiping water from the drinking fountain on his shirtsleeve. Lora twisted her sweating hands in her lap, irritated with herself when she realized her eyes kept landing on Deputy Ross when she wasn't staring at the wall in front of her. She was adrift in the currents of hushed voices flowing around the room. Other than Mr. Johnson, few people left, unwilling to risk losing their seats.

Her patience was rewarded when a door to her left opened and Eva, escorted by the flummoxed Sheriff Griffin, entered the courtroom. Lora slid to the edge of her seat, grasping the railing in front of her, and choked back the urge to burst into tears and laugh all at once. Never mind that Eva's arm was held tightly by the sheriff, or that her hands were cuffed in front of her, Eva walked into the courtroom like she owned the place. Her head was held high and her silver curls were surprisingly well maintained underneath the half-hat she still wore from yesterday. Her dress was only a little wrinkled. Despite Eva's outward composure, Lora suspected she'd barely slept in her cell to avoid mussing her appearance.

Eva's blue eyes immediately locked onto Lora's. She smiled confidently back at her granddaughter and mouthed, "Don't worry," before taking her seat at the defendant's table. Landon reached an arm around Eva's shoulders and gave her a quick squeeze. He leaned close to whisper in her ear, and Eva shook her head sharply. Her gesture was not the answer he hoped for and he withdrew his arm. Shaking his own head, he busied himself shuffling papers and muttering under his breath.

"All rise! The Honorable Judge Robert Underwood presiding!"

Everyone shuffled to stand as Judge Underwood once again took his place on the bench and motioned for everyone to sit.

"Well, glad to see everyone could make it this time. Mrs. Burnette, the court offers its apologies for any confusion this...delay," he looked pointedly at Sheriff Griffin, "may have caused. Let's proceed. Mr. Beatty, you have the floor."

Mr. Beatty addressed the bench.

"Your Honor, the charges in this case, brought against Eva Holder Burnette of Limestone County, are one count of voluntary manslaughter in the death of Ethelred Bumpus and one count of obstruction. Voluntary manslaughter due to a fit of passion and obstruction in the defendant's refusal to cooperate with the Sheriff's Department."

"Mr. Cook? Have you received a copy of these charges and the accompanying documentation in support of same?"

Landon quickly got to his feet. "Your Honor. We have received a copy of the charges. If I may, Your Honor, I would ask the prosecution to be more forthcoming with any supporting evidence they may have."

"So ordered. Mr. Beatty, I expect that information to be delivered to Mr. Cook's office by end of business today."

Mr. Beatty stole an almost imperceptible glance at a red-faced Sheriff Griffin and replied, "Certainly, Your Honor."

"Mr. Cook, does your client wish to enter a plea in this matter?"

"Yes, Your Honor."

With this statement and a nod from Landon, Eva stood, drew herself to her full height and did not flinch away from looking Judge Underwood directly in the eye.

"Mrs. Burnette, how do you plead?"

In a clear, firm voice, Eva said, "Not guilty, Your Honor." In a brief instant of uncertainty, she looked to Landon for what to do next. He motioned her to take her seat again.

"So noted. Now, I assume we need to move on to the question of bail. Mr. Beatty?"

Beatty pulled at his shirt cuffs and said, "Your Honor, due to the violent nature of the crime, whether intentional or not, we feel it would be in the best interest of public safety if Mrs. Burnette were to remain in custody until the conclusion of trial."

Landon Cook let loose an exasperated, dramatic sigh and turned a contemptuous sneer to his opponent while speaking to the judge. "Your Honor. Eva Burnette is a 66-year-old widow, mother, and grandmother. She attends services at Holley Hill Church of Christ every time the doors are open and is known to be a gentle, giving member of the community in Mooresville. She is no more of a threat to public safety than a butterfly lighting on a marigold. We request reasonable bail and a quick return to her daily life while this travesty of a manslaughter case is underway."

"Save your dramatics, Mr. Cook. I am inclined to agree that she poses no imminent threat to public safety. Bail is set at $10,000. Thank you everyone, see you on Monday morning." With a sharp rap of his gavel, he adjourned the court and before the bailiff could order everyone to rise, disappeared into his chambers in a flurry of black robes.

• • • •

THE COURTROOM ERUPTED in a mass of shuffling feet and disappointed murmuring. Hopes for a spectacle dashed away by a single gavel strike. Lora leapt from her seat and approached the knee wall which divided spectators from court officials.

"Ten thousand dollars?! How on earth is Gram supposed to pay that?" she demanded as she leaned across the gap to where Eva and Mr. Cook stood discussing their next steps.

Landon held up a hand and said, "She doesn't. You simply have to place a 10% deposit with the court clerk and then she is free to go home until Monday for the preliminary hearing. You'll need to work through a bondsman but I can help you with that." He gave Eva a warm look and squeezed her hand.

Eva said, "Lora, did you bring my checkbook?"

Lora nodded, gripping her purse to her chest.

"Good. I'll retire back to the jail with Sheriff Griffin. Go with Landon and just write the check. I'll see you shortly."

Lora was gobsmacked by the idea of writing a thousand-dollar check and suddenly remembered she'd forgotten to record the check she'd written for Mr. Cook's retainer fee. She fidgeted with her purse strap for a moment before reaching over the railing to pull Eva into a quick embrace as Deputy Ross approached to lead her out of the courtroom. She looked expectantly at Mr. Cook and said, "Well? Let's go."

He chuckled and shook his head. "You are most definitely her granddaughter. Let me gather my things and I'll walk you right over."

· · · ·

ONCE THE PAPERWORK was complete and the check written, Lora hovered around the courthouse square feeling triumphantly nauseous. Before taking his leave to attend to other clients, Mr. Cook said it could take three or four hours for the wheels of justice to roll back the bars of Eva's cell. All she could do was be patient. She was certain Sheriff Griffin would drag the process out as long as possible and hedged her bet against a five hour wait.

It was late afternoon before Eva emerged from the Sheriff's Office. Lora rushed to her side and almost bowled her over in a sweeping hug. "Gram! I am so so so glad you're out! Are you alright? Are you hungry? Thirsty?"

Eva laughed as she returned Lora's embrace. "Child, you're going to wear me out with these questions! All I really want right this minute is a bath and a clean pair of drawers!"

"Gram! You just said 'drawers' out loud, out here on the sidewalk! Somebody could hear you!" Lora was delightfully mortified.

The corners of Eva's eyes crinkled into creases at Lora's consternation. "The entire county is already talking about me. I doubt drawers on the sidewalk is going to make much of a difference. Besides, everybody wears 'em and right now, I need some clean ones. Let's go home."

Lora fished the truck keys from her purse and handed them over to Eva like she was being presented the key to the city. Eva bowed somberly in return, the twinkle back in its proper place, and took the keys. On their drive home, they rolled down the windows and sang "I Saw Her Again" at the top of their lungs the whole way home, making up words when they were unsure of the lyrics and laughing at their own silliness.

12

E va sped up for a car-chase style spin into her yard but hit the brakes with a jolt when she spotted an unfamiliar powder blue station wagon in front of her house. She raised an eyebrow at Lora.

"Oh. That's mom and dad's car. I called them on my way to town yesterday after you were arrested."

"Why on earth would you do a thing like that?"

"Gram! I had to! You're going on trial for manslaughter and you're innocent! Why would I not call them?"

Eva rolled her eyes and shook her head as she pulled responsibly into her drive and around back. "You don't have to tell everything you know, Lora."

Killing the ignition, Eva took a deep breath and slid out of the cab. Lora scrambled and quick-stepped her way to the back door behind her grandmother.

As soon as the screen swung open, Lora's parents flung questions at Eva like a verbal game of lawn darts.

"What happened?"

"Who's dead?"

"Why does Griffin think you did it?"

"Do you have an attorney?"

Eva ignored them and kept walking as she waved them off. "I'm going to take a bath."

With their mouths gaping, Charlie and Maeve rounded on Lora, circling like coyotes from either side. They were moderately gentler with her; switching from lawn darts to horse shoes. Still, they wanted answers and Lora wasn't well-equipped to dodge them.

"Bumpus was found dead in the cemetery a couple weeks ago. One of Gram's plates was found near his body. Sheriff Griffin thinks Gram cracked him over the head with it. Only, she didn't. She wasn't anywhere near the cemetery that day. Landon Cook is her attorney.

I don't know anything about him other than Gram asked me to get him and I did."

She said all of that in one long breath and sucked in a new, fresh one as soon as the words escaped her mouth. She shrugged her shoulders and blinked at them. The way they were standing, Charlie with his hands on his hips and Maeve with her arms crossed across her chest, she felt like a little girl again, caught in a lie with no way of avoiding trouble. She fought the urge to squirm and look at her feet. Instead, she alternated looking each of her parents directly in the eye. Her hands twisted behind her back to hide how tightly she was wringing them together. She'd thought Eva would have welcomed their support. She'd thought they would be calm and helpful. Apparently, she'd thought wrong.

"How long have you guys been here? I wasn't expecting you until tomorrow." Lora changed the subject, trying to dissipate the viscous tension in the room.

Throwing her skinny arms into the air, Maeve screeched. "You think we'd wait until tomorrow to get here after your phone call yesterday? No ma'am! We hopped in the car as soon as your daddy could get out of the plant! Do you have any idea how embarrassing it was for him to ask his boss for emergency time off?"

Lora's cheeks flamed.

Her mother continued, holding her hand up to her ear in imitation of a telephone receiver, her pitch and tone tightening higher and meaner by the syllable, "'Hi Boss, I need to make an emergency trip to Alabama because my mother has been arrested!' Yes, Lora, that was a great thing for him to have to do. Not to mention the loss of pay to come down here a day and a half early!"

Lora fired back. "Oh sure, Mom. Dad's loss of an extra day of pay and your precious image are way more important than Gram being arrested for a crime she didn't commit!"

She pivoted to her dad, who hadn't said anything while Maeve was ranting, "And you? Do you have anything to add? I'm here trying to help Gram and all either of you can do is worry about yourselves?"

Charlie's nostrils flared and his deep blue eyes narrowed at his daughter like she'd suddenly sprouted horns and a tail. He shifted his shoulders, pulling his lime green polo shirt taught across his chest, and leveled an angry finger at Lora. His voice was stern and demanding, "Now listen here young lady! You are not going to stand there and speak to us that way! We drove through the night to get here and if you think we're going to let you stay with all of this going on, you're sadly mistaken."

He took a single step towards her. She held up a hand, stopping him in his tracks. "Daddy. You aren't going to *let* me do anything. I'm 19 years old and don't need your permission to live with my own grandmother."

Charlie's head rocked back as if he'd run into a pane of glass. Maeve's head swiveled from Lora to Charlie and back again. "Lora Eve Burnette," she seethed, stalking across the kitchen to stand nose to nose with her daughter. "You are our daughter and you will do as we say. You might not like it, but you can get happy in the same pants you got mad in because that's the way it is."

Lora clenched a retort behind her teeth but refused to be cowed. She mimicked her mother's earlier stance and crossed her arms over her chest, one hip cocked out in what she hoped was an act of defiance. About that time, refreshed and rejuvenated after her bath, Eva came back into the kitchen wearing her favorite house dress and slippers. Pretending she hadn't heard every word and knowing she'd walked into a stalemate, she chirped, "Charlie, Maeve, it's so good to see you! Y'all hungry?"

Charlie ran his hands through his close-cropped, lightly salted dark hair in frustration, lacing his fingers together behind his neck. "No, Mama. We're not hungry. We're just here to pack up Lora's things and take her home. She doesn't need to be involved in one of your crusades."

Maeve tossed her heavily shellacked, perma-set, bleach blonde head in support of her husband and looked down her finely powdered nose at Eva. "That's right. Lora is coming home with us." She emphasized the word home as she said it.

Eva lifted one shoulder and brushed them off with a smirk. "Well, it seems we are, as usual, of two different minds. You see, in Alabama, a 19-year-old gets to decide these things for herself. And, seeing as we are in Alabama, I reckon what Lora says is what goes."

She pulled the door to the refrigerator open and peered inside. "Lora, didn't you say Myra left a pot of beans in here? And cornbread in the oven? I'm so hungry I could eat the south end of a northbound mule."

Lora envied the way Eva shut folks up with just a few words and the ease with which she dismissed nuisances. She regretted calling her parents. Instead of helping, all they'd brought was more stress and more problems to deal with.

* * * *

EVA BUSTLED AROUND the kitchen and set the table for four anyway. She warmed the beans on the stove and gently heated the corn bread, being sure to place a cup of water in the oven with the pan to avoid drying out the gritty bread. Maeve and Charlie continued their useless badgering, their words landing on selectively deaf ears. Lora navigated around them as best she could to help get the evening meal on the table. She took her cues from her grandmother and ignored her parents as she went about her business.

Once the beans were piping hot and the cornbread was butter-melting warm, Eva sat at the table and looked expectantly at Charlie and Maeve. "Y'all going to sit or not?"

Not waiting for an answer, she spooned beans onto her plate and began crumbling cornbread on top. "Lora, I couldn't find the piccalilli when I looked in the ice box. Did we eat all of that jar already?"

Lora nonchalantly shook her head and replied, "Oh, I threw that jar at Landon Cook's head."

"Not that he didn't deserve it, but why?" Eva cackled.

Charlie and Maeve exchanged resigned glances and sat. He pushed his plate to one side and folded his elbows onto the table. Maeve's hands gripped together in a strangle-hold wrestling match with her patience in her lap.

"He walked into the house unannounced and without knocking! The sun was behind him and I couldn't see who it was. I told him he was lucky I hadn't shot him with your rifle."

Eva spooned a bit of mash off her plate and made a tsk-ing sound. "Lord. That would have been terrible. What with me currently needing his services." The crinkling around her eyes proved she found the situation as humorous as it had turned out to be.

Charlie seized the opening and said, "Since you brought it up, Mama. Why don't you tell us what's going on?"

Eva lowered a hard stare at her son and said, "Charlie, now that you've remembered your manners and who's house you're in, I'd be happy to tell you. Although, I'm sure you've already heard the bones of it from Lora."

Lora didn't miss the way Eva's eyes slid her direction in disapproval, whether it was for calling them or for telling them, she couldn't be sure.

Eva reiterated what Lora had already told them in her trademark, matter-of-fact fashion. "Bumpus was found dead in the cemetery a few weeks ago. Sheriff Griffin found one of my plates near his body. He got a warrant for one of my plates from the house. My fingerprints were on both, not that that's a surprise. Early decided I must have conked him in the head and killed him."

Charlie interrupted. "Why does he think you'd kill Bumpus? Surely he doesn't think you're carrying a killing grudge all this time since Dot died?"

"Well, why he thinks it'd be me specifically, I can't say. Although you two know as much as anybody that I have more than a Dot reason to dislike Bumpus." She waved her fork at Maeve and Charlie. "Even so, Early and I have butted heads more than once over the years and I figure this is his one chance to rid himself of what he thinks is a problem. That problem being me."

Maeve insinuated herself into the conversation, pushing her empty plate away, leaning onto the table and seething. "Well, Eva, if you didn't insist on being a meddling old biddy, maybe he'd leave you alone."

"Maeve." Charlie's warning tone was lost on his wife.

"Mother!" Lora cried through a mouthful of food.

"Don't talk with your mouth full, Lora. It isn't ladylike."

"I couldn't care less what's ladylike right now, Mama. How dare you say something like that to Gram!"

Eva reached under the table and patted Lora on the knee. "Don't mind your mama, Lora. She's always been more concerned about other people's opinions than she should be. It's who she is and who she's always going to be. I'm not going to stop meddling simply because she don't like it."

Maeve spluttered for a retort, the flush of frustration creeping up her neck to find a home on her already pink blushed cheeks. "Eva, I will not have you talking about me like that to my daughter. And with me right here in the room!"

"Fine. I'll wait 'til you're gone. Is that better? Is it safe to assume you two won't be staying the night here?"

Maeve sucked in her cheeks and pushed away from the table, chair legs digging into the linoleum as she stood. She put her hands on her wasp-thin waist and looked sternly at her husband. "We will not be staying. We'll get a hotel room in town. Charlie? It's time for us to leave."

Torn, Charlie reluctantly eased his chair back and sighed. "Thank you for the invitation anyway, Mama. We'll be back in the morning for breakfast if you don't mind."

He rounded the corner of the table and leaned into Eva's cheek, whispering a faint "I love you" before squeezing her hand and kissing her cheek.

"I'll have it ready. Got a brand new jar of grape jelly with your name on it." Eva's wink and warm smile faded a bit as she caught sight of a scowling Maeve behind him, impatiently tapping her pointy-toed shoe.

13

O nce they'd gone, Lora choked down her dinner and cleared away the dishes, used and empty alike. Eva sidled up next to her at the sink, falling into the comfortable routine of washing and drying. Eva glanced sidelong at her granddaughter.

"I guess you have some questions?"

"Yes Gram, I do. But whatever it is between you and my mom can wait. I need to tell you about Mr. Cook's visit and what really happened last night.

"It's true that he startled me when he let himself in the front door. It's true that I hurled the piccalilli at his head. What I haven't had the chance to tell you is that Myra was here when he showed up. When he wanted to talk with me, I told him that anything he had to say could be said in front of her."

She rinsed the plate she'd been scrubbing and handed it to Eva. "I wasn't prepared for him to ask about the young Black man Mr. Johnson chased from his place. I understand Mr. Cook wants to provide the prosecution with a potential, different suspect but Gram..." Her voice trailed away into whisper.

Lora gripped the edge of the sink and braced herself, trying not to cry. "Myra had just told me all about what you and grandaddy did for her and her husband, how she helped you get through the death of both him and Walter, how you helped her cope when Mr. Edward died. But, when she heard Mr. Cook mention a young Black man, she got so...still. After he left, I tried telling her you'd never betray Leon for any reason but, I don't think she believed me. She said just the mention of a Black man being involved puts all the Black men around here in danger."

Eva paused, dishcloth and plate resting between her hands on the countertop. She took a ragged breath. "Myra is right. And you are too. I'll not be offering up Leon as a sacrificial lamb for slaughter."

She sighed. She glanced at the small clock over the door and said, "We still got time and I need to go see her. Come with me?"

Lora enveloped her grandmother in a quick, tight hug, leaving dishwater hand prints on Eva's back. "Of course I will."

• • • •

RATHER THAN DRIVING, Eva decided it'd be best to walk, no matter the creeping dusk, and approach Myra's place from the back door. Back doors on houses are reserved for friends and Eva needed to be a friend to Myra right now. She hoped Myra would let her.

Stepping into the pools of light cast into the yard from the kitchen window and stoop light, they heard a cacophony of laughter and jokes from inside the house. They exchanged wistful smiles, both wanting to be part of the happiness, if only for a moment, before knocking on the door.

At their knock, the house went silent. Amazingly, incredibly, it was Leon's face which peered out the window to see who was on the stoop. He let out a whoop and shouted, "It's Miss Eva and Lora!" Two quick footsteps, and the door swung open wide. Lora was pleased he'd dropped the "Miss" from her name.

"Come on in!" He tugged at their arms, a happy grin cracking his face nearly in two, as he drug them inside.

Two of Myra's younger boys gathered around them, chattering, and jostling for attention. The next oldest to Leon, 15-year-old Desmond, showed off the new baseball bat he'd gotten for his birthday, declaring himself the next Hank Aaron. Leon called him crazy and cuffed him on the back of his head, laughing. A shy, slightly built little boy, James, who appeared to be around seven or eight, tugged on Lora's arm and smiled sweetly. He opened his hand to reveal a tiny green tree-frog. Lora suspected he meant to startle her with his treasure but seemed delighted when she opened her own palm next to his to see if the little frog wanted to meet her in person.

He clapped and squealed with glee when the newly-freed, captive amphibian hopped from his hand to hers. She allowed herself a moment of ooh-ing and aah-ing before returning the precious green spot to James, who immediately ran outside to set liberate his friend. Another third boy, who looked to be twelve or thirteen, sat at the kitchen table, surrounded by books and scattered papers and pencils, quite obviously disgruntled by the sudden ruckus. Leon told him to stop scowling and clear away his mess so their guests could have a seat at the table. The boy huffed and rolled his eyes but did as he was told.

Leon rolled his eyes in return and shook his head, laughing. "Don't mind Cedric. He's jus' mad Mama's making him catch up on his studies over summer break and bothered by everything these days. What brings y'all over here?" He motioned for them to sit. "Y'all want some tea? We already ate but I'm sure I can come up with something if you're hungry?"

Eva said tea would be just the thing and asked if Myra was home.

"No. Mama had to work the closing shift at the grocery. She won't be home for another 15-20 minutes or so. I told her I'd manage these monsters tonight." He waved a hand in the direction of his brothers, still milling about the kitchen, his face breaking into a broad, indulgent smile.

Lora broke in, "Leon, why are you here? I thought you were in Chicago?"

Leon glanced at his brothers and shook his head, almost imperceptibly. "Well, I missed home, so I thought I'd come for a quick visit." Shifting gears slightly, he called out, "Hey Des! Get these hoodlums started on their evening chores. Let's get those done before Mama gets home."

With a muffled, "Yeah yeah yeah," Desmond herded his grumbling brothers out of the kitchen.

Once the boys were ostensibly out of ear shot, Leon sat and leaned closer to Eva, making a show of clutching at his gut while he spoke. "Mama called and said you're in trouble over Bumpus. I had to come see what I can do to help."

Eva and Lora both understood without asking that Leon hadn't had much choice in the matter. His own version of knowing insisted he return to Alabama and help however he could. All he'd done was follow the call.

Eva's lips curled downward slightly as she patted his hand. "Nu-unh! Nothing you can do to help me except go on back to your job in Chicago. I don't want you anywhere near this mess. But since you're here for the night anyway, and while we wait for your Mama to get home, tell us all about the big city!"

· · · ·

EVA SIPPED HER TEA and tried not to let her nerves get the best of her while Leon regaled them with hilarious and shocking tales of rail yard humor so rough it made his ears bleed, beef sandwiches with hot peppers that tasted like heaven on a French bread bun, fancy girls who thought he was handsome until they realized he wasn't interested in paying for their company, and the troubling discovery that Maurice had started snoring loud enough to wake the dead since he'd moved out. The younger boys drifted in and out of the kitchen, making excuses for drinks of water or forgotten shoes, even though it was clear they were simply eavesdropping. Leon, Lora, and Eva exchanged knowing, pinch-lipped smiles each time one of them dipped in and out of the room.

Before long, Myra huffed up the back steps, arms full of grocery bags and pushed the door in with her foot. If she hadn't already built up enough momentum to carry her into the room, Lora was sure the surprise of seeing her and Eva in her kitchen would have pushed her backwards into the yard.

Leon jumped up to relieve Myra of the shopping and said, "Look Ma! Miss Eva came to visit!"

"Boy! I got eyes. I can see! What I want to know is why?" Myra's expression would have wilted a pokeberry weed as Eva stood and smiled nervously at her friend. Before Eva could answer, the younger boys, hearing their mother's voice, barreled into the room, bouncing around Myra and sharing the events of their day. She hugged and laughed and scolded as necessary, enveloping them, collectively and individually, in the sure comfort and safety of her love. Eva and Lora were forgotten but fortunate bystanders.

Once the boys were shooed back to their chores, Myra turned to Eva, holding up one finger to make sure all attention was on her. "Imma ask one more time. What are you doing here?"

Eva twisted her hands together before reaching out to take one of Myra's. "Lora told me you were anxious when you left last night. I need you to know I will never betray Leon's involvement in all this. I would never risk hurting you or him like that. I am so, so sorry."

Myra snatched her hand from Eva's grasp as if she'd been burned and hissed. "Tell me why Landon Cook needed to know anything about a colored man!"

Before Eva could explain that she wasn't the one who'd told him, Leon, listening from his place leaning against the kitchen counter, interrupted, "Mama. When you called me yesterday, telling me Miss Eva'd been arrested, I knew had to come home. I intend to talk to Mr. Cook and set things straight. If that means Sheriff Griffin's attention is turned on me, well then, that's what it means."

As one, Myra, Eva, and Lora all rounded on him, each lobbing a different version of "Oh no you won't!"

Eva and Lora shared a horrified look at the idea of Leon interjecting himself into the case while Myra planted her hands on her ample hips and stomped across the kitchen. She grabbed him by the chin and pulled his face down to her level, forcing him to look her in the eye. "Leon, you will not be talking to Landon Cook. You gonna get on the first bus back to Chicago in the morning and I'm not listening to another word about it."

Leon gently pried Myra's fingers from his cheeks and rested his hands on her shoulders. "Mama, I'm not going back to Chicago tomorrow. I'm staying here for a few days. My boss at the rail yard thinks I'm here for a family funeral and told me to take a week. My job is safe. He's a good man."

"You lied to a boss you've only had for a couple weeks?"

"I did and I'd do it again. Miss Eva needs me. And, just to let you know, Maurice is coming in on the first bus in the morning. He had to finish his shift before he could get off. Makes sense if I needed off for a funeral, he would too."

Myra jumped back in shock, her breath heaving as she raised her hands in supplication to God for the patience to deal with headstrong children. "You dragging your brother into this nonsense, too? What has gotten into you son? You run up to the church and call him right now. Tell him not to come!"

Leon replied softly, "Mama, I can't do that. He's already on his way."

When Leon mentioned Maurice's name, an idea clicked in Lora's head. Not the painful flash or blurry vision of the knowing kicking in but a slow-sliding suspicion which made her speak up. "Leon, how about all of you...well, you, Miss Myra, and Maurice, no need to bring the little boys if Desmond can keep an eye on them for a bit, come over to Gram's around lunchtime tomorrow. I have an idea but need a little time to think it through."

Eva and Myra exchanged a perplexed glance and shrugged at each other. They were skeptically resigned to letting the young folks take the lead, at least until they heard Lora's plan. Myra squinted her eyes and whispered to Eva across the table, "I'm still mad at you but I won't stay mad for long."

Eva whispered back, "Okay," and grinned with relief at her friend.

Needing to make their way back home, Eva and Lora said their good-byes with hugs and squeezes for Myra and Leon. In the cool moonlit night, they were relieved to know at least some things were starting to get back to normal.

14

E va was up early the next morning, humming with the radio, squishing butter into the biscuit flour. She looked forward to having Charlie at her table again, even if it did mean Maeve was with him. She'd spent his high school years hoping his and Maeve's relationship would just fizzle out. It didn't. While he was overseas, Eva secretly hoped he'd get one of those "Dear John" letters telling him Maeve had moved on. But no, they'd endured through the traumas of war and violence on both fronts. Eva watched her second oldest son drift further and further away from his family. Losing his brother and father at the same time had wounded him deeper than any German atrocity he may have seen and she'd been in no condition to help him heal. She'd forever regret letting him down when he needed her most. Still, she reckoned she ought to be thankful. Without Maeve, she wouldn't have Lora to lean on.

When Lora bee-bopped into the kitchen, they shared a giggle and sang along with the radio. Eva had it tuned to the local popular music station and Lora showed her all the latest dance moves. The Watusi and the Swim resulted in fits of laughter. Dancing made Eva feel a little wicked. Her church frowned on dancing of any kind and, every spring, made waves in protest of proms at the local high schools. Dancing led to lascivious behavior. Eva thought that was a ridiculous idea and figured dancing was just a way of expressing oneself. Lack of self-control, lack of instruction, lack of good parenting led to lasciviousness, not dancing.

They were still twisting around the kitchen when Charlie and Maeve strolled in, casting a pall over an otherwise beautiful morning. Maeve, perfectly put together in black cigarette pants and a hot pink sleeveless button-up shirt cut to emphasize her figure, tutted, "Well I never!" Charlie, comfortable in brown slacks, a blue-and-white madras shirt, and slip-on dockers, laughed and started dancing right along. He was careful to avoid making eye contact with his wife.

Eva twirled from cupboard to table with a steaming stack of biscuits while Lora shuffle stepped behind carrying a platter of sausage patties and scrambled eggs. A hip bump whirled Lora to the fridge for jelly and mustard and Eva slid open a drawer for silverware. After hot-mitting a bowl of sausage gravy to the table, Charlie gambled on pulling Maeve into the impromptu dance party. She dodged out of reach and glared at him as she crossed to the window and switched off the radio.

"That's enough nonsense this morning," she said, settling herself primly into a chair at the table. Lora stifled a snort when she realized Maeve had chosen the one with a wobbly leg, knowing it would only irritate her mother more.

Charlie, with a slightly breathless flourish, gallantly pulled out chairs for his mother and daughter before taking a seat next to Maeve.

Pausing briefly to cover the meal with grace, the four of them sat in silence and filled their plates. When biscuits were split and smothered in gravy, or sausage sandwiched between halves slathered in mustard or jelly, Maeve spoke.

"Eva. Anthony will be here sometime before lunch. We hope he can talk some sense into you - and my daughter. "She glared and pointed her fork at Lora, her off-kilter chair thumping against the floor when she shifted in her seat. "We will be leaving this afternoon. With or without you."

Lora swallowed the bite she'd been chewing. "Well Mom, I hate you wasted a drive. I'm staying."

Eva's eyes disappeared into slits of irritation at the news that Anthony, her youngest son, was on his way but couldn't get a word in edgewise as Maeve's perfectly mascaraed eyes narrowed to throw an ultimatum at Lora. "In that case, don't expect us to send you any money to pay for school, or clothes, or anything else."

Charlie startled and slapped a hand on the table, making them all jump, "Maeve! Don't be unreasonable. We didn't discuss that at all."

"Unreasonable? Lora is openly defying us by refusing to come home and I'm the one being unreasonable?"

He set his jelly biscuit onto the plate in front of him. He blinked slowly and raised one dark eyebrow in a familiar gesture Lora called his "gathering patience" stalling tactic.

"That's exactly what I'm saying. Do I want Lora to come home with us? Absolutely. Do I think she'd be better off not getting tangled up in whatever trouble Mama's gotten herself into? Absolutely. But, she's an adult and can make these decisions for herself. Am I willing to make the price of her education a consequence of her decisions? Absolutely not."

He picked up his fork and stabbed a piece of sausage off his plate, silently daring his wife to disagree with him. Eva was pleased to see his backbone stiffening when it came to Maeve, even if it did only seem to happen when he was under her roof.

Speaking between chews, he looked at Lora. "Honey, you do what you feel is best. I don't agree with your decision to stay here while this plays out. However, I am not willing to punish you for that by refusing to cover the cost of your education. I will pay your school expenses and that's it. Nothing else. You're on your own for clothing and spending money."

"Fair enough, Daddy. Thank you." Lora tossed her ponytail and beamed smugly at her mother before turning her attention to Eva. "You think Monroe could use some help at the store?"

Maeve choked on her milk. "Monroe's? You want to work at Monroe's Store? No daughter of mine—"

Eva ignored Maeve's wheezing. "I dunno. Maybe. Won't know until we ask!"

Charlie wiped a glob of jelly from the corner of his mouth. "Now that's settled, Mama, I'd like to hear more than the bare bones of this Bumpus business."

• • • •

LORA FROZE AND HELD her breath. She was unsure how much Eva would share with Charlie and she worried about Maeve's reaction. She'd explained her idea for helping both Eva and Leon escape Sheriff Griffin's crosshairs to her grandmother on their way home from Myra's the night before. And honestly, she wanted her parents well on their way back to Detroit before Myra, Leon, and Maurice showed up. Eva was fully on board with placing the blame squarely on the shoulders of someone else as long as those shoulders didn't belong to Leon. But, the plan was dead in the water if the Strong's refused.

She drifted back into the conversation and was stunned to hear Eva telling them Leon had been delivering biscuits on her behalf. "Only one day, Hal caught Leon as he was leaving and chased him off. Leon ran into Bumpus in the graveyard and hid in my shed. Lora found Bumpus dead—"

On cue, Maeve shrieked, "You sent my daughter to a graveyard and let her find a dead body!"

No one acknowledged the outburst and Eva continued, "Leon didn't kill Bumpus. And I can't let him be accused of killing a man who wasn't worth the air he breathed anyway."

"How do you know Leon didn't kill Bumpus? You're believing him just because he said he didn't?" Maeve scoffed, throwing her napkin onto the table and crossing her arms over her chest.

Eva's head swiveled with the lethal certainty of an owl hunting in the dark. Her eyes narrowed dangerously.

"That is exactly how I know he didn't kill Bumpus. Because he says so."

"Good Lord Eva! Those people lie!"

"Those people? Let me tell you something Maeve," Eva rested her elbows on the table, giving her full attention to Maeve. "That boy don't know how to lie because he's never needed to, which is something I'm sure you will never understand. Besides, you of all people should be glad Bumpus is gone."

Maeve's mouth opened and closed with tiny popping noises, like a fish out of water, gasping for breath. She flushed from her shirt collar all the way to her perfectly set hairline. She scooted the wobbly chair away from the table and snatched up her plate, ranting and muttering to herself on the way to the sink.

Eva's posture relaxed as she folded her napkin in her lap and looked at her son, her face open and honest, waiting for his two cents. A unanimous, concerted effort was made to ignore Maeve banging dishes and silverware around while pretending to clear away the breakfast mess. Without an audience, her performance faded in intensity, as inconsequential as the clock ticking on the wall or the hum of the refrigerator.

Charlie rubbed a weary hand across his face and studied the ceiling. "So I was right, Mama. This is another one of your crusades."

He loosed a deep sigh and slid a sad smile her way. " I love you, you know I do. But, when are you going to retire from saving the world?"

Eva chuckled. "I don't know about saving the world but I can make sure Leon stays clear of Early Griffin. Nothing you say can change my mind."

"I didn't figure I could. But, have you even thought? You could go to prison for this, Mama. Prison!"

"I have. If the judge decides that's where I need to spend the rest of my days, well, I guess you'll get your wish. My crusading will be done. Ha!" Eva excused herself to run to the restroom and left the rest to stew in their juices for a bit.

Charlie rolled his eyes so far back in their sockets he might have been inspecting his brain. He shook his head, another long, low sigh escaping his lips as he chewed on the story. Lora was terrified at the thought of Eva spending even one more night in jail but, at the same time, was immensely proud of her for sticking to her convictions. She hoped she was made of the same stuff when push came to shove.

Recognizing an opportunity to change the subject, Lora said, "So, are you guys still planning to leave after breakfast?"

Maeve whirled from the dishes and jerked at the back of Lora's chair. She leaned around nose-to-nose with her daughter and squinted, "You couldn't wait for us to get here when you called and now you're running us off? Why is that?"

Lora sat up straighter in her chair and leaned away from the venom. "Mother, I thought you would be helpful or supportive, anything other than judgmental and hateful. But that's what you are so, you might as well leave."

She dug in a little and smiled sweetly at her father. "Daddy, I'll be sad to see you go. But since you're mom's ride, I guess you have to leave too."

It was Charlie's turn to splutter into his drink. He laughed and immediately grimaced with a nervous look over his shoulder to where Maeve stood fuming at the sink. "My mother's been fighting a private war against injustice for as long as I can remember. Feeding the hobos knocking on our door during the Depression, even when we didn't have much to spare. Helping young women who found themselves in the family way but not in the married way—"

Maeve fumbled the skillet she'd been drying with ringing clang.

Lora gasped and whispered, "Wait! Gram was, is...an abortionist? Is that what you just said?"

Charlie hid a quick grimace, lifted one shoulder, and risked a glance at his wife who suddenly snatched up the scrap bucket and stomped out the back door. He lowered his voice a notch, "No. She generally acted more as a mediator between the scared young woman and her parents. Sometimes she'd help them go away until after the baby was born or plan a quick wedding. I only know of one time she, well, did the other thing."

Hearing Eva's footsteps coming back towards the kitchen, he cleared his throat, indicating that the subject of premarital pregnancy should be tabled. He waved one hand in the air. "You know, Mama made sure to vote in each election since women were allowed. She even encouraged me and Walter to join the Army when she heard rumors of what was really happening in Europe."

Eva's step stuttered a little when he mentioned his time in the Army. She made her way to the sink as Maeve eased the back door open. Apparently she'd heard Charlie's comment about his time in the service too. Eva and her daughter-in-law stood still, the ice between them thawing for a moment, looking out the window and seeing anything but the yard outside. Charlie didn't see Maeve give Eva's hand a quick squeeze before choosing a plate to rinse.

Charlie took a deep breath as he thought of his brother. He rubbed at the spot on his thigh where he'd picked up a bit of shrapnel during the final days of the Bulge. He paused a moment before saying, "I'm really not surprised she's taken this stance with Bumpus and Leon."

Charlie wiped his face with his napkin and smirked at his mother's back. "I don't have to like it but I'm proud of her, even if it did make for some hard conversations and more than a couple fistfights when we were growing up."

Eva scoffed at the fistfight comment and fired at him over her shoulder, "I told you and your brothers not to fight over me!"

Charlie deftly parried in return, "Mama, we weren't fighting over you! We were fighting for you! You know that!"

Eva made a playful swipe at his arm which he dodged as he picked up both his and Lora's plates from the table to be washed.

Drawing her pride back tightly around her, Maeve made a show of checking her watch against the clock on the wall and said, "Since it's clear I'm not wanted here, Charlie, I think we should be leaving. It's a shame you're going to miss seeing Anthony when he arrives." She tapped her pointy-toed foot, smoothed her pants, and looked expectantly at her husband.

He sat down and poured another cup of coffee. "We've got plenty of time before we have to hit the road. I think I'd like to spend at least a couple hours visiting with my mother. Maybe Ant will show up before we go."

Maeve shook her head, annoyed with Charlie for insisting they stay even a second longer than she thought necessary. She retreated to the living room to sulk.

15

Lora made herself useful by wiping the table clear of jelly drops and biscuit crumbs. Eva relinquished the remaining dishes into Lora's care and turned her attention to Charlie. Lora enjoyed watching and listening to the two of them cut up and tease each other. He was a different person around his mother, without his wife around. She wondered if Maeve had always been a killjoy and wondered what had drawn her parents together in the first place.

A whiff of smoke from an Oasis menthol cigarette drifted into the kitchen from the living room where Maeve was huffing and pacing around. Lora hated that her mom smoked in Gram's house. Even though Dub had died before Lora was born, somehow, the house held onto the faintest whiff of Old Spice and his hand-rolled, filterless cigarettes after all these years. Lora worried the house would forget him and embrace her mother's influence instead. She knew it was a silly thing to worry about but still, the way the house smelled was the only real connection she felt to the grandfather she'd never known. And, after learning more from Myra about what kind of man he was, she felt more strongly than ever that Maeve ought to smoke outside.

"Mom," Lora called from the kitchen, "Gram doesn't allow smoking in the house anymore. You'll need to go out on the porch if you want a cigarette."

Eva's eyes widened at Charlie's look of surprise when Lora spoke out. They ducked their heads to their chests and barely avoided laughing out loud when they heard Maeve's, "My God. Fine!" and the front door slamming behind her.

Lora shrugged at them before turning her attention back to the dishes.

ANTHONY WHEELED HIS posh rental car into the yard just before noon. He'd cobbled together a dizzying array of connecting flights to get him from Sacramento to Pryor Field in Decatur. Yet another perk of working for the government. Swinging his long legs out of the driver's seat, he loped across the yard and up the steps, giving Maeve a quick hello and odd look, before letting himself in and tossing his suit coat over the arm of Eva's sofa.

"Anyone want to tell me why Maeve is on the front porch looking like she wants to burn the place down?" His question was the last straw on the smothered camel's back before Lora, Charlie, and Eva erupted in a cacophony of howls and giggles and snorts. The confused look on his face as Eva hurried to greet him only made the laughter more insistent.

Eva hugged his neck, grabbed his hand, and drug him into the kitchen. Charlie shuffled his mother out of the way to get to his brother before embracing him in a man-size bear hug. Lora, delighted to see Anthony for the first time in at least six years, bounced on her toes, twisting the dish towel around her hands as she grinned and waited her turn. She'd always thought Anthony cut a dashing figure in his tailored suits and perpetually disheveled, wavy dark hair. The fact that he was handsome and fun to be around didn't hurt her opinion of her favorite uncle either.

"Is this Lora? Good grief! Last time I saw you, well, you were just a kid! Gimme a hug!" He didn't wait for her to come to him, instead he took one giant step across the kitchen, lifted her off the ground, and swung her around like he did when she was small.

Setting his niece back on her feet, he looked at Eva and wasted no time getting to the business at hand. "I hear you got Landon as your attorney?"

"That she did," Charlie interjected, smirking at his mother. "No surprise there, huh?"

"I don't understand why hiring Mr. Cook is such a big deal," Lora said.

Eva flashed a warning glance at her sons and said, "That's a story for another time. Yes, Landon is my attorney and I have every confidence in his ability to represent my case."

Anthony turned a chair around backwards and straddled it. He held up a hand. "He called me right after Charlie did. I know he probably shouldn't have but I'm glad he did. I stopped by his place on my way here and we had a chat. Sounds like he's got a handle on things and, he's pretty good from what I gather. Although, seems like he's a little irritated with you, Mama."

Eva huffed with exasperation. "I'm glad to see you too Anthony but Lord have mercy, I wish you all would let me and him handle this!"

Charlie and Anthony shared a puzzled look before Ant continued, "He was finishing up some work on his truck when I left him. He's planning to stop by in a bit. Maybe we can all hash things out together?"

Lora and Eva stiffened with alarm. Myra and the boys would be there, literally any minute, and they'd hoped to chat with them alone. They certainly didn't want to worry Myra any more than necessary. Lora had no doubt that her mother would be less than helpful. Not to mention it made her anxious to think about how Landon Cook would react to seeing Maurice and Leon in Eva's kitchen when he so obviously wanted to point a finger at a young Black man in the community.

• • • •

SURE ENOUGH, BEFORE long a light knock lit on the back door just as Myra, Maurice, and Leon let themselves in. Not expecting the house to be full of Burnettes, they each paused mid-step and shot questioning eyes at Eva. Eva hopped from her chair, exclaiming, "Well now it's a party!" as she herded the Strongs into the kitchen.

"Charlie? Anthony? Scooch those chairs around, make room for everybody! Y'all remember Myra Strong? And these are her two oldest, Maurice and Leon."

Eva presided over the symphony of squeaking chair legs, shuffling feet, and jostling bodies with a cool head and graceful hand earned through decades of directing wiggling children and gruff farm hands into their places before each meal. She made a point of reserving a place for Myra without allowing her to sit.

"Myra? We can leave this bunch to get settled for a few minutes. I want to get your opinion on some squares I'm putting together for a quilt in the bedroom."

Leading Myra away from the growing din of voices in the kitchen, Eva pulled Myra into her room and pushed the door closed before whispering, "I know what this looks like, but you have to believe me...I had no idea Charlie, and Maeve," she rolled her eyes, "and Anthony would be here when y'all showed up!"

Myra whispered back, "Well, what are we supposed to do? Leave and come back later? That'd be suspicious, don't you think? When did Ant get here? Good Lord!" Myra heaved an exasperated sigh and leaned against the wall, staring holes through Eva.

"No, no need for y'all to leave. Anthony just got here a few minutes ago. They just told me this morning he'd be here today. Besides, I've already told Charlie and Maeve the story. Haven't had time to tell Anthony yet."

She cracked open the door to make sure no one was lingering in the hall. "What's worse, he said he stopped by Landon's house and asked him to come over too! I reckon he'll be here shortly."

"Well Lord Almighty! Eva, we gotta go! I can't let that man see me and my boys in this house!" Myra was shaking. Her ample frame rippled in nervous agitation.

"Hold on...Lora's got a pretty good idea for bypassing the sheriff on the running Black man bit, if he tries to bring it up. Let's go hear her out and see if we can at least get that story out of the way before Landon shows."

Myra calmed herself and squinted at Eva, measuring the strength of their friendship against protecting her boys. Making a decision, she slowly nodded and opened the door. "Eva, I think those colors look just fine on those squares. You let me know if you need my help with those inset-Y's. They can be tricky."

Eva, briefly forgetting her reason for bringing Myra to the bedroom in the first place, followed just a couple steps behind.

• • • •

BACK IN THE KITCHEN, Eva was surprised to see everyone, including Maeve, sitting around the table looking expectantly at Lora. Lora stood in the open space between table and stove, gesturing for Eva and Myra to take the two empty seats on either side.

"Dearly beloved, we are gathered here today," Lora began with a nervous grin, "to discuss the matter of the State of Alabama versus Eva Burnette in the matter of the sudden death of one Ethelred Bumpus."

Assorted chuckles, sighs, and one exasperated "Good Lord!" emanated from the table as she continued. "In all seriousness, we do need to discuss what happened that day, what's happened since, and what's going to happen in the very near future. I'll start. Please hold your questions until the end. This all needs to be said before Mr. Cook gets here." She looked at each of them in turn to make sure they understood the importance of what was about to be shared.

She cleared her throat, uncomfortable with being the center of attention but since it was her idea for the Strongs to come over in the first place, she figured it was her duty to carry on. "Here's a little back story. Gram has been making extra biscuits for Hal Johnson's family every day for the past several months. Leon has been delivering them. Sneaking them in the back door when no one was looking."

She slid an apologetic smile at Leon, who returned the favor and nodded for her to continue.

"One day, Mr. Johnson caught Leon coming out of his house, carrying an empty biscuit plate, and started chasing him. Leon, understandably, ran away as fast as he could. You all already know the shortest route between there and here is through the cemetery. Anyway, while running through the cemetery, Leon literally bumped into Bumpus, knocking him into a headstone, and dropping the plate in the process. He didn't stop to check on Bumpus because he could hear Mr. Johnson still chasing behind him. Instead, he ran here and hid in Gram's shed."

Leon continued to nod his head in encouragement.

"When Gram and I found Leon, and heard what happened, I ran to the graveyard and saw Bumpus was dead. We couldn't let Leon get in trouble for what was clearly an accident and together, we all decided he should go stay with Maurice for a while."

Maurice grinned at this and piped up, "And I sure do appreciate having somebody to split the rent!"

Myra shushed him with a thump on the head usually reserved for rowdy children in church.

"After seeing Leon off to Chicago the next morning, Gram and I went to Monroe's and told him we'd found Bumpus dead in the graveyard. We thought that'd be the end of it."

At this point, Eva took over the telling and Lora sat down, grateful for the reprieve.

• • • •

EVA, NOT BOTHERING to hold court like her granddaughter, remained seated. "That next Sunday, Lora overheard Hal Johnson talking to the men at church about chasing a Black man off his property. And, sure enough, Sunday evening, Early Griffin stopped by to ask if I'd seen anybody running across my place the day Bumpus died. That was the first time I'd heard any mention of killing. I figured everybody would assume he'd just passed out drunk and hit his head on the way down."

Anthony, drumming his fingers on the tabletop, glanced at the wall clock and said, "Mama, you ought to speed this along. Landon will be here any minute."

She nodded and kept speaking, "Wasn't a few days later that Sheriff Griffin was back out here demanding to have one of my plates. He didn't have a warrant, so I didn't let him have it. He came back the next day with a warrant for my plate and supposedly for my fingerprints. He took the plate, and I rode with him all the way to town before I realized I hadn't read the warrant. The warrant was for my plate only - not my fingerprints. I didn't let him have those either.

"The odd thing is that Hal Johnson nearly ran us over coming out of the sheriff's office that day, looking like he was wiping ink off his fingers. Anyways, Early was back out here the next day with a warrant for my arrest, accusing me of manslaughter, because he'd found my fingerprints on a broken plate near Bumpus's dead body and matched those prints to the plate he'd taken from the house."

Lora held up a finger, indicating Eva should pause in her telling, and looked at Myra. "I know you think Gram mentioned to Mr. Cook that a young Black man was delivering her biscuits. But she didn't. That was Mr. Cook's secretary, Lovenia Thigpen, who just happens to be Hal Johnson's sister. All the same, folks around here know he chased a Black man from his place that day and that can't be helped. Now, Mr. Cook wants to point the prosecution in the direction of another possibility. He thinks it ought to point to this anonymous running Black man. My thought is, wouldn't Mr. Johnson's prints be on the broken plate too? Why can't we point the possibility at him?"

The Burnettes at the table sat in stunned silence for a moment before launching into a dizzying volley of comments, arguments, agreements, and questions. Myra, Leon, and Maurice were stone faced and didn't say a word, splitting their gazes between Lora and Eva alike.

Finally, Anthony's voice overrode them all and he said, "I think Landon needs to hear all of this. I also think we need to know whether Hal's prints were on the cemetery plate. Anybody know how we could find out?"

Myra jerked up straight in her sea and threw up a hand to Anthony. "Hold up! I don't see why, if Hal's prints are on that cemetery plate, why does my boy's name need to be in anybody's mouth?"

Maeve took the opportunity to interject. "Because it's the truth! Your son may have been the one who killed Bumpus!"

Leon's head dipped slightly. Lora reached out a hand to him. Maeve's jaw tightened at the gesture.

Swiveling in her chair to face Maeve straight on, Myra bristled. "You obviously done forgot how quick people around here are to blame Black folks for everything. You done forgot what kind of man Bumpus was."

Never one to back down from an argument, Maeve opened her mouth to speak but was cut off when Eva said, "The sheriff's office was supposed to turn over all evidence to Landon's office by end of day yesterday. So we'll have to wait and see what he got."

She jabbed a finger into the tabletop and swept an "I-mean-it" warning around the table. "I'm telling you all, right now, Leon will not be dragged into this problem. Bumpus is better off dead. We all know it."

No one at the table disagreed with Eva's assessment of Bumpus. Nods from brown and white faces alike confirmed the consensus that the death of Bumpus was no great loss.

Lora chimed in, "I also think Mr. Cook needs to know everything. But," she said, pinning her mother in her chair, "what's said here, stays here. At this table. It is my understanding that attorney-client privilege means he can't tell anyone or discuss with anyone what we or Gram tell him. An alternative suspect could be enough to break the plate theory with a reasonable doubt hammer and, if Mr. Johnson's prints are on the plate, that might be the opening we need."

She turned to her uncle. "Uncle Anthony, you truly believe we can trust Mr. Cook? With Gram's life, and Leon's too?"

Anthony answered in earnest, without hesitation. "I do."

"Good. Then I say we tell him everything. And," she winked at Eva, "we support Gram running her defense the way she feels is best."

When Myra snorted and started to rise, Leon patted her back down into her seat, murmuring, "Mama, trust me too? It's going to be fine." Her face scrunched in desperation, even as she sighed and nodded. Leon recognized her expression. It was the same one she'd worn when his daddy died and it broke his heart.

• • • •

THE WHAT-IFS AND WHAT-abouts started up again as the families broke off into separate and mingling conversations about the revelations of the day. Lora, Eva, and Myra moved around the kitchen, putting away the air-dried dishes, filling tea glasses, and steeping a new batch in an effort to keep their hands and minds busy. Myra stole sidelong glances at her sons, fighting the urge to snatch them up and run as fast and far from Eva's house as she possibly could.

Figuring Anthony might be hungry after his travels, Eva sliced a garden-fresh tomato and made a sandwich with pillowy-soft white bread and mayonnaise. Just as she set the plate in front of him, Landon Cook's voice called through the front porch screen door,

"Hello! I'm here! Don't throw anything!" He kicked dirt from his boots while he waited for someone to answer. Lora and Myra smiled and Eva chuckled as she went to welcome him.

"Come on in, Landon. You hungry? I can make you a tomato sandwich, if you want?"

"Thank- you, Eva. I grabbed a bite before I left the house but, I wouldn't say no to a glass of tea."

"I think I can make that happen, go on and have a seat!"

Landon tucked a raggedy baseball cap into the back pocket of his grease stained jeans. He couldn't have looked less lawyerly if he'd tried. It was clear he hadn't expected such a large gathering. Charlie welcomed him with a handshake and one-armed hug. Anthony opted to feign a gut-punch before pulling up another chair for his old friend. The Strongs nodded in collective welcome. Maeve ignored him, picking at her peppermint red fingernails instead.

Once he was settled, Lora quickly re-told the story which had been shared earlier in all its detail.

Landon bit at a grimy hangnail on his thumb and studied Leon and Maurice. "So, I take it one of you is the young Black man Eva wouldn't talk about?"

"Yessir. I am," Leon replied. He'd picked up a tomato slice to snack on and barely managed to catch a yellow seed before it slimed its way down his chin. "Sorry, about that."

"Sorry about what? The tomato seed or helping Eva?"

Leon wiped his hands on his pants and rested his elbows on the table, lacing his long fingers together, and dropped a dead serious look on the attorney. "I would never regret helping Miss Eva."

Landon regarded the young man seated across from him with new respect on his open face. "Good. That was the exact right answer."

He shifted his attention to his client. "Eva, you're absolutely right. A running Black man has nothing to do with the death of Bumpus."

With a sigh of relief, Lora asked, "Alright, so we're square on that count. Can you tell us what information you got from Sheriff Griffin's office?"

Landon Cook smirked wryly and leaned back in his chair, knee bouncing from habit. He raised his arms and locked his hands behind his head. "I got exactly one piece of paper saying Eva's prints were on both plates."

A chorus of "What?", "Nothing else?", and "That's all?" rose from the congregation.

Landon waved his hands in an attempt to quell the tide. "Yeah, yeah, it's a bunch of horse shit and we all know it."

He gave Eva a cheeky grin over his shoulder and almost managed to dodge a swatting dish towel in return for his language. Eva didn't cotton to cussing for fun and Landon had spent enough time in her house to know it. He laughed as he said, "Don't worry though. I'll pull the rest of the information out of them on Monday at the preliminary hearing or, I'll sic the judge on them for failing to provide everything. Either way, we'll find out."

"Why don't we just ask Deputy Ross? Could he tell us? Would he get in trouble if he did?" Lora surprised them with this suggestion.

Landon propped his elbows on the table and thought for a moment. "As long as he doesn't tell us anything we wouldn't have gotten through a bona fide discovery disclosure, I don't see why he would. Legally, that is. Telling us anything outside that piece of paper could cause him some serious problems at work if Griffin finds out. It's worth a shot. I can't force him to tell us anything though."

Ever impulsive, Anthony shoved his chair away from the table and said, "Let's find out. I'll go down to Monroe's and call the station."

He twirled his keys and everyone shared an apprehensive glance when the screen door slammed a good-bye as he bounded down the porch steps.

• • • •

"MONROE WOULDN'T LET me call Deputy Ross myself. Said he'd make up some excuse to call him to the store and then send him our way. That way there's no official record of us calling."

Once again straddling his backwards chair at the table, Anthony shook his head and gave his mother an impish smile, saying, "I don't know what you did for Monroe to think so highly of you, Mama, but that man is scared to death. He's keeping his ear to the ground and says he's willing to do just about anything he can to put a stop to it—up to and including putting water in Griffin's gas tank."

Eva reached up and patted her gray curls, primping just a little, before replying, "Well, besides me and your daddy selling him the property for the store, once upon a time, ol' Monroe thought he was sweet on me. Followed me around like a lost pup! I let him down easy of course and introduced him to a friend instead. They been married for nearly fifty years now. It was the least I could do."

Myra rolled her eyes at gasps and exclamations of "I didn't even know he was married!" flew from the mouths of the young adults around the kitchen table.

Eva just chuckled and said, "Oh come on now! You'd have known if you'd been paying attention. Pfft! Besides, you all know his wife. She's the lovely lady who makes all the sausage biscuits and sandwiches he sells for the farm hands!"

More exclamations of "That old woman who yells at him from the back of the store?" and "You're joking! She's mean as a hornet!" erupted from the younger members of the conference.

Myra hushed them all and said, "Her name is Ellen and well, she may be prickly, but Monroe thinks she's the best thing to happen to him since Crisco was invented. And, y'all might not believe it, but when they close up shop every day, they go home and she babies him like he's the King of England."

Charlie and Anthony retreated into a corner and giggled like schoolboys getting their first peek at a girly-magazine. During a break in their wheezes, Charlie said, "I don't remember any Monroe kids running around! Is that because he's too fat to catch her skinny butt?" Anthony disintegrated into another round of laughter.

Eva shot them both a stern, chastising look. "No. They weren't blessed with children. But, if you were rude enough to ask why they don't have any, they'd tell you they were so happy just being together, they forgot to bother."

His mother's words had the intended effect. Anthony's laughter stopped abruptly, and Charlie said, "Well, I'm sorry for that." He glanced shamefaced around the room. "I never bothered to wonder much about Monroe's life outside the store."

Eva sniffed. "And that's a problem. Everybody is so busy these days. Folks don't take the time to find out about the people in their lives anymore. But seriously, Charlie, you and Anthony should be ashamed. You've been in and out of Monroe's store your entire lives. He's treated you and every other young'un who walks through that door like his own. In a way, he and Ellen had a hand in raising every last one of you."

Shaking her head, she got to her feet and waved her hands at them, scattering them out of her kitchen like chickens in the yard. She needed a few minutes to her herself. They could wait for Deputy Ross from other spaces in and around the house. It was agreed it would be for the best if Deputy Ross didn't see the Strong family when he showed up, so they planned to hide-out in Eva's room until the deputy left.

Myra, Leon, and Maurice decamped to the living room. Charlie, Anthony, and Maeve retreated to the front porch so Maeve could smoke. Lora snagged Landon's arm when he made to follow them.

"Can I talk to you? Outside?"

Curiosity piqued, the attorney gestured towards the back door. "Lead the way."

On the stoop, Lora shaded her eyes against the blinding afternoon sun with her hand and Landon pulled his cap on. Lora pointed at the deflated, headless body of Eva's dead mouse just beyond the bottom step and said, "Lovenia Thigpen."

Landon, leaning against the door, startled. "Yeah. What about her?"

"You've said it yourself. She's Mr. Johnson's sister and Sheriff Griffin's sweetheart." Lora's skin crawled with goosebumps just despite the scorching midday heat. "She knows everything that goes on at her brother's house. She knows everything that happens at the sheriff's office. And she tells you. Do you really believe she doesn't tell them everything that happens in *your* office? Do you trust her not to talk about this case?"

Landon scratched his chin, thinking. "She's been with our firm for ages and I've never had a reason to think she was breaching confidence."

Lora rolled suspicious eyes in his direction, one corner of her mouth twisting with derision. "And how many cases have you handled which involved members of her own family?"

Landon shrugged a shoulder in concession. "Good point."

"It's too late to keep her from telling Mr. Johnson and Sheriff Griffin everything up to this point. But, is there a way you can keep her from knowing what happens from here on out?"

The attorney chewed the inside of his cheek for a moment before nodding sharply in agreement. "I guess it can't hurt to be extra careful, can it?"

"Nope. Can't hurt at all. Better to pop the head off a mouse than let it ruin your pantry. Thanks, Mr. Cook."

Lora patted him on the shoulder before heading back inside.

· · · ·

CONVERSATION AND LAUGHTER, frustration and concern swirled around and through the little house while Eva watched the treetops sway from her kitchen window. She heard without listening to the sounds of a full house. Normally, the ruckus would make her heart happy. She knew her children were trying their best to be supportive, and that Landon was simply doing his job, but today she wanted them all to leave. She worried over her friendship with Myra and what damage may have been done to the trust they shared. She even wished Lora would go somewhere else for a few days. With a heavy sigh, she pulled a small spider web from the corner of the window and rolled the silk into a tiny ball between her fingers.

16

L ora meandered into the living room and sat cross-legged on the floor. Myra melted into Eva's rocker while Leon and Maurice sprawled on the couch. Maurice sat up and shifted a serious face at Lora. "Okay. I wasn't gonna ask this in front of the attorney but I know you asked for me to come over here today. Why?" His lanky, thin frame was perched on the edge of the cushion, his elbows on his knees, fingers steepled together under his chin.

The Strongs studied Lora and waited patiently for her answer.

Lora, squirming a little, fiddled with the end of her shoelace as she spoke. "Well, Mr. Johnson really hates Black people. I mean, really really hates Black people." She inhaled a stilting breath and continued, "I think he feels like he's got a good reason. See, his wife left him, and he blames a Black man. I can't say why that is or how I know exactly but, I'm pretty sure of it."

Maurice shifted slightly in his seat.

Lora looked briefly at Leon and then back at Maurice. "I also think he got a better look at Leon than he's letting on. I wouldn't ask you, any of you, to do anything you aren't comfortable with but, if Mr. Johnson's prints were on that plate in the graveyard, with your help, we might be able to upset him just enough to make himself a potential suspect, even if Sheriff Griffin doesn't want to consider him."

The brothers exchanged confused glances. Myra was quicker on the uptake and exploded from the rocker with surprising force and leaned into Lora's face, breathing heavily. "Absolutely not! You are not gonna use my boys as bait!" She whirled around to her sons, both of whom were now standing behind her, and pointed in their faces. "I ain't gonna be hearing nothing else about this out of you two neither!"

They each reached out and took an arm. "Mama," Leon began, "let's hear her out. I done said I'd tell Sheriff Griffin myself that I was the one running from Mr. Johnson's house. All I'm hearing so far is just letting Mr. Johnson get a good look at me and Maurice."

Maurice chimed in with, "That's all I'm hearing too." He peered over Myra's shoulder at Lora as she got up from the floor, his eyebrows raised in question.

Lora stepped closer to the trio, grasping Myra and Leon's shoulders, and said, "Mr. Johnson was at Gram's arraignment. I figure he'll be at Monday's hearing too. If he is, and if he acts like he recognizes Leon, well, the two of you look enough alike to maybe make him doubt himself. Certainly enough alike to cause a reasonable person to doubt him at any rate. So, I just want you two to be there. That's it. And, all this depends on whether Mr. Johnson's prints were on that plate. If they weren't, then neither of you should be there at all."

"See, Mama!" Leon jumped a little, "That's not too risky. Happy?" He grinned at Lora as he spoke.

Myra shook her head. "Nope. Don't none of this make me happy." Still, she huffed herself back into the rocker and folded her hands across her bosom, lacing her fingers together in a death grip. She closed her eyes and leaned back against the head rest. "Y'all need to take this scheming somewhere else. I am tired of wasting my words trying to talk sense into you." Her short legs pushed off from the ground with enough force to nearly tump her and the chair over backwards. Her eyes flew open wide as she jerked forward to counterbalance the chair and scowled when she realized the threesome was watching and struggling not to laugh. Her scowl sent them scuttling out of the room, through the kitchen, and out the back door.

• • • •

BLINDED BY THE SUNLIGHT, Lora, Leon, and Maurice decided to forgo the unsheltered stoop and made their way to the shade of a gnarled oak tree not far from the garden shed in the back corner of Eva's yard. Lora balanced herself on the dusty board of an ancient rope swing while the brothers flopped into the sparse grass, propping up on their elbows. Leon kicked a foot out towards Maurice and mumbled, "Go on. Say it. I can tell you got something on your mind."

Maurice spun a topless acorn around in his hand for a moment. "I ain't disagreeing with your idea but unless you got a way of keeping all Black folks out of that courtroom, I don't see why it matters whether Leon and me are there or not. You been coming down here long enough to know that most white folks think we all look the same. Hell, as far as they think, blaming one is just as good as blaming another."

"I know," Lora sighed, realizing the gravity of what she was asking him to do. She held the creaking ropes tightly and rocked on her heels. "Still, I thought it was worth a try. If Mr. Johnson's prints are on both plates, and I don't see how they couldn't be, it makes him a legitimate suspect. If we can catch him off guard, well, he might just act ugly enough to incriminate himself even more than his finger prints do."

Maurice closed his eyes and flared his nostrils. Momentarily, he looked at her and tossed the little acorn aside. "This is only if Ross says Mr. Johnson's prints are on the plate, right?"

Lora nodded.

Maurice wasn't finished though, "And if he do act up, how do you plan to keep the Black man business from being mentioned? If he recognizes us and acts out, that could be just what Griffin needs to drag us both in. He won't bother with no warrant for us, neither. He does that and Leon is as good as dead."

Lora didn't have an answer for him. She couldn't tell him that Arlene Johnson had left her husband for a Black man, or how she knew it in the first place. Keeping that secret was the only reason she could think of as to why Hal hadn't pushed the Sheriff to dig deeper into his morning trespasser the day Bumpus died. She gave a slight shake of her head and lifted a shoulder, acknowledging her loss for words.

Leon, situated slightly behind Maurice's line of vision, noticed Lora's discomfort and wondered if she was working on a hint provided by their shared uncanny gifts. He risked a surreptitious finger tap above his left eye and raised his eyebrows at Lora, silently asking her if that was the case. She answered the unspoken question with as small a nod as possible. Acknowledging the influence of her gift in asking the favor, Leon clenched his jaw in response. To her relief, Leon spoke up, "Maurice, we gotta do this. You know we do."

"We ain't gotta do nothing! You might think you do, but I don't!"

"Yes, you do. You're going to court on Monday with me and Mama. And, so are as many of our friends as we can round up. Like you said, we all look alike." He threw his brother's words back at him like a fastball over home plate. "Only the three of us will know the real reason he shows out. If he does. I doubt he got a good look at me anyways. I'm pretty fast, especially when I'm scared."

He flung this last bit at Maurice's feet, daring his brother not to go to court. Maurice took the bait and loosed an irritated sigh. "Fine. I'll be there. But if this goes sideways, you can bet I run faster than you, little brother." He stuck out his hand to Lora.

Before she could shake Maurice's outstretched hand, a vehicle slowed in front of the house and gravel crunched beneath tires in the drive. Leon and Maurice had no time to run inside to Eva's bedroom, instead bolting at a sprint to hide behind the garden shed. Likewise,

Lora ran to the backdoor, looking over her shoulder as she pulled it open to make sure the brothers were out of sight from the house.

• • • •

BREATHING HARD, THE brothers leaned on their knees to steady their nerves before squatting to lean against the back wall of the small building. Sticky catchweed grasped at their pants legs while prostrate spurge fanned deep, thick mats in all directions. Maurice plucked a tiny green snake from the brush and grass, letting the curious reptile curl through his fingers. Leon shuddered and groaned, "Why'd you have to do that? You know snakes give me the heebie-jeebies."

Maurice wheezed a short, quiet laugh, "Figured this was better than letting it crawl up your arm." He gently tossed the snake away from their spot. Leon watched the narrow emerald sliver slip out of sight and nodded.

"Mo? I got an idea."

Maurice turned slightly towards Leon and leaned his head back to look at the sky. "I ain't gonna like it, am I?"

"Not at all. But I think it'll work. Even better than letting Mr. Johnson get a look at us." Leon drew his legs to his chest, wrapping elbows around knees and sucked on his teeth. "You need to call her. Get her to come."

Maurice jerked upright in a spasm, lurching to his feet. "Of all the - you done lost your mind!"

Leon scrambled to his feet and reached out a calming hand. "Shh! You're too loud!"

Maurice pushed Leon's hand away and stepped close, chest to chest, heaving. "Risking our necks because some white girl asks us to is one thing but this? You want me to bring her - to this place - to these people?" He flailed his arms around making it clear he meant more than just Eva's little homestead. "I don't know this girl from

Adam's house cat and you gonna stand there and act like this is all just okay? Ask me to do more?"

"What you mean some white girl? This is Lora! She's been coming around every summer for as long as either of us can remember. You know her!" Leon leaned into his brother, eyeball to eyeball, staring him down.

"Oh, I know *Miss* Lora," Maurice growled, emphasizing 'Miss' as he said it. "I know she's from Detroit and she's Miss Eva's granddaughter. I know she's a white girl suddenly being extra friendly because she needs something from us. And now you asking me to sweeten the deal? No, I won't do it."

Leon stomped on Maurice's foot suddenly and with such force, Maurice crumbled to the ground, inventing cuss words as he did.

Squatting in front of Maurice, who'd taken his shoe off to better massage the offended foot, Leon said, "How on earth you think Lora was using us is beyond anything I can understand. This is ain't for her anyway. This is for Miss Eva."

Maurice glared at Leon and hissed through the small gap in his front teeth. "You can stomp all you want. It ain't happening. I'll go to the courthouse for Miss Eva, but I ain't asking her to come. It's too dangerous. And if you breathe a word to Mama about my white girlfriend, you'll wish all I'd do was stomp your foot."

Leon's grin spread from ear to ear, deep dimples piercing his cheeks as his eyes danced, "Not a word. Why would I waste good blackmail material like this?"

Maurice's stunned expression at his brother's underhanded retort set Leon thudding to his heels, whole body shaking with muffled laughter. Maurice's deep, low rumble eventually joined his and an easy camaraderie gently re-settled over them. Resting shoulder to shoulder, leaning against the shed, occasionally bothered by ants biting and climbing up their arms and legs, they listened for Deputy Ross to leave and waited for the all-clear to rejoin the others in the house. While they waited, Leon spoke with excitement about the Chicago Freedom Movement and Dr. King's recent move to the city. He planned to join the protests and beamed with optimism for the future. Maurice shook his head and muttered something about Leon getting his fool head bashed in, to which Leon replied, "I have to, brother."

• • • •

LORA WAS JUST COMING in the back door as Deputy Ross ambled into the kitchen. She noticed his hair was sweaty and stuck to his forehead in a clearly defined hat ring and her hand itched to sweep it back off his face.

Lora spied Myra peeping through the barely cracked door to Eva's bedroom and gave her a quick thumbs-up to let her know her sons were hidden and out-of-sight too. Myra nodded slowly and didn't move another muscle.

Deputy Ross spun his hat between his fingers. He was new to the badge and shifted awkwardly in the spotlight as the Burnettes gathered around the table and sat with silent expectation. When Landon Cook offered him his seat, Deputy Ross shook his head. "I'd rather stand if you don't mind. At least until I know why I'm here." He slid a questioning look at Lora, his eyes pleading for an explanation.

Lora took pity on him and smiled. "Oh! That's understandable. Deputy, we have some questions for you and if you can't answer them, well, we understand that too." She gestured for Mr. Cook to continue.

Landon raised a reassuring hand and said, "You're under no obligation at all to answer any question you're asked here." He flashed a mischievous grin. "Well, unless it's Miss Eva offering you something to eat or drink, not answering that question would just be bad manners."

Deputy Ross flushed at the implication he could be rude to anyone.

"See, I was supposed to receive copies of all evidence collected supporting Griffin's case against Eva and well, that didn't happen." Mr. Cook smiled crookedly at the discomfited deputy. "What we want to know, is who else's fingerprints were on the plate Sheriff Griffin collected from the cemetery when he recovered Bumpus's body?"

Deputy Ross hunched his shoulders, although no one could tell if it was from relief or pressure. Straightening, and looking Landon in the eye, he said, "I can and will answer that question." He slipped Lora a conspiratorial glance. "As long as you don't tell the sheriff I told you. I still need my job once this is all said and done, you know."

"Of course."

Lora noticed Myra stiffen in her hiding place behind the door and felt tensions tighten in the room. Breaths were held and subtle looks were exchanged. Behind the deputy's back, Lora patted the air with a surreptitious hand, hoping Myra would understand the gesture encouraging her to stay still and calm. Deputy Ross either didn't notice or noticed and decided not to ask any questions of his own.

"There were loads of prints on that plate but only a few we could match to anybody. Miss Eva's, Mr. Johnson's, and Mr. Bumpus. The rest don't belong to anybody in our records or anybody we can rightly call in for printing."

Those seated at the table were already anxious about the hidden Strongs and assumed Deputy Ross had heard the gossip about a Black man running from the Johnson place around the same time Bumpus died. If he discovered them at Eva's house, he could easily run the boys in for prints. If that happened, their safety net would develop some gaping holes which might not easily be stitched back together.

Mr. Cook sidled up to the younger man and placed a hand on his shoulder. "I know we said we had questions but that's really the only thing I wanted to ask." He clapped the deputy on the back as he made his way to the sink, shielding a smug smile from the rest of the group.

Eva stood, wiping her hands on her apron front, "John, how about you go on and have a seat? I'll get you some tea." She pulled a glass from the cabinet.

"I don't want to be rude Miss Eva, but I ought to go. My call was only to come out to Monroe's and if my car is seen parked in your yard for very long, well... you know how folks are."

His sheepish smile tugged at Lora's sympathies so firmly she was surprised to hear herself saying, "Of course! Here, let me wrap up a sandwich to take with you, it'll only take a minute."

He nodded obligingly and within three or four minutes, Lora was walking him to the door with a paper sack containing not one but two sandwiches: one bologna with cheese and one tomato with mayonnaise. Realizing they were alone as he and Lora stepped onto the front porch, Deputy Ross turned to her and asked, "Um, would it be alright if I was to call on you sometime? From what I've heard, you're planning to come live with Miss Eva?"

Lora laughed. "Let me guess, you heard that from Monroe?" She smiled. "I tell you what, if Gram gets clear of this mess with Bumpus without having to go to jail, you can call on me anytime." She felt brazen in her response but didn't really care. She thought Deputy John Ross was handsome and she liked the way he seemed to feel about the whole case.

He blushed and looked at his feet. "Well, in that case, I'm going to be praying hard this all goes away real soon."

He was still an adorable shade of pink as he pulled out of the drive.

Lora watched him go with relief and smiled to herself as she went back inside to let Myra know the deputy was gone. She needn't have bothered. Myra had popped out of the bedroom as soon as she'd heard the door close behind him and retrieved her sons from behind the shed. They were gathered back around the table with the rest of the family before John Ross's tires cleared the drive.

17

Lora slipped sideways into a rather heated discussion about whether or not Eva should attend church services the next morning. Eva held firm that as long as she was healthy, she'd be at church whenever the church was meeting. Myra nodded in agreement. Charlie and Anthony both landed firmly on the side of Eva not going to save herself any potential embarrassment. Maeve was silent and managed to look bored with the whole thing.

"Mama, those gossiping women will pester you to death and blab whatever you say to anyone who'll listen!" Anthony opined, disdain for the church ladies seeping into his tone. Charlie nodded in agreement.

"What do they have to gossip about? I didn't do anything wrong. Holing up here in the house will make'em think I've got something to hide. I'm going."

Landon Cook played both sides of the ball and made arguments both for and against her attendance. "Eva, you're right. Going sends a message that you are confident you'll be acquitted. Of course, it could also seem like you're overconfident and if word of that got around, well, it could bias a jury."

Eva swiveled in her seat like a jumping spider on a fruit fly to glower at Landon. "Why are you talking about a jury again? I've done told you I don't want a jury trial."

Landon's forehead wrinkled. "I know you don't want one, but I wish you'd —"

Anthony leaned his elbows on the table, thrumming his fingertips on the worn surface, his eyebrows scrunched together in thought and interrupted, "A bench trial? You can't think that's a good idea?"

Landon spread his fingertips wide on the tabletop and stared at them for a second. "No. I do not think a bench trial is a good idea.

But your mother is insisting I ask for one." He turned his attention to Eva, "Let me reiterate, a bench trial puts your fate squarely in the hands of a single person, Judge Underwood. If he finds you guilty, your appeal options are well...not great."

Eva crossed her arms under her bosom and said, "That's just fine. I want a bench trial if we can get one. Sounds like it'd be quicker anyway."

She stood, gifting Anthony with the special smile reserved for favorites, "Anthony, if you're planning to stay here, you're welcome. You can have Walter's old room. I didn't know you were coming, so you're going to need to make up your own bed. Linens are where they've always been.

To the rest of them she said, "As for the rest of you, you can stay or go, but I need to get my studying done for Sunday School tomorrow." She kissed Anthony's cheek as she left the room. "If y'all need me, I'll be in here," and closed the door to her bedroom.

Eva's departure caused only the briefest pause in the debate circling in point and counterpoint around the table. Myra chimed in every place she could to insist that Eva not going to church would make her look guilty, and to reiterate that it was Eva's decision to make after all. Charlie and Anthony vehemently insisted she'd be better off laying low until the whole issue was resolved. Lora, Leon, and Maurice looked as though they were watching a tennis match where no one was keeping score as their eyes bounced from one speaker to the next. None of them attempted to add anything to the conversation.

Maeve pleaded the need for a cigarette and excused herself from the table before slipping from the room.

. . . .

"EVA? DO YOU HAVE A minute?"

Eva sighed as her daughter-in-law's voice landed softly, like a hornet, violating the peace of her room. She'd barely gotten her bible and class book opened when the gentle knocking came. She snorted, setting her books aside and rolled her eyes to the ceiling. Maeve was normally insistent and loud. Her soft knock and subdued chords made it clear she was looking for a private conversation. Eva shifted her feet off the side of the bed where she'd been propped up to do her studying. "Come on in," she called back, matching Maeve's muted tone.

Eva's door swung thinly and quickly open as Maeve dipped into the room, closing it behind her and turning the knob to keep the latch from clicking. She stood along the edges of the lamplight from Eva's nightstand and pursed her lips. Maeve narrowed her eyes and said, "Eva. You need to let Leon's involvement be presented to the court. You simply cannot allow this thing to go to any kind of trial - bench or not. He thinks he killed Bumpus, so he needs to take responsibility."

Completely disinterested in entertaining any of Maeve's notions about much of anything, Eva stood, coming toe-to-toe with her daughter-in-law. "I'll do no such thing. And neither will you. We're gonna let this thing run its course. My way. Without involving Leon at all."

Maeve spluttered for a second. "If anything gets out about your...history, with Bumpus—"

"You mean *your* history with Bumpus."

Maeve's cheeks flushed as she sucked in a shallow gasp. Her perfectly manicured hands cracked as she gripped them together. "Eva! We swore we would never, *ever* mention that again. None of it. I couldn't stand it! I would die if anyone ever found out what that man did to me! Please. Leon owning this would keep everything quiet. "

Eva's eyes narrowed as she leaned in closer. "And you think letting him take the blame for something he didn't do, solves the problem? Why am I not surprised?" Eva stepped away in disgust.

"I'm sure I have no idea what you're talking about."

"Oh, yes you do. It's what you do. You hide. You think I forgot how you stole a pair of stockings from Ben Jaffe's and let that little Black girl take the blame?"

"I went back and paid for those stockings!"

"Mm hm. But not until Charlie threatened to break off your engagement and not before letting an innocent child be arrested for something you did. Something you'd have been able to pawn off as a simple mistake!"

Eva leaned a hip on her dressing table and whispered, refusing to look at Maeve. "Besides, you can't tell me you're losing any sleep over that man being dead. After what he put you through, you of all people ought to be relieved. I know I am. So, don't you dare come into my house preaching some hate disguised as fear nonsense. You are a coward." She balled her fists into the pockets of her dress, turned on her heel and settled herself back on the bed, popping her toes as she leaned back against the headboard.

Maeve blinked back tears before shaking her head and disappearing through the door as quietly as she'd entered, wringing her fists in frustration.

With an irritated sigh, Eva opened her Bible and workbook back to the appropriate pages and tried to concentrate on the lesson. After reading the same passage several times and not remembering a single word, she slammed them both closed and flipped them aside. She needed a moment to clear her head. Maeve had always felt to her like an old stump in the yard, refusing to give way no matter how much you chopped or pulled or burned at it. She wouldn't budge and the world was forced to go around her.

Eva felt a smidge guilty for thinking about chopping and burning Charlie's wife but felt the comparison was as solid as the old stump. Maeve was stubborn and hardheaded, absolutely immovable once she made up her mind about something. The only person Eva'd ever known to make any difference in Maeve's behavior was Charlie and even that wasn't very often or very much. She chuckled a bit to herself as she remembered the way Lora stuck up for herself the previous day and decided that maybe there were two people Maeve couldn't bulldoze over. Mollified, Eva returned to her studies and was a bit surprised to note that the passage for Sunday School was from the Old Testament, Isaiah 6: 8-9. It felt directed specifically to her.

"Also I heard the voice of the Lord, saying, Whom shall I send, and who will go for us? Then I said, Here am I; send me. And he said, Go and tell this people, Hear ye indeed, but understand not; and see ye indeed, but perceive not."

She closed eyes and her bible to think and pray. *Father, thank you for this. Thank you for sending this message to me today. You know the burdens of my heart. Borrowing a little from the words of Christ, let not my will but Yours be done. And, if it's not too much trouble, I'd appreciate it if you'd wallop Maeve upside the head with some sense. If you can't manage that, just put her on a bus back to Detroit. I'd be much obliged. Amen.*

Eva believed God had a sense of humor and had no compunction talking to him like he was a regular person. After all, if he'd created man in his image, she thought, that probably included enjoying a good laugh as much as anyone else. She also figured he could explain it to her when she got to Heaven if she got it wrong.

She quickly completed the answers in her class book, filling in the blanks with precise cursive handwriting. It was frowned upon for women to speak during Sunday School and so, most of the women didn't bother answering the questions at all. Eva, always a diligent student, answered the questions and kept notes on the answers discussed in class. She liked to think about what others said later. When Dub was still alive, they would often debate and rehash their own answers and those of others on their way home, sometimes for the rest of the day. It was a sort of game they'd played; never sharing their answers before class, enjoying the revelations and debate later on. This week's questions were interesting because they also seemed to be aimed directly in her direction.

Closing her study materials with satisfaction, she thought, *Sounds to me like Isaiah had a dose of the knowing too but I can't exactly write that down now, can I?* Lowering her stocking feet over the side of the bed once more, she slid into her house shoes and decided to see who was still hanging around and who might be hungry.

• • • •

EVA WAS GRATIFIED AND grateful to find no one had left. Knowing they all stood in solidarity with her, well, with the exception of Maeve, gave her a boost of strength and confidence she hadn't realized she needed. She was surprised to find dinner already made. Fried chicken, half a ham, okra, green beans, mashed potatoes, corn on the cob, macaroni salad, sweet potato casserole, rolls, and even a chocolate pie with an incredibly high meringue, all vied for attention. One look at Lora and Myra's delighted faces clued her in. After all, there was no way they could have pulled off such a feast in the short time she'd been holed up in her room.

Myra wiped her hands on a kitchen towel and cleared her throat. "I mashed the potatoes. Lora handled the okra. The rest...well, folks just started showing up at the back door and handing us food! Couple o' women from your church. Several from mine. Some I didn't know." She shrugged and pulled plates and silverware from the cupboards and drawers. "Your refrigerator is full too."

Eva laughed and grumbled. "Folks bringing food...Why? This ain't a funeral!" Myra shrugged again, shaking her head.

Lora grinned at Eva and whispered in her ear, "I'm betting Monroe has something to do with this."

Eva snorted in agreement and whispered back, "I wouldn't take that bet. You're probably right."

Myra's ears were better than most people gave her credit for and she startled them when she suddenly rasped in their ears, poking her head in between theirs, "There's a note from Monroe underneath the rolls. Ellen told me to make sure you knew."

Both Lora and Eva jumped at the sudden puffs of air blowing on their cheeks. Myra's laugh rumbled deep in her throat.

Eva looked out through the kitchen, to the living room and front porch, saw her family sprawled on couches and rockers. She gingerly lifted the platter teetering with freshly baked rolls and peeled off the note which was taped to the bottom. Wiggling her eyebrows at Lora, she stepped onto the back stoop to read the note in private.

E,

Griffin has deppitees watching you.
Lemme know if I can do anything.

M

Eva blew out a breath, flubbering her lips with the exhalation. She folded the note and slipped it into Myra's pocket when she went back inside. Seeing Lora's crinkled forehead and wide, quizzical eyes, she shook her head and said, "Just letting me know he's willing to help."

She raised her voice and yelled her usual come-and-get-it, "It ain't gonna eat itself!" noting with satisfaction that like always, hungry people tend to move with surprising speed.

Myra and Lora side-eyed each other behind Eva's back. Although neither believed Monroe's note was as innocent as Eva made out, neither was willing to dig into her to find out more. Their silence confirmed their resolve to let her keep her secret. They owed her that.

Charlie, Anthony, and Landon Cook jostled for position as they'd always done, laughing and cutting up like teenagers instead of grown men. Leon and Maurice rushed to the kitchen but stopped awkwardly at the threshold, unsure where they landed in the pecking order.

Lora laughed, pushing plates into their hands. "If you two want to make sure you get anything, you might want to jump ahead of that bunch!" She jerked her head at the tussle for dinnerware going on between her father, her uncle, and their friend, and gave the brothers a sneaky thumb gesture encouraging them to fill their plates. The Strong brothers grinned at each other and side-stepped the Burnette-Cook fracas to get first dibs on the best bits.

Eventually, everyone, including Maeve, filled their plates and their bellies, taking turns complaining about having eaten too much. After dinner, Charlie and Maeve shuffled out the door into the twilight heading to town and their hotel bed. Landon hugged Eva's neck and kissed her cheek, thanking her for dinner as he took his leave. Myra and her sons squeezed both Eva and Lora, disappearing into the moonbright darkness of the back yard.

Anthony, claiming jet lag and pants which were now too tight, took himself off to bed, leaving Lora and Eva to deal with the rest of the dishes in silence. Lora tossed a dish cloth on the counter and said, "Gram. I'm exhausted. I'm sure you are too. How about we leave these until in the morning and just watch TV?"

The last thing Eva wanted to do was a bunch of dishes. She'd forgotten the bottomless sink of dirty plates and forks and glasses that traveled in the wake when family came to town. What she remembered was that the *The Lawrence Welk Show* would be starting shortly. She couldn't get to the Magnavox fast enough. She clicked on the dial and tweaked the antenna before settling into her chair, rocking along with "Bubbles in the Wine" as the show started. Lora slipped off her shoes, curling her feet beneath her as she got comfortable in the corner of the brown corduroy sofa. Hearing more than a few random thumps from the back of the house, neither woman was surprised to see Anthony make an appearance. He leaned against the door frame, dressed comfortably in his plaid pajama pants and an undershirt. Judging from the mussed state of his hair, he'd obviously been in bed.

"Oh Mama. You know I can't let you watch Larry Welky by yourself!" He leveled a suave smile at his mother and held out his hand to Eva.

"Hey! What do you think I am? Chopped liver?" Lora yelped, chucking a throw pillow at his head. Her uncle smoothly dodged the flying pouf as he laughed and did a little foxtrot step to take his mother's hand and lead her around the room in a quick turn. Lora was delighted to see Eva's face light up. All the worries of the day melted away as she gave herself over to just a couple brief minutes of joy. Anthony was a surprisingly capable dancer and Lora wondered where he'd learned, even more interesting was the fact that Eva too seemed to know exactly what she was doing as Anthony led her through twirls and spins around the room.

When the song ended, Anthony dipped Eva in a most dramatic fashion, planted a firm kiss on her cheek, and said, "Watch me boot Liver off the couch." Eva laughed and sent him away with a sunshine smile.

In one swift motion he snagged the pillow off the floor and threw it back at his niece. Lora's reflexes weren't quite as quick as his and the pillow whopped her upside the face in spite of her flailing attempts at deflection. Coming in right behind the flying pillow, Anthony grabbed hold of Lora's hands and pulled her from her spot on the couch. Lora immediately went limp, trying to become immovable dead weight, but Anthony was not to be deterred. She finally gave up, opting instead to claim the other throw pillows from the couch and lay on the floor while Eva and Anthony enjoyed the show.

18

E va slept better Saturday night than she had in what felt like ages. The house breathed better with family in it. At least, that was her explanation for it anyway. Stretching the sleep out of her joints before rolling out of bed to tackle the left over dishes and making breakfast, she smiled to herself in the brief stillness of what promised to be a gentle morning if the soft light and sweet, grassy breezes flitting over the window sill were any indication.

The screen door squeaked through the open window and she sat up with a start. She hadn't heard any footsteps or creaking floorboards indicating Lora or Anthony were up and moving around. Easing herself off the bed, carefully avoiding any creaking boards underfoot which would give her away, she slipped her robe over her nightgown and eased her feet into her slippers. She pulled one of the boys' old baseball bats from underneath the bed, confident in its heft and weight. She gently turned the knob to her bedroom door, lifting up a little to keep the hinges from groaning as she pulled it open. Eva stepped gingerly into the short hallway before peeping around the corner into the living room towards the front door, bat raised high and ready to swing for the fences.

"God in Heaven! Charlie! I just about knocked your head off! What are you doing here so early?"

"Eh," he ran his hands over his face, scratching at the stubble shadowing his cheeks and glanced at the bag resting beside his feet. "Well, I thought I'd come stay with you for a couple days. Maeve and I had words last night after we left, and the upshot is I put her on a bus back to Detroit this morning." His tired eyes begged her not to push for too many details just yet and she obliged by swapping her bat for a weary embrace from her son.

"Shh...Of course you can stay here. Go put your things in your room. I'll come up and make your bed in a minute."

Charlie nodded in thanks and trudged up the stairs. There were two small bedrooms under the eaves of the little house. Barely big enough to hold a double bed or for a grown man to stand up straight in, but her children had thrived in those rooms and she was sure he would find the comfort he needed up there.

Lora poked her head out of her doorway as Charlie's foot hit the landing. Blearily rubbing her eyes, she said, "Hey Daddy. What are you doing here?"

"Your mother decided she'd go on home. I decided to stay for a few days. That's all."

She yawned and whuffed a sleepy, "Okay."

He gave her a crooked smile and ducked into his room. She heard the mattress springs creak under his weight as he flopped onto the bed.

It only took a few seconds for his words to register through the morning fog. Lora scrambled across the hallway and flung his door open, causing him to jump and hit his head on the low-hanging eave above the headboard.

"What do you mean Mama decided to 'go on home'? She's driving herself?" Lora couldn't imagine her mother making a road trip of that distance by herself. Maeve didn't drive anywhere, not even to the grocery store if she could help it, much less cross country.

Massaging the knot on his head, Charlie squinted at her and sighed. "No, I took her to Decatur early this morning to catch the first bus headed that way."

"Ha! Mama? On a bus? With other people?" Lora snorted and chucked him on the arm, "You're joking, right?"

Charlie sat on the edge of the bed, shoulders slumped, one elbow resting on his knee and the other hand digging at the lumpy scar on his thigh. Lora thought her father would like to crawl between the spaces of the floorboards and hide for a while.

"I wish I was. No, she's on the bus alright. Said she'd rather take a bus all the way to Detroit than wait around for all of us to come to our senses about your grandmother and this scandal over Bumpus. So, I let her do just that."

Lora sat next to him, wrapped her arms around him sideways and leaned her head onto his shoulder. "Oh Daddy. I'm sorry. Mama can be so difficult sometimes!"

"What was I supposed to do? Just run off and let you and my Mama handle this on your own?"

Lora straightened and gave him the most indignant look she could muster. "Well, we could have. You know that. Gram can handle anything."

He patted her on the knee and harrumphed. "Oh I am sure of that. You just shouldn't have to, that's all. Besides, I can't let Anthony get all the credit for helping out when she needs us most."

"Oh yes you can!"

Charlie and Lora both flopped back across the bed, groaning as Anthony's voice sang out in a strong tenor, announcing his presence on the landing like an overgrown child on the playground.

Anthony leaned against the door frame and slid his hands into the pockets of his pajama pants. He teased his older brother with a sneaky, superior grin causing Lora and Charlie to laugh.

Catching his breath, Charlie wheezed. "How'd you get up those blasted stairs without me hearing you?"

"Oh come on. You don't remember all the steps to the secret out-and-in dance?"

Lora interjected. "What is the out-and-in dance?"

Charlie gave his brother a stern fatherly look and said, "It's what we used to call it when we'd sneak out at night. We figured out which boards and steps creaked and learned how to avoid them so Mama and Daddy wouldn't know we were leaving."

"Or what time we were coming home!" Anthony snorted.

"You just think I didn't know but I did!" Eva's voice chimed as she grabbed hold of one of his ears and pulled him out of her way. Her other arm balanced a full complement of sheets and quilts for Charlie's bed.

Charlie and Lora both jumped to take them from her while Anthony rubbed his ear. "Ow Mama! How come you're up here making Charlie's bed and I had to make my own?" He teased her and stomped his foot the way he did when he was a little boy, his long, lanky body going all noodley as he swung his arms around the tight space. Eva shushed him with a grab for his other ear which he expertly dodged.

With the bed made, Eva declared it was time for breakfast and suggested Charlie lie down for a bit while she got it ready. Shooing Anthony and Lora out of the tiny room, she asked Lora clear the dishes they'd left soaking and neglected the night before. Anthony was voluntold to make himself useful by getting the coffee started.

· · · ·

LORA TUNED THE LITTLE window radio to the popular music station, hoping to get a good rhythm going for dish washing. Eva tutted and reached across the sink, changing the channel to WKAC which played gospel music on Sunday mornings for the sick and shut-ins to enjoy. Anthony caught Lora's attention as he measured coffee grounds into the electric coffee maker and crossed his eyes. She bit her lip in not to laugh.

California had rubbed off on Anthony. He was already the most unpredictable and irreverent of Eva's children and life in the Golden State hadn't helped. Instead of making a fuss with his mother over the music selection, he opted for singing along. He growled through rumbling basses and soared in full-throated tenors. Eva struggled not to smile when he breathed a piercing, airy falsetto through his nose, holding one hand to his chest, while exaggerating the emphatic syllables of "Oh, Victory in Jesus!" She turned her back to him as she eyeballed the measurements of flour, sugar, baking powder, salt, butter, and milk for biscuits. Red-eye gravy would have to wait until the coffee was brewed and the ham had been fried in the skillet. She figured red-eye was the best bet for Charlie. He looked like he'd been up half the night when he'd come through the door.

"Gram? What do you think really happened to make Mama go back to Detroit?"

"I think that's not really any of our business."

Anthony grunted. "It might not be any of our business, but I still want to know."

Eva smooshed her fingers through the flour and butter mixture. "Don't you go pushing him!" she hissed, continuing to incorporate the butter into the dry ingredients, "If Charlie wants to tell us, he will. What happens between married folks is usually nobody else's business."

Lora didn't miss the contradiction between this statement and Eva's effort years ago to extract Dot from her marriage to Bumpus. She supposed there were times when what happens between a husband and wife really are someone else's concern. She wasn't about to bring it up though. Eva was in an odd, tightly wound mood this morning, pretending everything was alright. Lora assumed she was worried about Charlie and probably a little anxious about her decision to attend church this morning. Lora couldn't blame her; she was worried about those things too.

Once the biscuits were rolled and cut and in the oven, Eva tossed several thick slices of ham in a skillet, making Anthony and Lora both swoon at the immediate sizzle and mouth-watering smell coming from the stove. Letting the ham do its work, Eva poured two cups of coffee from the pot, setting one aside for the gravy, gesturing for Anthony to make another pot. It wouldn't do for the pot to be empty or scorched when Charlie got up. Anthony and Lora made quick work of drying and putting away the dishes and were soon blowing across the tops of their full mugs and taking tentative sips from the tops, watching while she worked her kitchen magic.

Stepping on his cue, Charlie, still in his rumpled slacks from the day before, rounded the corner into the kitchen, and went straight for the coffee, sloshing the scant remnants around with a scowl, willing the pot to suddenly be full. Anthony made a gallant show of pulling the carafe from Charlie's hand and replacing it with his own cup. "Never fear, brother mine, I shall produce more of yon aromatic elixir for thine consumption forthwith!"

Charlie, unamused, dead-panned over the coffee cup and asked, "Why are you the way you are?"

Eva and Lora both let loose with whooping laughter when Anthony feigned a mortal wound to his heart and fell against the counter with all the drama of a silent movie hero. Charlie ignored them all and made his way to the front porch for some quiet time.

"Well, I see somebody is still grumpy in the mornings," Anthony huffed.

Eva hooked an arm around his waist and squeezed. "Oh my boy, I have missed your antics around here."

Lora took her own cup out to the porch and stood next to her dad as he looked into the woods across the road. He gave her a side-eye nod but didn't speak. Lora didn't say anything either, until she noticed his cup was empty and offered to top him off, saving him from any more Anthony action. She took his cup into the kitchen and shook her head when Eva raised an inquiring eyebrow. She could make out garbled singing coming from the bathroom and guessed Anthony was washing up before breakfast.

Returning to the porch and marveling at the early blooming heat of the day, she handed the brim-full coffee cup to Charlie and said, "Uncle Anthony is in the bath if you're interested in braving the kitchen again."

Charlie gave her a wry smile and said, "I won't be ready for Anthony until this cup is empty too."

She patted his arm and nodded in wide-eyed agreement. "He's a lot," she said before heading back in to help Eva get breakfast on the table.

"You have no idea." He raised his mug in thanks as he watched her go.

• • • •

"WHAT ON EARTH DO Y'ALL think you're doing?"

"Well, Mama. Judging from the ties around our necks, the Bible Lora's holding, and the keys in my hand, I'd say we're going to church with you." Despite two cups of coffee, Charlie's mood was not much improved.

After breakfast, Eva had excused herself to get ready for church. The brothers and Lora quickly conferred and agreed there wasn't a gnat's chance they were letting her go by herself. The three of them were dressed and primped in record time and waiting for her when she came out of her room.

Anthony offered to drive them in his flashy, convertible rental but Eva refused, choosing the safer option of Charlie's station wagon to get her where she needed to go. She squinted her eyes against the bright morning sun sparkling on the chrome of the black Cadillac El Dorado parked in front of her house, only stopping to say, "Well, it is pretty!" when she noticed Anthony's disappointment. Charlie's chest puffed up when he opened the front passenger door of his less impressive, but reliable and safe, Ford Falcon station wagon. Anthony grumbled as he folded himself into the back seat behind Charlie but didn't go so far as complaining. Lora scooched in on the other side behind Eva, glad the seats weren't blistering hot yet.

Charlie slipped the key in the ignition and swiveled a questioning eye at his mother before turning it. "You're sure about this?"

"As sure as I can be."

"Alright then, let's go."

He turned the key, rousing the large engine to life and turned the car out of the drive, avoiding the wash-out between the road and ditch with practiced ease. He cranked the air conditioning up to the setting Lora referred to as 'Arctic Breezes' and said, over his shoulder to Anthony, "Ooh! Just feel how nice! And no need to mess up Mama's hair to stay cool!"

Anthony sniped back. "I could have put the top up! The Cadillac has air conditioning too."

Charlie grinned at his younger brother in the rearview mirror and laughed when Anthony stuck out his tongue.

"Am I gonna have to separate you two before we even get to church?" Eva's exasperation made it clear that her patience was wearing thin. Lora was the irritation wasn't aimed at her.

They rode in cool silence the rest of the way to Holley Hill.

• • • •

CHARLIE FOUND A PARKING spot in the gravel along the edge near the tree line which he hoped would provide a little shade on the car by the time church let out. A lifetime of sweating through his good shirts on the way home from parking in the sun had proven the value of a shady parking spot time and again.

Every head under the portico swiveled to stare at the unfamiliar vehicle as it pulled in the church yard. Most of those heads made a show of putting on stone faces when they realized who was getting out of that car. Backs turned and conversations shifted to tight-lipped whispers. Anthony offered Eva his arm to escort her into the building. Charlie reached for Lora's hand, giving it a reassuring squeeze. Lora straightened her spine and held her head high. She was proud of her grandmother. Proud of her dad and uncle for sticking by their mother when she needed their support most.

As they approached the shade of the overhang, Hal Johnson sneered from the far corner of the building. He stubbed his cigarette on the red brick. "You got a lot of nerve showing your face here today, Eva."

Anthony's hands clenched into fists and his jaw set in a hard line. Lora winced as Charlie gripped her hand so tightly she could feel her bones rubbing together. Surveying the crowd, Lora noticed several heads nod slowly in agreement with Mr. Johnson and was surprised to see Agnes Crawford's was one of them. Eva drew up short and looked directly at Dale Fudge.

"Preacher? Does this man speak for this church? Am I no longer welcome here?" Her chin lifted in challenge, daring him to pass judgment on her before the congregation, before God, before the law.

Mr. Fudge's Adam's apple bobbed several times as he cast a shaky glance across the congregation gathered outside the church doors. His normally steady voice wavered just a bit, "Eva. You are always welcome."

He extended a hand to her, palm up in invitation. Anthony released his hold on his mother's arm as she stepped forward to take the preacher's hand. The preacher led Eva to her usual pew with the brothers and Lora following close behind. Nervous, judging twitters drifted along in their wake like dandelion parachute fluff after the flower went to seed.

Anthony and Charlie took seats on either side of Eva. Lora sat next to her father. Eva pulled her veil from her purse and carefully pinned it to her silver curls before settling her Bible on her lap. She motioned for Lora to grab Bibles for Charlie and Anthony from the racks on the back of the pew in front of them. The brothers exchanged eye-rolls behind Eva's head making it clear they had no intention of following along with the lessons of the day and laying the books on the seats beside them.

When the rest of the assembly filed into the sanctuary, the seats immediately surrounding the Burnettes remained empty. The void spoke volumes.

The song leader, a wormy looking young man with over-large ears and a booming tenor, led the church in a couple songs. Lora had always loved the warmth of the singing at Holley Hill. The church did not believe in instrumental accompaniment during worship. Instead, the church relied on the delicate four-part harmonies of a capella voices lifted in communal praise. Today's singing felt discordant and off.

After singing, prayer, and communion, Preacher Fudge climbed the dais and took his place behind the lectern, looking anxiously at his flock. He tugged on his collar, pulling it away from his bird thin neck and cleared his throat before speaking. "Brothers and sisters, there is a great dilemma plaguing us as Christians today. The Adversary is moving on the Lord's flock, dividing us and filling our heads with wrong-thinking. He is telling us we are all equal in the eyes of the Lord, that each of us is as important to Him as every other. Indeed, the Devil is using the Word of God to distort our understanding."

He held his well-worn Bible aloft and gestured to the audience, his eyes flashing with the conviction of his words. "Indeed, the Emissary of Hell twists our God's words to his own end. Turn with me to the Gospel of Luke, chapter 15." Pages rustled and whispered with thumbs and fingers searching for the passage while the preacher paused for them to find their places.

"Luke says, 'What man of you, having a hundred sheep, if he loses one of them, does not leave the ninety-nine in the wilderness, and go after the one which is lost until he finds it?' I see you nodding your heads in agreement. Yes! You would go looking for the one cow or pig that wandered off! Because that livestock is important to you! But I ask you, if that cow or pig was ill and in danger of infecting the rest of your herd, would you still seek it out? Would you bring it back into the fold? Would you risk the lives of the ninety-nine? No you would not! And I say the Lord would not either!"

From the corner of her eye, Lora noticed several heads, but not all, nodding along with the preacher. She glanced down the pew and was dismayed to see Eva, who normally took notes on the lesson, had dropped her pencil into the crease of the open Bible on her lap. Her hands were tucked up under her thighs like she was afraid they would fly up on their own in protest of the preacher's words. Charlie and Anthony's arms rested one on top of the other along the back of the pew behind her grandmother. Their grim, thin set faces expressions made it clear they believed the preacher's message was aimed directly at Eva.

"No! The Lord will not risk the health of His church. He will let that sinner go! Even as it says in Matthew 18, 'if he refuses even to hear the church, let him be to you like a heathen!' Jesus himself says if a believer sins and refuses to repent, cast him out! Just as Cain was cast from the family who loved him for the murder of his brother, I beseech you Brothers and Sisters, pull the weeds of sin from our garden before it takes root and is impossible to remove. Now, let us pray."

All heads bowed as Dale Fudge grasped the edges of the lectern, sweat dripping from his nose.

"Father God. Most Holy Lord. Look down on us and know our hearts are pure and our intentions good. Remove the veil from our eyes and let us see the truth of our actions. Show us the errors of our ways and convict us to repent, to honestly repent, so that You may welcome us back into the fold. In Christ's name we pray, Amen."

A soft chorus of echoing "Amens" followed the prayer and people shifted in their seats. Some rose to prepare for Sunday School classes, others to make a trip to the bathroom during the break. Charlie and Anthony stood to lean on the pew in front of them, on either side of Eva, glaring at anyone who looked likely to speak. Eva did not twitch a muscle.

Lora scooted down and whispered, "Gram, I think we should leave. Let's just go on home."

Although Eva shook her head, there were tears winking in the corner of her eyes as she gathered her things and whispered back, "I guess I know where I stand."

The four Burnettes left Holley Hill Church of Christ with their heads held high, dragging Eva's broken heart behind them.

19

As soon as they cleared the double doors, Eva wiped her eyes and exhaled a shaky breath she didn't realize she'd been holding. "Well, I suppose I won't be asked to cook for any potlucks any time soon."

Charlie responded with a sad, half-hearted chuckle. Anthony seethed and looked like he wanted to run back into the church and punch Dale Fudge in the nose. "Nothing better than church people for ruining church." He growled, "They don't deserve the scraps from your table, Mama."

"Exactly. Don't you worry. They'll be missing your chicken and dressing next time they're waking a body," Charlie agreed.

The effort to bolster their hurting mother did not go unnoticed or unappreciated. Eva reached an arm out to Charlie as she leaned her still-veiled head against Anthony's shoulder. Lora, a couple steps behind as they crossed the parking lot, felt her heart climbing into her throat. Not from fear or worry, but with complete love for the trio walking arm in arm ahead of her.

Charlie and Anthony rode up front on the way back to the house, tossing their ties onto the dashboard with exaggerated relief. Lora and Eva, pinched by stockings and pointy-toed shoes, rolled their eyes as the brothers simultaneously unbuttoned the top buttons of their collars and sighed with pleasure. Eva folded her veil into her pocketbook and reached across the back seat to pat Lora's hand. Although the gesture was intended to comfort Lora, she suspected it was just as much a boon to Eva.

When they got home, all four changed opted for fewer layers of clothes and more freedom of movement. Eva slipped into her favorite lavender flowered house dress with the big front pockets while Lora opted for denim pedal pushers and a button-up top tied at the waist. The brothers swapped suits for Havana shirts and slacks.

No one wore any shoes, preferring the cool hardwoods and linoleum underfoot after being stuffed into oxfords and heels all morning.

Eva stopped in the doorway to the kitchen and smiled gently at her family, flopped across the living room furniture. She leaned against the jamb and folded her arms. "You know, I don't much feel like cooking. Y'all mind fending for yourselves for lunch?"

No one minded.

Charlie dug up a years old, faded copy of *Popular Mechanics* from the magazine rack under an end table and stepped outside to read on the front porch. Anthony dozed on the couch, wadding the brightly-colored, nubbly afghan between his bony knees. Lora padded into the kitchen and made herself a plate of cheese and crackers to nibble. Eva poured a glass of tea and eased into her usual seat at the table.

Lora sat, crunching a cracker, and smiled at her grandmother, careful not to blow saltine crumbs through the crack between her lips.

Eva chuckled low in her chest and cupped Lora's face in her palm.

"What would I do without you?"

Lora's face flushed, her eyes watering as she chewed the dry mouthful of cheese and cracker. She blinked the tears away and opted for humor instead of despair. She shrugged her shoulders, flicked her eyebrows up and replied, "I don't know. Go to jail?"

Eva barked out a wheezy, surprised "Ha!" and clapped her hands together in delight. Her eyes disappeared into half-moon creases as she shook with laughter, trying not to wake Anthony from his nap. Lora sucked down a too-large chunk of cheese and choked a little, regretting not pouring herself a drink before sitting down. She clutched at her throat and covered her mouth, holding back her own laughter. Eva slid her tea over and Lora nodded in thanks as she brought it to her lips.

Catching her breath, Lora returned the drink and got up to pour a glass of her own. She said, "The better question, Gram, is what would I do without you? You're the binding and the rest of us are just pages in your book. You hold us all together."

Eva studied the beads of sweat rolling down the sides of her tea glass for a moment before leaning her elbows on the table and catching Lora's gaze. "No ma'am. We are each of us writing our own stories in a never-ending book. What matters is whether our stories are worth reading." She rubbed her fingertip along a hairline crack in the Formica. "Nobody is interested in ho-hum lives. We gotta live with our eyes wide open and do the scary things."

Lora nibbled the corners and edges off a cracker, right up to the edges of the slice of cheese on top, not caring about the crumby mess she was making. She set the cracker back on her plate and asked, "Okay, but everybody doesn't live exciting lives or have adventures. Loads of my friends act like I'm going on safari every summer, just because I come down here to stay with you. Still, that doesn't mean their lives aren't important."

"Everyday lives can still be interesting. The scary things, the interesting bits come about when we take the blinders off and study the world around us. It's just a matter of paying attention. We have to understand what happened so we can understand what is happening so we can understand what's gonna to happen."

"So, knowing that Sheriff Griffin thought Bumpus was a good man, and knowing he's not a fan of you, helps us understand why he decided to blame you for Bumpus's death instead of just letting it go. Is that what you're saying?"

Eva winked at Lora and said, "Exactly. Now, what do you think about clearing away the mess you made and playing some dominoes?" She waved her hand at the scattered crumbs on the table in front of Lora and got to her feet.

• • • •

CHARLIE AND ANTHONY roused themselves and shuffled into the kitchen when they heard Eva rummaging in the closet for the rattling box of dotted ivory. They poured glasses and settled into creaking chairs as Eva dumped the tiles onto the table. Charlie turned the pieces face down while Anthony swirled and shuffled them across the surface. Lora slapped away her uncle's hand when he reached for a cracker. "Get your own!" she laughed, sliding the plate out of his reach while choosing her hand from the boneyard. The Burnettes were a competitive bunch, even on lazy Sunday afternoons.

Eva's set was a standard double-six and was a gift from Monroe when he'd put a stop to the old men playing on the store porch. Some people with nothing better to do had complained about "no-good time wasters" hanging around, smoking, and swapping stories over a game. Some went so far as to claim Monroe was involved in illegal gambling. Ever the businessman, Monroe sulked and eventually caved to the pressure and boxed up his dominoes. He gave them to Dub. Dub often played at the store when the weather kept him from the fields. He and Eva would sit on their own front porch and play, chatting about all the everythings and nothings which made up a marriage.

Eva laid the first tile, a 1/2 which meant there were only four possible plays available. She flung her challenge with a smirk. Burnette family rules of play were cutthroat and indecipherable to purists. Double-doubles and blanks fell in line as the bones were thrown onto the worn table top and scores were tallied. Charlie and Anthony fell into their old roles of big and little brother; plotting and scheming, jibing and arguing, stealing and sharing. Eva and Lora took advantage of the distraction, racking up points at the brothers' expense. This simple communion was more comforting than sharing the Host.

Eva looked at the smiling faces around her table and thought, *Lord, surely this is holy too.*

• • • •

IN THE FINAL DREGS of the liquid afternoon, Anthony pushed away from the table and suggested they go for a top-down ride in his rented Cadillac. Eva rode in the passenger seat and leaned back against the headrest. Her eyes closed as the sun beat down on her face, protesting against the cooling breezes swirling around the open-topped vehicle. In the backseat, Lora and Charlie waved their arms and hands in rippling motions against the resistance from the wind like children pretending to fly.

None of them knew or cared where Anthony was taking them. The brief escape and carefree drive was a perfect departure from the gathering dread of court in the morning. The passengers were pleasantly surprised when Anthony turned off the main road into the shade of a dirt drive which led to the old cow ford on the Tennessee River. Generations of farmers and cattle once crossed the Tennessee at this shallow eddy. Since the Wheeler Dam was built in the 30's though, the old ford had become popular as a boat landing, swimming hole, picnic spot, baptismal pool, and place of reflection. Ancient and worn smooth tree stumps were put to work as seats and tables by everyone who visited. Today though, the Burnettes had the ford to themselves.

Anthony parked near a cluster of stumps. He waved Eva and Lora towards prime spots looking out over the glittering, muddy river and jerked his head at his brother to come help him with something in the trunk. Charlie's eyes crinkled around the edges like his mother's when he saw Eva's almost forgotten, red picnic basket tucked inside. His raised eyebrows asked an unspoken question to which Anthony's only reply was a single sweet word, "Myra."

Anthony pulled the basket from the cavernous trunk well while Charlie heaved a battered Coleman cooler out and over the edge. He grunted with the effort. "Brother, I think I got the loser's share of this bargain," he said, struggling to shift the heavy contents into an equilibrium suitable for walking. Anthony laughed and swung the lighter food laden basket in time with his easy strides towards the riverside.

The women made all the appropriate exclamations of surprise and pleasure as Anthony and Charlie spread their supper-time repast across the top of a large stump. Anthony explained he and Myra had conspired in the picnic planning before she'd left the night before. She'd taken Eva's basket home with her and filled it with fried chicken, corn-on-the cobb, turnip greens, and white bread. Sometime after her own church services were over, Myra had left it and the cooler, filled with an old milk jug full of sweet tea and four Cokes, in the deep shade behind the old chicken coop for Anthony to retrieve. Eva blessed her friend and sighed in deep pleasure as she sunk her teeth into a cold, but delicious, fried chicken leg.

"I can't deny it. This is good. And I'm not just talking about the chicken." She reached across and squeezed Lora's hand who in turn grasped her father's, who reached for Anthony's. Anthony took hold of Eva's free elbow, her hand currently occupied with the chicken leg.

Anthony murmured his agreement around a crunching mouthful.

Eva nodded and chewed, humming a snippet of hymn before speaking again. "I don't know what the next few days will look like but I'm feeling much better just having you all here with me right now."

The others smiled and shook their heads. "Mama, there's no other place I'd rather be," said Charlie. Anthony and Lora nodded in accord.

When the meal was finished and cleared away, Anthony and Eva walked to the water's edge. They took turns searching for perfect flat rocks and seeing who could skip them the furthest. Charlie and Lora put the picnic basket and cooler in the trunk, closing it firmly and leaning against the bumper. It was nice to see Eva enjoying her afternoon instead of worrying about everyone but herself. While they watched, Lora remembered something her father had said the day before.

"Daddy, yesterday when you were talking about Gram, you said she'd helped an unmarried girl with a, um, problem, and when you did, Mom stormed out of the kitchen. Do you know why?"

Charlie cleared his throat and crossed his arms. He walked away from the car several paces and stared into the waning sun for a moment. He scrunched his eyes closed and answered, "Your mother."

Lora gasped. "Mama? What? Why? You?"

Charlie bent over and rested his hands on his knees. His breath heaved, his back stretching and shrinking. Lora rushed around and knelt in front of him.

"Daddy?" She put her hands on either side of his face.

"No. Not me. I was gone, in Europe."

"Dad. I'm confused, if you were gone—"

Charlie straightened, taking Lora's hands in his own and pulling her to her feet. His face was stern but unashamed as tears leaked freely from the brims of his eyes. He tried smiling but managed little more than a grimace.

"Lora, let's just say your mother and your grandmother have more reason to be glad Bumpus is dead than anyone we know."

Lora snatched her hands from his grasp and covered her ears as she searched his face for a lie or a jest. Not finding what she was looking for, her mouth dropped open in a perfect shocked "o." She gulped in air, resembling a fish out of water, and whispered, "You mean, Bumpus? And Mama? He forced himself on her?"

Charlie shuttered his eyes and inclined his head in sad regret. "That's exactly what I'm saying and I wish I wasn't."

He reached up and gently pulled Lora's hands from her her ears, "But you can't let either of them know you know. Your mama has spent every day since then trying to put Bumpus behind her, trying to forget. Even though what he did to her, the choice she made, even though it's all unforgettable."

Lora nodded, "Of course. Of course, I won't breathe a word. But did you know? Before you got married? You were engaged, right?"

Charlie's shoulders slumped. He shoved his hands into his pockets and dug at a half-buried tree root with the toe of his shoe.

"Absolutely. I love your mama. Always have. Always will. What kind of man would blame a woman for something awful like that happening to her? What kind of man would walk away from the woman he loves because she was in an impossible situation? Come on now, I hope you know me better than that!"

Lora searched her dad's face and was immediately guilty, convicted of doubting him. "I'm sorry Dad. You're the best sort of man. I think I've been a little hard on Mom, though."

He chuckled deep and pulled her into a fierce hug. "Yeah, you have. But, for the right reasons. Your mama changed after...She lost her joy and spent most of her time trying to be... perfect. She has always felt like what Bumpus did was her fault. Even though it wasn't. Not a chance. Still, you were right to call her out about doing the right thing. She'll come around. She loves you." He kissed the top of her head. "Don't worry about it."

Lora squeezed his chest as tight as she could, finding comfort in the unique combination of Tide laundry detergent, clean sweat, and Brut aftershave which belonged just to him. She pressed her forehead into the hollow under his chin and breathed deep.

"Dad?"

"Yeah?" He pulled her ponytail.

"If you were still in Europe, how long did this happen to Mama before Uncle Walter was killed and Grandaddy died?"

Charlie pressed his chin into the top of her head, hard enough to hurt. She squeaked and pulled away from him.

He rubbed his hands across his face and went back to lean on the trunk of the car. His fingers, rough from building cars in the Ford factory, tugged on his face and neck until he looked like the painting, *The Scream* by Edvard Munch, that Lora saw on a school field trip once.

Charlie looked towards the riverbank, the corners of his mouth pulling up into a half-smile. Skipping rocks had turned into Anthony trying to throw Eva into the water. Eva threw rocks at him as she dipped away just out of reach, laughing as she went.

He shook his head. "I can't say exactly what happened on what day. All I know is that we all lost a helluva a lot in a real short period of time."

Lora hugged him again, gently this time and said, "It sounds like it."

She wrapped an arm through one of his and jerked her head towards her uncle and grandmother with a smirk.

"Come on. Let's go help Gram throw him in."

Charlie smirked. "Or we could stone him. That could be fun too!"

Within minutes, the brothers were tussling like overgrown children. Each trying for all he was worth to dunk the other in the reedy, muddy water near the shore, neither with any success. A sudden spray of gravel stopped their wrestling mid-motion. The Burnettes slid suspicious eyes towards a deputy none of them recognized emerging from the patrol car.

The deputy put his wide-brimmed, stiff hat on his head and stood on one leg behind the open door.

"How y'all doin?" he drawled.

Eva raised a level hand to her brow, trying to see more clearly in the retreating light of day and deepening shade of the trees surrounding the clearing. "I reckon we're doin' just fine, Deputy. Just clearing up."

She gestured towards the trunk, "We got some turnip greens left. You're welcome to them if you want?"

"No ma'am. I appreciate the offer though. I just saw a fancy car parked off the road when I drove by. Thought I'd stop to make sure everything's all right. Looks like it is. I'll be on my way." He touched a finger to the brim of his hat and stooped back into the patrol car. Raising a finger of farewell from the steering wheel, he carefully backed out the entrance to the cow ford.

Anthony let out a soft whistle, "You think Griffin has them keeping an eye on you?"

"Just like Monroe said." Eva shook her head and made a deep throated grunt of disgust.

Lora turned a round-eyed gaze at her grandmother, "Is that what his note said?"

Eva nodded and fended off Charlie and Anthony's barrage of questions about Monroe, the note, why hadn't she told them. "He let me know. Just like he said he would. That's all that matters."

Lora giggled. "Well, since the Sheriff lost you before your arraignment, he might figure he needs to know where you are at all times."

Charlie and Anthony barked in surprise. "He lost you?"

Eva filled them in on the snafu Friday morning at the courthouse and they laughed at the picture Lora painted of Sheriff Griffin sprinting out of the courtroom like a mortified daddy longlegs being chased by a broom. After some debate, it was agreed that Sheriff Griffin hadn't bothered to make arrangements for Eva's court appearance and had hoped the judge would proceed without her. Still, on their way home, they played a sarcastic little game of "Spot the Deputy" and racked up impressive scores of two each. Anthony wondered aloud when Griffin had hired so much help. Eva pursed her lips and agreed it was unusual to see so many lawmen running around her part of the county.

20

E arly Monday morning, with little time to spare before court at eight o'clock, the Burnettes were too nervous to do more than swallow a couple bites of day-old biscuits and scarf down a few swigs of pulpy orange juice to help the dry bread go down. Eva fiddled with her hair, her hat, her dress, and her stockings until Lora assured her for the thirty-fourth time she looked fine. Eva gave her an anxious smile and knit her fingers together.

"We ready to go?"

Lora and Eva turned to Charlie and nodded, clutching their pocketbooks tight to their sides. Lora brushed a few biscuit crumbs from the front of her black skirt and took a deep breath. She puffed her cheeks and let the air seep through her pursed lips like a balloon with a slow leak. She hooked her arm through Eva's and led the way to the car.

Without no discussion or arguing, Charlie and Anthony helped Lora and Eva into the backseat of the Falcon and made their way to Athens to see what more could be learned about the case against Eva.

• • • •

CHARLIE FOUND A PARKING spot near the west-side entrance to the courthouse and hoped the business of the day would be completed long before the sun's blistering rays could crest the top of the copper dome of the clock tower. Landon Cook's faded green jalopy of a truck rumbled into the space beside the Falcon as they were collecting themselves to climb the steep limestone steps. The bounce in his step and swing of his briefcase telegraphed confidence the preliminary hearing would go well.

"Hey there Burnettes!" he said, offering Eva his arm to help her up the stairs.

"Hey yourself Landon," Anthony replied, chucking Landon on the shoulder.

"That's Mr. Cook to you today. I am an officer of the court you know."

Their easy banter continued up the stairs, into the courthouse, and to the courtroom doors where they stopped briefly to settle themselves before going in.

Landon adjusted his brown-and-blue paisley tie and told them what to expect. "Eva, you and I will go in and sit at the same table as before. Charlie, Anthony, and Lora, y'all can sit just behind us but can't talk to us during the proceedings. Now, I'm going to be asking for all the evidence Griffin collected and a copy of your arrest warrant. I want to see what Griffin used as probable cause. The state's attorney should be able to just hand them across the aisle. If he doesn't, he ought to be ashamed of himself for coming to court unprepared. If that's the case, I'm sure Judge Underwood will be even more peeved than he was on Friday." He held up a hand when Eva raised a reminding eyebrow. "And yes, I will request a bench trial. Not sure he'll go along with it, but it won't hurt asking."

With that, he beamed an encouraging smile at his friends and reached for the door to escort them into the courtroom.

· · · ·

SURPRISED TO SEE THE room was already about half full when she and her father and uncle took their seats behind the defendant's table, Lora scanned the crowd. Sheriff Griffin and Deputy Ross were seated behind the prosecution. Deputy Ross did not look at the family as they sidled in and sat. Attorney Beatty was in his place at the state's table, busily making minuscule adjustment to papers placed neatly in rows across the polished surface. He had a crisp yellow legal pad situated directly in front of him. Flipping a pen through his fingers as he arranged and rearranged, he appeared as confident as Mr. Cook.

Lora was not surprised to see Hal Johnson and the Church Ladies ensconced in the same seats they'd occupied at the arraignment. Mr. Johnson caught her eye and puckered his lips like he was blowing her a kiss. He grinned when she shuddered and looked away. The Church Ladies wore varying shades of concern and morbid curiosity. Agnes Crawford was practically vibrating with anticipation. Margaret Clem dipped her pointy nose and chin at people she knew as others found places in the gallery. Helen Fudge clutched her Bible and was so pale, Lora thought she might faint before the proceedings even started.

Craning her neck further over her shoulder to see the rest of the room, she was pleased to see Myra, Leon, and Maurice seated in the back row. The family was surrounded by a sea of brown faces, people of all ages Lora assumed were from their church. She quirked a tiny smile in their direction and lifted her hand to wave when she noticed Hal Johnson tracking her gaze. Recognition bloomed on his face and his expression changed from smug satisfaction to silent fury at the sight of the Strong brothers seated beside their mother. He leapt to his feet and shook, staring at Maurice and Leon. Every sinew in his neck twitched as he tensed his muscles and trembled in mute rage. For a terrifying moment, Lora thought he might climb across the intervening benches and onlookers to attack one or both of them. Instead, he clenched his fists and clambered over his surprised bench mates, scattering purses and tripping on toes as he went. He pushed through the courtroom doors with enough force to leave impact gouges from the handles slamming into the hallway walls.

Mr. Johnson's dramatic exit set the gallery to buzzing louder than a swarm of bees. Landon Cook lifted a questioning eyebrow at Lora whose look of wide-eyed innocence was a clear sign she knew exactly what happened while his back was turned.

Charlie laid his arm along the top of the bench behind her and whispered, "Well, that was interesting."

"It was, wasn't it?"

He rubbed her shoulder and had just enough time to say, "You know you're going to have to tell me what you know about that," before the bailiff called for them to rise. She nodded as she stood, and Judge Underwood took the bench.

The undercurrent of whispers and low voices stilled when the judge gestured for the gallery to be seated and gaveled the court into session.

Lora glanced back at the Strongs as she smoothed her skirt underneath her. Myra's face had gone an ashen shade of caramel. Leon was smirking. Maurice looked defeated.

"Good morning Mr. Beatty, Mr. Cook. I trust we can keep this hearing short and to the point today?"

Both attorneys murmured their assent.

"Alrighty then, let's see. Preliminary hearing in the case of Alabama versus Eva Burnette. Mr. Cook? You have the floor."

"Thank you, Your Honor. I will start by asking the State to turn over all evidence regarding fingerprints discovered on the dinner plates recovered both at the scene of discovery and through execution of a warrant of seizure at Mrs. Burnette's home."

"Mr. Cook, you asked for this information on Friday. Mr. Beatty's office should have provided it by close of business of the same day. Are you telling me you did not receive it?"

"I believe my office received incomplete records, Your Honor. I received one piece of paper which says," he flourished a single piece of paper and read aloud. 'The fingerprints of Eva Holder Burnette were found to be present on a broken plate found in the immediate vicinity of the body of Ethelred Bumpus, deceased, and on a plate seized from her residence in execution of a search warrant.' Your Honor, I would posit this is scanty evidence on which to build a manslaughter case. It stands to reason that Mrs. Burnette's fingerprints would be on both plates, as they both belong to her."

Judge Underwood's face was grim as he shifted his gaze to Mr. Beatty.

"Mr. Beatty, I agree with Mr. Cook on this. Indeed, when you and Sheriff Griffin asked me to sign both the search warrant and the arrest warrant, you indicated you had substantial evidence to support your claim. If this statement is the sum total of the information you intend to use in this courtroom, I will immediately dismiss this case with prejudice. I do not enjoy looking stupid and will not abide my courtroom being turned into a circus of conjecture."

Mr. Beatty wiped his hands down his lapels and cleared his throat. "Your Honor, there was no intention to mislead you or subvert justice in this matter. The state does indeed have further fingerprint information on the plate but found it to be irrelevant. We also have witnesses who have come forward in support of our case."

The judge pinched the bridge of his nose. "Mr. Beatty, I would advise you to find copies of all the evidence in that tidy little arrangement of paperwork on your desk and place them directly into the hands of the defense. If you need to use the court mimeograph machine, I will gladly grant a brief recess. Bear in mind, copies made here are a nickel each."

The flustered state's attorney pulled at his collar while upsetting his well-ordered paper display and said, "No, that will not be necessary, Your Honor. Thank you though."

Finding what he was looking for, he shoved a stack of papers onto the defense table without bothering to look Landon Cook in the eye.

Somehow managing to keep a straight face, Mr. Cook said, "Thank you, Mr. Beatty."

"Mr. Cook, is that all you need?" Judge Underwood was once again cleaning his glasses with a corner of his robe and glancing at the clock.

Landon quickly flipped through the pages he'd just received. "Your Honor, the prosecution mentioned witnesses. I see neither witness statements nor a witness list. We would also request a copy of the attending warrants."

Judge Underwood's warning groan elicited a frantic shuffling of papers from the prosecution and a muffled, "I'm sorry, Your Honor. Just a moment, please," followed by a virtual rain of documentation flying across the aisle like manna from heaven.

After a tense moment, the judge dug his fingers into the corners of his eyes.

"Mr. Cook. Please tell me you now have everything you need."

Unable to avoid being smug, Landon quickly thumbed through the stack of papers and replied, "Your Honor, it appears we now have the required discovery documents."

Judge Underwood opened his eyes and stifled a laugh with a cough. The prosecution's desk was void of everything except the legal pad. The defense table however, looked like a paper mill had exploded across its surface. Landon Cook was happily straightening his newfound treasures into one big stack, turning and flipping pages like a boy playing with a fresh set of Tinker Toys.

"Excellent. Is there anything else?"

Landon, lost in his small victory, was startled by the question and winced at Eva's firm finger suddenly jabbing him in the ribs.

"Oh! Yes, Your Honor. The defense requests a bench trial at your earliest convenience."

"A bench trial?" The judge's hands tented on the bench, mimicking the pointed arch of his eyebrows over his glasses. "This is quite unusual, Mr. Cook. Are you certain?"

"My client is quite adamant, Your Honor. We maintain our request." Landon did not look at Eva when he spoke.

"Well, if you insist, I suppose I can accommodate the request. Does your client understand that, should the court find her guilty of the allegations, her options for appeal will be limited?"

"She does, Your Honor. She is confident in your abilities to discern the facts and render a true verdict."

"I'm flattered," Judge Underwood deadpanned. "Mr. Beatty? I assume you have no objections?

"No. Your Honor, the state is prepared to proceed." Mr. Beatty spoke with more confidence than his sweat-stained shirt collar indicated. He was still off-balance and throwing from his back foot after the fumbled discovery fiasco moments earlier.

Underwood muttered under his breath, "Hmpf. I wonder." Nevertheless, he motioned to his clerk, indicating he bring the court calendar to the bench.

Flipping through the calendar pages, he said, "Hunh! As unlikely as it sounds, it appears I have an opening on Wednesday morning of this week. Would the day after tomorrow work for you gentlemen?"

Court dates, even bench trials, generally took weeks to schedule. The sudden availability indicated Underwood's impatience with the proceedings. Both Mr. Cook and Mr. Beatty scrambled for their own calendars to check for conflicting obligations which could not be moved. Making notes to themselves in the calendar margins, each man frantically scribbled, grumbling to themselves.

Mr. Beatty was the first to recover. He cleared his throat and croaked, "Your Honor, the State can accommodate a Wednesday trial."

Landon Cook, nonplussed to be beaten to the punch, agreed he could be ready by Wednesday as well.

"Good. Shall we say eight o'clock in the morning then?"

The attorneys made further notes in their calendars and acknowledged the time.

Judge Underwood rapped the gavel on his desk and true to form, swept off the bench and into his chambers before the bailiff could instruct them all to rise.

• • • •

CHARLIE'S FALCON WAS still covered in a pool of deep shade from the trees on the west side of courthouse lawn. The Burnette family and Landon Cook stood in a huddle next to the vehicle, talking over each other, rehashing the morning's events.

Seeing the Strongs making their way down the gleaming white steps, Lora excused herself to dash over and speak to them. As soon as she approached, Myra cut her off with a chop of her hand and sharp shake of her head. "Not here, not now girl! We'll come by the house later."

Leon and Maurice, flanking their mother, gave her quick nods of encouragement and walked away without saying a word.

Lora knew she'd misstepped in public, in full-view of everyone who'd been in the gallery, all of whom were still milling about on the lawn or loitering near their cars. She suddenly felt as exposed as if she'd been caught sunbathing in her altogether. Squaring her shoulders, ignoring any eyes which might be following her, she walked calmly back to her family.

"There you are!" Landon Cook extended an arm, opening space for her in the huddle.

He set his briefcase on the ground at his feet and rubbed his hands together. "You want to tell me what you know about that scene Hal Johnson caused before Judge Underwood walked in?"

Realizing the watching eyes now belonged to her family, Lora wrapped her fingers together and shifted on her feet. "I'll tell you if the papers you got confirmed that Mr. Johnson's prints were on the graveyard plate."

Landon, surprised by her bargaining skills, wheezy laughed, and spluttered. "Indeed they did! Now, whatcha got on Hal Johnson?"

"Alright. We know Mr. Johnson is telling people he caught a Black man on his property the day Bumpus died. I just wondered how good a look he'd gotten at this alleged Black man and asked Leon and Maurice to be here this morning. I guess now we know he got a good enough look to recognize him. Or thinks he does anyway."

"Mm mm! Charlie, remind me to stay on your girl's good side. Lora, I'd say you're right. He most assuredly saw something he didn't like!"

Anthony couldn't resist. "Yep. She takes after her uncle."

Charlie elbowed him as Lora spoke up.

"Not something, Mr. Cook. Someone. And, because he acted the way he did, well, I've got to tell the Strongs to steer clear of court on Wednesday. I might even suggest they all run off to Chicago for a while!"

Eva squinted at her granddaughter. "Why's that?"

"Well, Gram, Myra is your friend and, according to Sheriff Griffin, the whole world knows it. So no one else would think anything of her and her boys being there to support you. And, there were plenty of other Black men in the room so Leon and Maurice wouldn't seem out of place. But, because Mr. Johnson stormed out, and Sheriff Griffin saw it, well, that may be enough for the prosecution to shift gears and focus on the running Black man thing if they think they're losing. Or, if nothing else, try to roll it all up into a bigger conspiracy ball and accuse you of outright murder instead of manslaughter."

Landon Cook whistled and ran his fingers through his previously slick-combed hair, tugging at the temples as he followed her train of thought. "Lora, you would make a fine lawyer. On either side of the aisle."

Charlie puffed up in pride at the compliment Landon had just paid to his daughter even though his words said otherwise. "Now Landon, don't go putting grand ideas into her head. I can't afford to send her to Alabama."

Lora sweetly smiled at her father and batted her eyelashes. "But Daddy, you've sent me to Alabama every summer for years."

Charlie feigned offense but soon joined in the hee-hawing laughter of his brother and friend. Shepherding everyone to the car, Eva called out an invitation to Landon to stop by for supper if he didn't have anything else to do that night. He hooted back that he wouldn't dare pass up the offer and he'd see them all later. Charlie rushed them into the Falcon. He was losing shade and for some weird reason, it mattered to him.

. . . .

MANEUVERING THE STATION wagon carefully into traffic, Charlie said his three bites of biscuit that morning had long since stopped doing their job and asked if anyone else was famished. At the mention of food, a chorus of loudly grumbling stomachs was enough to answer his question. Lora suggested hot dogs from Kreme Delite.

Anthony couldn't resist the opportunity to tease and twisted an arm over the front seat to tease his niece. "You only want Kreme Delite because you saw Deputy Ross walk over there after we left the courthouse."

Lora stuck out an indignant tongue and replied, "No he didn't! He went to the Burger Hut!" Realizing he'd caught her out, she clapped her hands over her mouth and shook her head, giggling like the young woman she was.

Charlie said he could go for a steak from Jerry's Restaurant out on Highway 31. Anthony heartily agreed, rubbing his hands together and pretending to drool.

Eva patted Lora on the knee and let out an amused snort. "I'd rather not go anywhere here in town. How about we head down to Greenbrier? I wouldn't mind some catfish and hush puppies."

"Greenbrier it is then." Charlie replied as he made the turn onto Jefferson Street towards the highway.

From the front seat, Anthony's sing-song tenor filled the car.

"Lora-and-the-deputy,

Sitting-in-a-tree,

K-I-S-S-I-N-G..."

Eva snorted and reached out, flicking him on the ear. "Are you ever going to grow up, son?"

"Ow Mama!" He rubbed his ear with such intensity, anyone else would have thought she'd flicked it right off his head. "But no, I won't. Where's the fun in growing up?"

In a more somber tone he added, "Charlie, you got eyes on the deputy following us?"

Charlie muttered an exasperated, "Yep, sure do," and turned on the radio, effectively drowning out any further conversation or antics from his successful but frustrating brother.

• • • •

THE LUNCH CROWD WAS packed tight as tree bark into Greenbrier Barbecue by the time the Burnettes arrived. The shaded parking spaces had all been claimed. Resigning himself to scorching hot seats after lunch, Charlie parked between a farm truck and tractor in the crushed gravel lot. He settled for rolling down all the windows and sent up a silent prayer of thanks for clear skies, even if the heat was suffocating. Better a warm bottom than trying to dry out wet leather he reckoned.

Still, in the short walk under a blazing sun across the parking lot, they were all uncomfortably sticky and sweaty by the time they reached the restaurant doors. They made quick work of dabbing their faces on napkins from the dispenser on the table once seated.

"I swear, if this isn't what being in the Devil's armpit feels like, then I don't know what is," Anthony grumbled.

"You're telling me California doesn't get hot?" Charlie asked.

"Oh, it gets hot alright. But it's different. You just don't need gills to breathe. The air is dry, and on a good day, where I live in Sacramento, the wind rushes down into the valley, off the mountains and it smells like Christmas and snow. Even in the summer."

Their waitress, whose embroidered shirt read "Marla," a girl around Lora's age with a neat, chin length blonde bob and giant glob of bubble gum wedged between her cheek and teeth, sidled up to the table with a tray of water glasses. Placing a glass and straw in front of each of them, she asked, "Y'all know what you want or do you need a minute?"

Eva smiled at the girl, whose name tag read "Marla," and said, "We'll have four catfish dinners, an extra plate of hush puppies, and four of the biggest sweet teas you got."

Anthony cut in. He was tearing off bits of wet napkin and rolling them into balls. "Now, Mama. You picked the restaurant. You don't get to order for us." He flashed a charming smile at Marla. "I'll have a pulled pork plate with green beans, slaw, and baked potato. Sweet tea too. Oh and don't forget the white sauce. Loads of it."

Charlie went for the catfish with extra lemon wedges. Lora passed on the fish and opted for barbecue.

"You got it!" Marla bounced away, making notes on her order pad.

Eva narrowed her eyes at the pile of ammunition gathering beneath Anthony's fingers and without saying another word, she swept the cache into her hand and took his napkin and straw from him. He managed to look sheepish for about two seconds before changing directions.

Anthony glanced around the dining room to see if there was anyone within earshot before leaning in to the table and whispering, "So, what do you think was in all that paperwork Landon got this morning? He already said it confirmed Johnson's fingerprints were on the graveyard plate. But what else do you think he got?"

"Well," Charlie mimicked his brother's posture and leaned in as well, "copies of the search and arrest warrants. He asked for those."

"Sure, sure. He asked for those. I mean, they said they had witnesses! Who do you think they're talking about?"

Eva's head drew back, looking like a turtle pulling her head into her shell, as her family stretched their necks to look at her.

"Lord have mercy! You don't expect me to know, do you?"

Lora pursed her lips and ventured a guess. "I bet Mr. Johnson is on that list. He had to know he'd been eating off Gram's plate every morning for months. And, that would explain why they didn't include his prints in the paper they sent over to Mr. Cook's office on Friday."

Anthony rubbed his chin. He was about to speak when Marla returned with four large styrofoam cups with lids, each with orbs of sweet tea bubbling out the straw holes. "These are the biggest we got. I figured y'all can take them with you when you're done. Your food should be out shortly."

They all said "Thank-you" as she walked away. Anthony held his hand out to his mother, asking for his straw back. Eva took the wrapper off herself before handing over the naked straw.

"So Mama, you want to tell us how much all this has to do with your special talent or not?" Anthony twisted his straw around his fingers, making an air popper for Charlie to thump. He didn't even glance in Eva's direction.

Lora choked and spluttered, dribbling tea down her chin.

Eva tossed a napkin in her direction before hissing at Anthony, "What are you talking about?"

Charlie chimed in, "Oh come on Mama. We've known our whole lives there was something different about you. Some of the things you did or said, well, sometimes it was like you were just inviting trouble. Me, Ant, Walter, even Mable...we all figured there had to be a reason other than just meddling in other people's business."

Eva's face flushed. She stared a hole straight through Charlie.

"Mama, it's okay," he chided. "Remember those fistfights I was talking about the other day? Well, I wouldn't have bothered fighting them if I hadn't thought what you were doing was right. Or that you had a choice."

Noise from the other diners, forks scraping on plates, bursts of laughter, oozed through the uncomfortable silence at their table like water through cracks in shale rock.

Lora found her voice first. "Daddy, is that why you said what you did about Mr. Cook being one of Gram's crusades?"

Charlie nodded at his daughter, then jerked his chin at Anthony. "Why don't you tell that story? Mama can fill in the gaps if she wants."

With a quick shh! from Eva, they noticed Marla heading their way carrying an over-sized tray piled high with their orders. Marla made sure they had everything they needed, including white sauce and extra lemon wedges, before swishing her way to another table.

As soon as the girl was gone, Anthony, ever the entertainer, launched into the tale of "Landon the Lost" with his usual aplomb and was soon gesturing wildly with his hands, eliciting gasps and laughter from his family.

21

"The story Landon told you is true enough. Although it wasn't on the first day of school, just early in the year. Anyway, I *was* trying to get another kid...that whiny little turd Morton Greenhaw, you remember him?" He dipped a glance at his brother and mother, who nodded.

"Anyway, I was trying to get him to eat a worm and Landon *did* step in to stop me. And yes, he did wind up being my best friend. But, not necessarily because that's the way things go with little boys who get into trouble together." Anthony scooped sauce over his pulled pork, mixing it into the pile of barbecued deliciousness.

"No, I thought Landon was a pampered, snot nosed brat who stuck his nose where it didn't belong. He showed up to the first day of school with brand new everything - shoes, books, pencils, paper, the works. And on worm-eating day, in my head, he wasn't trying to protect Morton but trying to prove he was better than me. Better than my hand-me-down shoes. Better than my beat up books.

"I wasn't fighting over a worm. I was fighting him for being uppity and trying to bring him down a notch. When Mama found out about the fight, I thought she was gonna faint. She clutched her chest and started whispering under her breath. I didn't have a clue what was going on. Once she came back to herself, well, she made me go cut my own switch - which by the way Mama, is a terrible thing to do to a kid. After thrashing my legs for fighting at school, she sat me down and said, 'Anthony, that boy you beat up today needs you. He needs you to be his friend. So, you're going to be his friend and that's all there is to it.' Can you imagine?"

Charlie chewed. Eva grunted. Lora giggled. Anthony waved his fork for emphasis.

"I'll never forget how mad I was. Sitting there on my sore butt, welts stinging up the backs of my legs and she was telling *me* I had to be friends with Landon! Next morning, she went to school with me. Walked right up to Landon and gave him a note to take home to his mother. I didn't know what the note said but you bet I figured it out the next morning when he told me he'd be coming home with me that afternoon!"

Anthony snurled his lip and shook his head in remembered disbelief. He snagged a crusty hush puppy from the communal plate of extras and popped it into his mouth.

"Sure enough, when I gathered my things at the end of the day, Landon was waiting for me outside with a stupid smile plastered on his stupid face. I didn't want to take him home with me. I didn't want him and his new shoes in our old house. I didn't want him to see our garden. I'd already seen the store-bought lunch box he toted and the perfect sandwiches he brought to school. I wanted to shove him off in a ditch and leave him. But, my stripes were still too new for me to risk the wrath of Mama if I did."

Eva hmpf'd. "That's one of what, five whippings you got in your whole life? Boy, you're holding on to a grudge something fierce!"

Anthony laughed. "Why do you think I learned to be so charming, Mama? I had to protect the switch bush from turning into nothing but a trunk with nubs!"

Charlie wiped crumbs from his lips and chuckled. "I always worried about that bush. Between Walter, me, and you, Mama probably should have had at least two more of those bushes!" He pinched lemon wedges over his catfish while Anthony was talking and, laying the latest spent rind on the edge of his plate, asked, "Mama, did Mable ever get a whipping? If she did, I don't remember it."

Eva dabbed the corners of her mouth with a napkin as she shook her head. "No. She never did. Not that she didn't get in trouble. She just operated differently than you boys did. Physical discomfort was the only thing that work with you and your brothers. Popping Mable on the rear just hurt her feelings. No, taking things away from her is what got her attention. When she misbehaved, all I had to do was take away her favorite doll for a day or two and she straightened right up."

"So you mean to tell me, taking stuff away was an option? I'd have gladly let you have my baseball glove if it'd have saved me a trip to the switching bush!"

Eva patted his hand. "I know, Charlie. And that's why it wouldn't have worked for you. It was the lesson, not the punishment that mattered. And, giving you something to remember was all I could think of."

Anthony, with a mouthful of barbecue, said, "Y'all gonna let me finish telling the story or not?"

Lora was fascinated both by Anthony's version of how he became friends with Landon Cook and by Gram's switch bush. She couldn't imagine Eva taking a switch to anybody. Then she remembered the little brown mouse from the cupboard, drying and deflated in the back yard, and adjusted her opinion.

"Please do! How on earth did you manage to make friends with Mr. Cook after all?"

"Well, Landon talked my ear off the whole way home. Told me about his Daddy's new car. Keep in mind, this was in 1930. Nobody I knew had two nickels to rub together much less enough money to buy a new car. But no, his daddy's new car, the horses they kept just for riding, the pedal-car airplane he got for his birthday, his favorite candy from the drugstore." Anthony rolled his eyes. "I was chewing the inside of my cheek so hard to keep from telling him to shut up I was eventually spitting blood.

"When we got home, Mama poured us both glasses of cold milk and gave us cornbread with honey. Walter was out in the field with Daddy. He was older and got to leave school early to help bring in the harvest during season. Charlie and Mable came in not too long behind us, chattering like magpies. They were just a little older and had homework to do before they could do anything else. They didn't even notice the extra kid at the table. Landon looked around with these big ol' eyes like he was in another world. Looking back, I guess he was. He looked at Mama, he looked at me, at Charlie and Mable, at his plate and said, I'll never forget it, he said, 'I love your house!'"

Anthony paused for a swig of tea. "I couldn't believe it. And if he hadn't looked so...awestruck, I guess would be the right word, I'd have thought he was making fun. But no. He really loved our house. Mama said thank-you and I just stared at him. I suppose that was the first time I really saw him."

He reached out and squeezed his mother's hand. "We finished our snack and Mama told us both to go pull some tomatoes for stew. I couldn't believe she was telling a guest to do chores! We left our satchels on the floor by the table and scooted out to the garden. Landon confessed he'd never seen a vegetable garden and he was so excited to see all the things Mama was growing. He kept pointing at plants and asking what they were, what we did with them, how they tasted, everything you could imagine. Then he asked who took care of all these things. When I told him Mama did, even though we all helped when she needed us, you could have knocked him over with feather. Not only had he never seen a vegetable garden, he said his parents had 'people' who took care of the plants and yard at his house!"

Lora looked at her grandmother and saw she was beaming. Her eyes were closed and she was smiling that easy, soft smile people get when they're remembering something particularly sweet, like a baby's first laugh or the effervescence of puppy breath. Charlie noticed too and nodded for Anthony to keep talking.

"I'd never heard of such a thing and couldn't imagine a life like his. I diddn't believe it and asked him 'What about chores? Don't you and your brothers and sisters have chores?' Landon stopped talking for the first time since we'd left school. Standing there in the dirt, in his unscuffed new shoes, with a fat, red tomato in each hand, he said, 'No chores. No brothers and sisters. No nothing.' His eyes welled up and he ran back inside.

"I was terrified I would get in trouble for making my company cry, never mind it was company I didn't want in the first place. I picked a couple more tomatoes and when I couldn't delay the inevitable any longer, wandered back to the house. Imagine my surprise when I walked in to see Landon sprawled across Mama, his arms wrapped around her neck like he was dangling off a cliff, and crying his eyes out! I started trying to tell Mama I hadn't done anything to him but she just hugged him tighter and shook her head. She whispered, "I know." Even now, I don't know whether she was talking to me, or him, or both of us. Mama?"

Eva opened her eyes, dragging herself away from the memory of that trembling life in her arms. "Mm hm. I remember that day almost as clearly as you do Anthony. Landon Cook was a lost little boy. He was drowning in loneliness and elegant neglect. I'll answer both your questions."

She shared a knowing look with Lora and took a deep breath.

"I was talking to both of you. I knew why Landon was crying and I knew you hadn't done anything to upset him. I knew he needed a family because this special talent you decided I have told me so." Eva stopped talking when Marla wandered by the table with a pitcher offering refills. When she'd meandered out of ear shot, Eva said, "We can discuss this more at home but it'll suffice for now to say Landon needed a family to love him and I happened to have one with love to spare."

She crumpled her napkin onto her plate and surveyed the table. "Looks like y'all are about done. Let's wrap up the rest of the hush puppies and take'em with us."

Enduring the jibes and teasing of Anthony and Charlie about her insistence to not let anything go to waste, she wrapped the crunchy, brown balls of fried cornbread in several layers of napkin and stuffed them into her purse. Reminding them to bring their drinks along, she scooted out of the booth and headed for the exit.

Lora expected an argument about who's wallet would be lighter after the meal and wasn't disappointed when her dad and Anthony each insisted the other should put his money away. She suppressed a snicker when Eva snuck around them and paid for the meal without waiting for her sons to sort it out. Lora and Eva left them arguing and waited in the shade of the overhang, sipping tea through their straws.

"How long before they figure out they're arguing over nothing?"

"Well, let me see, your uncle is forty-two years old so, I reckon it'll be a while."

Lora laughed and nudged her grandmother with her elbow. They only had to wait a couple minutes for Anthony's head to pop out the door and call out over his shoulder, "They're out here, Charlie." In another moment, they all piled into the station wagon, hissing and trying to avoid actually sitting on the blistering hot seats. Charlie eased the Falcon onto the roadway and waved at the deputy parked along the ditch in front of the restaurant.

22

By the time they got home, the conversation and teasing had retreated into comfortable silence. They'd ridden home with the windows rolled down, each lost in thought as vast acres of cotton, soy, and corn fields sped by in a hypnotizing blur occasionally interrupted by growling, industrious farm equipment. Crawling up out of a half-doze when Charlie turned off the engine, Lora hid a yawn behind her hand and smiled when she caught Eva doing the same.

"I'm going to lay down for a few minutes. But you all have to promise to tell me the rest of the Landon story after my nap!"

Eva and Anthony, arms around each other's waists as they walked towards the house, nodded in agreement and waved her on up the stairs.

Watching Lora go, Eva said, "I tell you Charlie. That Lora is something else. You and Maeve did a fine job with her."

"Thank you, Mama. We're proud of her." He swiped his sleeve across his forehead. "I wish Maeve was here to hear you say that though. I know she's...difficult...but she means well."

Anthony stopped in his tracks and grimaced. "Means well. Hunh! She's a termagant."

Charlie fists clenched as he whirled to face his brother, his temper flaring hot enough to rival the afternoon sun. "She's my wife and I won't have you running her down."

Holding his hands up in mock surrender, Anthony said, "Easy, easy. All I'm saying is Maeve isn't anything like the same girl you started dating back in school. That girl was high-strung but sweet enough. Maeve is not."

Charlie's shoulders slumped. "She's still sweet. She's just scared. Scared of everything. Has been for a long time."

Anthony's expression shifted from amusement to concern. He sat on the top porch step and patted the space next to him, inviting his brother to sit. They sat in silence, shoulder to shoulder. Eva went on inside. She knew why Maeve had changed. She didn't know how much Anthony knew about Maeve's story and thought it was best left to Charlie to make that decision. *Well, actually, it'd be Maeve's decision if she was here,* she thought, *but since she's not, I guess it falls to Charlie to keep or share their secrets.* Sparing a glance over her shoulder at her sons, she smiled to herself as they hung their ties from the newel post. Some things never change and she'd have to remind them to bring them in before bed. Just like she'd done when they were little.

• • • •

"SO, YOU WANT TO TELL me what Maeve's afraid of?"

Charlie unbuttoned his wrists and rolled up his shirtsleeves. "Like I said, everything. She's afraid of losing our daughter to Alabama. Afraid of what could happen to her. Afraid of getting old. Afraid of getting fat. Afraid of not being needed by anyone."

"Oh come on. We're all getting old. What is there to be afraid of?"

"Some of our friends just got divorced. The husband left his wife for a younger woman. That shook her up. I mean, we used to go camping with these people and now, " he snapped his fingers," just like that, it's all gone." He loosed a sad chuckle and rolled his shirtsleeves up.

"Surely she doesn't think your eyes are wandering?" Anthony asked.

"No. I just think she's afraid of being alone. Ever."

Anthony clapped his brother on the back and said, "Ah, man. That's rough. Come on, my sweat is starting to sweat. Let's go inside."

• • • •

"WELL, HELLO CHARLIE." Maeve perched stiffly on the end of the couch nearest the open door. The smell of scorched coffee hanging in the air was an appropriate backdrop to the look on her face which told him she'd heard every word. For a blistering split second, he wondered who forgot to turn off the coffeemaker. Whoever it was left a fair amount of work for whoever might want coffee next. Realizing the irrationality of his thoughts, he drug himself back to deal with the scorching mess he would be wrangling now that Maeve was back.

His eyes shot daggers of accusation at his mother and daughter for not saying something when they'd gone in the house moments before. In their defense, Eva and Lora shook their heads in apology, pale and mute like hostages. Charlie knew his wife well enough to know she'd probably shushed them into silence and bullied them into complicity. He quickly replayed the porch-step conversation in his head, trying to decide which parts would have made his wife the maddest. Not knowing what to say, he opted for delighted ignorance and pulled her from her seat, swooping her up in an exuberant embrace. "Hey Baby! What are you doing back here?"

"Put me down!" Maeve protested. Setting her on her feet, he stepped back.

Thinking her dad resembled a Thanksgiving Day parade float losing air by the second, Lora jumped into the uneasiness to seal the leak. "Yeah Mama! We thought you'd gone back to Detroit. I'm so glad you're back. What changed your mind?"

"No you're not —," Maeve stopped mid-sentence. She shook her head and adjusted. Shaking out her hands and rolling her head on her shoulders, like a boxer preparing for his turn in the ring. With a deep inhale and tentative hand, she reached out for Charlie. Confused, he threaded his fingers through hers. Finding strength and reassurance in his grip, Maeve turned to her daughter and answered, "You did."

She gestured for them to sit and winced as her family lit softly in their places, prepared to either fight or fly. Maeve gathered herself and knelt, speaking softly to her only child. "I was fuming mad when I got on that bus yesterday morning. Mad at you for not coming home with us. Mad at your daddy for not agreeing with me. Mad at your grandmother for not protecting you. Mad at —"

"Protecting me from what?" Lora's incredulous question stopped her mother mid-sentence.

Maeve took a shaky breath, "Please. Just let me finish. Please." The corners of her mouth quirked in apology as she looked around the room.

"Like I said, I was mad. But, by the time we'd stopped for a pick-up in Nashville, I'd cooled down a little bit."

She smiled softly at Charlie. "Yes, I heard what you said before you came in. In the yard and on the porch. And you're right. I have been scared for most of my life. And yes, our friends splitting up made me more anxious. But that didn't have anything to do with why I came back."

Maeve turned her attention back to Lora. "I realized I was really mad at myself. For running away. And, I guess I've been running away most of my life, spooking at shadows, and flinching for no reason. More important, I realized I was proud of you for *not* running away. For not being like me."

Maeve leaned across to Eva's chair and took her hand. "She learned that from you." She turned to Charlie and said, "And you."

"Anyway, I figured I owed you better. You deserve a better mother than me. I'm sorry." Maeve's bottom lip trembled.

Lora had never seen her mother so willingly vulnerable. Maeve wore her emotions like armor, wound tightly, guarding against any weakness no matter how small or insignificant. Lora realized her mother's shrill, overbearing antics were the shield she carried to protect herself. "Mama, you're one of the bravest people I know." She shifted to the floor and took both of her mother's hands. "I am glad you came back. How did you get here though? You were in Nashville at what, noon yesterday?"

Maeve blushed beneath her perfectly applied make-up and stood, her knees popping a little as she straightened her legs. "I got off the bus and cashed in the balance of my ticket for dinner and a ride back to Decatur this morning. I slept, well, half-slept, in the Nashville Greyhound station. When I got to the station, I called Monroe and he sent Ellen to bring me home."

With a sheepish smile for Eva, she said, "Ellen told me you were the one who taught her how make biscuits and encouraged her to sell them at the store in the mornings. She brought a couple with her when she picked me up."

Eva wheezed a little chuckle, "Mm hm. I made that man a fortune when I taught her how to cook!"

Anthony, who couldn't stand not being the center attention for very long, said, "If you're still hungry, Mama's got some cold, greasy Greenbrier hush puppies in the bottom of her purse. I'm sure she'd be willing to share them."

Maeve tittered a shaky laugh and scrunched her nose at the idea of eating purse puppies. "I think I'll pass. Thank you though."

Eva got to her feet and shooed Anthony upstairs. "That's enough of your sass, Anthony. Make yourself useful and take Maeve's bag up to Charlie's room."

Satisfied he was following her orders, she pulled Maeve to her feet and into her arms.

Lora and Charlie didn't miss the silent tears streaking ultra-black mascara down Maeve's face as she held onto her mother-in-law like a drowning person grips a life raft. Eva patted Maeve's back and, sheltering her under one arm, guided her towards the hallway. She discreetly pulled a handkerchief from a dress pocket and handed it to Maeve, indicating she might need to stop off in the bathroom for a quick refresher.

Maeve pulled away, shook her head, and laughed. "You all have seen me at my ugliest for years and my make-up was always perfect. I think I can let you see me just as I am for once." Adding quickly, "Unless I look like a raccoon! I mean, there's natural and then there's just ridiculous!"

Charlie, Lora, and Eva assured her she looked just fine. Nevertheless, Maeve surreptitiously wrapped the handkerchief around her index finger and swiped it briskly under both eyes to minimize the weepy damage. Charlie wrapped an arm around her waist, smiled into her hair, and whispered, "You are as beautiful as the day we met. I'm glad you're here too."

She wriggled in closer and stood on her toes to kiss his cheek. "I don't deserve you Charlie Burnette."

Charlie responded by picking her up and swinging her around the living room. This time she didn't protest. Instead, he was rewarded with a brilliant smile on the face he loved most and the sound of her laughter, merrily burbling in the same way that had stolen his heart twenty-five years ago.

Lora blushed when Anthony bounded out of the stairwell and hooted, "Geez! Get a room!" on his way to the kitchen.

• • • •

LEAVING CHARLIE AND Maeve to mend their fences, Eva hummed to herself and winked at Lora. Anthony had switched off the coffee maker and was busily scrubbing burnt grounds from the pot. Lora followed her grandmother to the kitchen and they bustled around the room, dodging Anthony at the sink, clearing away debris from their hastily eaten breakfast. Maeve and Charlie weren't far behind and settled around the table.

"Eva, let Lora finish that and tell me about court this morning?" Maeve sat next to Charlie, her hand resting lightly on his knee in a rare gesture of intimacy.

Eva ran a dishcloth across the counter, sweeping crumbs into the sink and said, "Oh there's really not much to tell. Besides, Myra and her boys will be here later. Landon too, I reckon. You must be exhausted from trying to sleep in the bus station. How about you have a lie down and we'll fill you in when everyone else gets here?"

She raised an knowing eyebrow at Charlie. "Charlie, maybe you could use a nap, too?"

To Anthony and Lora, she said, "Why don't we change and take ourselves down to Monroe's for a bit? Find out the latest gossip. I'm sure I feature pretty heavy right now."

Lora's face got hot and lit up like a bright red traffic signal when she understood what her grandmother was really suggesting. Her discomfort was exacerbated and mollified a little when she realized her parents' faces were glowing as brightly as her own.

Unusually circumspect, Anthony nodded sharply and meandered off to change. Lora rushed past him and barreled up the stairs, feet skimming on the treads. Eva laughed softly all the way to her own room. *What is it about children being unsettled by the idea of their mamas and daddies being friendly with each other?* She wondered. *How do they think they got here in the first place?* Still, she was happy to see Maeve's icy demeanor starting to thaw and wasn't about to inhibit any rift-mending between the couple by hanging around the house. A walk to Monroe's would work just fine.

• • • •

LORA SHIMMIED OUT OF her court clothes and into shorts and a sleeveless button-up in less than a minute. She ran down the stairs and out the front door in her bare feet, Keds in hand, with a scant passing glance into the kitchen. Charlie and Maeve sat by the table, knee to knee, foreheads together, fingers entwined, talking quietly. One brief look and Lora's face went all hot again.

She sat on the porch step and tied her shoes while she waited for her uncle and grandmother. As soon as the screen door slammed, she jumped up like someone had fired a starting pistol in her ear. "Well! Let's go!"

Anthony, comfortable in his summer slacks and another Cuban style shirt, snickered and leaned on the railing. "What's the hurry? Monroe isn't going anywhere. You that anxious to see his warty old face?"

Eva shushed him and teased, "You know the faster we get there, the faster we get back, right?" She cackled at the look of horror on her granddaughter's face.

Anthony couldn't resist casually poking the ant hill as he helped Eva down the steps, "Your shirt is buttoned wrong. Did you know?"

Lora squinted in the sunlight at him, her arms akimbo, strands of her ponytail sticking to the sweat on the back of her neck. She checked her buttons, which were buttoned just fine, and gritted her teeth, "Let's. Just. Go."

• • • •

FINALLY IN THE SHELTERING shade of the trees stretching over the roadway, Lora, more confident with each step away from Eva's house, said, "So, Uncle Anthony, you want to finish telling Landon's story?"

He shrugged. "Sure, why not? Not much more to tell anyway. Landon's daddy picked him up in his big, shiny car that afternoon without bothering to say more than 'Hello' to mama. Landon didn't want to leave but perked up when Mama told him he could come back anytime he wanted. He walked home with me every day after that. He pulled weeds like it was the best thing he'd ever done. He was so impressed with being asked to peel potatoes, he didn't even cry when he sliced his finger open."

Anthony kicked a rock with his shoe and belly laughed, "He ruined those fancy shoes! I took him off to the creek to hunt for crawdads and he just waded right in, shoes, socks, and all! I was sure he'd get in big trouble for it but no, he showed up the next day in another new pair of perfect shoes. Like it was nothing!"

Eva interrupted, "Landon's family was old money and didn't depend on farming for a living like the rest of us. The Depression didn't seem to hit them as hard. They owned a couple grocery stores and part of a steel mill in Birmingham. Landon's granddaddy was a state representative and most expected his daddy would be too. Money was all that mattered to his parents. Sometimes it seemed like they forgot they even had a little boy." She gave a sad shake of her head.

Anthony picked up the story again. "Eventually, he practically lived with us during the school week. Like we needed another mouth to feed." He pulled a face at his mother who gave him a side-eyed look of reproach.

"There wasn't a chance I could turn that child away, you know that."

"You want to tell me why you couldn't turn him away? How exactly do you know?" Anthony rubbed his hands together like he'd just discovered an unattended chocolate pie with mile-high meringue piled on top. He widened his eyes in innocent supplication.

Eva grunted as she swatted at his backside, and laughed when he danced out of reach.

In the end, unable to resist Anthony's hangdog expression and wistful sighs, she relented. Eva explained the ache she'd sometimes feel in the furthest, deepest reaches of her heart. She told him it felt like God's hand was squeezing it just a little tighter with each beat. She told him when God squeezed, she listened. She admitted she'd felt that squeeze when Dot was getting ready to burn her house down around her, when he'd come home after fighting with Landon. She said most problems weren't that big a deal; someone needed shoes, needed feeding, or a place to sleep when passing through. There was an unspoken need and she met it. Simple as that.

While she spoke, Anthony listened closely, watching the road pass beneath his feet as he walked by her side. He raised his head suddenly and stared at her. "Is that why you were sending biscuits to Hal Johnson's house?"

"Yes." She didn't elaborate.

Ever the quick thinker, he asked, "Then why was Leon Strong involved? Why weren't you taking them yourself?"

Lora choked on her breath, frantically waving her hands at her face, throat stretched tall and thin. "Bug! I swallowed a bug!" she gasped.

Eva and Anthony took turns pounding on her back as her eyes watered and she leaned over the ditch to spit.

"There you go! You alright?" her uncle asked.

Catching her breath, she nodded, "Yeah...I think so. Blech! Nasty!"

She saw Monroe's not too far in the distance and, hoping to distract her uncle from asking any more questions, she challenged Anthony to a race, saying, "I really need that Coke now! I bet I can beat you there!" and took off running.

Anthony grinned at his mother and dashed after his niece.

Eva figured Lora's sudden insect inhalation was a bid to change the subject and appreciated Lora's quick thinking. She hummed to herself and kept on walking, not bothering to hurry.

• • • •

CHARLIE AND MAEVE CRANED their heads in the living room window, watching the others head off in the shimmering heat to Monroe's. They were a handsome couple, standing together in the muted sunlight. Charlie, tall and trim, salt and pepper hair glinting in wayward sunbeams. Maeve, petite and elegant, even after spending the night in a bus station. He'd rolled the sleeves of his white dress shirt up to his elbows, the muscles of his forearms smooth and strong as he stood behind Maeve with his arms around her shoulders. She relaxed into his chest and breathed deep, her delicate hands grasping his forearms.

Maeve tilted her face up and to the side to look at him. "If she's staying here, maybe we should get her a car? I don't like the idea of her having to walk anywhere by herself. Even if it is just to Monroe's."

Charlie hummed into Maeve's hair. "We can do that. But, I'm sure she'll be fine."

Maeve's spine stiffened as she shivered. Her voice was low, almost a whisper, when she replied, "I'm sure my daddy said that too. He was wrong."

Charlie hunkered into his wife's back, his chin over her shoulder, and hugged her tight. "You're right. I'm sure he did. And he was. We won't make that mistake. Let's go to town early in the morning get her one."

Maeve snuggled deeper into his arms and sighed. "Thank you, Charlie."

"Of course." He loosened his hug and pulled her hand to his lips, his breath warm on her fingers. "Now, Mama said something about a nap. You tired?"

"Extremely." Her husky laugh told him otherwise.

. . . .

BUSINESS WAS SLOW AT Monroe's that afternoon. The lunch rush for sandwiches had passed and the last minute stops before heading home from the fields hadn't started yet. When Eva pulled open the door, Monroe beamed. Lora and Anthony sat precariously on stools by the counter, sweating soda bottles dripping onto the floor. Judging from Lora's hand gripping the counter and the foot Anthony kept solidly planted, the stools had apparently seen better, less wobbly, days before Monroe drug them out from the storeroom in back. He'd set out a stool for her. It looked to be made of sturdier stuff than the others and she realized it was his personal perch from behind the till. Monroe was standing, leaning on his meaty elbows, head ducked beneath the Camel and Lucky Strike cigarette displays hanging overhead.

Eva smiled back at him and said, "Looks like we got time to visit and places to sit while we do! Thank you, Monroe!" She pulled a Coke from the cooler and hopped up on the borrowed seat of honor.

"So, I hear ol' Hal got something stuck in his craw this morning?" Monroe relished his role as the community news reporter.

"You could say that, although I didn't see it. Lora did." Eva gestured at her granddaughter with the soda bottle and directed his attention towards her instead.

Lora took a swig from her own bottle and nodded as she swallowed, trying to figure out how to tell him about it without actually giving anything away.

Monroe could tell she was stalling. "Myra told me you wanted to see how he'd react to seeing her boys and, it sounds like you got the reaction you were looking for."

Anthony snorted and grinned at the trusty, old shopkeep. "Oh, we got a reaction all right. Just don't know what we should do with it now."

"Myra says you think just knowing Hal recognized Leon is enough to convince Leon to stay clear for a while?"

Lora said, "Well, that's what I'd like, and what Gram wants, but Leon may have other ideas."

Monroe grunted and stood up from his leaning posture, his back popping with the effort. "If Leon is smart, he'll keep hisself at home. Still, he's always been her reckless one. So who's to say what he'll do?"

He waggled one hand in a flip-flop motion indicating he had no idea what to expect from Leon before continuing. "Now tell me. What else happened this morning? You know folks tell me the gossip but not always the facts." He laughed from deep in his throat as he said this last bit.

Lora's laughter joined his as she said, "Oh not much. Judge Underwood found out that Mr. Beatty and the Sheriff hadn't turned over all the evidence to Landon like they were told. That was entertaining. I think Mr. Beatty was so flustered at being caught out he practically dumped his entire briefcase on Landon."

Monroe's jowly cheeks wobbled as he shook his head, trying to picture it. "Good Lord I'd have loved to seen that! Frederick Beatty is a tiresome son-of-a-gun. What kind of evidence did he get?"

Eva jumped back into the conversation. "Well, I'm not sure just yet but it was a whole lot more than Landon got on Friday. We'll know more later. He's coming by for dinner tonight."

"Good, good."

Changing the subject, Eva patted Monroe's hand and said, "Thank you for your note. We had a lovely surprise visit from a deputy while we were at the river yesterday. Thank you, too, for sending Ellen to pick up Maeve this morning."

Monroe blushed and waved away her thanks. "Psshh...Don't mention it. You know there's nothing I won't do for you."

He raised his eyebrows at her and squeezed a cheeky grin before adding, "Although, I didn't have many biscuits to sell this morning since she had to go to Decatur. Thought I was going to have a riot on my hands!"

Returning to the main topic, his face fell in seriousness. "Eva, I'll tell you this. If I'd a'known you were going to catch any grief over Bumpus, I'd have never called the sheriff in the first place. I'd have gone and rolled his sorry, no-good, useless butt into the first open grave I could find. Covered him over! Wouldn'ta thought twice about it neither."

"Pfft. Don't worry yourself. I didn't have anything to do with it and no one can prove I did." She reached across the counter and gave his hand a squeeze. "I'll be just fine."

Anthony and Lora were visibly weary of balancing themselves on their wobbly stools. Eva said, "I reckon we ought to head home. Charlie and Maeve's fences ought to be close to mended by now."

Monroe's eyebrows shot up and he teased, "Oh? There's fence mending going on at your place?" He giggled like a schoolboy. "Good for Charlie!"

Eva shushed Monroe with a stifled chuckle. She was pragmatic about intimacy between a husband and wife but was pretty sure neither Charlie nor Maeve would appreciate being the butt of off-color jokes.

Once again, Lora's face lit up like a beacon and the adults around her couldn't help but laugh at her consternation. In order to divert attention from her discomfort, she asked Monroe, "Hey, since I'm here, can I ask you a question?"

Monroe nodded, eyes wide with curiosity, laughter still playing along the folds of his face.

"Well, I'll be staying with Gram from now on. Daddy said he'll pay for my tuition and school expenses, but I need to find a way to pay for everything else. Would you happen to need any help around here?"

Monroe's eyes disappeared as his spreading grin cracked his face in two. He swallowed a belly laugh; his ample girth jiggling with the effort. He looked like a little boy who'd just gotten his most wished for Christmas present. "You askin' me for a job?"

Lora grinned back. "I guess I am. If you need any help, that is."

"I think I can come up with something for you to do if you don't mind getting a little grubby."

"Grubby?" Eva asked. "What you need doing that requires getting grubby?"

"Aw, nothing bad, Eva. You ought to know me better than that!" He waved her down with a lazy swipe of his hand. "Naw, Ellen and me was just saying the other day that we're getting too old and creaky to clean off shelves and keep up with the floors around here. And, since we ain't got any kids, it'd be nice to have somebody to take care of those things for us."

He turned his attention back to Lora, all business now. "I can pay you $1.25 an hour and provide breakfast or lunch depending on when you're here. I'm happy to work around your class schedule but need to know I can count on you to be here when you say you'll be. Until school starts, can you come by on Mondays, Wednesdays, and Fridays for four hours a day?"

Lora was amazed by the immediate offer. And the idea of earning her own money? Well, that was relish on the hot dog! She was thrilled and couldn't imagine she'd get any grubbier at the store than she would working in Gram's garden. Suddenly, she was immensely grateful for the time she'd spent on her hands and knees pulling weeds every summer. Hard work didn't scare her and now it looked sure to pay off.

She reached to shake his hand, saying "I sure can!" But, on impulse, she wound up leaning across the counter and hugging the old man instead. Monroe, obviously flustered and shocked, quickly thumped his hands on her back before disentangling himself and saying, "Um. Sounds good. Maybe let's not start off by hugging your boss."

Eva and Anthony laughed at Lora's excitement and Monroe's embarrassment, both slipping off their stools to leave.

Monroe rapped his knuckles on the counter and said, "I know you won't be able to work on Wednesday, what with the trial and all, but if you want to stop in for an hour or two tomorrow, I can show you around a bit."

Lora smiled and nodded. She even promised not to try to steal any gum. Monroe rewarded her joke by quickly retorting, "Oh don't you worry. I'll be keeping a close count on how many pieces are in the box before and after you leave every day." He laid a finger beside his nose and put on his best wizened old man expression.

Smiling, Monroe shifted his gaze to Eva. "I'll let you know whatever I hear. Ought to be easy now that I've hired a runner." He winked at Lora and she was even happier she'd asked for a job.

The screen door squeaked a warning. Deputy Ross stepped over the threshold.

"Well hello, Miss Lora!" The deputy sounded delighted to see her again.

Lora felt the tips of her ears go hot. "Hello."

Deputy Ross nodded over her shoulder at Monroe, Eva, and Anthony who made a show of ignoring them. The deputy smiled, pulling his dimples in towards each other. He leaned in slightly, fidgeting his hands around the brim of his hat. "I saw you in court this morning. Didn't get the chance to speak."

Lora's face tingled all the way to her hairline. "That's okay. I didn't feel much like talking." She waved a hand in Eva's direction and pulled a wisp of hair from her ponytail to chew on the ends. "I guess it's your turn to keep an eye on Gram?"

Deputy Ross flushed pink and said, "Oh I'm not keeping tabs on her. The sheriff had to call in the reserve deputies to do that."

"Why? What does he think she's going to do? Run off?" Lora's eyes bulged in irritation.

"I don't know what he thinks. I know me and the rest of us regulars think this whole thing is stupid. We wish he'd left well enough alone."

Lora relaxed a little and leaned on the counter, twisting the strand of hair around one of her fingers. "Since you think this is stupid, can you tell me why no one brought Gram to her arraignment on Friday? Like the sheriff said he'd asked?"

Deputy Ross's smile stretched from ear to ear as he leaned back and laughed. "Oh well, that. Yeah, the guy he asked decided that not bringing her would make Griffin look as dumb as this case. He was right, too, wasn't he?" His eyes crinkled. "The sheriff was hopping mad after court and blasted every one of us for it at the next roll-call. It was all we could do to keep straight faces on while he ranted!"

Lora let out a puff of air. "So, Griffin wasn't trying to make Gram look bad? That was the deputies...what? Protesting?"

"Yes ma'am. That's precisely what happened." He held his chest now, trying to keep his laughter to a low rumble.

His laughter was contagious and Lora giggled along with him. She found her breath and burbled, "Oh. Well. I guess that is pretty funny. He looked ridiculous sprinting out the courtroom to go get her!" She mimicked the sheriff's long strides and flailing arms, like a marionette whose strings were too short.

Deputy Ross lost what control he'd had over his laughter and roared at her antics.

Behind him, Monroe and company smirked, nodding their approval.

• • • •

A DUSTY, WHEEZING FARM truck pulled up to the gas pump as the Burnettes stepped off the store porch to head back to Eva's house. The driver waited until they'd made it to the tree line before getting out of the cab. Anthony commented on how fortunate they were to have had fifteen whole, uninterrupted minutes to catch up with Monroe. Eva burped, covering her mouth with her hand, and said, "Mm hm. He stays pretty busy. I hope his friendship with me isn't causing him any problems."

"Not a chance, Mama. He's the only store for miles. Folks have to shop at his place whether they like it or not," Anthony replied with supercilious satisfaction.

Lora beamed at her uncle. Despite the deputy induced smile on her face, Lora was unhappy with the idea that Eva would worry about anything other than herself for the next couple days at least. She piped up, willing to embarrass herself to keep the conversation from drifting into murky waters, "You think we've given Mom and Dad enough time to...whatever? I mean, should we just keep on walking?"

Her grandmother and uncle teased her, saying they figured they'd been gone long enough. By the time they'd reached Eva's front porch, Lora's discomfort subsided and she was glad to hear the radio playing when Anthony tugged the screen door open.

23

"Hey! We were wondering if y'all were lost." Charlie called out when he saw them coming through the front door. His shirttails were untucked and his hair a bit mussed but otherwise, he was relatively put together. Maeve waved at them as she pulled a skillet from the cupboard. She looked perfect as usual with the exception of being barefooted. Lora couldn't remember her mother ever walking around without shoes on. She even wore slippers on the beach when they went to the Lake St. Clair back home! Lora squinted with suspicion but kept her thoughts to herself. Some things, she decided, just weren't her business.

"Eva, I hope you don't mind but I scrounged around in your pantry and found enough ingredients to make something along the lines of Chicken a la King for supper tonight. You didn't have any mushrooms but that shouldn't matter too much. No rice or noodles either but it's good over biscuits and there's plenty of those left." Maeve stopped, realizing she was rambling, and quickly added, "I just thought you might enjoy a night off from cooking for all of us."

Eva marveled at the sudden change in her daughter-in-law. She was skeptical that merely facing the consequences of a temper tantrum was enough to turn Maeve around. Willing to extend the benefit of doubt, Eva again felt guilty for thinking so poorly of her daughter-in-law. Still, she had a hard time believing this particular tiger changed her stripes literally overnight.

"I'm sure it'll be delicious. Thank you, Maeve." Eva admired Maeve's preparations and made all the expected and appropriate noises about how good it smelled and tasty it looked.

Anthony flopped onto the couch and Charlie commandeered Eva's rocker to watch television. Lora landed the job of channel changer and antenna adjuster while the brothers debated and decided which of the two local afternoon news broadcasts they preferred. Anthony eventually declared the news was too boring to keep his attention and asked her to switch off the tube. Lora twitched an irritated eye at her uncle but did as he asked and went outside to enjoy the scant breeze in the shade of the front porch.

Sinking into one of the creaky rockers and propping her feet up on the railing, Lora looked up. She'd always loved Eva's 'haint blue' porch ceiling. When she was little, Eva told her some folks believed porch ceilings should be painted a pale blue because it kept evil spirits away. Eva enjoyed a ghost story as much as the next person but told Lora she didn't believe in evil spirits. Still, she did believe a sky blue porch ceiling kept dirt daubers, wasps, and swallows from building their homes in the corners and to that end, she entertained the blue porch ceiling tradition. Lora scanned the corners. Finding no evidence of nesting insects or birds, Lora concluded Eva must be right and thought it was a shame there was no special paint for keeping sheriffs away. She pushed her feet gently against the railing to recline the chair further back on its rockers and closed her eyes.

Lora had no idea how long she'd been dozing when she heard gravel crunching under tires as a vehicle pulled in Eva's drive. She opened one eye, saw it was Landon Cook's truck, and struggled to pull herself out of her half-sleep. She definitely wanted to be part of any conversations he was having.

"Hey! Whatcha doin? Checking your eyelids for holes?" he teased, bounding up the steps. He tugged his tie over his head and hung it on the post with the others left behind by Charlie and Anthony.

"As a matter of fact, yes. Happily, they are hole-free," she retorted.

She beat him to the door and they stumbled over the protocol for who should be opening the door for whom in this situation, both laughing by the time they managed to jostle across the threshold.

"Come on get up!" Landon chided his friends, waving his briefcase at Anthony and Charlie. "We have things to discuss!" He emphasized 'things' like a movie trailer announcer.

Eva leaned out of her seat at the kitchen table, where she'd been chatting with Maeve, peered into the living room and lowered her eyebrows. "Things? You got things that need discussing? Don't you think you ought to be telling me and not worrying with those two?"

Landon managed a chastised smirk. "Of course, Eva."

He looked back at Anthony and Charlie and said, "Change of plans. You two stay put."

Eva scowled at him. "You think you're so cute, don't you?"

Not giving him time to answer because she knew what his response would be, she sighed. "Come on y'all. Let's hear what things my attorney has to say!"

Her invitation to the table was unnecessary. They were making their way to their favorite seats before the words were out of her mouth.

Landon dropped his briefcase onto the kitchen table, removed the stack of papers he'd received from Mr. Beatty earlier. The entire pile was tabbed and organized into manila folders. Lora was impressed. Based on the state of his desk, she hadn't pegged him as being particularly organized.

Anthony propped his elbows on the back of the chair he'd straddled. "Okay, whatcha got?"

Landon hooted, "Everything."

He pulled out a paper-clipped set of documents. "These are the warrants. The one for your plate is on top; your arrest is underneath." He slid them to Eva.

"These are the fingerprint reports and they back up what Deputy Ross told us on Saturday. The only identifiable prints on the graveyard plate are yours, Hal Johnson's, and Bumpus's. Other prints are noted but as the examiner had no prints to compare them with,

they are unidentified." He slid this stack to Eva as well. She shuffled
the warrants to Maeve.

Landon asked Eva, "I assume at least one of the unidentified
prints would belong to Leon Strong. Is that right?"

She nodded.

"Do you think the others might belong to Hal's children?"

"Well, that would make sense. My plate of biscuits was in the
Johnson house."

"Mm hm. That's what I figure as well."

Eva fixed him with an expansive, stern look. "We are not about
to try and implicate any of those children either, Landon."

"No. No. I agree. I just want to know who could reasonably be
expected to have touched the graveyard plate."

"Following up on the fingerprints. You were right, Eva. The day
Griffin seized the plate from your house, and tried to trick you into
giving up your prints at the station, Hal Johnson was there being
printed. I checked the register and he signed in with the clerk. That's
important."

No one realized how intently they were listening to Landon
until everyone jumped at a sudden squeal from the back door. Myra,
Maurice, and Leon let themselves in. The Burnette family and
Landon tittered nervously and welcomed the three-some to the most
depressing party, outside of a wake, any of them had ever been to.

Quickly exchanging hello's while shuffling and scooting chairs,
Eva brought the newcomers up-to-speed on the information Landon
was sharing.

Myra raised a questioning eyebrow at Eva and jerked her head in
Maeve's direction, silently mouthing, "I thought she left!"

Eva eyeballed her friend and mouthed back, "Later," before
directing her attention back to Landon.

"Go ahead Landon. What else?"

He took a deep breath. "They matched blood and hair from the plate to Bumpus. All that proves is that someone hit him with it. Doesn't prove you did the hitting. But, here's the kicker. And most puzzling piece if you ask me. You remember Mr. Beatty said he had witnesses? Well, I have the witness list but none of their statements—" He held up a stalling hand as questions burbled to the surface.

"That in itself isn't unusual. It is only required that the prosecution disclose who is on their witness list. Not necessarily what they will say. Now, what I want to know is..." he looked at Eva. "What on earth do you think Agnes Crawford could have to say about this?"

Eva's face registered shock and betrayal. "Agnes? You're sure that's who it says?"

She took the witness list from him, her hand shaking as she reached for it. Disbelief took the place of shock as she shook her head, "I have no idea, Landon. Truthfully. I have no idea."

Eva put her hand to her heart and closed her eyes.

Lora hurried to her grandmother's side. "Gram, are you okay? Are you having another one of your spells?" She was hesitant to ask about Eva's gift in front of so many other people. Family, just-like family, or not, Lora knew everyone present didn't know about Eva's gift and she wasn't inclined to add that unsettling information on top of everything else.

Eva shook her head. "No. I'm fine. I just. Well, Agnes is my friend. I can't imagine what she would have to say against me. Or why she'd be willing to say it in the first place!"

Myra patted Eva's arm and understood. Some two-facedness stung more sharply than others. She didn't know what Agnes Crawford would say about Eva either but she was sure it was just as false as the cheery "Avon calling!" mask Agnes wore whenever she knocked on doors to make money off friends and enemies alike.

Eva covered Myra's patting hand with her own and in a thick voice said, "Thank you."

She looked at Landon and said, "Go on," as she straightened in her chair and lifted her chin.

"That's really about it, Eva." He looked around the table. "It seriously looks as though the state is hinging their entire case on the fingerprints and whatever Agnes Crawford might have to say. There's no mention of a young Black man, Hal Johnson's potential involvement, nothing."

Leon stretched a long arm out and jabbed a pointed finger into the table. "So, you telling us that this case is as flimsy as the paper you're holding? All you gotta do is mention that Hal Johnson's prints are on the graveyard plate and poof! It's all done?"

Landon smiled and waggled his hand in a so-so gesture. "Essentially, yes. It's not really that simple but pretty much."

Leon crowed in triumph and punched the air above his head. Myra jerked the back of Leon's shirt when he looked ready to jump up in a victory dance. Maurice rolled his eyes and Lora fought with herself. She wanted to jump and celebrate with Leon but read the room correctly and stayed seated. Still, their expressions were so similar, grins plastered across their faces, eyes dancing in delight, they could have been photo negatives of each other.

Charlie brought the tone back down to earth by asking, "This is all good but what are you going to do with it? You have to convince Judge Underwood, the man who signed these warrants, that Hal's prints matter. That he had just as much reason to konk Bumpus as Mama would. And I think it's safe to assume Agnes Crawford is going to speak to why Mama would want him dead." He gestured at the witness list. "I mean, surely Griffin can't speak to motive?"

Landon grimaced. "I think that's a safe assumption about Agnes Crawford. I wish we could figure out what she's planning to say."

He ran his hands through his hair. "But you're right. Without substantial evidence to back up his statements, any theory Griffin might have about motive would be pure conjecture.

"As for what I'm going to do with all this, I plan to point the finger long and hard at Hal Johnson. I plan to ask what the state did to seek out the owners of the other fingerprints on the graveyard plate. I plan to make it very, very clear that Griffin and Beatty were looking for an easy and sensational win. I will show Underwood that his court has been disrespected. That's what I plan to do."

Landon's face lit up when he spoke about his plans for Wednesday. They were shocked when he added "Oh, and I'm calling Hal Johnson as a defense witness."

"What?" Lora gasped, "Mr. Johnson hates Gram! Or acts like he does anyway...what makes you think he would be a good defense witness? Especially if you're going to accuse him of this!" The others echoed her questions and concerns.

Eva's attorney leaned back in his seat and laced his fingers behind his head. "I'm not going to accuse him. I'll just be suggesting he's as likely a culprit as Eva. He'll be as good a defense witness as Agnes Crawford will be a prosecution witness. Trust me."

Anthony snorted and shoved away from the table and exited out the back door, muttering "Trust me" the whole way. His dramatic exit adjourned the meeting and the table dissolved into discussion and gossip.

. . . .

LANDON STEPPED OUT to the front porch. His shoulders hunched in disappointment. He'd shoved his hands into his pants pockets and leaned against the railing, searching the woods across the road for answers that weren't there. Lora followed him outside, the screen door announcing her presence. He lifted his chin in her direction.

"Hey. You okay?"

"I just...well, after all these years, I hoped Anthony would trust me with this." He ran an agitated hand through his hair. "It is what I do for a living after all."

Lora hopped up on the railing, her back to the road. "If it helps at all, I trust you."

Landon grunted and smiled at her. "Actually, it does." His face brightened for a split second and then fell. "I need to tell you, you were right about Lovenia. Apparently, Hal stopped by my office after he stormed out of the courtroom this morning and told her what happened. I came back to a locked door and a resignation letter on my desk. She quit."

Lora gasped. "Really? Just like that?" She waved her arms in a conjuring flail and threw herself off balance, nearly falling off the railing.

Landon clutched her arm to keep her upright. "Yep. Just like that. Which means, I have a problem. I need someone to help out. You have a good head on your shoulders. Would you be interested in working for me?"

Jumping down from the railing to keep herself from falling over again, Lora's eyebrows shot up and her mouth popped open. "Are you serious? You want me to work for you?"

Landon, delighted by her reaction, chuckled. "Completely serious. Well, what do you say?"

Lora steadied herself and gushed, "I'd love to work for you, Mr. Cook. But, I have no idea what to do in a law office. What about school? And the phone? I can't be there all the time."

Landon held up a finger to interrupt. "All I really need is someone to type things, transcribe dictation, organize documents, that sort of thing. It's just me in the office nowadays so the work load won't be too much and we can work around your school schedule. You're enrolling in the secretary program, right?"

She nodded.

"Wonderful. This will let you use what you learn in the classroom to work and will help me out tremendously. I'll put a note on the door telling folks to come back later when you can't be there. I'll either answer the phone myself or people can call back. Heck, you can work on assignments there when I don't have anything for you to do."

Lora lifted her chin and arched an eyebrow at him. She squared her feet and crossed her arms over her chest in challenge. "Monroe just offered me $1.25 an hour plus whatever I eat or drink for free while I'm working. Your job will require driving to town everyday, which means gas money, and I'm guessing bringing my own lunches and drinks. Not to mention I'll have to buy new clothes. Professional clothes."

Landon smirked and planted his hands behind him on the railing while he sized up his opponent. "I see. I can offer you $1.50 an hour, all the coffee and water you want, space in the refrigerator for anything you bring to eat or drink, and...I'll buy your textbooks each quarter."

Lora hesitated for effect, making a show of considering his offer before she grinned. "If you tell Monroe you just stole his first employee, you'll have a deal." She thrust her hand out to seal the deal.

Landon grinned and whistled through his teeth. "You drive a hard bargain. I think I can still outrun Monroe. Let's hope so anyway."

A firm handshake clinched the agreement. Lora would come to the office for a couple hours in the morning to get the lay of the land.

Lora bounced into the house, twisting a thick chunk of her ponytail through her fingers. Lost in thought, she ran headlong, nose-to-chest, into Leon as he was making his way across the living room. Leon hadn't been paying attention to where he was going either, although his reason was more serious than any new job excitement. He was on his way to find Landon Cook himself when his mother distracted him, calling out for him to bring Lora inside.

"Heya! There you are! My mama's looking for you." Leon gripped her shoulders to steady them both and jerked his head in the direction of the kitchen. The vision of her left eye went dark and she lost her balance as pain bloomed behind the socket. His hands were warm on her upper arms, supportive through the momentary swoon.

Lora shook her head, her vision clearing and blue eyes going wide, searching Leon's coffee browns. She gasped. "Oh. Oh my! Really?"

Leon nodded gravely, before breaking into a wide, smirking grin. "I wondered when you'd figure it out. Keep it to yourself for now, please? Don't worry. I got you."

Realizing they were hanging on to each other like debris in a whirlwind, they awkwardly jumped back a step apiece, both laughing nervously.

"Sorry about stepping on your foot, Leon."

"No problem. I got nine other toes." He said, stepping to one side for her to pass. He intended to have his own conversation with Eva's attorney.

· · · ·

LANDON, LOST IN HIS own thoughts and pleased with himself, was staring into the woods again. He jumped when the screen door slammed behind him. Expecting Lora, he was surprised to see Leon leaning against the wall, picking at a hangnail.

"Hey there Leon." Landon stuck his hand out.

Leon shook Landon's hand, sure to grasp firmly and look the other man in the eye.

Landon straightened, not missing the challenge in Leon's handshake. "What can I do for you?"

"Well, Mr. Cook, can you tell me how sure you are that this case is going to go Miss Eva's way?"

Landon leaned back against the rail and crossed his arms over his chest, considering his answer before speaking. "It'd take a slam-dunk witness statement from Agnes Crawford to sway the Judge into a guilty verdict. Everything else is easily explained away or so completely circumstantial, it's not worth considering."

"What if I told you I could make anything Miss Crawford said completely useless?"

"If you're suggesting I put you up as an alternative—"

Leon chuckled and batted the suggestion away like an irritating gnat. "Oh. No no no. You and me both know Miss Eva wouldn't have that. Even if it would work out better and easier for her. Naah, I'm interested in saving her. And, I'm working on something that oughtta work just as good. Can you come to our place around 7:00 tonight?"

This, the planning and guessing and strategizing, was the part of his job he enjoyed most. Landon smiled conspiratorially at Leon and said, "Sure. Why not? What have I got to lose?"

Leon glanced quickly back into the house through the door and snickered. "You might lose something if you eat whatever Lora's mama made for supper. Chicken la Something." He snurled a nostril in the attorney's direction. "You gonna want to eat at my house."

Landon grinned, clapped Leon on the shoulder, and agreed dirt from Myra's floor would probably be better than Maeve's Chicken la Something.

24

E va, Myra, and Maeve stayed in the kitchen while everyone else dispersed and Anthony stomped around the backyard. Myra, unwilling to wait for Eva's explanation, fired an inquiring shot at Maeve.

"So, how come you decided to come back?"

Maeve stifled the immediate, automatic urge to tell Myra what she did was none of her business. Instead, she swallowed her pride and said, "Well, I realized I made a mistake by leaving and wanted to come back to help however I can."

Myra's nostrils flared as she crunched the ice from her glass. "Is that so? 'Zactly how do you think you gonna be able to help? I've known you a long time and you ain't never been one for helping nobody if it didn't help yourself too. What's different now?"

Eva, startled and amused by Myra's directness, inhaled a sharp, stabbing breath and held it, waiting Maeve's response.

Maeve took a long, deep drink, clutching her glass tightly in both hands. She stared at Myra over the rim. She swallowed and sucked on her teeth for a moment before answering.

"You're not wrong. I am not the most charitable person. And, you have good reason to distrust me—"

Myra jerked forward and slapped her hand on the table. All pretense of friendliness gone as she glared at Eva's daughter-in-law. Realizing she was in one of very few safe places a woman like her could let loose, she allowed a lifetime of resentment and frustration at third-class citizenship to froth around the edges of her words as she spoke.

"You right about that! Do you know it took my cousin two years to find a job after that stunt you pulled at the Ben Jaffe's? Two years! Do you even care? Two years of being called a thief! Two years of not being able to help her family. Two years of feeling like a burden! All because you wanted a pair of stockings you couldn't afford." Myra's sneer gave face to palpable disdain oozing from the pores of her skin, mingling with the temper-driven sweat gathering at her hairline.

Maeve lowered her hands into her lap and willed herself not to fight back or cry. She whispered. "No. I didn't realize any of that. And since I'm being honest, I haven't given it or her a second thought in years."

She blinked several times and looked up at the ceiling, determined not to let any more tears fall than she'd already lost that day. "I can't do anything now to make it right, except apologize. I'm sorry. Truly."

Myra snorted, still fuming, and leaned back in her chair with a thud, the back supports creaking in protest. She was seething. "You didn't bother taking responsibility for what you did until you thought it was going to cost you Charlie. Steep price to pay for a pair of stockings. Still, even that wouldn't have been nearly as steep as the price my cousin paid for no reason other than your selfishness. It ain't me you ought to be apologizing to...but, since she's moved off all the way to Mobile, I guess I'll just have to tell her what you said."

Maeve stretched an open hand across the table to Myra, imploring the other woman to accept her meager olive branch. "I know it's not much in the grand scheme of things but I hope you will give me the chance to prove I'll do better from here on out."

After a tense moment of hesitation, Myra grudgingly took Maeve's hand in a tight squeeze, even if her face still looked like a thundercloud ready to burst open at any moment.

Maeve's gaze swept to meet Eva's. Eva nodded gently. She'd been silent through the exchange, watching her dearest friend and her daughter-in-law hammer out a thin peace after more than twenty years of scantily clad tolerance.

Breaking the tension and searching for a way to calm the maelstrom of emotions swirling across her kitchen table, Eva patted her hands on her knees and asked, "Did either of y'all see where Lora got off to?"

The other women shook their heads. Myra called to Leon in the living room, where the men had retreated to do whatever men do when there's nothing that needs doing, and asked him to find Lora.

. . . .

LORA'S AMUSEMENT AT her run-in with Leon in the living room died when she entered the kitchen. Although the ladies were seated where she'd left them, Lora could tell she'd walked in on the tail-end of a reckoning. She just wasn't sure who won and who lost.

Myra beckoned for her to join them at the table and smiled. She shuffled her chair underneath her to make room for Lora to pass behind. Lora slipped easily into the seat next to Myra and asked, "Leon said you were looking for me?"

Myra slurped an ice cube out of her glass as she nodded. Shifting the cube to one cheek, she said, "Mm hm. I saw the way you hopped-to when Deputy Ross was here the other day and wondered if you might be sweet on him. I figured now was as good a time as any to ask you about it. You know, seeing as how we got nothing to do now but wait."

Maeve's jaw dropped as she looked from Myra to Lora. The blush blooming on Lora's cheeks told on her and Maeve wondered how she could have missed it.

"Um. Well. I don't think it'd be accurate to say I'm sweet on him but...he is handsome. And, he doesn't agree with the way Sheriff Griffin has handled this whole Bumpus thing."

Eva chuckled. "Oh he's handsome. That's for sure."

Lora attempted to smile but managed a half-grimace as she kept talking, the tips of her ears warming up. "And, he asked if he could call on me sometime once the trial is over. I told him yes. On the condition that Gram is found not-guilty." She clapped her hands over her face in embarrassment, trying to hide the secret pleasure she'd felt when Deputy Ross had asked.

"Lora!" Maeve interjected. "Why didn't you tell me?"

Unwilling to take her hands away just yet, Lora's muffled reply was a quick reminder to Maeve that she'd missed quite a bit, even when she was in the room. "There wasn't time and you wouldn't have listened anyway!"

It was Maeve's turn to blush and stammer, "Apparently." She tossed a wicked glance at Myra and said, "So, Myra, tell me what I missed and all about this hopping-to my daughter did."

"Mother!" Lora scrambled out from behind the table and darted out the back door, leaving behind a trail of cackling women in her wake, news of Landon's job offer temporarily forgotten.

• • • •

ANTHONY DOZED UNDER the oak tree. His arms folded across his chest, head leaned back against the deep grooves of the ancient bark, legs stretched out long in front of him. Lora stomped her way through the sweltering afternoon heat to join him.

Without opening his eyes, Anthony warned, "If you're coming out here to talk my ears off, you need to just keep on walking."

"Fine," she grumbled and huffed herself onto the ground beside him and imitated his pose, their shoulders just barely touching.

"Uuunhhh...don't touch me. The air is too thick today for being so close to another person. Scoot over."

Lora huffed again and scooted over a few inches, refusing to give him a reason to run her off.

After a few minutes contemplating the busy kind of silence one hears in the country, Lora sighed heavily. She shifted her shoulder blades against the rough tree bark and sighed again.

Anthony opened one eye and swiveled his head around to look at her, "What?"

"Oh, nothing."

He closed his eye and resettled himself, slouching lower against the tree. Lora listened as his breath slowed, flowing in and out like the tide. The cicadas were tuning up for their evening serenade. Birds whistled and chirped, declaring undying, seasonal love for each other. In the underbrush along the property's edge, Lora caught the gentle cooing of doves as they scurried to and fro in search of tasty morsels hidden in the leaves. Occasionally, a truck or tractor would rumble by in front of the house, unseeing and unseen by either the tree-sitters or tractor drivers.

Eventually, Lora couldn't stand the noisy stillness any longer and said, "Uncle Anthony?"

He groaned and scrunched his eyes more firmly shut. Lora wasn't sure whether he was listening or just wanted her to stop talking. She opted for the former and forged ahead.

"Why'd you storm out when Mr. Cook said 'Trust me'? I thought you trusted him to defend Gram?"

Anthony groaned again and heaved himself upright. Pulling his legs up, and resting his arms on his bent knees, he said, "I trust that he will defend her to the best of his ability. And, knowing him as long as I have, I know his abilities to be pretty convincing, I guess is the best word. But, I don't want him to go into that courtroom on Wednesday thinking this is an un-loseable case. If he goes in all arrogant and cocksure, he might miss something important. Mama has decided to let Judge Underwood pass judgment and if Landon misses a single trick, that weasel Beatty could pull a magic rabbit out of his hat and win."

Lora hadn't considered Mr. Cook's confidence in this light before and wished she hadn't asked.

She got to her feet, brushing away the moss and leaves which had stuck to her sweating legs.

"I'm sure it's getting close to supper time. Mom made Chicken a la King for us. You ought to think about coming in and washing up."

Anthony, none too excited about eating any of Maeve's cooking, waved her on ahead and muttered something about taking himself into town for a steak dinner from Jerry's instead.

. . . .

SURE ENOUGH, PREPARATIONS for the evening meal were almost complete when Lora returned to the kitchen. Pulling open the backdoor, the inviting aroma of rich fresh tea steeping on the stove enveloped her in a warm embrace. She always looked forward to watching the tornado of sugar crystals dissolve in the concentrated hot tea as it was stirred before being mixed with cold water. It was her favorite part of making tea. Eva and Maeve were working in tandem heating the chicken, fixing the sides, and warming the biscuits.

"Where's Miss Myra?" Lora asked.

Eva glanced up from the pot she was stirring. "Oh, she and the boys had to go on home. Myra said something about Desmond burning the house down if he tried making dinner."

Maeve shot a reproachful look at her daughter, "We certainly understand that concern, don't we, Lora?"

Lora's lips thinned, pulling down at the corners, making her look like a pouting toad. She was not pleased about being reminded of the time, several years ago, when she'd started a grease fire in their kitchen while cooking bacon. The kitchen curtains were a complete loss and the entire house smelled of smoke and scorched Formica for days. Insult was added to injured pride when Maeve insisted Lora clean up any remnants of salt and baking soda left along the cracks and crevices after the fire had been extinguished.

Eva chuckled under her breath. "Everybody has to start at least one grease fire on their way to being a good cook."

Maeve rolled her eyes but laughed and surprised them all when she clicked on the radio and tuned it to a country-and-western station. Recognizing the entirely wrong-for-the-situation, yet catchy, strains of Johnny Cash's "Folsom Prison Blues" thrumming from the speaker, Lora hustled to the window to change the channel. Radio static filled the silence while Lora fiddled with the tuning knob. She was horrified to hear Eva singing the words softly in the background.

Settling on the only other clearly received channel, Lora was thankful when the upbeat, easy twang of Lovin' Spoonful's "Did You Ever Have to Make Up Your Mind?" drowned out Eva's singing. She did not want to encourage her grandmother's contemplation of spending time in prison. One night in jail was more than enough.

Maeve and Eva stood in the middle of the kitchen, in wordless consensus, with their hands on their hips and surveyed the meal. Eva nodded sharply and said, "Maeve, how about you do the honors and call 'em to the table?"

Knowing it was a small gesture that wouldn't matter to most, Maeve flushed with pride. To her knowledge, Eva had never asked anyone else to ring the proverbial dinner bell before. A broad smile etched it's way across her face as she channeled her inner-southern mama and hollered, "It ain't gonna eat itself!" before disintegrating into laughter so silly and giddy it took her breath away.

Eva and Lora laughed along with her and prepared for the inevitable rush to the table.

Anthony swung the back door open and sauntered into the kitchen, the back of his shirt wet with sweat, dirt and leaves clinging to the seat of his pants. He made his entrance so soon after Maeve's yell that Lora suspected he'd been sitting on the stoop, waiting for the call. It didn't look like he was going to Jerry's after all. Charlie stumbled in from the living room, an unruly sprig of hair sticking straight up from the crown of his head and the sleepy startled expression on his face indicating he'd been napping.

Lora peered into the living room and asked, "Did we lose Mr. Cook, too?"

Charlie cleared the sleep from his throat and said, "Yeah. He left not long after Myra and the boys. Said he needs tonight and tomorrow to go back over the details."

He scratched his head, smoothing the wayward sprig, and looked at his mother. "He said he might come out tomorrow night but, if he can't make it, he wants to meet up with us at his office at 7:00 in the morning on Wednesday. You know, to go over everything."

Eva's brows furrowed. She didn't like the idea of showing up for her own trial without knowing the plan exactly. Trusting someone is one thing; blind faith is a whole 'nother animal.

While everyone helped their plates and found their seats, Lora turned the volume down on the radio and said, "In other news, Mama, Daddy, you're looking at the new secretary of Cook, Cook & Puckett, Attorneys at Law. I start in the morning." She sat primly in her seat, pleased at the shocked expressions on her parents' faces.

Their reaction was precisely the one she hoped for. Her feathers had been more than a little ruffled by their prickly stance on her education and expenses after moving in with her grandmother. And, her mother's almost violent protest to the idea of her daughter working for Monroe made this small accomplishment a little bit sweeter. Not only had she gotten a job, on her own, she'd gotten a good one with an understanding boss, who, she was sure would never take advantage of her inexperience or begrudge her time spent in class.

Maeve coughed, choked on her chicken, and pounded a hand on her chest as the too-large bite worked its way down her throat. She grimaced. "A job at Landon's? Tomorrow?" She gulped some tea and wiped away the tiny tears which clustered at the corners of her eyes when her chicken momentarily rendered her breathless.

Lora smiled in triumph and nodded. "Mm hm. He's paying a dollar-fifty an hour, will work around my schooling, and agreed to pay for my books each quarter."

Charlie was impressed. "Look at you! That's a pretty good deal. When did this happen?" He flipped a questioning eyebrow at his mother to see if she'd known anything about this new development.

Eva shrugged her shoulders and dabbed a napkin to her lips.

Lora answered him. "Today. When he and I were chatting on the porch. Of course, this was after Monroe offered me a job helping out at the store."

Maeve spluttered a little more at this news, choking out, "When did Monroe offer you a job?"

"When me, Gram and Uncle Anthony walked down to the store while you and Daddy were...doing whatever it was you were doing." Lora willed herself not to get flustered at the thought of her parents' unsupervised time alone.

"I asked him if he could use any help around the store and he said I could come by a few days a week. Of course," she scooped a spoonful of chicken onto a warm split biscuit, "I won't be doing that now." She shoved a heaping bite of biscuit and chicken into her mouth and smiled at her father with cheeks full enough to rival any autumn squirrel.

By this time, Maeve had gotten her swallowing sorted out and reinserted herself in the conversation. She held up her fork to get their attention. "Well, this is a lot to digest. Two jobs in one day!" Maeve blinked wide brown eyes around the table. "So, when are you going to tell Monroe his first ever employee has quit on him?"

Lora gazed smugly around a mouthful of chicken and biscuit. "I'm not. I made telling Monroe a condition of my employment with Mr. Cook. He has to tell him!"

Everyone laughed and wished they could be a fly on the wall to watch Monroe's reaction. They knew he'd lay into Landon with thick theatrical betrayal for no other reason than entertainment and dramatic effect. They also knew Landon would play along.

Charlie reached for his tea and dropped a wise gaze on his daughter. "That's great, Honey. You really ought to stop in and talk to Monroe yourself, though. He won't begrudge you an office job but it's only right that you go see him. If you're old enough to ask for a job, you're old enough to explain why you're not taking that job after all."

Heads bobbed in agreement around the table, including Lora's. "Of course, Daddy. Even if I wanted, which I don't, I couldn't exactly avoid the store or Monroe. I just thought it'd be fun to put Mr. Cook in the frying pan for a bit." She rested her fork on the edge of her plate. "Can I use your car tomorrow?"

Charlie felt Maeve studying his face for any sign he was going to ruin the new-car surprise they'd planned. He didn't look at his wife, instead tossing an apologetic half-smile at Lora. "I'm sorry but no. Your mother and I have some errands to run in the morning. Maybe Mama will let you borrow her truck?"

Eva wiped her mouth and nodded enthusiastically. "Sure thing! I was planning to stick close to home all day tomorrow anyway. No need to go traipsing all over the place when there's work to do around here. Anthony can help me with the laundry."

Anthony grumbled into his plate. "This is why I don't come home more often."

Eva just smiled and patted his hand.

Maeve winked at Charlie across the table and raised both her eyebrow and her glass in his direction, giving him the silent toast of parents who know which battles are worth fighting and which are best left alone.

Anthony, sensing an opportunity to change the subject, interjected, "Speaking of school, have you registered yet?"

"No, actually. With all the hub-bub and drama lately, Gram and I haven't had a chance."

Anthony waved an understanding fork in her direction while he chewed. "You might want to think about doing that after you're done at Landon's in the morning. Classes will be starting soon and you'll need time for them to get all your transcripts and records from your school back in Detroit."

Lora hadn't thought about the need for records and felt a bit panicked at the thought she might not be able to enroll for the fall quarter. She resented Bumpus for dying and Sheriff Griffin for making such a stink about it. The sour look on her face made Anthony laugh. "Don't worry. I'm sure you're fine. Still, no harm in going ahead and getting it done."

Charlie and Maeve agreed with Anthony and said they'd drive her to the admissions office after lunch the next day.

25

Landon heard Myra yelling before he'd even turned off his engine. He couldn't quite make out the words but her fury was blistering and made him reluctant to knock on her door. He took his time gathering his briefcase, checking his reflection in the rear view mirror, picking his teeth, doing just about anything he could to put off getting out of the car. Once he did, he made sure he slammed the door with enough force to be heard two farms down, hoping someone inside would hear him and Myra would collect herself before he mounted the porch steps.

The slamming car door didn't stop the yelling but when a child's voice sang out, "Mama! They's a white man in the yard!" the sudden rush of quiet from inside the house almost took his breath away.

Leon's guarded expression dissolved into a welcoming smile when he appeared through the screen. He chided his younger brother, "Aw James, that ain't no white man, that's Landon Cook, Miss Eva's lawyer."

James chirped a quick "Hello Mr. Cook!" and darted into the brilliant pinks and oranges of a lowering sunset, obviously thrilled for an excuse to remove himself from the path of his mother's wrath.

Leon watched James escape and laughed as he opened the door wider to shake Landon's hand. "Don't mind him. He hasn't figured out Mama is more bark than bite yet."

Landon ran a hand through his hair and winced. "I find that hard to believe. If her bite is half as bad as the bark I could hear, I imagine she can do some serious damage!"

Myra swooped in from the kitchen, her eyes blazing, one hand on her hip and the other flailing a dish towel in Leon's direction. She'd gone pale around the lips in her rage and Landon took a step backwards, afraid he'd just stepped into her line of fire. He was right.

"Landon Cook!" she bellowed. "I hope you gonna tell my fool son that this plan of his is the most dangerous, reckless, craziest, brash, careless, irresponsible, dumbest thing in the world! And if you ain't, you can just march yourself right back out to your truck and keep on driving!"

Landon held both of his hands up in surrender. "Miss Myra, I can't tell him that without hearing the plan first!"

"Oh yes you can! You can just take my word for it and that's enough!" She was within striking distance now and Landon cut a sidelong plea for assistance in Leon's direction. Leon let him sweat.

"Don't you be looking at him! You got to deal with me!" Myra threw both her hands up in his face. She was real close to laying violent hands on a white man, a thing she'd never done before in her life. The only thing that stopped her was the tiny voice in her head reminding her that this particular white man was responsible for keeping her best friend out of jail.

She stretched up on her toes, jabbed a finger into his chest, and hissed, "These is my children. I don't care how old they are or how grown they think they are. It is my job to protect them. Even if it means protecting them from themselves. You hear me, Landon Cook?" Her fingertip made dents in his shirtfront with every syllable.

Landon rested his hands on her shoulders for a split-second before pulling her into a tight hug. "Yes ma'am. I hear you. I don't want to do anything that will put Leon in danger either."

He could feel her trembling fear and fury when she clutched the back of his shirt. Her muffled voice vibrated against his chest when she spoke, "It's Maurice. Not Leon."

Confused, Landon gripped the now sobbing woman a little tighter and looked to Leon for explanation.

Leon gathered his mother from Landon's arms and led them all into the kitchen, where he explained his plan to Landon while they shared a meal. Maurice was conspicuously absent.

26

Tuesday morning crept gently over the windowsills. Dawn danced in morning breezes across sleeping Burnette faces. Eva stretched and wriggled into her housedress. Peeking through the window sheers, she decided the weather would be just fine for a day spent on laundry and gardening. If Anthony didn't dawdle or grumble too much, she might be able to get most of it done before her stories came on. Deciding not to hold her breath waiting for that to happen, she flicked the sheers back into place and sighed at the idea of Anthony doing any housework without protest or threat. She figured his California apartment was a disaster zone and wondered if he'd hired a cleaning lady.

She was still chuckling under her breath as she measured scoops of grounds for fresh coffee. Bed springs complained and protested from the bedrooms when the first drops dripped and sizzled into the pot. Before going to bed the night before, Charlie had shared his and Maeve's plan to buy a car for Lora and Eva was looking forward to the surprise. Her heartstrings sang along with the growing hum of anticipation in the house. New cars, new jobs. Progress. Breakfast would be fast and simple this morning. Everybody but her and Anthony had places to go and things to do.

"What are you laughing at so early in the morning, Mama?"

In her musings, Eva hadn't heard Anthony padding barefoot into the kitchen behind her. She jumped and scattered coffee grounds across the countertop. She swept the mess into the sink before stoking the embers in her old cook stove and feeding fresh logs into the firebox.

Charlie sauntered into the kitchen, scratching at the shadow of stubble running along his jawline. "Mama, why don't you use the electric oven and get rid of that thing?"

"Because the biscuits don't seem to taste right out of the electric, Charlie. You know that. Besides, I'm just warming the rest of yesterday's and scrambling some eggs. It won't take long." Eva playfully jabbed a small stick into his gut when he walked past her.

He skittered out of the way, pushed Anthony into a chair, and assumed guardianship of the percolating coffee pot.

Anthony leaned back, stretched his legs out long, toe-knuckles popping with the effort, and yawned. "I'm exhausted. Lora was killing me going up and down the stairs at all hours. Charlie, we have *got* to teach her the dance. What was she doing in the middle of the night anyway?"

"Ah, the posh life of a government employee," Charlie mused, lifting a shoulder and smirking. "I heard the bath running really late. My guess is she decided to wash her hair before starting her new job."

Anthony kicked a foot in his brother's direction but couldn't help grinning.

"So, what's on the agenda today?"

Eva replied, "Well, me and you are going to do some laundry and pull weeds." She yielded the floor to Charlie with a pointed look.

Charlie, snagging a mug from the drying rack, whispered. "Maeve and I are going to town to buy Lora a car."

Anthony grumbled and whined. "Laundry and weeds, Mama? I don't want to do that. Can I go with Charlie?"

Charlie handed a brim-full cup to Anthony. "Nope. Mama needs help and you're the only one available." His smirk earned him a baleful look from his brother who took the proffered cup without a word of thanks.

"Fine," Anthony snorted and pinched the bridge of his nose. "What kind of car you gonna get?"

"I dunno. The car thing was Maeve's idea and I'm all for it. I'm sure she'll want her to have something safe and ugly." Charlie blew across the top of his own coffee and mischievously said, "I want to get her a Mustang. This year's models are beautiful."

Anthony whistled. "A brand new Mustang? Aw man...Can I be your kid?"

Eva laughed and spoke up. "I think I'm on Maeve's side of this debate—"

"My side of what debate?" Maeve asked as she rounded the corner into the kitchen. Her hair was set and her make-up was done. She'd pulled a pale yellow, satin robe over her nightgown for breakfast.

Charlie smiled at her and handed over his coffee. He poured the last into cups for himself and his mother before brewing another pot. He once more leaned against the counter and with an air of innocent nonchalance, he splayed his hands. "Well, we were discussing what kind of car to get Lora. I figured you'd want something large and clunky but I think we should get her a new Mustang."

Maeve leaned next to him and gingerly held the hot coffee mug with the fingertips of both hands. "Oh? It just so happens, I think a Mustang would be perfect." She arched an eyebrow and raised one corner of her mouth at her husband to let him know he'd played his cards right and she knew it.

Anthony hooted softly. "Ha ha! She just called your bluff Charlie!" He pointed a finger at his brother. "Still, looks like the only one who wins is Lora!" He pasted on a serious face as he studied his sister-in-law. "No joke though. Can I be your kid?"

Maeve shushed him with a slap to his arm and set to helping Eva get breakfast on the table.

• • • •

MOMENTS LATER, LORA flew down the steps in a blur of long, dark hair and flailing arms and legs to the bathroom underneath the stairs. She was running on pure adrenaline from staying up late while her hair dried. With a fresh scrubbed face and chirping good mornings to her family, she raced into the kitchen for coffee and a buttered biscuit before zooming back upstairs.

"Mom? Can you come up here? I need your help!"

Maeve lifted her coffee cup to the ceiling like she'd pulled Excalibur from the stone before climbing the stairs. The others raised mugs and biscuits in salute as the hem of her robe disappeared from sight. Crackling stair treads provided progress updates with each step towards Lora's room.

• • • •

"WHAT'S UP?" MAEVE RESTED a shoulder on the door frame and peered inside, blowing across the top of her steaming coffee. If closets and dressers could vomit, it looked like Lora's had. Dresses, skirts, pants, shorts, blouses, jeans, undergarments, and shoes covered every surface in a kaleidoscope of cloth and color. Lora, wearing only a full-slip, long strands of ponytail wrapped around her neck, stood twitching in the middle, eyes wide, twisting a hunk of hair and chewing on the ends.

"I don't know what to wear. What do you wear to work? At a law office? Was this a mistake? Should I tell Mr. Cook I can't do this?" Her words ran together in an anxious mush with scarcely a breath between them.

Maeve nudged Lora's toiletry case aside, making room for her mug on the small vanity just inside the door. Picking her way through piles of textile debris on the floor, she tip-toed to stand in front of her daughter. She tugged the hair from Lora's neck and pulled the ends from Lora's mouth.

"Do you think Landon really cares what you wear?" she laughed, swinging Lora's hands from side to side like she had when Lora was little playing London Bridge with neighborhood friends.

"Mom! I'm serious. He might not care but I do!"

"Naturally. I'm just saying as long as you're clean and put-together, it really doesn't matter." Maeve struggled to compose herself and couldn't resist petty dig. "Besides, you could wear a flour sack with muck boots and look better than Lovenia Thigpen."

Lora wrinkled her nose. "And I don't smell like onions."

She settled on a sleeveless, navy shift dress with a boat neck and white button accents. Completing the look with a low ponytail and white sling-back flats, she and Maeve went downstairs to proud whistles and approving nods from her family. Lora kissed cheeks and pulled the truck keys from their hook by the back door.

As soon as she'd gone, Charlie and Maeve dressed quickly and dodged renewed pleas from Anthony, begging them to save him from laundry and weeds. They all but skipped out of the house debating available options for Lora's new car the entire way. Cruise-o-matic or manual? Console? Eight-track or simple radio? Air conditioning was a necessity and non-negotiable.

· · · ·

AFTER AN INTRODUCTION to the workings of Landon's office, Lora eased the old International over the driveway culvert. Her eyes narrowed when she spotted the shiny, powder-blue Mustang holding court in Eva's front yard. She'd stopped at Monroe's on her way home to tell him about working for Landon. The old store-keep teased her but agreed the attorney's deal was to good to pass up. Lora suggested he offer her spot to Maggie Johnson and was pleased by the surprise and approval which flitted across his broad face. He said he'd do just that and congratulated her with an RC Cola and a moon pie, adding a lowered brow, cryptic remark that she might want to hurry home.

With her hands full, she thumped the truck door shut with a hip and walked slowly across the yard. She was oblivious to the dehydrated crunch of noontime grass under foot, blinking at the

Mustang's chrome twinkling in the midday sun. Her reflection in the paint was as clear as a new mirror. She didn't see anyone on the porch or in the yard and couldn't resist the temptation to get a closer look. Careful not to let dripping condensation or sugary crumbs mar the dazzling finish, Lora sidled up to the driver's side door and peered inside. The pony embroidered, blue leather seats offered no clues to who owned the gorgeous car.

She slumped away to head inside and change clothes. The front door banged open and her family poured out of the house.

"Surprise!" Her mother called, quick-stepping her way down the steps and across the yard to catch her daughter up in a happy little dance.

"Wha—? Surprise?" Lora dropped the moon pie and looked at her dad, who'd followed Maeve into the blinding sunlight.

Charlie shielded his eyes from the glare and pressed the keys into her hand. With a face splitting smile, he said, "It's yours."

Lora plopped down, cross-legged, in the grass and stared at the car. Stunned, she tore her gaze away from the car to her parents. "What? Really? Mine?"

Anthony and Eva yelled out congratulations as they barreled off the porch. Charlie pulled Lora to her feet and guided her to the Mustang. He pulled the handle and opened the door for her.

"Ooh! Get in! Get in!" Maeve scooted around to the passenger side and slid into the front seat. "Let's go for a ride! Just me and you!"

Maeve pulled the passenger door closed with a loud thump and rolled the window down, dangling her arm out the window. Her smile was almost as bright as the chrome trim lining the windows.

Lora, still in shock, whirled around to Charlie and leapt into his arms. "Oh Daddy! Really? Thank you! I love it!"

Delighted, Charlie spun her around in a tight hug, her ponytail flying behind her. "Yes! All yours, sweetheart. Now, your mama wants to go for a ride. Think she'd mind if I came along?" He winked and set her down.

"I don't care if she does or not," she giggled, handing her half-finished cola bottle to Anthony. "You said it's mine and I say you can!"

Charlie tweaked the lever to release the front-seat and folded himself into the backseat. Lora felt like her cheeks were meeting on the back of her head from smiling so big. She let loose a jumping whoop and waved at her grandmother and uncle as she fired up the engine. All thoughts of being tired were carried away with the breeze as she sped out of Eva's drive and onto the road. She honked the horn when she zoomed past Monroe's store.

• • • •

THE AFTERNOON PASSED in a blur of joyrides. Anthony, hoping to avoid more housework, tried to take everyone else's turn. Charlie insisted he and Maeve accompany Lora to Calhoun to get her enrolled for the fall quarter. Lora ran Eva up to the store. She didn't need anything from Monroe's but was tickled by his schoolboy appreciation of Lora's new ride. He even showed Lora where she could park it out of danger from flying gravel when she stopped in.

As the day wound down and the sun's rays weakened, Eva asked Lora and Maeve to bring the wash in off the line. Despite the new car excitement, Eva could not shake the feeling she needed to see Landon and get a better idea of what he expected to happen in court. She was perturbed with him for not coming out to her house or at the very least, sending a message with Lora asking her to come to his office. Eva changed into a clean skirt and blouse. Slinging her purse strap over her shoulder, she asked Anthony to accompany her in tracking down her attorney.

Anthony threw up his hands in relief. "Good Lord yes! Anything is better than folding clothes, or pulling weeds, peeling tomatoes, moving rocks, or whatever else you come up with to keep me busy! Give me three minutes to change." He sprinted to his room.

Charlie folded his arms across his chest. "Where you going to look? He could be anywhere, you know?"

Eva harrumphed. "This time of day? If he ain't still at his office, I'm going to park outside his house until he comes home."

Charlie laughed. "Of course you are. I take that to mean we're on our own for dinner?"

Eva, hearing Anthony hopping around to put on his shoes, stepped to the door. "I'm sure you will be fine with whatever Maeve can put together."

Ignoring the skeptical look on his face, she called out, "Anthony! You're driving. I'll be in your car!"

• • • •

EVA'S IRRITATION WAS palpable when she and Anthony pulled into the yard just after dark. She clomped into the house, flung her purse onto the couch, and stomped to her room without saying a word. Her door slammed, rattling the windows, and making them all flinch. Charlie, Maeve, and Lora looked to Anthony for an explanation. He shook his head and shrugged his shoulders. "Couldn't find him. We went to the office first. Locked up tight. We went to his house. Same thing. Sat there for an hour and a half before I convinced her to just come home."

"I see," Charlie said. "Did you have to listen to her opinions about wayward lawyers the whole way back?" He knew how aggravated his mother got when things didn't go according to plan and didn't envy Anthony his time alone with her. He figured she ranted the entire way and nothing Anthony said made a difference.

Anthony grimaced and nodded. "Wayward lawyers, party line telephones, inconvenient drunks, twenty-four hour days, you name it, she's mad about it." He kicked off his shoes and flopped onto the couch, shifting Eva's purse to the end table, and closed his eyes.

"Did y'all eat?"

Anthony clutched his gurgling stomach and moaned. "No. I'm starving. What'd y'all have? Is there anything left?"

Maeve laughed. "Nope! Lora drove us up to the Burger Shack. We had burgers, fries, onion rings, and strawberry milk shakes!"

Anthony opened one squinty eye and glared at her. "You're mean, you know that?" He lurched off the sofa and made a show of stumbling to the kitchen, groaning the whole way.

Charlie and Maeve rolled their eyes.

Lora, wincing through the flash of a sudden knowing burst behind her left eye, whispered "I know where Mr. Cook is. He's at Myra's."

Her parents stared in alarm while she dug the heel of her hand into her eye socket.

Maeve rubbed Lora's arm. "Did he tell you that this morning?"

Guarding the secret of how she knew, Lora agreed with the convenient lie presented by her mother. "Yeah. That's it. Should we tell Gram?" She leaned into Maeve's arm for support.

Charlie, suspicious of Lora's sudden headache, eased himself onto the sofa on Lora's other side, moving like he was afraid she'd either break or run away. "I don't see much point in telling her tonight. She's mad enough as is." He squeezed her shoulder. "You're exhausted. Why don't you go on to bed?"

Lora nodded. Her vision clearing as the pain ebbed. The long and exciting day had worn her out and she couldn't begin to dissemble.

Charlie placed a comforting hand on her back, pushing her up and off the couch.

Lora gave her parents a grateful, weak smile and made her way to the stairs. She weaved her way to her room and fell onto the bed.

She hadn't realized exactly how tired she was until her dad sent her to bed. Still fully clothed, with her shoes still on, she dropped instantly to sleep.

• • • •

ANTHONY WALTZED BACK into the living room with a mouthful of bologna sandwich, a smear of mayonnaise glistening on his cheek in the lamplight. "Where's Lora?"

Maeve stood, smoothing her pants. "She was tired and went on to bed. I'm pretty tired too. I'm turning in." She dropped a lingering look at her husband before disappearing up the stairs.

Anthony wiped his face and took advantage of the empty rocker. "Huh! Mama's sulking, Lora and Maeve are tired. Looks like it's just you and me." He sucked at a gob of bread stuck to his teeth.

Charlie got to his feet and chucked Anthony on the shoulder. "Nope. Just you. I'm going to bed too."

"Well, if you're abandoning me to my own devices, can you at least turn on the television?"

"Nope again. You gotta get up to change the channel anyway."

Anthony grumbled while he chewed but didn't bother turning on the television.

27

The Burnettes rushed to get out the door Wednesday morning. Five people, one bathroom, and three generations of anxiety rubbed everyone's nerves the wrong way. Maeve twisted her watch around her wrist every ten seconds in a not-so-subtle hint that they should hit the road soon. Eva, after one watch twist too many, hissed. "Yes, Maeve. We know, Maeve. We'll get there. We're just going to Landon's office, remember?"

Maeve twitched slightly. Evidently, she'd forgotten they were going to the office first. She loosed a nervous laugh. "Oh. You're right. I forgot."

"Stop twisting your watch and pacing the floor. You're going to wear a hole in the carpet and screw your hand clean off. I'm telling you right now, if you do, I just might smack you with it," Eva threatened.

Maeve escaped to the porch where she could twist her watch to her heart's content. The screen door bounced in its frame behind her, sounding like gunshots in her head. She lit a cigarette and inhaled as deeply as she could, desperate for the momentary high of the first drag of the day. Her guts tied themselves in nervous knots and she wound up vomiting the few bites of dry biscuit she'd managed to swallow over the railing into Eva's day lilies instead. She crushed the cigarette on an upright and flicked the butt into the yard. She had just turned to yell through the door that they really should have left five minutes ago when everyone else poured out of the house.

It had rained overnight and the steam rising from the grass promised a sweltering day. There was a bit of confusion as to who would be driving into town. No one liked the idea of being squashed together in one hot car on the way home afterwards. Neither did anyone want to split the group into two. No one mentioned that there might be one less of them when they left the courthouse.

Eventually, it was agreed that Lora would ride in the very back of the station wagon so long as Charlie didn't toss her around too much with his driving.

Conversation was stilted and awkward on the way to Athens, soon lapsing into road noise silence as each of them took refuge in their own thoughts and worries. Maeve twisted her watch until Eva reached across the seat and grabbed hold of her wrist, not letting go. Charlie white-knuckled the steering wheel, leaning forward in his seat, dodging potholes like a fighter pilot dodging flak. Anthony fiddled with the radio, the power windows, the in-dash cigarette lighter. Lora pushed her feet against the passenger side wall of the station wagon's back-back and stared at the roof.

• • • •

CHARLIE PARKED NEXT to Landon's truck in front of the law office. He left Anthony to open the doors for Maeve and Eva while he popped the tailgate for Lora. Landon swung the office door open to the sidewalk and ushered them inside. His smile was tight and belied his cheerful greeting.

"Come on in."

The Burnettes clumped into a small, defensive knot in the center of the cool waiting area and looked expectantly at Landon.

Remembering his manners, he asked, "Y'all want any coffee? Water? I think we've got some cokes in the back fridge..." His voice trailed off into a near-whisper, evidence that he was more nervous than he wanted to let on.

As a group, the Burnettes declined his offer. Heads shaking, a murmur of "Thank-you, no," and "We're fine," floated through the outer office.

"In that case, why don't y'all follow me to the conference room?" Landon pushed open a dark-paneled door behind Lovenia's/Lora's desk and flipped on the light. A large oak table with ten high-backed leather chairs, five on each side, and leather wing backs on either end, anchored the high-ceilinged room. A richly polished credenza stood on the opposite end of the space, underneath the oil-painted watchful eye of Landon's great-grandfather, Mr. Herman Cook, founder of the firm back in 1888. Landon's case notes were spread across one end of the polished table top and he took his seat, gesturing for them to make themselves comfortable.

Scooting the heavy chairs from underneath the table, Charlie and Anthony made sure Eva, Lora, and Maeve were seated before claiming their own places.

"The way I see it, our only real concern is Agnes Crawford because we have no idea what she's going to say. Eva, you're certain you didn't discuss anything about the day Bumpus was killed, or the day you found him, with her?"

"Positive," she replied. "She tried asking me about finding him in the graveyard at church but I didn't answer her. I have no idea what she's going to speak to."

"Alrighty then. We'll just have to wait and see, I guess."

He glanced around the room, making eye contact with each of them before continuing. "When we get there today, the judge will call the court to order and read the charges aloud. He will then open the floor for opening statements from both me and Mr. Beatty. Once those are done, the prosecution will build its case. I get to question any witnesses he calls. Likewise, he'll get to question mine. Looks like we can expect to hear from Sheriff Griffin, Deputy Ross, the coroner, the fingerprint technician, and unfortunately, Agnes Crawford. I can only assume the prosecution is using her as some kind of character witness. Since she's testifying for the bad guys, we can assume she won't have anything good to say. To off-set whatever that is, I decided to call Dale Fudge as a character witness for you. Preachers usually make excellent character witnesses."

Charlie slapped his hand on the table and shook his head. "That won't work. Dale's sermon Sunday morning was aimed right at Mama. He is not on her side. He—"

Landon interrupted him. "Look, I spent a good part of yesterday with Dale. We discussed his sermon. Turns out he wasn't preaching at Eva. He was preaching against Hal and Agnes."

Charlie's lips curled and he muttered, "I don't believe it, or trust it, for a second."

Anthony and Lora nodded in agreement. Anthony picked up Charlie's thought and ran with it saying, "You should have talked to Mama before you just up and decided to use Dale Fudge as your counterweight for Agnes Crawford. I don't trust him either." He raised a questioning eyebrow at his mother.

Eva was torn between agreeing with her children and trusting her attorney, a man who felt almost as much like one of her own as they did. She fidgeted in her seat and studied Landon for a moment before slowly nodding. "If Landon trusts the preacher, I guess I need to do the same."

Charlie and Anthony both ran their hands across their faces and stared at the ceiling. Lora reached across the table and splayed her fingers on the surface, reaching out to her grandmother. Eva gave her hand a quick squeeze before withdrawing it back to her lap. Maeve, who hadn't been at church on Sunday, sat silently, staring at the table and twisting her watch.

Landon mouthed silent thanks to Eva and continued, "Once the prosecution rests, we, the defense will have the opportunity to refute the prosecution's claim and build a case for reasonable doubt."

He shifted his focus directly to his client. "Eva, I may or may not call you to testify. That will depend on how everything else is going up to that point. If I do call on you, you will be last."

"Are you still planning to call Hal Johnson in my defense? You're telling me I might not get the chance to say my piece?" Her volume rose as she leaned forward in her chair, eyes popping in disbelief.

"That's exactly what I'm saying." The attorney raised his eyebrows at her and lowered his chin. "If the prosecution's case is as heavily dependent on the fingerprints as I think it is, you won't need to."

Eva snorted and leaned back in her chair, arms crossed tightly over her purse against her chest.

Landon hid a smile to himself.

Anthony, still concerned that Landon was overconfident, said, "And what if their case turns out to be more than just the fingerprints?"

Eva spun in her chair to glare at her favored son. "What are you saying? You know something I don't? I did NOT kill Bumpus."

"Well Mama, I'm sure we in this room aren't the only ones who know how you felt about the man—"

Eva held a hand up to cut him off. Anthony clutched her hand and and kissed her fingers.

"No one in their right mind could think you killed Bumpus." He tried to lighten the mood a little and grinned. "Even if you do pop the heads off innocent mice and toss them out the back door."

Lora gasped and clamped down on a startled giggle, covering her mouth. No one else thought Anthony was funny. His joke landed on the table as dead as the mouse outside Eva's back door.

"Mama, my concern is that enough people know your opinion of him and the state could have rounded up enough of them to convince the judge." Anthony looked at Landon, "Do they have to tell you who all they're calling to testify?"

"Yes. To my knowledge, those five are the only ones testifying."

"Do you have to tell them who you're calling?"

"Yes. I've prepared them for Dale Fudge, Hal Johnson, and possibly Eva."

Charlie leaned an elbow across the table and jabbed his index finger in Landon's direction. "So no surprise witnesses from them. But, your entire defense strategy is resting on Dale Fudge, Hal Johnson, and 'maybe' Mama? You have lost your mind." Charlie stood and began pacing the conference room behind his daughter and wife. He pressed his hands against his lower back and stretched, vertebra cracking loud enough for everyone to hear. "Mama, you need to fire Landon. He's going to get you sent straight to jail."

Landon jumped to his feet, knocking his chair over with a thud to stand toe-to-toe with Charlie, gripping his friend by the shoulders. "Charlie! You have got to trust me. I'd rather swim through a ball of cotton mouths than let Eva go to jail. For this or anything else. Ever!"

The tips of Charlie's ears blistered red and his fists clenched as he stared into Landon's pleading eyes. Rather than punch him square in the face, Charlie pushed Landon away, hard enough to make the attorney stumble backwards a couple paces. Charlie swallowed hard. He straightened his tie, cinching it tight around his neck, and stalked out of the conference room. Maeve rushed after him, glad to exit the conversation, even if it did mean dealing with a very angry Charlie. The rest of the family, Landon included, froze in place as the door clicked shut behind them. Landon fanned his suit coat behind him, re-tucked his shirttails, adjusted his own tie, and smoothed his hair.

"Sorry about that," he apologized, setting his chair back upright at the head of the table. "Now, where were we?"

Anthony, figuring Charlie had used up the morning's allotment of drama, arched a dark eyebrow and flatly replied, "You were saying you plan to use Dale Fudge as a character witness, even though the rest of us think that's a bad idea. You will also call on Hal Johnson for reasons none of us understand. And, you may or may not ask Mama to testify on her own behalf. Does that about sum everything up?"

Landon cleared his throat and rested his elbows on the table. His deep brown eyes were flat. He matched Anthony's detached tone and said, "Yes. That is an excellent summary."

Anthony planted both hands on the table and slowly stood. His eyes didn't leave Landon's face. He shoved his hands into his pockets, jacket sleeves rucked up around his wrists, and shook his head. After a heartbeat's pause, he followed his brother's footsteps out the door.

Landon glanced at Lora, then turned his attention to Eva, reaching out to hold her hand. A sad smile danced around his lips when he spoke, "You know? I've heard folks say to never mix business and family. I know we're not related but I am starting to understand exactly what they mean."

Eva chuckled and cupped his face in her palm. "Landon, family isn't always about relation. You are family and I trust you. Charlie and Anthony are just frustrated because this is a problem neither of them can fix. They'll come around."

She patted his cheek and said, "Judging by the clock on the credenza, it looks like we ought to be on our way. What do you say? Walk an old lady to court?"

She stood and smoothed her dress. Landon gathered his documents, careful to keep the tabs straight and in order, and placed them in his briefcase.

He held out an arm to Eva and said, "Eva Burnette, it would be my honor."

Lora trailed behind them. She herded the others from the outer office as Eva and Landon strode silently out of the building into the morning heat of the late summer day.

The courthouse square was always busy on Wednesday mornings. Today was no different. With the exceptions of the drugstore and sheriff's office, all the businesses circling the courthouse were either closed altogether or would shut their doors at noon. Although it was still early, pay by-the-hour parking spaces were filling up and greedy parking meters were being fed. Store patrons bustled about on the sidewalks perusing the sale-boards advertising the day's sales and specials. "64-count Crayola Crayons with SHARPENER - 35 cents! Today only!" at Ben Jaffe's Department Store, "Buy Two Yards Get One Free!" at Wilson's Fabrics, and "Free Shoe Polish with Shoe Purchase" at Smith's Menswear. Eager teenagers, with anxious parents in tow, skipped across the courthouse lawn to take the driving test and hoped to get their driver's license.

Pedestrians crossed streets at the corners, tipping hats and nodding hello as they went. Eva gripped Landon's arm for stability she didn't usually need as the two of them led the somber group to the intersection of Washington and Marion Streets. While they waited for the light to turn and oncoming traffic to stop, Eva had eyes only for the courthouse steps. Even so, when the signal changed, indicating it was safe to cross, she hesitated.

"Gram? Are you okay?" Lora asked, stepping up next to her grandmother and putting an arm around her waist.

"Not really but there ain't much can be done except getting this over with." Eva fanned herself for a second and raised her chin. With a weak smile, she let go of Landon's arm and took the first step across Washington Street alone.

28

L andon led them up the limestone stairway and paused at the courtroom doors. "Okay. I know you are all nervous. I am too. But, I have faith in my plan, faith in Judge Underwood, and faith that Mr. Beatty's case is as inconsequential as he is." He checked his watch. "We're about ten minutes early so if anyone needs to go to the restroom or step outside for a cigarette, now would be the time to do it." All eyes turned to Maeve but she surprised them, shaking her head and motioning to the courtroom entrance. Landon tugged on the heavy oak doors and held them open for the group before following closely behind.

Landon nudged the barrier gate open with his knee and settled Eva into her place at the defense table. He nodded in greeting to Mr. Beatty and his array of neatly sorted supporting documentation. Mr. Beatty responded with a curt nod and mopped his head with a dingy handkerchief. He was already sweating. Charlie, Maeve, Lora, and Anthony shuffled into seats on the bench directly behind Eva.

Maeve looked around. She leaned towards Lora and whispered, "Are there always this many people here?"

Lora glanced over her shoulder and surveyed the gathering crowd. She was relieved Myra, Leon, and Maurice were not in attendance. She shook her head. "No. Usually there's more."

"Really? Don't people have anything better to do?"

Lora shrugged and chewed on her bottom lip. She had no interest in small talk with her mother.

Charlie reached his arm around Maeve and squeezed Lora's shoulder.

Anthony rested his forearms on his thighs and stared at the floor.

Sheriff Griffin and Deputy Ross filed in and took their seats a few minutes before eight o'clock. Griffin was tight-lipped while he shook Mr. Beatty's hand. Deputy Ross glanced across the aisle at

Lora and lifted a finger in greeting. She flicked her eyebrows up and flashed a quick smile in return.

When the bailiff called for the audience to rise, the chamber was filled to standing room only. The temperature crept higher. Hints of Pine Sol and Murphy's Wood Oil permeated the stifling air.

Judge Underwood's robes flew behind him as he took the bench and gestured with his glasses for everyone to be seated. "My. Did all of Limestone County show up today?" Chuckles and twitters eddied around the room over the scuffling and creaking of the crowd resettling. He cleaned his glasses and took a few moments to flip through the case file on the desk in front of him.

"Okay. As this is a bench trial and my courtroom, I am going to dispense with the performance elements today." He perched the spectacles on the end of his nose and peered over the top at the two attorneys. "There is no need for opening and closing statements. I know why we are here and what's at stake. Any objections?"

Mr. Beatty grimaced and slipped two handwritten pages of notes into the open briefcase in the seat next to him. Suppressing his disappointment, he replied, "No, Your Honor. No objection from the State."

"Good. Mr. Cook?"

Landon grinned. "No objections at all. Thank you, Your Honor."

"Alright then. Mr. Beatty, you may call your first witness."

The state's attorney stood and steepled his fingertips on the desk, the tips turning white from the pressure. "The State calls Sheriff Early Griffin."

Sheriff Griffin unfolded himself from his seat and navigated through the barrier gate, even though he could have just stepped over the partition. The creases ironed into his shirt were stiff with starch. Sweat streaked white salt rings on the khaki fabric under his armpits which puckered with every swing of his arms. He climbed the witness stand and placed his hand on the Bible; swearing to tell the truth so-help-me-God.

Mr. Beatty paced the space between the prosecution desk and witness stand. His hands clasped behind his back, his round belly straining the buttons of his gray and black checkered vest and jacket.

"Good morning, Sheriff. In your own words, tell us what you found in the cemetery in Mooresville once you were notified of a dead body in the vicinity."

"Well, we received a call from Monroe's store around one o'clock in the afternoon advising us the body of Elthelred Bumpus had been found earlier in the day, in the graveyard, by Eva Burnette and her granddaughter." Griffin pointed a long finger at Eva and then at Lora.

"When I arrived on the scene, Bumpus was sprawled against a tombstone with a pool of blood around his head."

"I see. For the record, it is commonly known that Mr. Bumpus was regularly drunk and spent several nights in your custody, courtesy of the tax-payers of Limestone County, correct?"

"That is correct."

"Would it have been reasonable to assume Mr. Bumpus was drunk and had tripped or fallen into the tombstone, effectively killing himself?"

"That was my original assumption, yes."

"What made you change your mind?" Mr. Beatty spread his feet and leaned back on his heels, hands still clasped behind his back.

"While we waited for the coroner to come collect the body, I walked the area and discovered a broken dinner plate behind the marker where Bumpus had fell."

"A plate? That's an odd thing to find in a cemetery, isn't it?" Mr. Beatty spread his hands wide at the absurdity of the notion.

"It's not unheard of. Sometimes churches have picnics in the cemeteries on clean-up days. You know, the congregation meets to clear out debris. Fallen tree limbs, dead flowers, and the like. Occasionally things get left behind."

"Oh? Is that so? Was it possible that was the case in this instance?"

"No. The graveyard was overgrown, dead flowers everywhere. It obviously hadn't been cleaned in a while. Besides, I checked with the preachers of nearby churches and none of them had held a clean-up since early in the spring."

"Who did you check with?"

"Dale Fudge from Holley Hill Church of Christ and Otto Winters from First Baptist of Mooresville."

"No others?"

"No. Those are the two churches who bury their dead there most often. The two closest to the cemetery and the two most likely to take on the job of maintenance."

Mr. Beatty adjusted his cuffs and interlaced his fingers beneath his belly. "So, you found a dinner plate near Mr. Bumpus's body and confirmed there had been no dining events in the cemetery. What did you do next?"

"There was a marker on the back of the plate with the initials 'EB' beneath the maker's mark. I intended to find out who the plate belonged to."

Mr. Beatty retrieved a piece of flat, white pottery from the clerk's desk and held it aloft. "Is this a piece of the plate you found in the cemetery?"

Sheriff Griffin reached out for the shard and examined it. "It would appear to be, yes."

Mr. Beatty handed the plate piece to the clerk and said, "Please record this as Exhibit 1," before turning back to Griffin and the judge.

"Why did you think that was important, Sheriff?"

"The plate had blood and hair on it when I found it."

"That's a gruesome thought."

"It was. Mr. Bumpus was a fine man who lost his way and to think someone had taken advantage of him, hit him, while he was at a low point, it just—"

Landon Cook jumped to his feet. "Objection, Your Honor. The sheriff's opinion about the deceased is irrelevant and prejudicial."

Judge Underwood nodded. "I agree, Mr. Cook. Objection sustained. Sheriff, you will keep to the facts. Mr. Beatty, carry on."

Mr. Beatty pulled on his collar and shot the sheriff a warning look. "Um, yes. Sheriff Griffin. What made you think the plate belonged to Mrs. Burnette? Surely there are other 'EB's' around. Ethelred Bumpus for one!"

Griffin chuckled slow and low. "True enough but I couldn't figure out why or how Bumpus could have hit himself over the head with his own plate. No, since Eva Burnette was the one who reported finding his body and she is the closest 'EB' to the cemetery, it made sense to start with her."

"Sounds logical. Please continue." The prosecutor waved a hand.

"I went to her house to look at her plates and compare the markers. They matched. She was officially a person of interest in the matter."

Eva nudged Landon with her elbow and widened her eyes at him, encouraging him to speak up. Sheriff Griffin violated the rules of unlawful search and seizure when he came out looking at her plates. Landon patted her hand, leaning in to whisper in her ear. "I'll ask him on cross. I got it."

Mr. Beatty propped on the witness box. "So you were able to confirm the cemetery plate belonged to Mrs. Burnette. Now, why would you think she had injured or harmed Mr. Bumpus in any way?"

Sheriff Griffin cleared his throat and said, "Mrs. Burnette spent years pestering my office about Bumpus. She hated him."

Landon spoke up, "Your Honor, this is speculation. Sheriff Griffin cannot possibly know how my client felt about the deceased."

The judge didn't bother looking up from cleaning his glasses and said, "Sustained. Mr. Beatty, I advise you and your witness, again, to stick to the facts."

"Yes sir. Sheriff, were you able to obtain fingerprint information from the plate and compare it to the defendant's fingerprints?"

"Yes. I got a warrant for a intact plate from Mrs. Burnette. By comparing the prints on it to the pieces left in the cemetery, we discovered the only set of overlapping prints between the two belonged to Eva Burnette. At that point, I got a warrant for her arrest."

"Seems pretty clear to me. Thank you, Sheriff." Mr. Beatty hitched his pant legs up, sat down at his desk, and slid another piece of paper into his briefcase.

Judge Underwood waved a lazy hand in Landon's direction. "Mr. Cook, your witness."

Landon stood, buttoning his suit jacket and smoothing his trousers. "Good morning, Sheriff."

Griffin nodded and leaned back in his seat, crossing his arms and tucking his fingers into his armpits. He quickly pulled them back out and wiped them on his pants' legs.

"Sheriff, you said you went to my client's house to look at her plates yet you fail to mention that prior to obtaining a warrant, you broke into her house when she wasn't home and rummaged through her cabinets without her being there. Do you remember that?"

"I do. It was an oversight on my part and one that turned out to be irrelevant."

"Irrelevant? Are you saying that you are above the Constitution or that the ends always justify the means?"

Sheriff Griffin's cheeks colored and his beady black eyes thinned dangerously, pulling the skin on his skull tight under his close-cropped hair. "No. I would have gotten the evidence anyway. The order doesn't matter."

Landon undid his jacket buttons and slipped his hands in his pockets. "Eh, you also didn't think it was important to Mirandize my client when you arrested her but I'm sure you're correct. As long as the end justifies the means, right? Although I think the Founding Fathers would disagree but I digress. We'll leave that alone for now."

Judge Underwood cleared his throat impatiently. Landon took the hint. His point had been made.

Mr. Cook skimmed the notes he'd taken during the Sheriff's testimony. "Sheriff, you also indicate that you had fingerprint analysis done on the plate from the cemetery. That's good police work. Who else's fingerprints did you find on the plate?"

Sheriff Griffin eyeballed Mr. Beatty before answering. "Aside from Mrs. Burnette, we discovered the identifiable fingerprints of Hal Johnson and Mr. Bumpus. We also found a whole bunch of prints we could not match to any body."

"Hal Johnson, you say? Why on earth would Hal Johnson's prints be on one of Eva Burnette's plates?" Landon crossed one arm across his chest and rested the other elbow on his wrist, his fingers tapping on his chin in deep thought, as though he was trying to figure out the answer to his own question.

"I spoke with Mr. Johnson and he indicated Mrs. Burnette had been bringing biscuits to his house every morning for the past several months. That would explain the presence of his fingerprints on the plate."

Still tapping his chin, Landon asked, "Mrs. Burnette brought biscuits to Mr. Johnson's house every single day for months? That sounds like a very nice thing to do and certainly not at all like someone who would wallop another person over the head, wouldn't you agree, Sheriff?"

Sheriff Griffin's already thin lips disappeared as he realized Landon had just backed him into a corner. A corner which required him to say something nice about the woman he was trying to put away for manslaughter. He gritted his teeth and said, "Yes. It does sound neighborly. As to why? Who knows why any woman does anything?"

Landon slid his hands back into his pockets and turned his back to the witness stand. He winked at Eva. He'd just introduced Hal Johnson as an alternative suspect and exposed the Sheriff's bias without much effort at all. "Why indeed. That will be all for now, Sheriff. Your Honor, if it please the court, I reserve the right to recall Sheriff Griffin."

Judge Underwood, bored already, grunted. "That's fine, Mr. Cook. Mr. Beatty, call your next witness."

Mr. Beatty ran the point of his pen down the witness list, scratched out a name, and said, "The State calls Sanders Powers, County Coroner."

29

L ora glanced across the aisle at Deputy Ross when Mr. Beatty skipped over him and called the coroner to testify instead. Deputy Ross cocked his head to the side and examined the brim of his hat, scratching at a bit of dirt along the edge. Still, his shoulders relaxed in relief under his shirt and a dimple flashed on the side of his face she could see.

Mr. Sanders Powers was a surprisingly young man, slightly built with strawberry blond hair. From the waves and swirls on the back of his head, it was plain he wore his hair extra-short to combat a head full of tight curls. He wore a black suit, white shirt, and black tie. His sleeves and pants were about an inch too short and he walked like his shoes hurt his feet. His kind, ruddy face smiled, frowned, and smiled again when he looked out at the audience after swearing in. Mr. Powers was uncomfortable.

Mr. Beatty wasted no time on pleasantries. "Mr. Powers. You are the coroner here in Limestone County, yes?"

"Yes. I was elected last year." His voice cracked and his face turned a deeper shade of red.

"Congratulations. Did you retrieve the body of Ethelred Bumpus from the cemetery in Mooresville?"

"Yes."

"And you examined the body once you got it back to the morgue?"

"Yes."

"What did you find?"

Mr. Sanders loosened his tie and said, "Ah. Well, Mr. Bumpus smelled strongly of alcohol suggesting he'd been drinking. He had two wounds to his head. One very deep on the back. Appeared to have been caused by a sharp blow from a corner. I believe this wound was caused by striking the corner of the tombstone. There was blood and hair on the stone."

"Blood and hair on the stone," Mr. Beatty shuddered. "What about the second wound, Mr. Powers?"

"The other wound was relatively shallow but long. Stretching from temple to ear. Not much meat on a person's skull, you know?" His smile faltered when he realized no one was smiling back. "Like I said, it was shallow but deep enough to result in substantial bleeding."

"Enough to cause Bumpus to bleed to death?"

"No. But head wounds bleed profusely. This in addition to the other wound could make him pass out. Passing out from blood loss because of head trauma, in combination with his age and being drunk, would have been enough to kill him."

Mr. Beatty put one hand on his hip. "Was there anything particularly interesting about this second wound? You said the one on the back of Bumpus's head was caused from striking the tombstone. What caused the second wound?"

Mr. Powers was apologetic when he softly answered. "I found pieces of ceramic in this wound which matched the plate Sheriff Griffin found in the cemetery."

The state's attorney jumped like an evangelical preacher at a tent meeting. "You did? Pieces of a plate, owned by Eva Burnette, were embedded in the head of Ethelred Bumpus?"

Sanders closed his eyes. "Yes."

Mr. Beatty beamed a wolfish, triumphant grin at Landon Cook but addressed the judge somberly. "The state is finished with this witness, Your Honor."

Underwood pointed at Landon, who stood and addressed Mr. Powers. "Hello Mr. Powers. Thank you for being here today. You have a tough job and, from what I understand, you do it well." He smiled and Mr. Powers relaxed a little.

Landon continued. "Mr. Powers, you found pieces of my client's plate in one of Mr. Bumpus's wounds. Did you find anything which indicated she was the one who hit him with it?"

"Um. No. I did not." Mr. Powers straightened in his seat. That kind of evidence did not fall under the purview of his office. Realizing Mr. Cook had just let him off the hook, he smiled and shook his head to reinforce his answer.

"Thank you again, Mr. Powers. Your Honor, I have no further questions for this witness."

Landon reclaimed his seat next to Eva. Eva flashed him a quick smile. Mr. Powers was just doing his job and no one could blame him for that.

Judge Underwood, pleased with the pace of the trial so far, twirled a forefinger in the air and said, "Mr. Beatty, let's keep this moving."

"Yes, Your Honor. The state calls Albert Romine, fingerprint technician for the Limestone County Sheriff's Department."

Landon held up his pen and interrupted, "Your Honor, unless this witness is going to testify to something different from what Sheriff Griffin said earlier, the defense is willing to concede that Mrs. Burnette's fingerprints were on both plates and that the cemetery plate also contained the prints of both Mr. Hal Johnson and Ethelred Bumpus."

Judge Underwood took a break from cleaning his fingernails with a small pen knife. "I agree. Mr. Beatty, will Mr. Romine's testimony add anything substantive to the proceedings or are you calling him as a matter of formality and procedure."

Mr. Beatty, annoyed his time in the spotlight was shrinking, inhaled deeply through his nose, producing a nasally, whistling sound. "No, Your Honor. Mr. Romine's testimony confirms Sheriff Griffin's earlier statements and is procedural in nature."

Judge Underwood laid the pocketknife on the bench. "Good. As long as his witness statement and paperwork back that up, and I have copies of those items," he leveled a serious look at the state's attorney, "I think we can dispense with Mr. Romine's services for today."

Mr. Romine hovered midway down the aisle, unsure what to do. Judge Underwood addressed him directly. "Mr. Romine, you are free to go," and dismissed him with a wave of his hand.

"Mr. Beatty, you still have the floor."

"In that case, Your Honor, the state calls Agnes Crawford to the stand."

There were several gasps from the gallery. The sounds of shuffling feet and occasional mutterings of "Pardon me" hummed through the courtroom as Agnes Crawford cut a wide, fragrant path to the witness stand, like a spice ship on rolling ocean waves. She did not look at Eva. Landon leaned his elbows eagerly onto the defense table. His deep brown eyes as shrewd and discerning as a hawk.

Mr. Beatty gently took Ms. Crawford's hand to help her into the raised box. Once she was seated, he smoothed his comb-over and straightened his jacket like a nervous suitor on her doorstep. He smiled. She smiled back, her heavily rouged cheeks squinching her mascaraed lashes together until they resembled dried up earthworms resting on hot coals.

"Ms. Crawford. Agnes. May I call you Agnes?"

She tittered and rocked in her seat. "Of course."

"Thank you. Agnes. You have been Eva Burnette's friend for many years. Most of your life, correct?"

"Yes. Eva and I have gone to church together all our lives. She's a little older than me but I don't remember Holley Hill without her."

Mr. Beatty pursed his lips, acknowledging Ms. Crawford's age-divulging dilemma. "I see. In all the time you've known her, has she ever said or done anything, er, untoward regarding Mr. Bumpus?"

Landon's ears perked up and he raised a hand to the judge. "Your Honor, this is bordering on hearsay."

Judge Underwood folded his arms on the desk in front of him and addressed Ms. Crawford. "Ms. Crawford, before you answer this question, I would like you to understand that you can only testify to words Mrs. Burnette said directly to you or actions which you, yourself, actually witnessed. Is that clear?"

Agnes breathed an inappropriate giggle and pushed at her tightly set hair with a pink-gloved hand. "Yes, Judge. I understand."

"Excellent. You may answer Mr. Beatty's question."

"Alright," she looked at Mr. Beatty, "Eva Burnette once told me that some people just need killing."

The state's attorney placed a hand over his heart in a mockery of shock and dismay. "She did? And she said this about poor Mr. Bumpus?"

Landon groaned, "Your Honor! The question is leading and again seeks to paint a prejudicial picture of Mr. Bumpus."

Before the judge could respond, Mr. Beatty obligingly offered to rephrase the question. "Ms. Crawford, who was Mrs. Burnette specifically saying needed to be killed?"

Agnes clicked her tongue and said, "Mr. Bumpus."

"I see. And did she tell you why she felt this way about Mr. Bumpus?"

"No. Not that I recollect, it seemed to come out of the blue." She wrung her gloved hands in her lap and sniffed.

"Thank you, Ms. Crawford. I can see it troubles you to expose the horrible things your dear friend said about the deceased. Your Honor, I have no further questions for this witness."

Judge Underwood shifted his gaze to the defense table and circled a finger in the air again, indicating Mr. Cook should get a move on.

Landon stood and cleared his throat. "Ms. Crawford, good morning."

Agnes inclined her head.

"You tell us Eva Burnette said, to you, that some folks just need killing and that she was speaking about Mr. Bumpus, correct?"

"Yes." Her voice no longer held any warmth. Landon needed to tread carefully in order to get Ms. Crawford to stumble.

"How did you know she was speaking about Bumpus? Did she say 'Bumpus needs killing?'"

"Well, no. She didn't say it like that. She showed up at church one Wednesday night, agitated, all red-faced and angry. I asked her who she was mad at and she said, 'Bumpus!' After services, she was still mad and I told her she needed to pray for him. She laughed at me. Said she'd do no such thing and that's when she said some folks need killing. I was horrified!" Agnes sniffed again and ran a finger under her nose.

Mr. Cook turned his back to Agnes and searched Eva's face. Her expression could have been carved from granite for as much as she was giving away. Eva met his gaze and mouthed a single word question, "When?"

He flicked his eyebrows upwards and pivoted back to Ms. Crawford. "I imagine so. A lady of your...sensibilities...Did she say this recently?"

Agnes flushed under her make-up, making her look like a fuzzy peach left laying in the hot sun for too long. She covered her mouth and coughed.

"Ms. Crawford? Do you need a drink of water?"

"No. I'm fine. Eva said this to me, um, twenty-two, twenty-five years ago?"

Lora, enthralled by the proceedings, felt Maeve stiffen in her seat. When she looked at her mother, she was alarmed to see the color had drained from Maeve's face. She gripped Charlie's leg, nails

SAVING EVA   301

digging in like claws. Charlie wrapped his arm around Maeve's shoulders and pried her hand off his leg, weaving her fingers in his. He leaned into her ear and whispered something Lora couldn't make-out. Maeve took a deep breath and shook her head.

Lora turned her attention back to Mr. Cook, who was saying, "Ah. So, you felt a statement my client made in a fit of anger, which you described for us, more than twenty years ago would have bearing on this case?"

"Well, not immediately. Mr. Beatty and the Sheriff seemed to think so when they came around asking all of us who go to Holley Hill about Eva and Bumpus. And the more I thought about it, the more I thought why not? People can hold grudges forever, can't they?"

Landon approached the witness box and dug a handkerchief from his suit pocket. He handed the soft linen square to Ms. Crawford and said, "Twenty-five years is a long time, Ms. Crawford. Has Eva ever, ever said anything else about Bumpus to you?"

"No. She has not. Maybe she's joined in when others complained about his drunkenness but nothing like that again, no."

"Ms. Crawford, we're just about done here. Bear with me. I'm going to summarize what I understand from your testimony. You tell me what I got wrong and then you can go. Okay?"

She nodded, pulling the handkerchief through her fingers.

"Alright. Twenty some odd years ago, Eva was angry with Mr. Bumpus, for a reason unknown to you, and in a fit of anger, said some folks need killing. She has not since, to your recollection, which is uncommonly good for something which happened so long ago by the way, said anything to you along those lines. Is that accurate?"

"Yes. That is accurate."

"Thank you ma'am. Your Honor, I have no further questions for this witness."

Landon took his seat next to Eva.

Judge Underwood ran a hand over his face, reaching up under his glasses to wipe at his eyes. "Mr. Beatty? Call your next witness."

Mr. Beatty stood, his swaggering confidence somewhat lessened. "The State has no further witnesses at this time, Your Honor."

Underwood echoed under his breath, "At this time," and shook his head. "Very well. Mr. Cook, unless you have any objections, we will take a 10-minute recess before you take over." The judge didn't give Landon time to object before banging his gavel and skittering off the bench, nearly catching his robes in the door to his chambers as it closed behind him.

● ● ● ●

LANDON TURNED IN HIS seat to address both Eva and her family at once. "Now's your chance to smoke or make use of the facilities. Underwood looks unimpressed with the State's case, don't you think?"

Lora and Maeve excused themselves to briefly step out. Landon advised them not to speak to anyone in the hallway. Eva stayed behind with Landon and her sons to discuss the proceedings so far. Landon gestured for the bailiff and asked for a glass of water. Bailiff Boeswetter, a spindly shadow of a man with a startling, booming voice, grumbled but did as he was asked. Landon thanked him without looking up and the bailiff resumed his place by the judge's chamber door.

After the fastest bathroom break in their lives, Lora and Maeve returned with just moments to spare, whispering sharply for Charlie and Anthony to fill them in on what they'd missed.

Anthony turned his back to the larger audience, shielding his face from prying eyes, and whispered back. "Landon still plans to call Dale and Hal to the stand. He hasn't decided whether or not to call Mama."

Lora glanced at the gallery over her uncle's shoulder. Hal Johnson flitted around the doors, watching every move she and her family made. Unlike previous court appearances, he'd combed his hair and dressed for the occasion in a white, short-sleeved dress shirt, without an undershirt, and a tie which looked to be at least as old as she was. His rawboned cheeks rippled as he clenched and unclenched his jaws. She was glad to be snugly bracketed between her parents and uncle.

30

Boeswetter's voice cut through the crowd noises as Judge Underwood took the bench again. The judge motioned for them to be seated and leaned in the bailiff's direction. After a moment's consultation, the court officer disappeared through a side door and quickly re-emerged carrying a large, oscillating pedestal fan. He plugged it into the wall behind the clerk's desk and stretched the cord as far as possible, placing it so the breeze would hit both the judge and the attorneys' tables alike. The gallery would have to sweat.

Judge Underwood undid the top button of his robes, and said, "Mr. Cook. It is sweltering in here. I apologize for the fan noise but it can't be helped. You're going to have to talk over it."

Landon grinned at the Judge and spoke up. "Not a problem at all, Your Honor. I appreciate the consideration. Rest assured, I will try to be brief without compromising the defense of my client."

"Much obliged, Mr. Cook. When you're ready, you can proceed."

"Thank you. The defense calls Dale Fudge, preacher of Holley Hill Church of Christ."

Like the other witnesses, Mr. Fudge had taken care with his appearance that morning. He wore his best wedding and funeral suit with enough Brylcreem in his hair to hold it in place through the most violent of tornadoes. He carried his own weathered, leather bound bible in his hands and laid it on top of the one offered by the clerk when he was swearing in.

'Good morning, Mr. Fudge. Thank you for being here. I won't keep you long. I'm sure you have much to do in preparation for tonight's church meeting."

Dale Fudge sat ramrod straight in the witness seat and graciously inclined his head. "Not a problem at all, Mr. Cook."

"Wonderful. I asked you to come in as a character witness for my client. You've heard what Ms. Crawford had to say for the prosecution. Tell us, how long have you known Eva Burnette?"

"Thirty years."

"That's a long time. Have you been her preacher for all thirty of those years?"

"No. I was a member of Holley Hill before taking over the pulpit after my father passed on about ten years ago."

"I'm sorry for your loss. So, you've known Mrs. Burnette both as a fellow worshipper and as her spiritual leader, correct?"

"Yes. She has always been an active and regular member of our church. She helps members who are struggling, often without being asked. She's taught Sunday School classes, sewed wedding dresses, carried food to shut-ins, driven folks to doctor's appointments, and sat with the grieving."

"It sounds like she is a vibrant member of your church family. Would that be a correct statement?"

"Yes it would. Eva has always been ready and willing to step into the gap, so to speak, for anyone who needed anything."

"Would that include Ethelred Bumpus?"

Mr. Fudge snorted in amusement. "Ah, Bumpus. I heard what Mrs. Crawford said and I won't call her a liar. Although, I never heard Eva say anything of the sort. Even so, if she did say those things, I firmly believe if Eva thought she could have helped Bumpus, well, I doubt she would have hesitated." He paused for a long second, "Bumpus was a...challenging...member of the community to say the least."

Landon considered this for a moment, hands in pockets and said, "So, what you're saying is that the Eva Burnette you know would be more likely to help Bumpus than harm him, no matter how she may have personally felt about the man. Is that correct?"

"Yes. That is correct."

"Thank you, Mr. Fudge. No further questions."

Judge Underwood fired a finger and thumb pistol at Mr. Beatty, "You're up, Counsellor."

Mr. Beatty spread both hands across his desk, now almost completely devoid of paperwork, and said, "The State has no questions for this witness, Your Honor." Cross-examining a preacher-cum-character witness was a minefield the prosecution had no intention of crossing.

"Wonderful! Mr. Cook, call your next witness."

"The defense calls Mr. Hal Johnson to the stand."

A collective inhalation sucked in the walls of the courtroom. The Burnettes were the only audience members prepared for this interesting choice of witness. Most of the others, like Hal himself, had been present for Eva's other court appearances and witnessed his antagonistic attitude towards the proceedings firsthand. To his credit, Hal jumped from his seat and moved with alacrity to the witness stand. He rushed through his oath and sat, staring holes in the wall over the heads of the riveted audience.

"Good morning, Mr. Johnson. Thank you for coming."

"Hmpf. I don't reckon I had much choice."

Landon paused mid-step and narrowed his eyes at Hal.

"Fair enough. This shouldn't take long—"

"Good!"

Landon growled low in his throat. "Mr. Johnson, if you would let me ask a question, we can get through this unpleasant business much faster. Now. We have learned that your fingerprints were also on the plate recovered from the cemetery after Bumpus's body was discovered. Can you explain why your prints would have been on the plate in the first place?"

"Like the Sheriff said, Eva Burnette had been bringing biscuits to my house every morning for the last few months."

Landon stopped. He faced Mr. Johnson square on. "Why would she do such a thing? For that long?"

Mr. Johnson shrugged his shoulders, refusing to answer aloud.

Landon leaned on the railing of the witness box. "Mr. Johnson, did you ask Mrs. Burnette to bring biscuits to your house every day?"

"I did not."

"Did your children ask her?"

"I'd have whipped 'em if they had."

"Did your wife ask her?"

Mr. Johnson froze in place but didn't answer.

Judge Underwood cleared his throat, losing patience with the recalcitrant Mr. Johnson.

Landon stepped away from the witness stand, giving Hal Johnson a clear view of the audience, before asking his next question. "Mr. Johnson, where is your wife?" No one moved a muscle. Hal Johnson blanched.

Mr. Beatty opened his mouth to object but had no chance to squeak out a single word. As soon as Landon asked the seemingly irrelevant question, the muffled silence, stirred only by the whirring fan blades, shattered when the courtroom doors opened. All eyes swiveled to see who was disturbing the tension.

In the witness box, Hal Johnson lurched to his feet. Pointing his fingers at the newcomers, he shouted, spit flying from his mouth, "Heya! That's my wife! Get away from her you—"

Half a dozen men, and more than a few women, stood and shouted in protest.

Judge Underwood's gavel rang out like gunshots, impotently calling for order. If anyone heard him, they didn't listen.

Landon Cook turned to the door and raised a grateful, welcoming hand.

Along the back wall of the crowded courtroom, Leon Strong stood next to Maurice. Maurice bravely held the hand of a very white, very nervous, Mrs. Arlene Johnson.

For several eternal seconds, the courtroom was a pressurized powder keg. One errant spark would provide all the energy necessary to set the place ablaze.

Shouting from his diaphragm at maximum volume, Judge Underwood and Bailiff Boeswetter managed to wrest everyone's attention from the trio at the back of the room. The judge, red faced from the exertion and sudden excitement, kept banging his gavel, even as the crowd took their seats. Swinging his arm like he was chopping kindling, he emphasized each word with an accompanying report.

"I. Will. Not. Tolerate. This. Kind. Of. Outburst. In. My. Courtroom!"

He pointed the gavel at Landon's head and sucked a deep breath in through his nose. "Mr. Cook. I hope to God you can quickly get to some kind of point with all this." He waved his arms around, robes flapping, indicating he included the entire room in his gesturing.

"I hope so too, Your Honor. Thank you for your patience."

Landon confronted a seething Mr. Johnson, who was still standing and glaring daggers at his wife.

"Mr. Johnson. Your wife left you for a Black man, didn't she? And you didn't tell anybody because you were too proud to admit it. Mr. Johnson, sit down and look at me."

Hal Johnson did not sit. Confused, he had difficulty tearing his gaze from the sight of his wife holding hands with Maurice Strong. "What? What did you say?"

"I said, your wife left you for a Black man. Mr. Johnson, look at me."

Mr. Johnson hardly glanced at Landon. Hal's hands trembled. His red face would rival any turnip pulled from the garden. He drug his eyes from his wife's face to Eva's attorney.

"Mr. Johnson. Did you see Bumpus on the day he died? Did you speak to him?"

Hal Johnson, still seething, barely scratched out, "Yes."

"Yes to which question, Mr. Johnson? Yes you saw him or yes you spoke to him?"

"Both."

"Where did you see him?"

"In the graveyard."

"In the graveyard?"

"Yes. I was chasing a nigger—"

"Mr. Johnson! That language is not allowed in my courtroom! And you will sit down!" Judge Underwood bellowed, lifting up a little from his seat to glare at Hal, threatening him with a gavel-shot upside the head.

Still standing, Mr. Johnson leaned away from the judge and flung himself into his seat, nodding. "I was chasing a Black man off my place and run up on Bumpus. He was bleeding from the back of his head but he was laughing! Pointing and laughing at me!"

Landon's lips thinned and his face tightened. "He was laughing at you? Why?"

Mr. Johnson hung his head. In any other space, his low-pitched voice would not have been heard, but, except for the whirring fan, the room was silent. Every ear heard him swallow before he spoke. "He knew Arlene had run off. He knew she'd left me for a ni-...Black man. He was laughing because I wasn't man enough and couldn't keep her!"

Unwilling to lose this momentum, Landon leaned onto the witness box railing. He feigned sympathy for Mr. Johnson. "That sounds awful. What happened then?"

Mr. Johnson closed his eyes and raised his face to the ceiling. "Ol' Bumpus was laughing and waving Eva Burnette's plate around like a gypsy tambourine. I wrestled it from him and smashed'im over the head. He went down like a sack of potatoes!" Hal was crying, tears streaming from his clenched eyes, mingling with the sweat rolling from his forehead. "I didn't know he was dead. I didn't know I'd killed him until I heard Eva'd found him the next day."

In a gesture of humanity and genuine sympathy, Landon pulled another handkerchief from his jacket pocket and handed it to the trembling man in the witness box. The gallery held its breath as Hal's gut-wrenching confession rolled over the gathered crowd. The Burnette family held hands and stared wide-eyed at Hal Johnson.

Recovering himself with a shake of his head, Landon stepped away from the witness stand and addressed the bench. "Your Honor. I think we have heard enough to dismiss the case against my client."

Judge Underwood, as stunned by the revelations as anyone else, nodded and found his voice. "I think you're right. Mrs. Burnette, you are free to go with the apologies of this court for the imposition on your time and wallet. Sheriff, I'll leave Mr. Johnson to you. Try not to screw this up." He rapped the gavel one final time and looked blankly at the bailiff.

"All rise for the honorable Judge Underwood!" Mr. Boeswetter boomed.

Amid a startled shuffling of feet and scraping of benches, Judge Underwood vanished into his chambers. Leon, Maurice, and Arlene sprinted out the courtroom doors as quickly as their feet would carry them. Eva was engulfed in a tidal wave of family and laughed as they hug-danced around her. Landon gathered his paperwork and was just putting it in his briefcase when Anthony created an opening for him in the family circle.

Sheriff Griffin collected a broken and unnoticed Hal Johnson from the witness stand.

Several of the men watching the proceedings ran out of the courthouse, looking for the Strong brothers and Mrs. Johnson. The Church Ladies, minus Agnes Crawford, hovered around the periphery of the celebration, trying to break in and be part of this momentous occasion. Dale Fudge reached a hand to Eva, over Lora's head, and squeezed her shoulder before taking his leave.

Mr. Beatty sat in disbelief at the prosecution table. He held his head in both hands, pulling his eyes into deep slits. His entire case had just fallen apart. He looked like a fool and knew it.

31

The courthouse corridors were packed elbow-to-ankle with people of all ages and skin colors pretending to have business with the numerous offices and departments which called the courthouse home. The surrounding lawns crawled with families, both Black and white. Blankets and coolers blossomed on the sparse grass beneath the towering oaks. Children ran and froze in endless games and iterations of tag, screaming in excitement, threading frantically through knots of chatting adults. Fathers played catch with their sons and pounded fists to gloves in anticipation of the next throw. Mothers swayed with heavy, sleeping, sweating toddlers on their hips while they ooh'd and aah'd over newborns. Finding three people in the milling crowds proved to be as impossible as herding cats. The men from Courtroom 1 who chased after Leon, Maurice, and Arlene came up empty handed.

Landon Cook all but skipped as he led a triumphant Eva Burnette and her family down the steps on the east side of the courthouse. Several bystanders stopped what they were doing, pausing their conversations to smile in Eva's direction. Some dipped their chins in solidarity. A minority few scowled and turned away. Weaving their way back to Landon's offices, Lora spied Deputy Ross leaning on a lamp post at the corner of the courthouse. He lifted his hat with a congratulatory wave, his deep dimples casting split-second shadows near the corners of his mouth. Waving back, she hoped he would make good on his promise to call on her.

Away from the crowded lawns, Lovenia Thigpen stepped suddenly from a recessed doorway, directly blocking the party's progress. Her orange hair was in disarray and mascara-tinged tears tracked down her cheeks. Lovenia's carefully crafted facade of superiority had crumbled, leaving a gritty, hardscrabble rage in its place. All celebrations and laughter came to a screeching halt. Her bony hand shot out like a viper and she slapped Landon across the face. She screamed at him, spit gathering in the crevices of her lips. "You just couldn't leave it alone! You had to push! You had to—!"

Landon reeled in shock, covering the blooming hand print on his cheek with his palm. "Lo?"

Running footsteps thundered up the sidewalk as Deputy Ross swooped in, wrapping the sobbing, heaving Lovenia in a bearhug restraint. His hat fell to the pavement, immediately crushed by Lovenia's stomping, flailing feet. When she'd settled a bit, the deputy, still puffing from his sprint, huffed at Landon, "Mr. Cook. I saw the whole thing. You want me to take her in?"

Landon rubbed the shock from his face and shook his head. "No, John. She's upset and lashing out. No need to make it worse. Let her go." Shifting his gaze to Lovenia, he held a hand up, bidding for calm, like a lion tamer with a dangerous new cat. "Lo, I need you to take a minute. Think about what needs doing. Your brother, his children. They need you to be strong. You're all they have."

Lovenia wilted and fell apart in Deputy Ross's arms. She covered her face and collapsed into keening heap when the deputy loosed his hold.

Eva handed her purse to Maeve and knelt next to Lovenia, ignoring the concrete snagging her stockings when her knees met the sidewalk. She glanced up at her family, their silhouettes stark in a nimbus of sunlight behind them. Laying a gentle hand on Lovenia's juddering shoulder, she said, "Lovenia, I know I'm the last person you want to hear from right now. But, I'm gonna say this and I hope you'll hear me."

Lovenia wiped a bare arm across her splotchy cheeks and sniffed.

"I had no idea about Hal. And I hate more than anything that this has landed in your lap. It's not going to be easy but, you can do this. And, you might not want it, but if you need help, anything at all, I'm willing." Eva patted Lovenia's hand between hers.

"Dammit if I don't believe you," the other woman barked in a laughing sob. Her face twisted in a sneer, "Bumpus."

Eva hummed low in her throat and nodded in agreement. "Bumpus. If that ain't a new cuss word, I don't know what is."

She helped Lovenia to her feet, both sets of knees popping on the way up.

Ms. Thigpen smoothed the front of her jeans, wiping off her wet hands, and turned to face Landon. "I'm not sorry I slapped you but I do appreciate you not letting the deputy arrest me." She squared her shoulders and dug her keys out of a hip pocket. "I'd better head out to Hal's. Like you said, I'm all they got."

She turned on her heel and marched away around the corner.

Landon, finding himself with no more handkerchiefs stashed away in pockets, used his coattail to blot sweat from his forehead before opening the door to his office, inviting the Burnettes, and Deputy Ross into the cool, dark air conditioning.

• • • •

TURNING THE CORNER from Monroe's store onto Eva's road, Charlie uttered, "What in the—." Eva's yard was crammed with cars, trucks, and even a couple small tractors, parked at odd angles. Automobiles and milling people blocked the well-beaten tracks leading to the back door. Every available shady oasis, under trees and on the porch, was occupied. Charlie slowly maneuvered the station wagon into the drive and grumbled as he squeezed the car into a narrow space along the ditch at the road. The family would make slow progress to get indoors.

Myra Strong bustled off the crowded front porch and shouldered her way through clumps of people to Eva's side as the car doors opened. She wrapped her arms around Eva, laughing and crying at once, bouncing up and down in a jubilant dance. With their arms locked around the other's waists, the old friends worked their way through the crowd, back to the house, taking time to stop and speak with each person along their path.

Charlie and Anthony, making their own meandery ways around the yard, shook hands with the men, innocently flirted with the women, and thanked everyone for coming. Maeve and Lora did the same, working in smaller and smaller circles, towards the house. Monroe and Ellen, squeezed into the thin mid-day shade cast by the porch roof, chatted with Dale and Helen Fudge next to the steps. Lora was surprised to see the rotund storekeeper away from his corner throne. Lunchtime was busy for the store and his presence at her grandmother's house was telling. She was pleased to see Deputy Ross pull over in front of the house on the far side of the road. She flipped her ponytail and waved as he got out of his patrol car. He smiled, squinting into the sun, and returned her wave. Lifting her chin in invitation for him to join her inside, she opened the front door.

Lora inhaled a shaky breath, thankful for the quiet calm and dim light filtering in through the window sheers. As her eyes adjusted, she was thrilled to see Leon and Maurice grinning at her from the cased opening into the kitchen. Arlene Johnson shifted from one foot to the other, smiling nervously from just behind Maurice.

Lora ran to them. She jumped into a hug, managing to catch both brothers at once. They smiled and fiercely hugged her back. Lora stretched out a hand to Arlene to pull her into the fellowship. After a moment, the four of them let go and stood, grinning at each other like Cheshire cats. Lora, blinking back tears and breathless for words, could only whisper, "You are the bravest people I know. You saved her. Thank you, thank you, thank you."

Arlene's hand found Maurice's, her head resting briefly on his shoulder. She laughed softly and said, "Your grandmother tried to talk me out of marrying him. I should've listened. Still, when Leon called and told me what was going on, I had to come. I won't go back to Hal but, none of this would've happened in the first place if it hadn't been for me." Maurice lifted his shoulders in a tired shrug and shook his head.

Leon took Lora's hand in his and said, "No thanks necessary. It's not perfect but it is right."

Lora gulped and swallowed a sob of relief. "That it is."

Acknowledgements

Storytelling is a work of community. Tellers must have an audience; an audience needs tellers. In the intervening spaces, a wide and motley crew of critics and cheerleaders are woven into the threads of each story, creating a vibrant and timeless tapestry of expression. And so, a few thank-yous are in order.

Heartfelt thanks go to my mentoring professor, Cindy Skaggs, for her repeated banishment of persistent, chronic imposter syndrome.

To my beta readers, Carson Wakefield, John St. Clair, Larry Penton (thank you for the knowing!), Eric and Lynnette Larmore, your precise questions and margin doodles helped me focus on the good stuff and cull the meh.

Carrie Dalby and Quenby Olson. Thank you for writing such beautiful historical fictions and most of all, for saying yes when I asked you to read my book. Your feedback means the world to me.

To the Before We Go Blog team – I cannot begin to express how grateful I am to be part of such an incredibly talented group of readers, writers, reviewers, jokers, champions, and genuinely good people. You guys are the best!

Harlyn and Deacon – thank you for being super cool people and believing in your mother when she doubted herself.

And most importantly, Dave. Every word I write is yours and will never be enough. You're too good for me.

About The Author

Whitney Reinhart is a native Alabamian and regularly eats pintos and cornbread for dinner. She is a graduate of the University of South Alabama and Southern New Hampshire University. Life has been kind and provided opportunities to live in several places across the USA in the past decade. She currently lives in West Virginia with her most excellent husband and two very spoiled and entitled Siberian Huskies. This is her first (but hopefully not last!) novel. Visit her website at www.meanderyme.com or follow her on Twitter @WhitneyRReads and Instagram @whittabit

www.ingramcontent.com/pod-product-compliance
Lightning Source LLC
Chambersburg PA
CBHW020935260626
47169CB00006B/1735